Twisted
LOST IN OBLIVION
BOOK TWO

COPYRIGHT

Dedication

To my Mom, who thinks I'm a rock star.
To Taryn, who buys me bats and keeps me company on the many nights when I'm still awake to see the daylight. The music of friendship is the sweetest melody there is.
To Erin and Diane, who are the best friends and cheerleaders we can ask for.
To our Word Wenches, who keep us fueled with mancandy.
And most of all to our readers, thank you for coming along for the ride with Oblivion.

"Sugar Kiss"

G. Duffy, N. Crandall, S. Kagan

Up against the wall
Or on the floor
I'll take what I need
Anytime at all
Watch me lick my lips
Because you already want my kiss
Up and down and side to side
One long taste brings you bliss
Don't act so shy
I taste the flavor on your thighs
You know you want my
Sugar kiss, baby
I'll dive between those lips
Oh so sweet
Lick my plate clean
And all the places in between
Feel my fingers
Take my hard drive in your dock
Beg me, beg me to stop
I'll keep on giving you my
Sugar kiss

Chapter One

"Gray, your new sister is here."

Gray rolled over on his stomach and dragged the pillow over his head. He was still hungover from the party last night and wasn't in the mood to play nice. Not while there were cymbals crashing in his skull. "Can I talk to her later?"

"No. You can talk to her now."

He groaned. "Brent's home for the weekend. Let him play welcome wagon. I'll take the night shift."

"Brent already went back to campus."

Figured. His older brother swung in for a night then swung back out again before the fawning stopped. Leaving everything to Gray as usual.

"Besides, I think you're more suited in this case." The mattress sank as his mom sat down at his side. "This one's not had an easy time of it. I think a friend would do her good."

Instantly guilt twisted in Gray's already knotted stomach. Damn Mad Dog. He was never drinking that crap again, no matter how often Jimmy tried to tell him getting loaded would help their band. Bullshit. All it had done was given him a fucking headache and put him in a pisser of a mood. He rolled over and tossed his arm over his eyes. "How bad?" he asked tiredly.

"Pretty bad. Her mom kept her sister but turned Jasmine over to the state. Said she'd gone wild and she couldn't handle her anymore. Since then, she's bounced from place to place."

"So she's trouble." He didn't have time for that. He could stir up enough of his own.

"I think she's just lonely. You have to meet her."

The foster kids his mom and dad took in had usually come from rough environments. Some of the children were friendlier than others, which was understandable. It had been six months since the last one, and he'd begun to think that the Duffys had taken in their last kid. Brent was off at college now, and he would be too in a couple of years. Maybe his parents were looking forward to their empty nest.

But now they'd taken in Jasmine.

"Jasmine, huh? Like the flower?"

"Yes. Jasmine Edwards. You two actually have a lot in common."

He snorted. "Oh yeah? Like what?"

"You'll see." She stood up. "I'm going to give you two some time alone. I'll be in the den, okay?"

He grunted and waited until she left to haul his ass out of bed. He checked his appearance in the half bath off his bedroom. Lovely. Bloodshot eyes, check. Way too long hair that looked like someone had gone at it with shears, check. Dragon breath from puking in the bushes before he'd crashed that morning, triple check.

He brushed his teeth a couple of times, pushed a hand through his hair and sniffed his Dokken T-shirt before taking another run at his pits with his deodorant. Good enough. He headed downstairs, taking the steps two at a time. It wasn't like he was meeting anyone he needed to impress.

Five minutes with this chick and he could consider his duty done. Then maybe he could get some practice in on Krystal Sword's new material. He'd been writing this new song—

Halfway into the living room, he came to a halt.

Everything stopped. His feet, his breath, his heart.

Curled up in one corner of the couch sat a tiny brunette, a guitar stretched across her lap. It dwarfed her, making her seem even smaller. Her fingers moved like a blur, coaxing out the most beautiful music from the antiquated acoustic. Scratches and welts covered the cherry wood, but it didn't matter. She might as well have been playing the finest instrument that ever existed.

Head bent, she strummed and sang a song about a woman on her wedding day. Hope, fear, excitement. Crying tears of joy. He didn't know the song—folksy type music wasn't his thing—but he couldn't stop listening. Or watching the way her perfect pink lips curved around the words she sang so effortlessly that she became one with the melody.

When she finished, she glanced up and flushed. "Oh."

Her eyes were bright blue, like the sky on a sunny day. Surrounded by blue-flecked lashes, those stunning irises bored into his and left him mute. He couldn't say a damn thing.

"I'm sorry. I guess I shouldn't have been playing." She set the guitar aside and brushed her hands over her skintight white jeans. The denim had been sliced all the way up and down her legs, and through the holes he could see glimpses of color on her skin.

He cleared his throat. "Tattoos?"

Her flush only worsened as she followed his gaze to her legs. "No. Markers." She pulled open one of the gaps on her knee and a drawn-on daisy appeared in the hole. "When I get bored, I draw on my clothes. And on myself, since I'm easier to wash off." She gave a little hitching giggle and stood up, sticking out her hand. "I'm Jazz. You must be Gray."

He clasped her hand, not the least bit surprised when heat flared between their palms. But she didn't seem to notice. She just kept smiling at him, her huge eyes locked on his.

"Yeah." He swallowed hard. "I'm Gray."

"Nice to meet you. How old are you?"

"Sixteen." Not for too much longer though. "You?"

"Fourteen. But I feel way older."

He looked her up and down. "You don't look older."

She threw back her shoulders. "Yeah, 'cause I'm little. But I could still grow. It could totally happen. I take my vitamins. I work out." She flexed her tiny biceps under the pink sleeve of her T-shirt and he couldn't help grinning.

"Sure. I bet you'll end up six-feet tall."

"Nah. That's as tall as you are. I'd settle for five-two."

Gray glanced down at her red Chucks. "You could wear heels."

"No way." She scrunched up her perky nose. "I'd rather be short."

He laughed and gestured to her guitar. "So how long have you played?"

"All my life."

He tried to take a deep breath and realized his lungs were still seized up like he'd just run a mile. God, she was cute and she was into music? And she'd be living in his *house*? *Down, boy.*

Talking to chicks wasn't difficult. Well, before today. He'd never had any trouble acting cool around them in the past. Besides, this one was too young. Fourteen-year-old girls weren't going to be as easy to coax up into his bedroom, something he did on the regular. He loved girls. The way they smelled. Tasted. Felt under his hands. They were like guitars, all smooth lines and perfect curves. He adored pulling different sounds out of them, just like he did his axe.

But this particular one would be his sister. Sort of. Which made this awkward.

"Me too. I'm in a band," he said, preening a little.

"You play too?" Her eyes lit. "What instrument?"

The nerves finally disappeared as he slid his hand down the neck of her guitar. The wood felt good under his hands. Like it was meant to fit his grip. He grinned. "Guitar."

Chapter Two

Now

The stage throbbed with the bass. Confetti from the New Year's Eve celebration littered the stage and colored strobe lights swung back and forth, landing on each member of Oblivion in turn. The lights bounced over the crowd, revealing individual faces caught in various stages of excitement. The first time they'd played at Frenzy, back home in Carson, California, the crowd hadn't been nearly as enthusiastic, at least at the beginning. They'd had to seduce them into the music.

Tonight they were all ready to fuck.

Gray Duffy closed his eyes and threw back his head, letting the beat take him. His head was spinning, his heart pounding with every crash of the drums behind him. Jazz was killing it. He followed Deacon's lead as he always did, tracing that heartbeat bass line that led into "Taste of Candy". The song wasn't his favorite, but he didn't care. When the sweat was coursing down his face, the salt burning on his lips and tongue, and his fingers were climbing the frets, so fast he wondered how any skin still covered the muscles and bone, he tasted every note. *Became* them. Even the dueling guitar played by the guy against his back—Nick—only heightened the experience.

They were a unit again. They'd sewn the group back together, in spite of the fraying threads. But when they were playing for their fans, especially in their hometown, none of the shit that had transpired the past few months mattered. The grin Nick flashed him as he goaded him into the solo near the end of "Taste" was as genuine as the shoulder nudge Gray gave him when he tried to cut him out too soon. They weren't friends, exactly, but they weren't enemies anymore either.

Simon slung an arm around Deacon's neck and shoved the microphone in their bassist's face, earning a growl that somehow fit the song. Simon laughed and pranced away, swaying his hips in his best Mick Jagger imitation. He hadn't even zipped his leather pants. Why bother? He'd be screwing some chick the instant he finished the set. Maybe before, if the brunette in the front row who kept flashing her breasts actually made it up on stage.

Jazz banged her heart out on her kit, her wild multi-colored curls flying, the sticks in her nimble fingers colliding with the skins with a beautiful poetry he never grew tired of watching. Every time she smiled, his chest caught, the breath in his lungs stalling out until he looked away and his heart eventually gave in and started beating again.

The vibration of the stage under his boots brought him back to himself, to the solid reality of the instrument in his hand. The heat climbed up his spine, matching the fiery pressure in his fingers as he raced to keep up with the music inside him. Building, building. As potent as any orgasm, swelling to the point it finally exploded.

And when Simon's voice sliced through the screams of the fans, the tension inside Gray snapped, forcing him to his knees while he played for his fucking life.

Two hours later they dragged themselves into the back, higher than they'd been in months. Laughing, joking with each other. Deacon grabbed Jazz and swung her up on his shoulders, making her squeal. Gray grinned and tweaked her bare foot, pulling on a candy pink-tipped toe, and she kicked out at him, thrusting her hand in his hair while she struggled closer. He leaned up to meet her mouth, knowing the kiss wouldn't be anything but a glancing blow. Just friends being friendly. His blessing and his curse. Then his gaze flickered to the woman off to the side, smiling at him with determined promise.

He stumbled back, mumbling an apology to Jazz. He didn't see her face because he was focused on the woman dressed in the blue tube dress, her blonde corkscrew curls fountaining from the top of her head.

About goddamned time.

"Where the hell have you been?" he asked once he was at her side, gripping her arm to pull her close. "I called you five times last night, Cricket."

"Oooh, such an appetite you have." She leaned up and spoke against his ear. "Got a new supplier, handsome. You'll be ready to go tonight." She reached down and grabbed his cock through his jeans. He gritted his teeth, hating for once in his life that playing always made him hard. "You're ready to go right now."

He grabbed her wrist. "Stop it. We're not about that."

"But we could be." She licked her vamp red lips. "You have no idea what I could do to you."

"Not interested." He wished he could walk away. But she had something he needed more than he needed his pride. "All I want is what I pay you for."

"You haven't paid me for anything in quite a while. Your tab's getting pretty long." Her gaze drifted below his waist. "Let me help you settle your debt."

Christ. It would be so easy to say yes, to just spread her legs and drill himself inside her until she stopped begging. But he was on the verge of begging himself, and not for the well-used landing strip between her thighs. "You'll get your money. Now it's your turn to deliver."

"Fifteen minutes. Outside." Cricket looked pointedly over his shoulder. "Just you, handsome." Turning on her razor-sharp heels, she left him standing there.

He turned, knowing who would be waiting. Goddammit. He needed a hit before he faced those liquid blue eyes, so full of accusation. "Who is she?" Jazz asked, crossing her arms.

"A friend." The words tasted bitter on his tongue.

"What kind of friend? A groupie?"

"Does it really matter?" He stabbed his fingers into his eyes. "I need a drink."

A moment later, a damp bottle bumped his arm. "Here."

He opened his eyes and accepted Jazz's offering. Water. He couldn't help smiling. Simon was guzzling whiskey right out of the bottle, but Jazz was drinking water. So that meant he was too.

He popped the cap with his thumb and tipped it back, sloshing the water into his mouth while he pulled her against his side with his other arm. He pushed the bottle at her next, holding it up for her as she swallowed. A few drops splashed her bare chest over her sharply V-necked top, but he wouldn't give in to the urge to study the pattern of droplets on the tops of her breasts.

He'd spent enough time torturing himself over Jazz Edwards.

Before she could question him further, he finished off the water himself and turned away, crushing the bottle in his fist. "Be back later," he muttered, knowing she'd never hear him over the chaos backstage. Knowing it wouldn't be enough. Nothing he ever said or did was.

"Gray." Her abrupt cry cut through the noise and he stopped, expecting her small hand to close over his forearm. She had a crazy intense grip from playing the drums and a thrill of anticipation always buzzed down his spine when her strong fingers pressed into his flesh. Every time he imagined her touching him somewhere else, like she had that one time—

The one time he wouldn't let himself think about, because it hadn't been right. In all his fantasies about his first time with Jazz Edwards, there was never another guy there too.

But he hadn't walked away. Even a saint couldn't have turned away from those needy blue eyes, and God knows he wouldn't be fitted for a halo anytime soon. The burn in his nose and muscles jangling under his skin proved that more than anything else.

He pivoted to face her and discovered she hadn't moved from her spot. Her pale bare feet gleamed against the floor covered in spilled liquor and sweat and who knows what else, those pink-tipped toes speaking of the innocence she still possessed. She was the drummer for a band on their way to superstardom and she had a freaking clit piercing, for God's sake, but the woman before him would never lose that inner core of sweetness and purity. He wouldn't allow it.

"Where are you going?" She stepped closer, silently imploring him to stay. "The guys are heading out to Sharkey's for an after-party in the VIP room."

Gray snorted. "What VIP room? That place is a dive."

"They remodeled it, I guess. We've been away for a while."

Talk about an understatement. Their whirlwind tour had ended up getting extended when they switched management and record companies and their new team had wanted them to be seen in a few more key venues before they packed it in for a few months. Not that they'd be on vacation. They had a new album to cut, which meant studio time as well as serious hours spent writing new material. They didn't have nearly enough to go into the studio with yet. That also meant they'd need to put away the shit between the band members long enough to actually sit still and work on some words and melodies together.

Long meet shot.

"Simon's got a disguise too," Jazz went on, clearly oblivious to Gray's disinterest. He hadn't been all that fond of hanging out with most of his fellow band members before the big contract mess that Nick and Simon had instigated. Now he definitely couldn't be bothered.

Especially when there was all that pretty blow, just waiting for him. Maybe. All depended if Cricket really would come through without him having to do her. Some females just had a thing for rock stars, even sweaty, hyper ones who were more interested in powder than pussy.

Still, he had to try to pay attention to this conversation and possibly even show up at the after-party. For Jazz if no one else. "A disguise? What the hell?"

"You know, so he won't be recognized." She rolled her eyes. "I think he stole your hat too. I swear he was carrying that around with this freaking curly red wig that makes him look like Carrot Top."

Gray frowned. "I was wondering where it went."

She smiled faintly. "I was amazed you could go on without it. In the old days, you would've refused to play."

In the old days, I would've refused a lot of things.

He rubbed his hand over the back of his damp neck. "Babe, I need a shower."

"So? I do too. That doesn't mean you can't come to Sharkey's."

Rather than stand there and envision things he had no business envisioning—namely his best friend naked and soapy under a stream of hot water—he stepped back. "Why don't you go ahead? We can connect later."

She gave him a pleading look that never missed its target. "It's New Year's Eve. A fresh start. Please, Gray."

And those words right there? His undoing.

He sighed. "I'll meet you there, all right?"

"No. Not all right." Eyes narrowed, she closed the distance between them again. Apparently she had no intention of giving up easily. "Who is that woman? I don't like the looks of her."

"You don't like the looks of anyone." He couldn't resist tapping the side of her head, right above one of her bedraggled rainbow ponytails. "Very suspicious mind you have in there, young lady."

"Someone has to watch out for you."

"Oh really?" He cocked a brow, still a little sore from the ring he'd had put in yesterday. Pain was his new thing. At the rate he was going, he'd have tattoos and piercings all over his body. "I think that's my job."

"No, it's mine." She wet her lips and grabbed the lapels of the leather vest he'd worn over skin onstage. That skin was currently soaked to the bone from their crazy-ass set under the lights, but she didn't seem to mind. Why would she? Her bangs stuck to her forehead in a thick clump. Even her lashes had tangled in the heat.

And that wet look only brought him right back to thoughts of her in the shower, her body pressed tightly to his from the tips of her full breasts to her shapely thighs and everywhere in between.

His dick veered against his zipper. Christ. He needed to get his head straight or else he'd make some serious mistakes while he was waiting for his fix.

Like indulging in an even darker, more dangerous one.

"I've been watching out for you since I was fourteen, Grayson Duffy." Her fingers tightened on his vest, as if she suspected he was on the verge of pulling away. "Nothing and no one will make me stop now. So get your ass into that shower, get cleaned up and presentable, and come with us to Sharkey's."

The devil on his shoulder—or in his pants—made him lean close to speak against her ear. No less than six miniature hoops cupped the curve of her lobe. "What, you don't think I look presentable now? I think there are some ladies here who might disagree with you."

She sucked in an audible breath before releasing him and taking an obvious step back. "Like that chick who was groping your dick in front of everyone?" Her eyes flashed. "I bet you didn't think I saw that."

"No. I didn't." Wished she hadn't.

He didn't have any reason to tread gently around Jazz, other than how much of a worrywart she was. They weren't a couple nor had they ever been. Deep down, he still had a niggle of hope that things could change. That one day she'd stop looking at him as her best friend and see him as more.

Or at least he had hoped that, before. Now he didn't want her anywhere near him. He loved her enough to know she deserved better.

His gaze darted to Nick, his arm slung around some random redhead wearing shorts that almost exposed her crotch. Jazz deserved way better than that jerk too. He knew all about the backstage blowjobs she used to give Nick before shows. Hell, he'd practically walked in on one once. What they had done after them was more than he wanted to think about.

It was bad enough that he'd never be able to scour the image of her riding Nick from his brain. Lord knows he tried every time he lined up coke on a mirror and shut his eyes. But nothing made the picture disappear.

"I see more than you think." Jazz reached up to let down her hair. Tumbled, wavy rainbow strands fell down around her shoulders, making her look even younger than usual. "I'm heading back to the bus to get ready. If you're not at Sharkey's by eleven, I'm hunting your ass down. And you can tell that skank that I'm not afraid to use my drumsticks."

He couldn't help grinning. "I'll be along soon. I promise."

"You better." She bounced from foot to foot, seeming to hesitate, then arched up on her tiptoes to kiss his jaw. The contact seared him straight to the bone as it always did. "It's hard for me too," she whispered.

For a second, that same stupid hope surged. That perhaps this was it. The moment he'd been waiting for since he'd realized he had fallen for the one woman he would never allow himself to have.

"Is it?"

"Yes. They hurt both of us. Deacon too." She sighed and rubbed her eyes, her exhaustion evident in even that simple gesture. "I don't think Simon and Nick understand how much they fractured the band when they accepted that agreement. To them it was just about percentages. They don't get that they hurt us by not trusting us enough to make us full partners."

Of course. She hadn't been talking about *them*. She was referring to Oblivion.

Where he wanted to be himself, as fast as humanly possible.

"Yeah." He cleared his throat. "I'll catch up with you guys at Sharkey's soon."

Before she could say anything more, he headed out to find Cricket. She and her blow were guaranteed to improve his mood.

Better yet, maybe he'd finally feel nothing at all.

Chapter Three

Then

Gray shielded his eyes with the side of his hand to block the sun's glare as he searched the pretty tree-lined campus of Shadyside High. Where the hell was she? This was only Jazz's third day of classes at her new school. How could she have figured out where to hide out so soon? Unless she was a stoner. Their hangout at the back of the parking lot by the gym was pretty obvious. He frowned. He didn't think so. She didn't strike him as the druggie type. She was too smart for that.

He swiveled around, gripping the neck of his guitar loosely in one hand and juggling books and a lunch sack in the other. He'd gotten the guitar from his car, hoping he and Jazz could play during lunch. It was a gorgeous California spring day and he'd packed something that morning for them to eat. Nothing fancy, just bologna and cheese sandwiches and green grapes, but Jazz always acted like he'd given her jewels when he gave her anything. It made him want to give her stuff all the time.

So where was she?

Doing another scan, he spun in a circle, his gaze drifting over the scattered groups of students. Several friends called to him, two of them girls he'd dated at one time or another, but he waved them off with a smile and a promise to catch them later. He finally spotted his quarry under a big leafy tree, her guitar in her lap, her dark hair obscuring her face.

He jogged over to Jazz and dropped down at her side. "What are you doing sitting way over here by yourself?"

"Gray!" she exclaimed, as if it had been years since they'd seen each other rather than the four hours since he'd dropped her off before first period. She hugged him tightly, pressing her face to his neck for one painfully long moment. Painfully long because she smelled like wildflowers and watermelon and felt like the softest, sweetest heaven in his arms.

Even more painful because she pulled back.

Get it together, man. "Hey," he said huskily before clearing his throat. "You didn't answer my question."

"Oh. I'm just...here."

"Great explanation," he teased, tossing aside his books.

"It's a nice day. I like this tree. It's huge." She tipped her head back and studied the leafy canopy above her head, so dense that it barely let any sunlight through. "How old do you figure it is?"

"At least a million years."

"Jerk." She laughed and looked at him again, setting those amazing eyes back on his with a seriousness that pulled at his heart. "Why are *you* here?"

"I have to eat lunch, you know. Speaking of that..." He dumped out the contents of the lunch sack on the grass. "Look at this fine feast I put together for us. Deli meat and slightly brown grapes. Check it."

She plucked a grape out of the baggie and popped it her mouth. "I've never had finer."

"Uh-huh. Sweet talk will get you nowhere."

"So what would get me somewhere?"

He cut a glance her way but she wasn't looking at him anymore. She'd set her guitar aside and was now digging through her battered backpack. "I have drinks." She pulled out two cans of grape soda, tossed him one and opened her own can before taking a long swallow. "I raided the machine this morning."

"And you gave *me* one. I'm honored."

"Who else would I give it to?" She grabbed another grape.

"Oh, I don't know. All the new friends you must be making. I expected you to be holding court like any good Queen Jazz should do." He grinned and unwrapped his sandwich.

She looped an arm around her up-drawn leg and picked up her sandwich. "Don't think that'll be happening anytime soon."

"I bet you've been fighting the adoring hordes off all day." Fighting the guys off especially. Not that he was thinking about that. She was his foster sister. Completely off-limits, even if she tilted her head and licked grape soda off her lips in such a naturally sensual way that he couldn't help shifting where he sat.

"Nope. No fighting off."

"So you let them have their way with you?" he asked with a grin, hoping she would grin back. Jazz not smiling seemed like a crime against humanity. The sun dimmed even more on their little patch of grass until he had to do something—anything— to make the sunshine come back. He reached out to tip up her chin, expecting to see her usual smile. Instead he found tears.

"Hey. Hey," he murmured, thumbing one of them away. "What's the matter?"

She launched herself into his arms, nearly pitching them back onto the grass. "I hate this place."

He patted her back awkwardly, his hand still full of bologna. "Huh? Why?"

She shifted back on her knees and rubbed at her blotchy cheeks. "This school is horrible. I don't fit in."

"Says who?" he asked, setting aside the sandwich in case his arms were needed again.

"The whole world."

"That can't be true. You're just imagining things." Hearing his father's thread of lawyerly doubt in his own voice, Gray sucked in a breath and tried again. "What happened?"

"What do you mean, 'what happened'?" She gestured at herself. "Just *look* at me."

He already did far too much. "Yeah, and?"

"I shouldn't be here with all these California perfect blondes with tanned skin and mile-long legs. My skin's so pale you can see my bones. My hair's almost black. My legs—"

"Are perfect," he interrupted quietly, trying to stop his gaze from drifting past the hems of her cutoff jean shorts as she plopped her butt on the grass. But when he glimpsed the smiley-faced daisy she'd drawn on her calf, something twisted inside him that wasn't desire. For once. "Tell me who upset you. I'll talk to them." He'd do more than that if necessary. Gladly. Hell, he'd take on the whole football team if he had to.

"It's not just one person." She swiped at her chin. "It's everyone. I don't belong."

"Stop it. You belong just where you are. On the grass, with the sun behind you. With a flower drawn in marker on your leg and crushed grapes under your foot."

"Oh no." She winced and pried the baggie out from under her heel. "Shit, I'm sorry."

"I like them better like this." Taking the baggie, he scooped his fingers through the green mush and sampled. Then he offered her some. "See? Perfect."

Hesitantly, she slid her lips over the tips of his fingers and eased back. Smiled. "Yeah. Perfect."

Chapter Four

Now

Jazz stepped inside the VIP room at Sharkey's and smiled at the plastic palm tree covered with Christmas lights beside the entrance. Nope, it no longer looked like a dive. It also didn't look like the typical Ripper Records shindig put together by their scarily efficient manager, Lila. In fact, after taking in the attire of the waitresses with their low-cut tops and skimpy red velvet skirts, Jazz did a double take to make sure she hadn't wandered into a more upscale version of the strip club down the block.

Curved leather couches wrapped around low tables bearing flickering candles and lovely displays of poinsettias and greenery that were largely wasted on this bunch. Jazz wondered if Deacon's new wife Harper, Oblivion's in-residence chef, had helped out with the menu, because the offerings on the buffet table defied description. God, so much food. Colorful bottles lined the wall behind the glossy bar to her left. It nearly sagged under the festive Christmas lights that seemed to drip from every surface. Long ribbons of lights even hung from the ceiling.

And people were making out, approximately everywhere.

A pair of redheads had wrapped themselves around Simon. She'd seen one of them on their bus before. Monica, maybe? Deacon and his wife were kissing much less lewdly than Simon's reenactment of a porno, but they were tangled up too. Even a couple of the roadies had cozied up with their conquests for the night.

Love and lust were everywhere. Except anywhere near her. Figured.

She needed a drink, fast.

Bellying up to the bar, Jazz plastered on a smile. "I'd like a Zombie, please."

The bartender leered. "You like a strong drink, little lady?"

Oh Christ. One of those. She tried to keep her smile in place. "Sure. I'm really thirsty."

He licked his lips. "Oh, I just bet you are."

Though she rarely drank, she made an exception on New Year's Eve. After he deposited her drink in front of her and disappeared down the bar, she took a hefty swallow. She grimaced. Rum. Ugh. She tried again with a smaller sip. Still toxic, but manageable. Why did people do this to themselves again?

Oh yeah, to have a good time. Right.

She sucked off a cherry on her swizzle stick and spun around on her stool to survey the packed bar. Familiar faces mixed with strangers. Still, the usual suspects stood out. Simon and his women had stopped playing tongue twister and were doing some jumping thing that Jazz supposed counted as dancing. Deacon and Harper had snagged a high-top table and were sharing a plate of chicken wings. Harper was gesturing wildly and Deacon was just grinning, looking utterly content. The new husband and father-to-be seemed pretty pleased with himself. Who could blame him? He was in the market for a cute little house for his family and he'd left the bed-hopping scene behind. Simon probably never would.

Donovan, the head of Ripper Records, had opened a bottle of champagne and was smiling as a perky blonde poured for him and a couple of the other execs. Lila watched the entire scene with a cool gleam in her eyes, waving off the bubbly in favor of bottled water. She gripped her ever-present tablet, but she'd ditched her usual business suit for slim trousers, a silky blouse and what looked like real pearls. Everything about her from her wardrobe to her bone structure gave her a haughty, sophisticated air. Even the purse of her lips looked regal.

Nick was around too, wandering from group to group, never landing anywhere for long. Since the show he'd been texting Jamie from Brooklyn Dawn, their opening act. He claimed he was scoping out the rest of Brooklyn Dawn's winter touring schedule because they "brought a different dynamic" to the stage—AKA an excess of boobs—but Jazz hadn't pursued the subject. She had other things on her mind.

Like where Gray was.

He's probably showering with Busty Blonde Babe.

Jazz pried off her other cherry and chewed, trying to ignore the sinking feeling in her stomach. The sensation had started in her chest, right where her racing heart was doing its best impression of a kick drum.

He wasn't coming. Why had she pretended otherwise?

So what if it was New Year's? He didn't know she'd made a resolution to stop dancing around what she wanted and finally go for it. The *it* being Gray. She'd worn her version of something classy—a little black dress, patterned tights and chunky heels—and she intended to march up to him at midnight, grab that rock-cut jaw and kiss the holy hell out of him. Then she would strut away.

Lots of marching and strutting. The plan hinged on that. If he followed, well, they'd just see where things went. If he didn't...

If he didn't, she was going to throw up this disgusting drink and sob herself to sleep. Probably right on the bathroom floor.

She hiccupped and took another sip. Maybe if she kept drinking, she wouldn't feel so miserable. Even nausea was better than this. All she kept picturing was Gray and that woman. Him smiling at her and her fingers stroking him for that instant before he tugged her away.

"Give me another one," she said to the bartender as soon as she'd finished the first. It took everything she possessed not to look at her watch. It was getting closer to midnight. He wasn't going to show.

Maybe it was just as well.

Every time one of her friends stopped by, she made small talk and giggled, fulfilling her role as group cheerleader/clown. But she didn't try to get her pals to stick around. For once, she didn't do anything possible to avoid being alone. She put on a good show of being Ms. Happy Go Lucky, and a lot of the time it was even true. But ever since the contract debacle that had almost leveled the band, a lot of her happy had gone missing. Considering Gray's no-show, her lucky seemed to be on the lam too.

She swallowed more of her cocktail. All signs were pointing to one inevitable conclusion: she wasn't going to have someone to kiss at midnight. At least the someone she wanted to kiss. And if she couldn't kiss Gray, she'd just keep her lips attached to the rim of her glass.

"Whatcha drinking?"

She turned her head at the voice near her ear. Nick. More friend than foe, most of the time. "It's called a Zombie. I looked it up online. They said after three of them you'll need a stretcher," she shouted over the music and laughter. "This is number two."

He leaned in and sniffed. "Sounds promising."

"Can't say I'm a fan."

"So why are you drinking it?" He looked around for an empty stool, which was basically a joke. The place was packed from wall to wall. Giving up, he edged an elbow on the bar and awkwardly eased himself between her stool and her neighbor's. The position put him between her legs—a place he'd been before. On his own, and with Gray.

Swallowing hard, she peered at her fruity drink. Best not to look at him right then. She was certain her face had to be six shades of red. An experienced woman of the world, she was not. She could fake it with the best of them though. At least when her heart wasn't breaking.

"Maybe I want to get drunk," she said under her breath.

"Then be more decisive about it." He ordered two more Zombies, making her smile in spite of herself. He set her spare drink aside and tipped back his own. Grimaced. "Well, that's interesting. A bit girly for me, but I've had worse."

"Yeah?"

"Back in the projects, hell yeah. Simon and I had our drugstore special. Every cheap bottle of shit we could buy, all mixed together. Guaranteed to make you puke." Because he was grinning, she grinned too. The alcohol was starting to swim through her bloodstream, loosening the muscles in her shoulders and back that were tensed from their set.

And from picturing Gray in the arms of a sexy blonde with breasts that made up approximately four of hers. Which was saying something, because the boob fairy had made a stop at Jazz's house too.

Wanting visual affirmation, Jazz studied the cleavage popping over the top of her dress and sighed. She'd never complained about her cup size before tonight, but perhaps an extra handful or two would snag Gray's interest. Couldn't hurt. He'd barely even looked at her chest when they'd had their threesome with Nick.

"Are you checking yourself out?" Nick sounded amused.

"Maybe. Are you done checking out the sexy brunette guitarist from Brooklyn Dawn?"

"Nah. It's not like that. Brooklyn Dawn might be doing a few shows with us if we can make our schedules mesh." He fingered her hair. "Though I do have a weakness for brunettes."

Yeah, she wasn't going to acknowledge that comment.

She brought her glass back to her mouth, sloshing some over the side. She licked the alcohol off the back of her hand and glanced up to see Nick eyeing her too closely.

"Need some help with that?" His voice matched his gaze. Warm heading toward hot.

She waited for her belly to flutter. God knows it had fluttered plenty around him last spring. She'd had a crush on Nick that had quickly turned into more and just as quickly flamed out. But now there was nothing. She started to reply, then realized there wasn't a chance he'd be able to hear her over the din. How had the bar gotten so much noisier and more crowded in the last few minutes? She couldn't even find Simon and his bright red wig anymore. All she could see was Nick looming a little too close, his golden eyes too intent.

Someone's snorting giggle snapped them out of the moment. Thank God. She wouldn't have kissed him, but she really didn't want to get stuck in the position of having to turn him down. Her own feelings were entirely too bruised. If she could distract him from whatever madness had sent him pinging back her way, that would be much better.

"Um, Nick..." Her attention veered right and the words died on her lips. Gray stood at the end of the bar, arms crossed. He didn't look happy.

That made two of them.

"Let me up." She stumbled off the stool, barreling into Nick in the process.

"Hey." Nick laughed as he caught her arms. He smelled of smoke and leather, the scents she most often associated with him. "Guess I shouldn't have gotten you another one. You're already locked and loaded." He spoke close to her ear. "You tired of this yet? We could—"

Gray yanked hard on his shoulder. "Get the hell away from her, Crandall."

Nick turned his head, but he didn't look pissed as much as amused again. "Duffy. Back to this, are we?"

Jazz put a hand on each of their chests, ignoring the call of her fingers to curl into Gray's shirt. He'd swapped his leather vest for a black T-shirt that clung to his pecs. "Guys, tonight's not the night."

She wasn't even sure why Gray was in Nick's face. He usually wasn't so openly confrontational, especially since nothing was even going on. But Gray's eyelid was twitching and he clenched his jaw so tightly it had to hurt.

Nick only aimed a mild look at her hand. "I'm good, Jasmine. No need to restrain me."

"No, that's not what you wanted her to do to you, you stupid prick. She's not just some receptacle."

Heat flooded Jazz's cheeks. Jesus. "Gray, stop it. What's gotten into you?"

Nick's nostrils flared as he tossed a look at Gray. "I have some idea," he said almost too low for her to hear.

She frowned. What was that supposed to mean?

"You got something to say to me, Crandall?" Gray shoved Nick against the bar, upending Jazz's third drink in the process. "Go right the fuck ahead."

Nick slammed his hands against Gray's shoulders. "Back off, you fucking moron."

Gray grabbed his upper arms, pinning him to the bar for one humming moment before Nick sent him careening backward. Jazz's stool went flying with her still on it. She landed hard, her glass miraculously still in one hand, the other attached to the sticky floor with what felt like superglue. Ick. She'd have to burn this dress.

A little dizzy, she looked around at the people that surrounded her—some still dancing, some standing still to show off their incredibly hot shoes, some taking the opportunity to get into shoving contests of their own. Her ass hurt. And damn, she really felt short way down here.

All of a sudden she was pulled upward, so quickly that her unsteady head threatened to spin right off her shoulders. *Whoa.* Her dizziness only got worse when she realized she was being carried through the laughing, jeering crowd by Gray. Her stomach wobbled and she tried to get her bearings.

Before she could, he planted her on a stool at the far end of the bar, then summoned a glass of water and pressed it into her trembling fingers. "Are you okay?"

Gray's shoulder-length wavy dark hair brushed the round collar of his shirt as he leaned closer to peer into her eyes. His *wet* dark hair. Looked like he'd taken that shower. Alone?

Forget it. Not relevant.

"Just bruised my pride." She drank the water because it gave her something to do other than try to bite that sexy-as-hell jaw of his. Not that she'd be able to manage it at this angle. But if she stood up on the rungs of the stool for a little boost—

"Jasmine, are you okay?"

She shut her eyes at Nick's voice. He never knew when to let incensed dogs lie. "Fine," she said weakly, praying he would just leave. "When I was on the floor, I saw some shoes I need to find. Strappy silver sandals with a wedge heel. Super cute." When she opened her eyes and caught Gray's narrow-eyed expression, she decided she'd used the heel to wedge her own mouth shut. "Just making a joke," she muttered.

"Not the time."

"Yeah, well, when is the time?" Anger and embarrassment welled up inside her and she pushed him out of her face. "How dare you? You show up late after promising you'd be here. I ask for one little thing and you can't even give me that." She pushed him harder. "Then you get in my face if some guy dares look at me, but you can't even see me when I'm standing right in front of you."

He moved in and grasped her throat before she could block the move. The wide plane of his thumb tipped up her chin until she had no choice but to meet his furious gray eyes for one frantic second before she fixated on the movement of his lips. "You think I don't see you, Jazz?" His voice was quiet. Too quiet. She didn't know how she could hear him over the crowd. Maybe because she couldn't drag her gaze from his mouth.

God, that mouth. She wanted it so bad she couldn't think. Couldn't tell herself to calm down or save it for another time when there weren't so many people watching. They weren't just two anonymous kids anymore. They were in a semi-famous band. Together. How they behaved in public affected the others.

But none of that seemed to matter. All she could do was prod him harder.

"You were with her, weren't you? While I was waiting, you were probably fuc—"

"Shut up." He shook her lightly. So lightly she wondered why it felt like her bones were rattling under her skin. Those blunt, scarily strong guitarist's fingers slipped around to the back of her neck, digging into flesh. "Just shut the hell up. For once, stop talking to me. I don't want to hear your voice in my head anymore."

Hurt slammed through her, slicking ice over the burning fury. "So go. No one's forcing you to be near me if it's so repulsive to you. I'm sure she's waiting anyway, right? She has something you need." His pupils flared and the truth cut her so deep that she went limp in his hold. She hadn't wanted to believe it. But the reality burned in his eyes.

Those eyes had never lied to her. And they weren't lying now.

Don't cry. Not here.

She yanked at his hold, desperate to get away. Things had quieted considerably in their corner of the bar, probably due to all the spectators watching *them*, but she didn't give a shit. Let them listen. Let them do what she always did and record it all for Twitter. She was tired of being the cute, spunky, easily dismissed Oblivion chick.

If that meant she had to have a meltdown in the center of a New Year's Eve party, she was entitled.

"Let me go," she whispered when Gray's grip only tightened, taking her right up to the point of pain but never beyond. "You want me out of your head. I'm gone."

"You don't get it. You never did." He brought their faces close, so close that his breath fluttered over her lips. He'd been drinking too, something dark and rich. "I could walk out of here and never see you again and it wouldn't make one fucking bit of difference. I could screw every woman I see blind and I'd never shake that sound from my mind. You. Always you."

Each word hit her heart like a blade. Any more of them and she'd be left quivering on the floor, impaled by his obvious disgust.

All this time, she'd believed they were a team. Sure, they'd had their rough patches. Joining Oblivion for one. That insane threesome for another. He'd pulled further and further away until she'd felt like she was losing her best friend, but she hadn't panicked. Because she'd known way down deep that he would always come back to her. He was her constant. The center of her life. Without Gray, nothing made sense.

But now *with* Gray, nothing made sense anymore either.

"Let me go," she breathed again, her throat as raw as her eyes. "Just let me go."

He stared at her for so long that she started to shake. This was really it. He was going to release her and they would be over, without really ever having been anything. This had all been a long dream. She'd just imagined he'd ever loved her—

"Never." He crushed his mouth down on hers.

Chapter Five

Then

"Okay, now do it again."

Jazz sighed. She'd been playing guitar for years, but he took it to another level. He was crazy good. Almost Kirk Hammett-in-Metallica good. "My fingers are tired."

"Aww, poor baby." Gray grinned. "I thought you wanted to be in a band."

She snorted. "Like that's ever actually going to happen."

They'd been practicing for hours in his parents' basement rec room, which was fancier than the house she'd lived in with her sister and her mama in Glenview. Expensive artwork decorated the navy walls and leather furniture filled the space. The huge TV and high-end stereo were fascinating enough, but the row of antique pinball machines always drew the bulk of her attention. Ms. Pac-Man was starting to look really appealing.

She wasn't a gamer and normally she loved playing her music more than anything, but Gray had been teaching her some complicated finger combinations on his spare Stratocaster since they'd gotten home from school. Between his endless instruction and the reverberation from the amp, she was starting to get a headache.

And she still had three hours of algebra homework to do. Three hours of pretending she didn't hear the feminine laughter coming from Gray's end of the hall as he "tutored" his latest student in French. Literally.

She'd almost walked in on him and the last one. They'd gotten so quiet in there that she'd thought Shelly or Sally or whatever her name was had gone home, so Jazz had stopped outside his door, prepared to knock. The moan had taken her by surprise. As had the red lace bra on the floor when she'd given in to curiosity and quietly nudged the cracked-open door.

Yeah, Gray knew his French, all right.

"You're right, it won't happen if you don't start practicing more. You think Krystal Sword will take on just anyone? We have qualifications."

"I'm sure you do." Like tongue-testing all the female applicants. If they even had female applicants. Krystal Sword was a band of six loud, smelly boys.

He went on, oblivious to her sarcasm. "Jimmy's already told me he's not going to replace Stevie unless we can find exactly the right fit. You're good, but not better than Stevie. He doesn't just play, he writes music—"

"I write music." She set aside the guitar and dug through her backpack, prying out two brightly colored notebooks. The first she tucked under her bent leg. Nope, he wasn't getting to see that one. "Here."

Eyebrow raised, he flipped open the peace sign-covered notebook she'd handed him. He read the pages of lyrics quietly, his face devoid of any reaction.

She toyed with the slouchy top of her DayGlo yellow socks then blew out a breath and folded her hands in her lap. So what if he didn't like her lyrics? That wasn't her best work. The best work was in her other notebook, the one with way too much personal information.

Like songs about a boy she'd once been in love with. *Once* because it was safer. Because she'd never tell anyone the truth.

He continued to flip pages with his agile fingers, reading silently, his expression blank. The other guys in the band all wore guyliner. He refused. The one time he'd put on makeup for a show at open mic night at a local club he'd looked almost too pretty. With that lush mouth, super-long eyelashes and thick, wavy hair, he'd been prime rocker material. The chicks had gone nuts for him, but he'd immediately gone back to his own personal style—jeans and concert tees mixed with the occasional leather vest. Hair gel was about as far as he went toward the whole musician look.

Not that it mattered. He already had groupies, both male and female. Guys wanted to be his friend. Girls wanted to do him. When any of her classmates bothered to talk to her, they always asked the same things.

"What's it like living with that hottie?"

"What does he wear to bed?"

"Have you ever seen him naked?"

Her mental answers were always the same. *Amazing, when it's not hell. Nothing. Absolutely not.*

She'd die if she saw Gray naked. She'd seen him shirtless and that was bad enough. The dude was ripped. Not that she'd seen tons of male bodies to compare him to, but his torso alone could cause serious drooling. Since he'd told her he slept totally nude—who did that?—she made sure to avoid his bedroom on weekends until early afternoon. Just in case. Not because she didn't want to see, but because she did. Really fucking bad.

"Well?" she demanded when she couldn't take another second.

He held up a finger and continued to read.

"Oh God. Forget it. I'm going to watch TV." She started to stand up.

"Sit." Gray grabbed her thigh and yanked her back down. He continued to read. "By the way, Mom told me you have math homework to do. TV's for later."

Yeah, she'd known the parental nets would drop down on her after her first midterm report had revealed her D in math. And biology. Her C in Government wasn't much better. "Jeepers, are you my guardian or what?"

"Or what. Shh."

There was one sure way to break his concentration. "So is Shelly your girlfriend?"

His lips twitched. "No."

She smoothed her palm over her other notebook. The one he would never see unless she dropped dead. If he didn't tell her what he thought of her music soon, that could be anytime now. "So you just have sex with her to pass the time?"

He tilted his head to look up at her from under the curve of dark hair that fell over one moody gray eye. "You been spying on me, squirt?"

Squirt. The most hated of all nicknames he could give her. "No. Of course not." She tried not to blush. "She just moaned a lot."

A satisfied smile drifted across his lips before he looked back down at her notebook. "Doesn't mean we had sex."

Curiosity ate at her while she gnawed on her nail. Yeah, she definitely wasn't going to show him her other notebook. She'd taken some guesses at what the "not sex" stuff was and her songs weren't exactly fit for church. They made her squirm a bit but she'd had to get the words down. "So she's not your girlfriend?"

"I just said she wasn't." He closed her notebook and returned it to her, along with the Stratocaster. "Do you have a melody for 'Captured' yet?"

"No."

"Let's figure one out."

"Does that mean you liked the lyrics?"

He fingered his own guitar, plucking the strings with a deftness she both envied and admired. "I liked them," he said simply. He lifted his head and caught her gaze with his. "Let's get to work."

Chapter Six

Finally.

Gray pushed his hands into her crazy braids. Her soft mouth tasted of rum. Of everything he'd ever wanted and told himself he shouldn't take.

Before now.

He tried not to rush, to let the moment spin out naturally. But when she moaned and parted her lips, inviting his tongue inside, he couldn't resist. He wrapped her hair around his wrist, dragging her up off the stool until she was half standing against him, her full breasts pressed to his chest. Her nipples imprinted his flesh even through their clothes. She wanted this. Wanted him, even if it was because she was a little tipsy and more than a little pissed. Her nails clawed down his side as she sucked on his tongue with an urgency that matched his own.

Come with me. Be with me. The words clamored loudly in his head. He was so tired of fighting his feelings for her. If it was wrong, if he'd go to hell for this, at least he'd take them on a long, hot ride through heaven first.

He eased back a fraction and dragged in a breath, already diving back down when the singe in his nostrils registered. The moments before he'd walked into the bar flashed through his mind in stark Technicolor.

Face close to a mirror, eyes shut. Too many memories crowding his head until he inhaled, slow and deep, and they all faded away. The high rushing through his veins, filling the vast, empty spaces that had gone to rot inside him.

No. God, no. He couldn't let that filth touch her.

You're the filth.

He shut his eyes and dug his fist into his forehead. Already the rush was receding, the edges of his consciousness blurring as reality encroached. The warmth that had exploded inside him from her kiss wouldn't last long.

She'd been about to kiss Nick when he showed up. Fucking Nick. *That* was the truth. More proof of what he'd never been able to accept.

Jazz would never be his. And now he'd made it so he didn't even deserve her.

Her sleepy blue eyes opened and she blinked, clearly confused why he'd stopped. Her lips were swollen and wet. So wet. "Gray?"

His hand was still embedded in her hair, fisting it at the root. He pulled it away, unsurprised when a tangle of rainbow-streaked dark strands snarled in his fingers. He must've hurt her. Again.

God, not again.

His gaze shot to hers and he swallowed hard at the hazy desire reflected back at him. He'd never been good enough for her, and he sure as hell wasn't now.

"That's enough. Party's over." The sharp female voice cut through the crash of noise in his head. He hadn't even realized that the people around them had quieted. It was still so loud in his brain. He pressed his fists against his ears and stumbled away.

Right into a coolly furious Lila.

"Easy." She gripped his forearm to hold him still when he would've kept going and stared into his eyes for a beat too long. Her lips pursed. "Band meeting in five."

Gray tried to process what she'd said. The words hung in the air between them, pulsing with a meaning he didn't get. What meeting? His vision wavered. Since when did she have three mouths? Jesus, she looked like a Venus flytrap with bright white teeth, ready to bite.

Someone bumped his shoulder, hard. "Oh Jesus. Right fucking now?" Nick. Naturally. "It's New Year's fucking Eve—"

"I don't recall asking for your opinion, Crandall." Lila's focus whipped to Nick for a fraction of a second, though she didn't release Gray. Good thing, because he wasn't entirely sure he could've remained standing if she had.

What had been in Cricket's shit tonight? He'd taken an extra hit, yeah, but he'd done this much before. He'd just wanted a little extra buzz to get him through the party.

At this rate, he'd be laid out before their meeting was over.

"We're not punching a freaking clock."

"We'll discuss it in private," Lila snapped at Nick. "Now."

She called something out to a passing waiter before leading Gray and the others—he assumed the others were behind him, but he didn't dare turn his head—from the packed VIP room into a narrow hallway. Halfway down it, she opened the door to an office crammed with a conference table and a few file cabinets, then grabbed the nearest chair and pushed him into it.

He didn't protest. All the fight had gone out of him the moment he'd dropped back into his body and realized he was ripping the hair out of Jazz's head like an animal.

Remind you of someone else who mistreats women?

"Gray."

He didn't lift his head. It took more energy than he had left. His thoughts played on a constant loop, taunting him.

You hurt Jazz. Just like he did. You're no better than Brent.

"Dammit, Duffy, get it together." Lila got right in his face. "You think I can't see it on you? Smell it on you? Get yourself straight. I'm not tolerating this."

He opened his mouth to reply then snapped it shut as the other guys shuffled in with Jazz in tow. Deacon had his arm around her shoulders and she gripped his waist as if she needed the assistance to walk.

Gray's heart lurched into his throat. He half rose out of his chair. "Jazz."

"Sit your ass down," Lila said flatly.

"But—"

"I said sit down and now I'm adding 'shut up' to that." She stalked to the door and slammed it closed. When she turned back, her lips curved. "Fun little party, hmm?"

Nick slumped into a chair at the head of the table. "Bipolar much?"

"I can assure you I'm not. What I am, however, is angry. Do you think being on our label is a right? That you can use and abuse our good faith—" her gaze landed on Gray before darting to each of them in turn "—and we'll just stand back and smile?" She stopped behind Nick's chair and aimed a death ray at the back of his head. "If so, some of you have grossly miscalculated."

"Lila, it was just a small scuffle. They probably had a little too much to drink." Deacon aimed a hard stare at Nick.

"Oh fuck that. I didn't start a damn thing. I was talking to Jazz, that's all."

Gray swore. "You weren't just talking to her, you frigging pri—"

"Grayson," Lila warned. "Now would be a really good time to learn to listen."

Gray scraped a hand over the back of his head and glanced at Jazz, who sat between Simon and Deacon. Between those two, she looked tiny. Deak still had his arm around the back of her chair and even Simon kept nudging her with his leg, clearly trying to annoy her into smiling.

It was good she had them. She needed someone else to rely on besides him. God knows he'd tried to be everything to her, but he'd failed. Over and over again.

"I'm listening." Gray shut his eyes.

Maybe then he wouldn't have to see the expression of disappointment Deak wore or the pinch in Jazz's smile. Simon wouldn't look too deeply into what had happened, if he'd even untangled himself long enough from his hookups du jour to notice. And Nick wasn't his friend anyway.

But Deak mattered. Jazz mattered. He hated letting them down.

Lila...well, yeah, she mattered too. She was his boss. Sort of. But he couldn't drum up much concern about PR nightmares and whatever icicle their manager had up her panties while he could still smell Jazz's watermelon-and-wildflowers scent clinging to his clothes.

Lately he hadn't been able to smell much. Even walking into the bar, where the scents of smoke and spilled beer and sweat were commonplace, he hadn't picked up anything until he reached Jazz. Somehow she'd gotten through.

"That goes for the rest of you too. Gray and Nick were the instigators of tonight's fiasco, but in case any of the rest of you decide to get cute, consider yourselves preemptively on notice. You're on Ripper Records because you're stars on the rise. But make no mistake. If any of you become a liability to this label and my reputation, you'll be out the door faster than you can say 'at-will termination clause'. Got it?"

Nick pushed back his chair. "We signed contracts. You have no right to threaten us."

"Read the fine print. Then go look up a band in the annals of pop culture called Menudo. They had a revolving door of talent. Oblivion could become the same."

Simon dusted his nails on his black sleeveless shirt. Gray was pretty sure it had sleeves before they arrived at the bar. One of his lady friends had probably torn them off. "Can't have Oblivion without the lead singer," Simon said airily.

Lila leaned forward to plant her hands on the table. "Keep telling yourself that." Her blue eyes were on fire. And in Gray's current state of mind, he half expected them to pop out of her head and hurtle like mini-missiles right at his face. "You're expendable, every one of you. You think your talent will save you? Look around Los Angeles. See how many of you there are and then come talk to me about how your ability makes you exempt."

"What the hell's the point of having a contract if you're holding it over our heads constantly? We walked away from fucking Trident's morality clause and it sure as hell sounds like—" Nick ground the heel of his hand into his eye. "Forget it. Different dancers, same tune. Guess you didn't save us from much, huh, Boy Scout?" He directed the last bit at Deacon.

Rather than shoot back a retort, Deacon steepled his fingers over his stomach. Placid to the last, except for the stone stare he leveled on Nick.

"You could try saving yourself," Lila suggested, propping a hip on the table next to Nick while she consulted her ever-present iPad. "You know, just for a change of pace."

For once, Nick didn't say anything. He cracked the knuckles on his left hand, his jaw working as if he were fighting to remain silent.

Gray understood the feeling.

"Wow. I'm impressed. This may be an Oblivion record for no sniping. And since we're all getting along so well, I've decided to spring something on you all that I'd planned to save until after the holiday. But why put off what you can do today?"

"My Magnum says we can put it off," Simon said in a low voice.

Jazz elbowed him. "Magnum or Magnums plural?"

Simon flashed her a grin and yanked on one of her disordered braids. She grimaced more than she normally would have and guilt arrowed straight into Gray's gut. He'd been too rough with her. Hell, he didn't know how *not* to be rough after wanting her for so fucking long.

Which was exactly why he needed to steer far away. Reason one of a million.

Simon flipped her braid between his fingers. "Both, pink passion fruit."

"Your Magnum is empty. Consider your New Year's Eve party over, Kagan."

"Aww, Brianna and Monica will be so disappointed." Simon's frown pulled down his cheeks, giving him a hangdog expression.

"I doubt it. Monica was already crawling all over one of the roadies when we passed her." Nick shook his head. "Some staying power you have, man."

"Hey, his fist never complains."

Everyone glanced at Gray. Christ, had he spoken aloud? He always thought stuff like that, but he never actually opened his mouth. Not anymore.

Jazz shot him a smile, her lashes sweeping down to hide her eyes before she shifted her attention back to Lila.

Simon grinned and thumped the flat of his hand on the table in front of Gray. "I got two fists. And I use 'em both."

Lila cleared her throat. "As charming as this detour into your personal recreational activities is, Simon, I'd rather we get back to business. Shall we?" Without waiting for his response, Lila tapped her tablet and directed a sunny smile at the group. "Ripper Records prides itself on being a different kind of record company. We take an active interest in growing our artists for reasons other than money, but let's face it, green always talks. Oblivion is booked for studio time beginning in late January for an as yet unnamed album. I'm sure you've come up with a few choices. Let's hear them."

Silence reigned.

"We just got off tour, for fuck's sake," Nick muttered.

"I didn't realize you'd nominated yourself as the spokesperson of the band." Lila waved her hand at the table. "But I'm all for group politics. All in agreement say 'aye'."

"Aye." Simon raised his fist.

"Shut the hell up. If you were closer to sober, you wouldn't want him to speak for shit."

Nick lifted a brow. "Oh, and who should be our spokesperson, Saint Deacon? You? In between knitting booties and shining your wedding band?"

"Not going there with you." Deacon directed his attention at the glittery landscape outside the window. "Miserable pricks suck as company."

Nick kicked back in his chair. "I'm not even sure you *have* a prick, never mind a miserable one."

"He must. I've seen his missus's baby bump," Simon affirmed.

Jazz poked Simon's shoulder. "Shut up. You're all looking like a bunch of jackasses."

"How dare you taint Papa Smurf's reputation, Jasmine?" Nick slid a crushed cigarette pack out of his jeans pocket. "And here I was just about to light up in his honor."

Lila plucked the remaining cigarette from the pack and tossed it to the floor. The crunching noise that followed proved she'd disposed of it with one of her wicked heels. "Consider that me doing you a favor," she said to Nick, who hadn't yet wiped the shock off his face. "First and last time."

Nick's lips twisted and he bit off whatever he'd been about to say. "I think it's you who needs a favor," he said softly. "Too bad I forgot my extra-long ice pick."

Simon snorted. "You forgot your extra-long everything, dude."

"I've had enough. Maybe you guys don't care about this band enough to stop cracking jokes, but I do." Jazz bounced to her feet, heat and energy vibrating off her in almost visible waves. "We don't have a name for our album, Lila. We haven't even made a list. As far as songs go, all we've managed to do is gripe at each other. We have some lyrics and chord progressions, but nothing much useable. Our material blows and no one seems interested in changing that fact."

"Are you interested in changing it?" Lila asked.

Jazz hesitated, then nodded. "Yes, I am."

"Do you have some songs you'd like considered?"

Jazz's gaze darted around the table before she crossed her arms and nodded again. "I have some stuff that could work."

"Oh yeah? Like what?" Nick leaned forward with an insolent smile. But Gray saw the gleam of curiosity in his eyes. He'd never admit to wanting to know what musical notes Jazz had up her sleeve.

"Like 'Captured'," Gray said quietly. "That's a great song. We could both play that in our sleep."

"Gray—"

"Let's do it, Jazz." He swallowed hard and focused on her face to block out the cacophony in his head. "You and me."

Chapter Seven

Then

"Mmm, guess it's a good thing I finally gave in to you."

"You guess?" Gray teased.

"Well, you were so persistent. Coaxing me no matter how many times I said no..."

Gray grinned and lifted his head, staring down at Melissa Peachtree spread out beneath him on his bed. He'd been trying to get her there for so long that he wasn't about to speed up the process, even if his mom was due home soon from work. Maybe he could make time stand still if he stared at the clock long enough.

Nah, scratch that. He'd rather stare at Melissa's tits.

"I think it turned out to be worth your while."

"Yeah, I think you're right." She lifted her shoulders off the bed. "Do that again. Harder."

"Your nipples are already red enough to match your lipstick. Sure you want more?"

"You know it, baby." She tugged on his hair, walking the fingers of her other hand up his chest to toy with the chain around his neck. She was a toucher, and he couldn't say he minded. At all. "Though there's something even better you could do for me with that mouth." Her dark eyes lit up with her suggestive smile.

His favorite thing. Some guys hated going down on a girl. He thought they were idiots. If he had his way, he would've been happy to eat pussy for breakfast, lunch and dinner. From the tiny pink string bikini stretched between her narrow hips and the dizzying scent of her arousal, he had a feeling this one would be particularly delicious.

"Is there?" He thumbed her nipples. "I think you're going to have to be a little more descriptive. Tell me what you really want. And don't play coy like you used to do."

She laughed, all throaty seduction, and leaned up on her elbows to study the movement of his mouth over her breasts. She wasn't some high school chick who was too young to understand what he craved, never mind want the same thing.

Melissa was a freshman in college, one of his friends' older sisters, and she'd drawn out their flirtation so long that his cock pulsed between his legs, thick and hard. He'd unbuttoned his jeans to give himself room, but he might as well not have bothered. There would never be enough room in his pants when Melissa was beneath him.

"So you want me to talk dirty." She fisted his hair to drag his mouth to hers. "Before you do me dirty."

His fingers continued working, unable to keep still. "Sounds about right."

"I want you to use those wicked-fast fingers to make me come. Then when I'm coming, I want you to replace them with your tongue." She bit his lower lip, dragging it between her sharp white teeth. "Slide it way deep inside my pussy until you lick me dry."

His heart kicked hard. "I like the way you think." He smiled and turned his head, burying his face in the thick ribbons of her blonde hair. She smelled like strawberries and sex. He didn't want to forget a single detail about having her this first time.

"Oh, and don't worry," she purred. "I always return the favor."

"I'm not worried." He shimmied down her curvy body. "All I want is that sweet pussy on my mouth."

A movement in the connected bathroom caught his eye and he shifted his gaze to the doorway, his hand fisting in the sheet beside Melissa's hip. Jazz stood just inside the threshold of the other doorway, utterly still. With her pigtails, cutoffs and bare feet, she looked like a kid. All she needed were scuffed knees. But her eyes weren't young. They watched him with an understanding way beyond her years.

Dull horror and embarrassment and something else, darker and edgier, coursed through his veins. He waited until Melissa turned her head and mouthed the word, "Go."

She held her ground. Not moving. Barely breathing from what he could tell.

Obviously she needed a nudge to get the hell out of where she had no business being. Short of getting up to shoo her away—which would be bad on too many levels to count—he had no choice but to continue and hope she got the hint. Fast.

Melissa flicked her tongue over her teeth. "Do I need to draw you a roadmap? Go south."

"I know right where I'm headed. No detours." Bracing his hands flat on the mattress, Gray ducked his head and caught the eager tip of her breast between his lips. He sucked harder than he had before, more than a little off-center from the knowledge that they had a spectator.

Fuck, if he closed his eyes, he would swear he could smell that watermelon-scented lotion Jazz was always smearing all over herself. She'd sat on his bed last week and he'd had to run his sheets through the wash twice to get every last trace of the scent out. Now she was filling up his bathroom with that same damn smell.

Whose bright idea had it been to move her into Brent's old room? He couldn't share a bathroom with a spy.

A spy who was still standing there, head tilted, eyes narrowed, as he slid down Melissa's body and yanked at her panties. He rolled them over her uptilted hips and practically attacked her pussy, so pissed off and turned on he didn't know what the hell he was doing.

Jazz shouldn't *be* there. He shouldn't be getting harder from knowing she was.

She was too young, a girl who'd seen and survived way too much. She wasn't ready for this. If he wasn't some kind of pervert, he'd get up and slam the door he'd accidentally left open.

Even though he knew she liked to come into his room that way. Even though he'd never locked a door to keep Jazz out in the months she'd lived in his—*their*—home.

Even. Even. Even.

Melissa moaned as he speared his tongue deep, completely without skill. He'd lost the rhythm. The beat to their movements was gone. He raised his head, not to seek his lover's expression, but Jazz's.

Their gazes locked. And held.

She fumbled behind her for the doorknob and stumbled into the room at her back. She looked for all the world like a doe who'd crawled off into the bushes to die after being hit by a car she'd never seen coming.

Fuck.

Shutting his eyes, he lowered his head to finish what he'd started.

Chapter Eight

Now

"You two can play your little song. Nice." Nick snorted with obvious derision. "Too bad we're a band and not Sonny and Cher, huh?"

"I'd like to hear it," Deacon said.

Jazz dropped back into her chair and groped for the chain around her neck. Gray glimpsed the flash of purple she flipped between her fingers and smiled behind his hand. She'd never taken that guitar pick necklace off in all the years since he'd given it to her, though he'd never actually seen her use it for its intended purpose. "I'm not sure I remember—"

"I remember." Gray hoped like fuck he remembered. Before, he would've been able to bring back the melody without even looking at the sheet music they'd scribbled together during those long nights in his basement. But *before* was a long time ago.

A wrinkle appeared between Jazz's brows. If he'd been closer, he wasn't sure he would've been able to stop himself from leaning in to kiss it. "We set it up for two guitars."

"We have two guitarists," Gray replied, well aware of her nerves whenever the spotlight shifted her way. There was a reason Jazz had drifted behind a drum kit rather than choosing to focus on guitar, and it sure as hell wasn't talent. She had it in spades with whatever instrument she picked up. Keyboards, drums, guitar—she was proficient in all three.

What she didn't always have was confidence, though no one but Gray knew that. He would've bet his last dollar that no one in Oblivion had seen beyond her wild-colored hair and iPhone stunts and crazy antics to the girl beneath who still never felt quite good enough.

Except him. He always saw all of her.

"And a drummer and a bassist and a...Simon," she trailed off, worrying the end of one of her braids.

"So we'll make it work. We've adapted how many songs?"

She bit her lip, making his head throb in tandem with his dick. He'd had that lip between his teeth less than ten minutes ago. And where was he now? Surrounded by his band and Lila and his own insecurities, pretending he didn't feel them pressing cold hands against his spine.

Unlike Jazz, he never doubted his talent. Everything else, yes. His worth as person, every fucking minute. But when he played his guitar, *he* was the drug. It was afterward, when he had to go over the same damn song sixty times, or when he had to sit across from the guy who'd screwed his girl right in front of him, that the darkness came back, tearing open the scabbed-over holes. So many holes. He didn't even know where they'd all come from anymore.

Maybe it didn't matter. He had a way to make them go away, so he used it. He went elsewhere to handle his shit, hoping she wouldn't ever find out. That she would never look too close. If that made him pathetic, weak, he'd take the label as long as he got the cure.

"Yes, but that was before." She implored him with her eyes to drop it, to let it go. Why she didn't want him to share that song, he didn't know. He couldn't think straight when those San Francisco Bay-blue eyes leveled on his.

Hell, who was he kidding? He couldn't think straight, period. The high was already wearing off, leaving nothing behind but exhaustion and misery.

"I have newer stuff." She shifted toward the rest of the band with hope in her voice. "Let me show you."

"Show us 'Capture'. If Vapor over there," Nick nodded toward Gray, "thinks it's so adaptable, bring it on."

She stared at her empty hands. "I don't have my notebook."

Gray smiled in spite of the anvil drumming at the base of his skull. She'd carted the same composition notebook around for years. Since Jazz had the smallest handwriting he'd ever seen, she'd filled those pages with hundreds of songs. If she ever lost it, she'd be screwed.

Someday he should scan it into a digital file for her. She definitely liked her technology, even if she went old-school when it came to her songwriting.

"It's in the van with our gear." Simon gestured toward the door. "If you need a couple of guitars, grab mine and Nick's and run it through for us."

"Here?" She shot a look at Lila, who nodded.

"I'll get the gear." Gray bolted to his feet, eager to get outside in the fresh smog. The air in this room was stifling him. Maybe the short walk would help him clear his head enough to fumble his way through the song.

He'd promised himself he'd never play high, and so far, he'd kept that vow. Practice, yes. God, he'd practiced high more than sober over the past year. But he'd never gone onstage with that buzz in the blood, even if sometimes he timed things all wrong. Some shows, the ones where even the music hadn't been enough to carry him away, he shook so bad that he played like a demon was climbing up his back just to distract himself from the agony.

Now he'd have to play the song that he and Jazz had refined so long ago, repeating it so many times they'd worn grooves in the strings of his old guitars. She rarely touched a guitar anymore, but he doubted she'd require more than a couple of minutes to get back her groove.

The girl—woman—was a freaking wonder in so many ways.

He headed out of the room before anyone could stop him, letting the door slap shut in his wake. As he pushed through the teeming crowd in the VIP area, all the more frenetic as the clock ticked closer to midnight, he glanced longingly at the line of shots a pair of glammed-up girls were doing at the bar. He'd never been a big drinker, other than a few misspent weekends in high school and college. Still, anything was better than the dry, jittery sensation in his veins like dry leaves blowing over his grave.

Somehow he kept moving. Past the liquor, past the women with their candy smiles and hungry hands. It had been so damn long since he'd fucked. Weeks. Months. Who even knew? The days blended together, spinning out into an endless chasm of music and money and blow.

At first he'd only taken a hit during the long nights of practice to keep up his energy. He'd hauled around the baggie Ziggy had given him for weeks. It scared him enough he'd told himself he wouldn't try it. After growing up with Brent, he'd seen exactly what kind of addictive genes ran in his family, even if his older brother's poison of choice was alcohol. One mistress or the other, they always screwed you sideways. He knew better.

Then he'd seen Jazz come out of a closet with Nick before a show at the Blue Rhino, and lo and behold, all his reservations had fallen away.

Halfway across the parking lot to the van, a sleek black vintage Mustang pulled up beside him. The passenger window slid down and Cricket leaned across the seat, her lips curved with such pleasure he half believed she was happy to see him.

"Hey there, handsome. I tried your cell. Thought you might be ready for a lift back."

"Phone's off." He scraped a hand over the top of his head, squeezing his palm until the prickle of his short, crisp hair centered his meandering thoughts. All the gel had a purpose. He could've cut glass with the spikes on his skull.

"What about the lift? I'm here now." She waved a plastic baggie, her smile widening. "I even brought a party favor."

He'd taken two long strides to the window before she let out a tinkling laugh and tucked it out of reach. "Not so fast, handsome. Come with me and we'll share."

Share. Yeah, fucking right. Like any good dealer, she never touched the stuff. She just used it as the powdery hook at the end of a very long rod.

Sucking in a breath, he tipped back his head. "I already partied tonight, remember?"

Partied. Talk about ironic. The parties she threw only lasted fifteen to twenty minutes, and the crash hurt like a motherfucker. But God, for that high, for those brief, golden moments where nothing hurt anymore, nothing crowded his brain until he couldn't think...he would've sold his soul.

Maybe he already had.

"I do. But this is premium stuff. I saved it just for you." She waved the bag between two slickly polished nails, that smile taunting and luring him both. It would be so easy to just *go.*

Why should he sit in that room with those jerks? He'd thought they were good guys once. Deak was, yeah. But the other two, they only cared about themselves. That was obvious after what they'd pulled with their old record label.

Nick was even worse. He didn't only want to steal their music and hijack the band, he wanted to take the one thing away from Gray that had kept breath coming in and out of his lungs for years. He'd built a life out of taking care of her, out of righting all the wrongs that people he'd never met had done to her when she'd been too innocent to fight back.

And Brent. Fucking Brent.

He squeezed his eyes shut, focusing hard on the memory of Jazz's mouth on his. So soft and wet. For that moment, she'd wanted him. Sixty seconds out of his life he would cling to with both hands, despite the promises he'd broke by even touching her.

"I'll never let anyone hurt you again."

For years, he'd waited for the day she saw him as someone other than her protector. Her buddy. Her music partner. He'd given her all the time in the world to make her move, determined not to force her hand by possibly guilting her into a relationship she didn't want. He knew she loved him, but was it the way for her it was for him? Sure, she'd made what seemed like a few tentative steps in his direction. She just never followed through.

Eventually he'd begun to think she'd slotted him firmly in the big brother zone, with the occasional exploratory side trip into "what if?" That didn't work for him. He couldn't be her friend with benefits. He honestly didn't think he could even casually date her.

After all these years, it was all or nothing.

Now, with the choices he'd made, even if she did want more, even if she could love him the way he loved her, it didn't matter because he'd ruined everything before they ever had a real chance. He wouldn't let the drugs touch her, even peripherally. So he couldn't touch her either.

His promise to keep her safe came before all else.

Gray cleared his throat. Rust filled his airway, gathered on his vocal cords. "So give it to me and get out of here before she sees you."

"*She*?" Cricket laughed again, harder-edged this time. "That sweet little thing that was hanging on you at Frenzy? She's Oblivion's drummer, isn't she?" She slipped her tongue in the corner of her mouth. "She also belongs to the group, so I've heard."

He slammed his hand against the car, making her jump. "Don't fucking talk about her like that. It isn't that way."

Images of that night with Nick and Jazz flashed through his mind, stark and bleak like the churning sky. Her undressing, tugging off her bra and baring her breasts. Crawling on Nick's lap to kiss him, driving her fingers through his hair. Her slipping onto Gray's lap, facing away from him. Gray helping her to open her legs wider so Nick could get a nice long lick.

Of *his* girl. His Jazz. The only thing he'd wanted for so long he'd had to become numb to the need or it would've killed him.

"Mind the car," Cricket said in a low voice. "I like you, but if you dent my baby, you'll be cut off. Because we both know you can't pay, handsome."

He rubbed against the pressure pounding in his temples. "I'm good for it. My money's tied up right now, but once we meet a few benchmarks with the band..." He trailed off, hoping that would be enough.

He didn't waste money—other than on blow—but there just wasn't a whole lot of it to be had yet. They were still a relatively new band on an up-and-coming label. Ripper Records wasn't Trident. They didn't get to live in a swank pad rent-free. It wasn't as if they were roughing it, but they were all paying and rent in LA wasn't cheap.

Picking up a few overnight shifts at the transport company he'd worked at for the past few years helped fill in the gaps, but he was only in town for a few weeks at a time. This break between the holidays and the beginning of March—minus studio time, which would be extensive, and a short club tour to keep them visible—represented Oblivion's longest break since they'd been signed. If he budgeted his time well, he'd be able to earn enough to pay back some of his debts. He just needed to juggle the separate halves of his life a little longer.

"I don't operate on promises. Even if I wanted to, the boss lady wouldn't allow me to."

Cricket had mentioned her a few times before. Supposedly she was especially ruthless because she was relatively new to the game. Made it all sound so nice and tidy. She was just a hungry businesswoman, trying to get ahead.

"She's not as forgiving as I am," Cricket continued, uncapping the bottle of water in the cup holder to take a long swig. "Look, let's be straight with each other. The only reason you're still walking around and not laid up in a hospital somewhere is because I like you. You're talented. You just keep working those fingers of yours, and you'll return what you owe with interest, won't you?" When he didn't do anything but continue to breathe hard and fast, she repeated, "Won't you, Grayson?"

"I said I'd get you your money."

"I have faith in you." She capped the bottle, set it back in the holder. "But there are other ways you could work off some of your debt." She smiled, slow and sure. "I'm open to...alternatives."

Gray rested his hands on the hot roof of the car and closed his eyes. Why was he making such a big deal about this? Sleeping with Cricket wouldn't make him a whore. He'd just be a guy who slept with a pretty girl. Simple. Uncomplicated. The rest was his business and his alone.

Not the band's. Not Jazz's.

In fact, doing this would lessen some of the pressure on him for the money. Maybe get Cricket to back off a little. In a way, he'd be buying Jazz's innocence for a while longer. It would kill her to find out what he'd gotten into, so she couldn't ever know.

He was the one illusion she had left. He'd be damned if he took that from her too.

Before he could talk himself out of it, he yanked out his phone and tapped out a quick text to Jazz. Then he opened the car door and slipped inside.

* § *

Sorry, something came up. I had to leave. Notebook's still in the van. Good luck. You're going to nail it.

Jazz gazed at her cell until the words swam. It wasn't surprising, since her shock swiftly turned to tears. Big, annoying ones she could feel hovering in her eyes, ready to spill if she so much as blinked.

Or looked up at her band mates, all sitting around the table, watching and waiting.

She swallowed. Swallowed again. There was anger beneath the sadness and pain, and way down deep below that lived fear. Something was very wrong with Gray. She couldn't put her finger on it, and she wasn't sure if it was because he'd become a skilled liar when she wasn't paying attention or if she was just fooling herself, pretending not to see the writing on the wall.

He was sleeping with that blonde chick, and she had him all twisted up. Plain and simple.

It was like high school, part deux. Gray had the sexy girlfriends, and she had a little vibrator she never even used out of sheer terror one of the boys would hear. She would never live it down. They could bang babes in stacks of twos and threes but her quality time with her bullet would be front page news.

Especially if Simon got too handsy with his phone while he was drinking some night.

"Well?" Nick nodded at her cell. "Is he coming back sometime this century?"

"No." The word shocked her as much as she could tell it surprised Nick. Acknowledging that Gray had made her believe that they were a team then let her down once more caused the tightness in her throat to return full force. Her stomach roiled and she clutched her phone to it as she dragged in a breath. "He had to...go. It was an emergency," she added, looking at Lila.

"What kind of emergency?"

Pussy. He needed it really bad. Obviously, since he was horny enough to even kiss me.

"His grandmother," she said instead, as solemnly as she could manage. Even pissed as hell at him, she would defend Gray with her last breath. He had done things for her that nothing short of murder could erase. Even this confusing past year couldn't touch the bond that had wrapped them tight all those years ago.

If he wanted to cut loose, break the chain so to speak, he'd need to get out the bolt cutters and cut more of the links than this.

She knew he banged other girls. Hell, she'd heard and seen it back in high school. What was one more? So what if his lips still tasted like *her* lip gloss when he laid them on someone else?

The ripping slash through her midsection caught her off-guard. She dropped her phone and doubled over, gasping as if someone had punched her square in the gut.

The abrupt metallic scrape of a chair made her look up. It took so much effort to just lift her head and focus on Nick. He was talking to Lila, his voice a dull hum.

"...leave us alone for a few minutes. Granny's so sick. Hard on the family..."

Holy shit, Nick was defending Gray. She knew he was doing it for her benefit, considering the concerned glances he kept aiming her way.

No wonder, since she hadn't yet managed to sit up straight again despite Simon and Deak's comforting touches—Simon's hand on her shoulder, Deak's on her other arm. They were offering her their support and silent solidarity without knowing why they needed to.

Hot tears blurred her vision and she lowered her head, wishing for once that she'd just left her hair down and not braided it back out of her face. She had nowhere to hide.

Nowhere to go to outrun the torment Gray's text—and his kiss—had caused.

"I understand family dilemmas and I'm sympathetic, really." Lila's voice had gone soft around the edges and the glance she directed at Jazz reflected compassion, not annoyance. Okay, yeah, so there was a little annoyance too. "But Gray has a responsibility to this band and for him to just up and leave in the middle of a meeting without giving a proper explanation proves exactly why I need to take the step I have in mind. Now."

"What are you saying?" Nick asked, his gaze still centered on Jazz.

Lila gripped her iPad to her chest. "I'm splitting you up."

Chapter Nine

Then

Outside the doorway to the Duffys' formal dining room, Jazz pressed a hand to her shaky stomach. If her belly knotted any more, she'd throw up for sure. "I'm so nervous."

Wide hands cupped her shoulders. "Why?" Gray spoke near her ear, his warm breath wafting through her hair and causing goose bumps to pop up on her neck. "We're your family."

Though the words helped settle some of the manic fluttering in her stomach, she rolled her eyes. "I've lived here a few months. Before then I was a complete stranger. It takes a lot longer than that for someone to become family."

Not for her with Gray, but she wasn't about to tell him that. She was already half in love with him and his parents. They made it so *easy*.

Now there was someone new she had to win over—Gray's older brother, Brent. She supposed she could use the reminder that nothing was guaranteed, nowhere was safe. There were always new challenges and higher hurdles.

Including smirky-mouthed frat boys who scared the hell out of her even in a photograph.

"Says who?" Gray tugged her back against his chest. She closed her eyes and savored, relieved he couldn't read her mind. "The best family is what you make when you get to choose. We chose you."

Her lips curved in spite of the pang between her breasts. How could words that filled her up also tear her down? She didn't want to cling. Didn't want to need him or his parents too much. This situation, like all the others in her life, was just temporary.

Wonderful, absolutely, but temporary.

She was being silly. Brent was giving her his room, for God's sake. He was probably a great guy. He had to be, didn't he, coming from such an amazing family? The twist in her belly whenever she glimpsed his face in family pictures didn't mean anything. He just looked so much like Gray that it was disconcerting. They had the same thickly lashed gray eyes, the same dark hair that tended to curl if not cut super short. Matching strong jaws and lush lips. They could've practically been identical twins if not for the fact that Gray was growing his hair out past his shoulders and had more definition in his arms and shoulders. He had a guitarist's upper body whereas Brent had a bit of a beer pooch. Otherwise, they were scarily similar.

But hey, that should make it easier to get to know Brent, right? That he looked like someone she lo—cared about a lot had to help. Besides, he would only be home for the weekend to pack up the rest of his stuff to take back with him to his off-campus apartment. She was getting his room permanently...for however long forever lasted here.

His bedroom was large like Gray's and the enormous space overwhelmed her in the best way. She could already picture having her girlfriends over to sit on the fluffy white rug in front of the bay windows that overlooked the backyard with its kidney-shaped pool and brightly colored deck chairs. Their voices would fill the room with their laughter and happiness, chasing away the monsters that lived not in Jazz's closet, but in her head.

If she actually *had* any girlfriends, she would've pictured that.

Instead she visualized sitting on the bed with Gray, notebooks and music composition books spread out between their knees, guitars on their laps, surrounded by the scent of erasers and Cherry Coke and Gray's minty aftershave. She'd never seen him anything but clean-shaven, which was why it was a surprise to feel his stubbled cheek scraping over hers.

"Stop thinking so hard. You're making *my* brain hurt."

"Sorry. Bad habit." She laughed and shifted to kiss his cheek, something she'd done a million times. She'd kissed his cheek the morning before she'd watched him go down on his latest girl, kissed it again the next day when he'd come down to breakfast and looked at her with heavy, brooding eyes. They'd never spoken of those moments when she'd played voyeur. If it was up to her, they never would.

But now there were new moments, a new tension unwinding between them as her careless cheek kiss glanced off the corner of his mouth, so close that she swore she tasted cherry cola. His wary gaze shot to hers and he hooked his arm around her waist, drawing her in even as his mouth twitched with all the things he didn't say.

"Sorry," she repeated. God, her cheek was still tingling from the imprint of his stubbled jaw. "Missed."

"Stop apologizing, Jazz." Gray eyes so like the mists over the San Francisco Bay drifted over her face. But they weren't cold. They were the day's warmth burning off the fog until only heat lightning remained. She felt the sizzle and simmer in her bones, in her blood. "You have nothing to be sorry for, ever. You're perfect." His lips were a heartbeat away. He angled his head and they skated closer for a fraction of a second. Lifetimes passed in that instant yet they weren't nearly long enough to feel all of *this*. "Absolutely perfect."

She lifted her hand but she wasn't fast enough to hold him still. That was Gray. Life. Movement. Pure energy captured in human form. He was already moving away, striding through the dining room doors and calling out to the guy who waited on the other side with his parents. His brother. His family.

She wasn't truly his sister and could never—would never—be more.

Chapter Ten

Now

Splitting up the band? What the hell?

Deacon lumbered to his feet. "What is that supposed to mean? You can't split us up. That's not your call to make."

One of Lila's pale blonde eyebrows lifted. "Oh, you'd be surprised what calls I can make, Mr. McCoy. However, in this case, you misunderstand me. I'm not splitting up the band." A hint of a smile crept across her mouth. "For long."

"I've had enough of this shit for one night. Call us back when you're done speaking in riddles." Nick shoved out of his chair and had made it halfway to the door when Lila barked out a command.

"Sit. All of you. And listen with the things on the side of your head instead of the big gaping maws under your noses."

Jazz sniffled and tried to discreetly run her thumbs under her eyes. Simon bumped his chair into hers then slid his arm around her shoulders, giving her an excuse to lean into his embrace. After the near band breakup a couple of months ago, things weren't the same between her and Simon anymore, but she wasn't about to fight that battle right now. She was tired of fighting to hold on to the pieces of her life.

It was nice, just now, to be held.

Her gaze connected with Nick's across the table. His Adam's apple bobbed in the stubbled column of his throat but he didn't look away.

After tonight, she had a feeling he was willing to hold her too, in a much different way than Simon or Deak. Somehow he still was, even after that mess that had been the threesome with Gray.

And what was stopping her from taking that comfort if it was offered? Why shouldn't she feel good too?

Because he's not who you want and it's not fair to either one of you to settle.

God, she hated that reasonable voice in her head sometimes. All the time lately.

"When I said I intend to split the band up, I meant temporarily. For the ultimate good of Oblivion."

"Should we pull our pants down and bend over now or should we wait?"

Jazz tried not to smile at Nick's question but Simon choking his laughter into her hair didn't help. Deak, on the other hand, sat stoic, stone-faced to the end. He was the best negotiator of all of them and wouldn't concede even a smile until he knew what Lila had in mind.

Jazz had to admire him for that, just as she admired him for managing to build a family in the middle of the craziness that was life for a new band on the road. If a little envy snuck in there from time to time, she figured that was natural. Harper would be starting to show soon. Hell, she was already glowing. They both were, Deak in a much more mansterly way, of course. They were new too, their marriage, their life together. But they were a unit.

She wanted that so fucking bad.

Kinda crazy that she'd achieved the dream of being in a semi-famous band but the one of settling down with a husband and family seemed to get farther away by the day. Not just any husband. It would always be Gray for her. Always.

Lila sent Nick a withering look. "Please, don't drop trou on my account. I'm not sure my heart could take the thrill. Now if we can continue..."

Jazz blinked away the renewed prickling in her eyes and tried to focus on Lila. "Shouldn't we discuss this when Gray's here?"

"I intended to do just that until Granny fell ill. Unless you can get him back here in the next ten, we proceed without him."

"No," she whispered. "He's gone."

"Then we'll continue now." Lila eased a hip on the table, putting Nick at her back as she tapped away on her tablet with her gleaming nails. "As of tomorrow, Oblivion is being sent away on a working sabbatical for a couple of weeks to get your shit straight. You'll be split into two groups. Group one will have accommodations at the Santa Monica Inn and Spa. Group two will be stationed at a luxurious cabin. Thanks to some generous agreements we have with the owners of said properties, all expenses will be paid by Ripper Records, assuming you come back with material we can use for the record. If you don't, your future monies will be deducted at an appropriate rate of repayment for the debt you have incurred. A brief document outlining terms will be presented for you to sign forthwith."

"Forthwith this," Nick exploded. "You're breaking us up to send us to Disneyland and then if we don't come back with the biggest toys, we gotta pay out the ass?"

"Nicholas," Deak said in a low voice. "Let the woman speak."

"Oh, I'm quite done. This is not optional. This is not a vacation. You are being sent to optimal locations in the hopes that maybe a change of venue will help you return our investment in you. I would advise all of you to be productive in the teams you're assigned and come back with usable material in the time allotted."

"Or else what?" Simon wondered.

"We'll just leave it at *or else* for now." Lila gave Simon a blinding smile and glanced at her watch. "Well, look at that. Almost midnight. You kids should go enjoy the rest of your evening. I'll meet you at eight a.m. sharp with your team assignments at Ripper Records. Gray too," she added to Jazz.

Jazz nodded. Yeah, rounding him up after his sexathon would just put the capper on her night.

"Happy New Year, Oblivion." With another smile and a pat on the head for Nick that had him snarling, Lila sashayed out of the room.

"Finally," Simon muttered, gently extricating himself from Jazz and bouncing to his feet. He made a beeline for the door. "See you party people later. I'll catch a ride with the girls. You can take the van, Nicky," he said over his shoulder on his way out.

"I'm out of here too. Harper's probably ready for bed by now." Deak unfolded himself from his chair and cast a worried glance at Jazz. "You okay, pix? Want to get a ride home with us?"

"Nah, I'm fine. Thanks." She squeezed Deak's massive forearm. "I rode over with some of the roadies. I'll just—"

"I've got her." Nick kept his focus on Jazz while he spoke to Deak. "Have a good New Year's, man."

Deak stroked a big hand over her hair. "You good with this?"

Jazz heard the question within the question and smiled. *You good with dealing with him while he's in full dick mode?* She'd always felt like she understood Nick, even before they'd had the bright idea to spend some time together naked. "Yeah." She reached back to squeeze his arm. "Tell Harper to call me tomorrow, k?"

"Will do. Happy New Year, pix." After a minute, he sighed. "You too, Nick."

Then he was gone.

"So." Nick flexed his fingers. Like the other guitarist she knew, he seemed unable to keep his hands still. "Where did Gray really go?"

"I don't know."

"C'mon, you have to know that I won't make trouble—"

"How do I know that? Based on your history of, oh, I don't know, making trouble at every opportunity? Especially when it comes to me and Gray."

"You're a unit." When she only stared at him, he knotted his fingers together. "You and Gray. Can't have one without the other."

She didn't say anything. It didn't feel very much like that at the moment, but that didn't change the reality that her allegiance to Gray couldn't be broken. The past year of mostly suck couldn't erase all the millions of good memories they shared.

Besides that, she didn't want to hurt Nick. If even a shred of his feelings toward her remained from their...whatever the hell it had been, she didn't want to twist the knife. She'd cared about him too, enough to have sex with him. Still cared despite what he'd done—tried to do—to the band with Simon.

"You know our history," she said, rubbing her gritty eyes. All she wanted right now was to check out from the world for a few hours. Morning and the class field trip would come all too soon.

"I do. I also saw your future tonight."

"What future?"

"The one where he runs off and leaves you holding the bag, and you'll make any excuse in the world for him while he violates everything you think he stands for."

Her head snapped up. "You don't know him like I do."

"No. I don't. I don't know you all that well either. But I know people. He's...not in a good place," he said finally, directing his attention out the window.

"You don't know him like I do," she repeated, ignoring how the words echoed in her chest. So they were having a rough patch. That didn't change who they were together. Gray was the best friend she'd ever have. She trusted him with her life. Her body. Her heart.

He might not have much use for the second two things in that list, but she wasn't going to demolish their relationship just because he didn't want her like she wanted him. Too bad, so sad. She'd lived through worse in her life. So much worse.

Besides, his shutting her out stung more than anything else. Even the sex. She might not have watermelons for breasts, but she'd been Gray's confidant for years. His lying about needing to leave wounded her in a way nothing else could. And now she was sitting alone with Nick.

Déjà vu was a freaking bitch.

"You want to practice that song? 'Captured', was it? We can go back to the apartment, run through it together. You can use Simon's guitar."

"Is that all you're willing to let me use? I mean, let's be clear about what's going on here. You're not just being a helpful bandmate. You have an agenda, right?"

He cracked his knuckles and sprawled back in his chair, sending her a disarming smile that would've fooled most people. She'd gotten to know him better than most, not because he wanted to share himself with her, but because she'd made a study of him in the quiet moments when he didn't know he was being observed. Partly to distract herself from Gray, partly to see if she'd been wrong that Nick had some good inside him in spite of how frigging hard he tried to prove that he didn't.

"That depends on you."

"Why?" she asked softly, trying to understand. "Why would you want to get involved in my mess again?"

Something shifted in his golden eyes. "You look like you could use a friend tonight." He shrugged. "Doesn't have to be any more complicated than that."

Oh, if only that were true. "What about you? Can you use a friend?"

His mouth crooked into a semblance of a smile. "Damn sure better than having an enemy."

She smiled and rose. "Let's get out of here."

"So I'm guessing that's a maybe?" He crossed the room to open the door and ushered her out ahead of him.

"That's an 'I'm sorry, but it's not fair to you'." She sighed. "Said with plenty of regret."

"Do you see me worrying about what's fair?"

"One of us has to. I didn't before and you got caught in the middle."

His mouth lifted again. "Sometimes the middle's a pretty hot place to be."

"Hell's hot too. That doesn't mean you want to hang out there for eternity."

"Nah. But for an hour or two, why not?" He shot a grin over his shoulder and led the way into the VIP room.

Her smile faded as they stepped into chaos. The loud countdown by the guests indicated it was almost midnight, as did the number of faces turned toward the flat screen TVs tuned to the ball dropping in Times Square.

Almost a new year and she didn't have anyone to kiss. Yet again.

Nick glanced at her, his expression miles more sympathetic than she would've given him credit for. "Your call, Jasmine," he said quietly enough that only she could hear.

Not a lot had felt like her call lately. She was tired of being tugged along in the wake from Gray's ship. That didn't mean she would make another colossal mistake just to avoid her loneliness for a little while longer.

She leaned in just as the countdown hit one. "Happy New Year, Nick," she murmured, kissing his cheek.

He gripped her shoulders and offered her a cheek kiss as well, then eased back and shook his head. "I hope he realizes one of these days how lucky he is."

"Not sure about that." She tucked her hair behind her ear and glanced toward where Deak and Harper were wrapped up in each other, smiling and kissing while he protectively cupped her growing belly. She wasn't jealous. Nope, not even a little.

Liar. She was so green Oscar the Grouch would think she was a long lost relative.

"Hey. Look at me." Nick tapped her chin until she did what he asked. "You can't keep doing this to yourself. You need to tell Gray once and for all how you feel and force him to make a move."

She tugged him toward the corner of the room and leaned up on her tiptoes to speak near his ear so he could hear her over the noise. "Are you honestly giving me dating advice?"

"Please. You two are so far past dating it's insane. Just fuck already or get out of the bedroom."

It took a minute for his words to sink in. When they did, she let out a startled laugh and gripped his shirt, moving in close to speak once more. "You ready to split this party and head home to practice?"

The grin he flashed her was pure sin. "Can't imagine a hotter New Year's Eve."

"Me either." She grinned. "I'm totally lying."

"Me too." He smacked her ass and dragged her toward the exit. "Now get a move on, Edwards. We have magic to create."

Things weren't that bad. She had friends. She was part of a successful band. She could do anything she put her mind to. Which meant Nick was right. She needed to stop pretending she was going to make a move on Gray and actually *do* it, big-boobed-blondes aside. Whether he said yes or no, at least she wouldn't be wondering anymore.

Time to let the sticks fall where they may.

* § *

He was having a nightmare. That could be the only explanation for the litany of shit currently infiltrating Gray's brain via a tinny voice on TV.

"In entertainment news, we have the scoop on up-and-coming hard rock band Oblivion. Word on the street is that a red-hot love triangle is about to split the band apart. The band's drummer, Jazz, looks like she has all she can handle of Oblivion's guitarists in this undated pic. Last night's show at Frenzy provided another opportunity for this scorching triangle to generate some heat, though from these pictures snapped at Sharkey's Bar, it looks like Oblivion's two guitarists aren't as fond of each other as they are of the pint-sized drummer."

"Pint-sized?" Gray groaned. "Jesus." He wasn't even going there with the rest of that crap.

"Well, now, that must be mighty difficult, facing both of your love interests day after day. Wonder how long it will be before Oblivion implodes like so many great bands before them. What do you think, Pete?"

"I think it's too bad. But she is pretty cute. Guess I can see why those boys are pulling each other's hair out over her."

Gray cocked open an eye and ascertained that yes, the voice was coming from the TV. And no, seeing himself punching Nick on a 60-inch widescreen wasn't any improvement over listening to that ridiculous morning monologue spewed by two geriatric types sipping coffee and beaming greasy smiles.

"Had enough?" Cricket purred next to his ear. "Because I have more." She dropped a newspaper in his lap, considerately turned to a black-and-white photo of Nick hugging Jazz at Sharkey's. She was gripping his shirt front and leaning up to talk to him—or kiss him. If that wasn't bad enough, the smaller inset photo showed Nick's hand on her ass.

On her fucking *ass*, right there in the middle of the club.

Gray shoved the paper away and ground the heels of his hands into his eyes. "What the fuck is this, Cricket?"

"Aww, you didn't read the article." She made a *tsk tsk* noise. "One of the 'special friends of the couple' said they were giggling and groping each other as they left, and Nick mentioned something about 'making magic together'. Sounds like those two are a real item, doesn't it?"

"Stop it." He pushed his hands through his hair and locked them behind his neck. His head was pulsing like a freaking strobe light. "Leave me alone."

"No can do, handsome. See, you crashed here last night without giving me...well, anything. I thought maybe this visual would get you to finally pull your head out of your ass long enough to acknowledge the facts." Her candy-sweet breath fluttered over his cheek and he shrank away as if it was the foulest stench he'd ever encountered. She only laughed. "Your little drummer girl isn't yours anymore, loverboy. She belongs to someone else now." Her fingers danced over his bare torso—why the hell was he half naked?—on their way to toying with his belt buckle. At least he still had his pants on, thank God. "And you belong to me."

"I don't belong to anyone." But he didn't push her away, because he'd noticed something even more disturbing than her meandering hand.

The lower part of his stomach burned, as if it had been branded. A quick investigation told him why. Apparently he had a new tattoo, and it was a classy one. A small black arrow started right below his navel and pointed downward, captioned with a charming slogan—*this way to Oblivion*. The O in Oblivion had been adorned with a skull and crossbones, in keeping with each of the band members' decision to get an Oblivion tattoo.

Nice to know that even when he was clearly out of his mind, he still followed the acceptable band tat format.

"Christ almighty. What did you do to me?" He traced the words while he flipped through his memory banks of the night before. All he remembered was Jazz. Kissing her. Holding her close for a brief snatch of time. That irritating band meeting before walking away from her to get more blow. Snorting it the moment he'd arrived at Cricket's, because he'd been desperate to forget finding Jazz with Nick. Again.

After that, nothing.

"I didn't do anything to you. Nor did you do anything to me. Unfortunately." With a heavy sigh, Cricket rested her arm on the back of the sofa and toyed with the ends of his hair.

He elbowed aside the pillow wedged against his hip. Apparently Cricket's living room couch had been his bed last night. So much better than waking up in her actual bed.

"So, ah, just to clarify, we didn't have sex." He glanced at her. "Right?"

"No. You worked your way through my stash, demanded Jeremiah do a new tat for you on the spot and passed out halfway through. How many days had you been up straight?"

"I don't know. A lot." Probably three or four, minus a couple of short naps. He'd forgotten what it was like to just go to bed at a regular time and sleep. When he did manage to doze off, nightmares usually woke him up in a few minutes. Sometimes they were of crazy horror-movie type shit. Other times he dreamed of the day he'd burst into Brent's room at the sound of Jazz's screams, only to find her pinned beneath his brother.

That memory never left him, no matter how much he snorted.

"I could tell. As hot as you looked with your eyes rolling back in your head, I went up to my own room alone."

He let out a grateful breath. "Good."

"Not so good. You still owe me. Actually, you owe me even more than you did before." She tapped her bright red nails against her mouth. "Any ideas on how you're going to start repaying me? And when?"

Jesus. Not this again, first thing in the morning. He rubbed his hand against the throb in his temple and swallowed the dust in his throat. He'd need to brush his teeth with a Brillo pad to get that toxic taste out of his mouth.

"You managed to cough up the cash for this," she said lightly, tracing a nail over the arrow that led south. As humiliating as the tat was, he couldn't deny the flare of interest beneath his waist the farther down her nail crept. And that shamed him more than being in her debt.

He didn't want Cricket. He didn't want to want her or what she stood for. That probably made him a hypocrite. Or just a delusional junkie.

Fuck, he wasn't a junkie yet. He still had control. Maybe it didn't seem like it, but he could walk away from the coke anytime he chose to. He just hadn't chosen yet.

"See, I saw your wallet last night. That tattoo just about tapped you out. But the offer I made you still stands. For now." She leaned back and parted her legs, revealing the tiny scrap of panties she wore under her miniskirt.

Pink lace. Christ. "Why would you be willing to let me off that easily?"

"Who said anything about letting you off? You'll be getting *me* off." She laughed and tugged on his hair. "You have a reputation for fast fingers. Let's see how fast and we'll talk about how much you still owe me when you're finished."

When he didn't respond, she leaned closer and licked the side of his throat. He shuddered before he could check the urge. Hell, his dick should be soft right now, not hard enough to hold up her prissy glass coffee table. Cocaine dick could be a problem for some, though luckily—or unluckily, considering his lack of a sex life—his usual side effect was inhuman staying power.

A fuzzy memory from the night before flashed through his mind. Jeremiah, the tattoo dude, had slipped him a baggie of male enhancement drugs along with a stash of supposedly primo weed. Those had been bonus gifts to go along with the reduced rate tattoo. Signs of true friendship right there. Gray hadn't taken the pills or the weed last night but he'd held on to them. Never know. He might fuck again someday and need the pills to combat the coke effects. Or he might finally run out of Cricket's good graces and be forced to become a stoner.

"You want me. I know you do." She reached down to stroke his cock through his jeans and he couldn't hold back the groan. Damn, it had been so long since he'd had hands on him that weren't his own. It had even been a while since he'd touched himself. "And I definitely want you. You should've seen yourself last night. So hard and pulsing just from doing the line that I could see it in your jeans. Jere turned on that porno and started the tat gun and I swear, you were ready to go right there."

God, it was all coming back to him now. Moans from the TV, Jere laughing as he told stories about rubbing coke on his girlfriend's pussy to get them both off faster. Gray laughing too, because when he was high everything was so fucking funny.

Now it wasn't. Nothing was funny about what she was doing to his dick through the denim, squeezing the head of his shaft, tracing the edge of the tip with one of her wicked nails. His balls felt like knots. He had to come. It had been too long.

"Come on, handsome. We can make each other feel so good." She nipped the tendon in his throat and his length jerked in her hold. "Besides, you know your little drummer girl's getting some of her own right now. You don't need that stupid bitch."

He shoved her back and stumbled to his feet. In a minute he'd have to adjust himself but right now touching his cock wouldn't be smart. "I gotta go."

"Go how?" She rested her arms on the back of the sofa and spread her legs wider, offering him a glimpse of the wet spot on her panties. Jesus. "You came here with me, and I'm not taking you anywhere."

"Fine. I'll call a cab." One way or another, he was getting out of there. She wasn't allowed to talk about Jazz that way. No one was.

She let out a tinkling laugh as he lurched toward the door. "Do you even know where you are?"

"I have my phone." He patted his pockets and glanced around wildly. "Where the fuck is my phone, Cricket?"

She waved it between two fingers before dropping it between her parted thighs. "Come and get it, handsome."

Chapter Eleven

Then

"Everyone, let's hold hands and give thanks for this wonderful night we can spend here together."

Jazz snuck a glance at Gray under her lashes as she tentatively gripped the hand he held out. He grinned at her and laced their fingers together while the family said grace.

On her other side sat Brent, Gray's older brother. He gripped her other hand without any of the playfulness, his lips quirked in an expression closer to a sneer than a smile.

She had no reason to dislike the guy. She even kind of owed him for being nice enough to give up his room for her to use. But something about the way he stared at her for a little too long skeeved her out. Especially when Gray was around. He seemed to enjoy antagonizing his brother by teasing her with his lewd jokes. He didn't mean anything by it, she was sure. Gray just tended to get a tad overprotective.

A few moments later, they moved on to the Thanksgiving meal itself. As soon as she cut into the thick slab of turkey Mrs. Duffy had given her—technically, Conchita, the housekeeper, had given it to her—she decided she couldn't hold back her gratitude any longer. "May I say something?" Jazz asked.

"Of course, honey." Mrs. Duffy smiled. "This is your home too."

"That's just it." Jazz set down her fork to avoid attacking the succulent meat like a wild animal.

She'd gone through enough lean times in her life to have to struggle not to leap on food when it was presented to her. At the Duffys', it was presented often. Breakfasts were luxe affairs with mounds of scrambled eggs, stacks of sausage, piles of crispy bacon and jugs of fresh-squeezed orange juice. Dinners were the same.

And Thanksgiving dinner blew both out of the water. Food seemed to weigh down the table. She'd poured a moat of gravy around her turkey and Mrs. Duffy had only laughed.

"What is it, honey?"

"You've made me feel like I really belong here. I've been shuffled so many places I didn't think that was possible anymore. I just wanted to say thank you. For me, it really is Thanksgiving."

"Aww, how sweet," Brent said under his breath. When she shot a look his way, he smiled and forked up more potatoes.

Gray squeezed her hand. "You do belong, J. How many times do I have to tell you that?"

J. He so rarely called her anything but Jazz, though when he did she always got a warm burst inside her belly. "Apparently a lot, *G,*" she teased, lowering her head.

"Aw, y'all are so adorable together," Brent put in just before Mrs. Duffy spoke.

"Jasmine, sweetie, we love you. You know that. Mr. Duffy and I always wanted a daughter."

Jazz only smiled, so moved she couldn't speak.

Brent waited until Mr. and Mrs. Duffy headed into the kitchen to get pie and coffee—and probably to sneak a kiss, since those two were so lovey-dovey it made Jazz blush—to drop his next zinger.

"Gray, would you say you feel brotherly toward our cute little Jazzy?" He tipped his head to the side. "Because I'm not so sure. I think I'd call it something else."

"Shut up," Gray said, voice low.

Jazz frowned and reached for her water glass. What was Brent getting at? He couldn't mean what it sounded like. Gray didn't have feelings for her. That was perfectly obvious to her every time he brought home some new chick.

Brent smirked. "Jazzy, I'm sorry. I shouldn't interrupt a nice meal with such talk. Guess I'm just choking on all the hormones in the air."

Gray shot to his feet. "You want to take this outside?"

Brent giggled like a teenage girl despite the fact he was over six-feet tall and built like a linebacker. "Oh man. This is hilarious. You're really torqued."

"Gray, sit down," Jazz said, still not getting what was going on. Brent was just being a jerk as usual but why was Gray getting so pissed off? "Your parents will be back in a minute."

Gray didn't seem to be listening to her anymore. "Her name is Jazz, not Jazzy," he said to his brother, opening and closing his fists at his sides.

"Is that so?" Brent glanced at Jazz. "You have any problem with me calling you Jazzy?"

She bit her lip, her gaze drifting to Gray again. She didn't want them to fight today of all days. This was a day for family, and she didn't ever want to get between the two brothers after the Duffys had been so wonderful to her. "N-no, I guess not."

"You heard her." Brent dragged his chair closer and threw his arm over her shoulders. His breath smelled disgustingly of beer and chewing tobacco. "She likes whatever I give her, don't you, Jazzy?"

Caught in the trap of his arm, she tried to smile for Gray's benefit. "It's Thanksgiving. Let's not argue, okay?"

It took Mr. and Mrs. Duffy's reappearance for Gray to drop back into his chair. His gray gaze defiant, he snatched her hand, pulling her closer to him and away from Brent.

Brent only chuckled and let her go.

That time, he let her go.

Chapter Twelve

Now

The hour of reckoning was at hand. Oblivion was about to be broken up and sent to opposite camps—and one member of their ranks was nowhere in sight. As expected.

"Where the hell is Gray?" Lila demanded.

Everyone turned toward Jazz. She pursed her lips and dragged out the speech she'd rehearsed when numerous texts to Gray had gone unanswered.

"He's very sorry, but—" she began.

"Don't bother." Lila set her tablet down on the long table in conference room C at Ripper Records. Framed gold albums lined the walls around them, shooting off sparks that would blind Jazz if she dared look away from Lila's furious blue gaze. "Evidently Gray thinks you're his happy little parrot, but perhaps I didn't make myself clear enough last night. This meeting is not optional. Either he gets his ass here now or he's suspended from Oblivion."

"Hold it," Deacon said, pressing one big palm to the tabletop. "Aren't you being a little hasty? He had a...serious issue come up." He raised his brows at Jazz as if it was her fault he was forced to cover for her best friend. "He'll be here as soon as possible. Won't he, pix?"

Jazz darted another glance at her phone. She didn't know what to do. She'd texted Gray twenty times, the messages becoming increasingly frantic the closer it became to eight a.m. He hadn't replied.

The fact that he wasn't there because he was probably getting laid had ceased to be important in light of his being kicked out of the band. She couldn't do this without him. He was the one who'd pushed her to make something of her music when she'd been content to play just for the sake of playing.

Then, like a miracle, her cell vibrated with an incoming text.

"It's him." She blinked at the words on the screen until they made sense.

I'm outside. Pay my cab? I'll pay you back.

She scrambled up from her seat, waving the phone. "He's outside. I've got to go get him. I'll be right back."

"Jasmine, you're under the same warning he is," Lila said. "This is serious business and I need everyone here in the next ten or we're going to have a problem."

The not-so-subtle threat landed a barb in Jazz's chest but she shook it off and moved to the door. "I'll be right back. I promise."

Outside, she found Gray leaning against a yellow cab. He wore the same clothes as last night, though they were more wrinkled, and his hair stood straight up. The bags under his eyes were so puffy they looked painful. No matter how she tried, she couldn't *not* think about why he looked so exhausted.

Worst of all, the nearer she got, the more she smelled the perfume that clung to him. Not the cheap kind either. Nope, this was high-class scent.

Even after last night, she'd tried to pretend that he hadn't gone off to fuck that blonde. Perhaps there was another explanation. He wouldn't leave her high and dry for a simple booty call. Maybe that was where her logic had broken down. What was between him and that woman wasn't simple. It couldn't be. He wouldn't have left her in the lurch for someone insignificant.

So that meant she didn't need to make a move at all. He was taken. She'd had her chance and she'd wasted it. Period.

Ignoring the fist that wrapped around her throat, she pulled out some bills and thrust them through the open window of the cab. Then before Gray could speak, she turned and headed back toward the building.

It was his choice to follow her or not. She'd done as much as she could.

"Jazz, wait."

She didn't stop walking until his brutally strong fingers clamped around her upper arm. "What?" she snapped.

Obviously surprised by her tone, he let his hand drop and shoved it into the pocket of his baggy jeans. "I wanted to explain—"

She started walking again. "There's nothing to say."

"Yes, there is. I'll pay you back. I just ended up short."

If she didn't look at that face she'd loved so long that her pulse sped every time she saw him, she'd be okay. She'd get through this. "Yeah, whatever. It's no big deal."

"Is that what you said to Nick about kissing me last night?"

Stunned, she stopped and stared at the splashy record company logo on the building while she struggled not to let the lid off her temper. By nature, she wasn't a volatile person. She worked hard to be happy, to keep the demons at bay. She fought to count her blessings rather than her disappointments. But Gray affected her like no one else ever had.

"You have a lot of nerve," she whispered, afraid to raise her voice in case it came out as a scream.

"Do I? Apparently not enough, because I should've done that years ago." He grabbed her arm again, and this time she slapped him back, nailing him in the chest hard enough that he immediately released her.

"Should've done what years ago? Ditched me to run off with some blonde who takes baths in perfume? Consider this your invitation to do just that."

"And if I do, then what? You get a free pass to go back to giving Nick closet blow jobs?"

Before she could toss back a response—or even wipe the shock off her face that he knew about the blow jobs she used to give Nick before shows to help him with his stage fright—he held up his hands, palms out. "I shouldn't have said that. I apologize."

"No, you shouldn't have. It's none of your fucking business when you've spent the night balling some babe."

"It wasn't my business long before last night," he said quietly, the words ripping equally quiet gashes inside her. They wouldn't gush blood but trickle it innocuously until she bled out.

"Nick and I haven't been anything in months." She shut her eyes. "*You* ended us."

"Oh yeah, how did I do that?"

"By changing what we had. It wasn't fun anymore after you—after we—" She couldn't finish.

After they'd had that stupid threesome, she and Nick had broken up and it had opened up immeasurable stress fractures in her relationship with Gray. Their situation was an even bigger question mark than what she'd had with Nick.

"What?" he murmured, stepping closer. Their bodies brushed and she shivered, hating the effect he had on her. Fighting it only bought her so much time. The longer he pressed his advantage, the closer to crumbling she came.

"Nothing."

"Jazz." He brushed careless fingers over her cheek and she swung her gaze to his, unable to check the tears brimming in her eyes. They seemed to catch him off-guard. He opened his mouth to speak then clenched his jaw and shook his head, backing off. "This isn't the time."

"No, it's not."

"But you should know that the papers and the TV shows have picked up on the story."

"What story?"

His head came up but he still wouldn't meet her eyes. "Don't play games with me."

Nerves began to flicker in her belly. "What are you talking about? Tell me."

"About you and Nick. How he smacked your ass and the way the two of you were cozied up in the club last night after I left."

She choked out a laugh. "Some newspaper actually wasted ink to print that? Wow, they're getting desperate."

"There's more. On the television, they were talking about our supposed love triangle breaking up the band."

"Love triangle, my purple push-up bra. A triangle usually means three interested parties. Nick and I went home to practice 'Captured' after you took off. We didn't have sex or anything approaching it. In fact, I didn't even let him share my grape soda. So whatever." She started walking up the pathway, unsurprised when he fell into step beside her. That he reached out to take her hand did surprise her—mainly because she let him.

"If I jumped to conclusions, I'm sorry."

"Yeah, well, too late now."

He rubbed his thumb over her knuckles. "Why is it too late, baby?"

God, he couldn't call her *baby* or rub her hand or make her wish for even a second that maybe she hadn't lost her chance with him. Her chest hurt too much to take it right now.

"I smell her all over you," she said tiredly. "Look, forget it. Let's just go inside and deal with Lila. She's pretty mad at you and now she's annoyed at me too."

"I didn't have sex with her. She pushed several times and I said no. This last time, I caught a cab that I couldn't afford from her place rather than spend another minute in her company."

"Right. I'm just supposed to accept that, no questions asked."

"That's why you're so angry with me? You think I nailed her?"

She had to laugh or she'd cry. "You left me in the middle of a band meeting after promising you'd rehearse a song with me that you knew I was nervous about doing. Then you stayed out all night and show up here in yesterday's clothes, smelling like you rolled around in Blondie Boop's bed for hours. How do you expect me to feel? Elated?"

"I guess maybe I didn't realize you'd care that much." He tipped back his head to stare at the cloudless sky. "Whatever you think is going on between me and Cricket, it's not like that. I swear to you that we aren't lovers."

Some small part of her rejoiced. The rest only longed to ask more questions. *Then what are you? Why did you chase after her last night? When did she start having this hold on you?*

But asking would prolong this awkwardness, and they had to get inside before they both had to look for new jobs. "Okay."

"Do you believe me?" He fixed his gaze on her face. The intensity behind his storm-cloud eyes surprised her into a rapid nod.

"Yeah." She was trying. For him, she would never *stop* trying.

"Can we start over?"

If only. She would erase much of the past year if given the chance. "Before which part?"

He scuffed his boot over the ground. "Before we stopped being best friends and started trying to find ways to hurt each other."

Jazz nudged her hip against his to make him stop scuffing the ground. Fidgeting tended to be his number one evasive maneuver, and today, she wasn't tolerating it.

It was past time he faced their reality.

"I cover for you when you ditch meetings. I make up lies and I pretend I'm not bleeding inside when you don't even give me the courtesy of being honest. If that's not being a friend, maybe I don't understand the concept."

He twined his fingers through hers and brought their joined hands to his mouth for a kiss. "I'm sorry."

She wanted to stay angry. Hell, she had every right to be pissed for a good long while and to nurse her hurt feelings even longer. But she loved him too much. "Me too," she said finally, offering him a weak smile. "Now you better look lively because Lila's ready to barbeque your balls and use them to garnish her pot roast."

His laughter rumbling against her knuckles smoothed over the worst of her irritation. She simply didn't have it in her to stay mad at Gray for long. Whether that was her greatest strength or her biggest weakness, she didn't know.

"Thanks for the advice. And for having my back."

"Always." It was sterling truth. She would always protect him.

Even if it broke her in two.

* § *

Evidently the length of a conference table still wasn't enough of a buffer from a peeved Lila Shawcross.

"Where the hell have you been, Grayson?"

Before he could answer, a small notepad pinged off his chest and hit the table. "Let me make my displeasure clear. I don't appreciate people walking out of my meetings. I appreciate even less those who make up bullshit stories about dead grandmothers when you smell like you've been in the back of some groupie's van all night. You're lucky to have someone who's willing to cover for you." She shifted her attention to Jazz. "But make no mistake, if you go down, you'll bring her down with you. I'm assuming you don't want to do that?"

"Jazz isn't my keeper." He lifted his chin and met Lila's gaze head-on. "She has no say over my choices, which means you can't hold her responsible for them."

"You might want to clue her in to that fact. And that one over there," she jutted her chin in Nick's direction, "because he was just as willing to recite your excuses."

Gray glanced at Nick and got a flat stare in return. That look told him exactly what he'd suspected. Nick hadn't been covering for him, but Jazz.

It always came back to Jazz.

"Your bandmate's willingness to help you is a surprise in light of what came across my desk this morning." Lila popped open her slim soft-sided briefcase and pulled out a newspaper, slapping it on the table face-up. The picture of Nick's hand on Jazz's ass seemed to have grown even larger. "The airwaves are blowing up with this love triangle bullshit, and I want it stopped now. Are we clear?"

Nick leaned forward and clasped his hands between his knees. "Correct me if I'm wrong, but you're our record company rep. Don't you think you're overstepping your boundaries just a smidge?"

"Time for a reality check. Your success as a band partially depends on your ability to get the girls' panties wet. Sorry, Jasmine," she said without sparing Jazz a glance. Her attention remained fixated on Nick. "That's why we don't want all of you marrying off too soon, because every time one of you gets hitched, your popularity slips. You're too new of a band to risk much of that. One band member married works. He's the good, steady one that the little girls find safe. The rest of you are the sex appeal that fuels your rise up the charts."

Nick's lips twitched. "I get it. You're afraid Vapor over there and me want to marry Jazz. That'd be some story." He draped an arm over the back of his chair and sprawled out his legs.

"Don't worry, sweetheart. I'm not planning on marrying anyone. Ever."

"I'm not your sweetheart," Lila snapped, "and you're not impressing anyone here with your big-shot routine."

Nick's smile gleamed for an instant before he held up a hand in apology. "Sorry. I'll try harder next time."

Lila ignored him. "A little of this type of gossip doesn't hurt the band. Too much starts to get the focus off the music and on your backstage antics. That makes it my problem, especially when I think those antics have a very real possibility of causing serious trouble with Donovan's investment." She shoved the newspaper back in her briefcase. "I mentioned splitting you up to work on the album. After last night's events, I've changed the bunking assignments. The five of you need to be able to work together like a well-oiled unit, and I want you to focus on what you're here for—the music." She nailed Nick with a brief look. "And *only* the music."

"So let me get this straight." Simon braced a fist on the table and squinted out of bleary eyes. "As long as we don't marry anyone or screw around with our bandmates, we can fuck anyone we want?"

Lila appeared to weigh his words then nodded. "Essentially, yes."

A grin split Simon's face as he relaxed in his chair. "Sounds like a great deal to me."

"Good. I'm glad to hear you say that. You, Jazz and Deacon will be spending some quality time at the inn and spa. Which leaves the cabin and—"

Gray shot to his feet. "No. You're not putting me with him."

Nick matched his stance on the other side of the table. "Absolutely fucking not."

Lila gave them a bland smile. "Perhaps you missed my memo that these assignments were not optional. You two represent the biggest problem in this band. Therefore, you will take this time alone to get your shit straight. Alone, without any pretty drummers to distract you from what's important."

"You have no right to do this," Jazz said, her chin quivering. "We're adults. How can you try to run our personal lives?"

"From the looks of things, *you're* an adult, Jasmine. These two? That remains to be seen." Lila planted her hands on the table and leaned forward. "I don't give a flying fig who you bring into your bed, unless it has to do with this band. Then it becomes my mess to clean up. Right now? The three of you have mess all over you."

"Lila, I'm not sure exiling Gray and Nick is the answer." Deak tucked his hands under his biceps, his expression tense. "Maybe I should go with them, leave Simon and Jazz on their own."

"Oh yeah, now that sounds like a recipe for fun. Living with Gray and having Saint Deacon around to run interference." Nick shook his head. "Let me go get a pack of enemas from the drugstore and I'll be all set."

"Thank you for the offer, Deacon, but I have my reasons for the arrangements I've made. You'll have three club shows during your time away to keep you in front of the public eye, and so I can evaluate the success of this experiment. Then, after you've each bonded within your individual groups, you'll get a weekend all together to solidify the progress you've made. At that point you'll be booked for serious studio time." She consulted her tablet. "You all have two hours to head home to pack and be ready to leave. A car will pick each group up at that time. Bring only the essentials and anything you need to work."

Deacon frowned. "What about Harper?"

"What about her? Is she a member of this band?"

"The guy should be allowed to bring his wife, for God's sake," Gray said, unable to stay silent any longer. "She's pregnant."

"I'm well aware of that fact. She's not due for six months, correct?"

Deacon gave a reluctant nod.

"Then she's fine to stay home for a couple of weeks while her husband travels to a neighboring town for a work trip. That's what this is. It's not for recreation." Lila's smile turned feral. "In case I didn't make myself clear about that last point, let me spell it out. Nick, Gray, you're both to stay away from Jasmine outside the boundaries of Oblivion business. Keep your hands—and your other parts—to yourselves. Are we clear?"

Gray tightened his jaw until his bones cracked. "If we say no?"

"Then you're choosing to put your spot in Oblivion at risk." She consulted her tablet. "Pursuant to section 2.3 in the contract you all willingly signed with Ripper Records, you are to abide by a morality clause that includes, but is not limited to, restricting behavior that jeopardizes the position of the band in the public eye. That refers to excessive intoxication, drug offenses and personal involvements with other band members, et cetera. It's all right here."

It wasn't the personal involvement section that shut Gray up, but the drug offenses. If he skidded on any more thin ice, he'd end up falling through the cracks.

Nick glared at Deacon. "Yeah, what was that about this being our dream contract, Papa Smurf?"

"Hey, if you could keep your dick in your pants, this wouldn't be a problem."

"His dick hasn't been out of his pants with me." Jazz got to her feet, her cheeks flaring pink. "Not recently anyway. All we did last night was practice. I thought that was what we were supposed to do. But I guess I'm the problem here, so I'll just go."

Gray rose, his hands in fists. When it came to protecting Jazz, logic went out the window. "If she goes, I go. End of story."

"Newsflash, your contract says neither of you are going anywhere." Lila sighed. "Look, people, just try this my way. See what you come back with and we'll go from there. Okay?" She glanced from one member of the band to the next, landing on Gray last. "Okay?" she repeated softly.

Gray focused on Jazz. She lurked by the door, her eyes huge and stricken, her cheeks still flushed. She gripped the guitar pick necklace he'd given her like a lifeline. "You willing to do this, J? It's your call."

She shut her eyes and nodded. "Yeah. I'm in."

Gray returned his attention to Lila. "Guess we're going on a field trip."

Chapter Thirteen

Then

"So what do you think of Shadyside High?"

Jazz smiled at her new friend Stacey and tucked her leg up closer to her chest on her new bed. So much new. Mrs. Duffy had taken her shopping last week to buy stuff to redecorate Brent's bedroom and she'd gotten to choose a bedroom set, rainbow sheets and a dresser for her early Christmas gifts. Not thrift store finds either but brand new.

She could hardly believe all the wonderful things happening to her. Now this. She'd finally made a friend at school. It had only taken three months. Stacey was super popular too and had promised to introduce Jazz to all of her cool friends, including Toby Daniels, last year's prom king. Stacey claimed to know "for a fact" that Toby had been asking questions about Jazz.

Jazz figured it was too good to be true, but she didn't care because she wasn't looking for a boyfriend. School and her music kept her busy enough. Still, it was nice to pretend Toby might've taken notice of her for a positive reason instead of a negative one.

"I like it. It's too huge, though. Kind of overwhelming. I only stopped getting lost on the way to my locker just two weeks ago—" Jazz broke off and frowned as Stacey pointed at Jazz's knee. Today's artwork included a G-clef and a stack of books. "Yeah, I draw on myself when I get bored." She tried to laugh. "Weird, huh?"

"A little, but you're like, creative, so that's part of the deal, right?" Stacey flopped on her back and spread out her arms.

"Wow, this room is just so amazing. You must freak living here."

Jazz leaned back against her headboard, looping her arm ever so casually over the top of her knee. "It is pretty sweet."

"Sweet? That pool out back is gigantic. I even saw a frigging Benz in the garage. Your family has serious moolah."

Jazz started to explain that the Duffys were her foster family, not her real one, but she pressed her lips together and nodded. What did it hurt to pretend for a couple of minutes? She wanted them to be her family more than anything. This was the closest she'd had to a real home since she was little, back when things had been semi-okay with her mom and grandma. Her mom had worked long hours, but she'd always come back eventually and Nana had been so much fun.

After her mom hooked up with Jacob and gave birth to Molly, things started to change. By the time Nana died, they were moving from house to house. It wasn't long before her mom started coming home from nights out with Jacob with a black eye. When her mom had begun talking about moving them in with her boyfriend, Jazz had rebelled hardcore. She knew they shouldn't live with a guy who was abusive, but her mom had refused to listen.

Then she'd thrown up her hands and Jazz had ended up in foster care.

Stacey giggled. "I mean, if you gotta be a foster kid, it's better to land with a rich family, right?"

Jazz smothered her sigh. No point in pretending after all. She should've known that word had traveled all the way through school. "I don't really care about the rich part." She stroked her silky pillowcase. "The Duffys are incredible. They've made me feel so welcome." Except Brent.

"You've gotta tell me what it's like." Stacey rolled on her stomach and propped her chin on her fists.

Jazz smiled, glad for the distraction from her thoughts about her mom and Mol. She tried not to dwell on them, but sometimes she couldn't help it. Where were they now? Did they ever think of her?

"Jazz?"

"Yeah, sorry. What did you say?"

"You have to tell me what it's like to live with Gray. He's so...gah." Stacey grinned and grabbed her chest.

Jazz's smile faltered. She should've known this was coming. Only she would be dumb enough to think she'd actually made a genuine friend when she hadn't managed to make any in three months. "He's pretty awesome," she said, dropping her arm to her side.

Screw it. Why should she hide herself when people weren't paying attention to her anyway? She was just the girl who got to live with Gray the hottie.

"I went to see Krystal Sword once and he made out with a girl right on stage. Touched her boob and everything. I got so hot I did it with my boyfriend Craig the first time that night."

Jazz's eyes widened. "You're not a virgin?"

"Nope, haven't been for months. Are you?"

Jazz nodded. Despite what her mom and her caseworker had believed, she'd stayed out past curfew to go to clubs and hear live music most of the time, not run wild with boys. Guys had been involved a couple of times, and she'd definitely made it past second base and halfway to third, but no one had gone near what her mom used to call her "inner sanctum" yet. "Yeah."

"You should do it with Gray."

"What?" Jazz clapped her hand over her mouth to keep her laughter from spilling out. "He's got...girlfriends."

She couldn't say he had one in particular, but even so, the idea was ludicrous. In spite of that weirdness with Brent at Thanksgiving a few weeks ago, she'd never believe for a second that Gray had feelings for her beyond friendship. He saw himself as her older brother, she was almost sure.

Thank God he never read her *other* notebook. The sexy one, where she did things with Gray in her songs that she'd never ever tell anyone.

"So?" Stacey nudged her arm. "You could be one of them too. Nothing wrong with hooking up with a guy. Then another guy. And another one."

"Didn't you just say you had a boyfriend?"

"*Had*. Now I'm checking out my options." Stacey did a hip flex that made Jazz giggle again. "Hey, my friend Beth is having a party next Friday night. I'm positive Gray's going. You should come too."

"What about Toby?"

"He'll be there too. Throw out a couple arrows. See which one hits." Stacey grinned and grabbed her arm. "Come on, say you'll come. It'll be so much fun."

"Okay, sure. But my curfew's at ten. I gotta be home before then."

"Absolutely," Stacey said before bouncing up into a sitting position. "Let's go raid your closet and find you something hot to wear."

Jazz took a deep breath. She didn't have to do anything crazy. It was just a party. Maybe she'd make some new friends, dance a lot, drink a little. But she wasn't having sex with anyone.

Especially not Gray.

Chapter Fourteen

Now

Jazz faced her closet, hands on hips. "Fuck."

How was she supposed to fit that many days' worth of clothes into one suitcase? Essentials only. *Pfft.* They were going to a spa. That required fabulous outfits to go with her hair and makeup makeovers. Plus, she needed her gear. She couldn't be ready for serious work without her stuff. This was technically a writing/bonding session, so she wouldn't need her regular kit. She had a portable drum kit that she could use in a pinch, as well as her keyboard, but she'd have to bring both guitars since she couldn't decide between Gray's old Stratocaster or her newer Fender. She couldn't write music without a guitar in her lap. Probably a holdover from her days spent in the Duffys' basement with Gray.

Everything circled back to him eventually.

Before she could check the impulse, she called the one person who could understand her dilemma. The minute she heard Harper's voice, she swore. "Oh fuck. I forgot you had to get Deak ready to go. Sorry, I'll catch you later."

"Hold it," Harper commanded. "We can talk for a minute. He's a grown man. He can get himself ready for his trip. It's not like he's going to war." She gave an uncertain little laugh. "It's only a week."

"Ten days."

"Hello, I'm trying to be chill. Don't ruin it."

Laughing, Jazz tugged her hot pink mini dress off the hanger and tossed it in the direction of her bed. "Shutting up now. Except I can't, because I need your advice. Should I bring—"

"About freaking time. I've been waiting for you to go after Gray once and for all."

"My navy halter—wait, what?"

"You heard me. If you're asking me if you should go for it with Gray, the answer is hell yes. When is going to be a better time than right now?"

Jazz sank onto her bed. "Any time would be better, considering we've been banned from going near each other."

"Say what?"

Jazz ran through Lila's diatribe at the meeting and sighed. "I'd decided to do it finally last night, but he didn't show up. Then we kissed and he ran off to bang some girl, except he didn't, I don't think, and oh God, pass the Excedrin. It's so much frigging drama. I hate drama." She flung herself backward on the bed and stared at the glow-in-the-dark star decals she'd affixed to her ceiling. "Maybe this thing with Lila is the best thing that could happen. Maybe I'm not supposed to throw myself at him."

Harper snorted. "*Throw*? I think if you even swayed in his general direction, he'd snap you up in a hot minute."

"Did Deak tell you about that stupid gossip rag article? They had a picture of Nick's hand on my ass. We didn't even do anything. Yeah, he smacked me, but we just practiced and had a bit too much to drink."

She must still be suffering from the aftereffects since she'd developed a bitch of a headache. Having to collect Gray from the cab and Lila's meeting hadn't helped.

"Oh yeah, ouch. I saw the stuff online. If you hadn't called, I would've texted the minute big guy left. Love triangle, huh?" Harper whistled. "That's inaccurate."

"No kidding. Lamest love triangle ever. I haven't had sex with Nick in more than six months, and I haven't had sex with

Gray since ever. My vagina gets less action than any of the guys' hands and I get all the shit."

"Sorry to say, but I think that's part of being the only girl in a group of guys. You'll always get slut-shamed while they get exalted for doing much worse stuff. It sucks."

"Meh." Jazz threw her arm over her eyes. "I'm tired, Harp. I think I'm pathologically allergic to angst." Yet it kept chasing her, like a freaking fungus.

"You had enough to fill ten lifetimes before you joined Oblivion."

"Yeah. Maybe I should just channel my frustration into writing some dirty songs. Think the guys would be cool with calling the new album, 'I'm horny'?"

Harper snorted. "Simon would be, no doubt."

"Lila made it pretty clear that I'm enemy number one to all the guys' penises in the group. Excluding your guy's penis, of course. And Simon's, because it belongs to about five thousand other women."

"Ugh. And seriously? You're adults. You should be able to do whatever you want as long as it doesn't affect the band."

"That's the problem. It is. Plus I think Lila's afraid someone else is going to settle down like Deacon did and screw the single guy dynamics with the fans." Jazz grimaced and sat up. "Oops, sorry. I didn't mean to bring Deak into it."

"He is into it, and it's a valid point. But people fall in love and get married. What're you going to do? Put people in chastity belts until Oblivion's gone platinum a few times?"

"Lila would love to, I think. Simon's harmless. He'll screw his way across the country and never settle down."

"Like Nick would?"

"Yeah, that would be a no. But Gray and me, we're the wild cards."

"You think she can smell your baby fever on you?" Harper teased.

"Ugh, probably. I can't help it." Jazz grabbed a pillow and dragged it to her stomach. "You're already adorably cute and you're not even showing yet."

"Aww, thanks. I don't think it'll be too long before I am, though. My jeans are already getting snug." Harper sounded so content that Jazz would've hated her if she hadn't loved her so much. "But we're talking about you. You're just going to let Lila tell you what to do?"

"What choice do I have? I think I need to lie low with her for a bit. Hopefully the gossip rags will forget us if we stay separate for the length of band camp. The paparazzi has a short attention span, right?"

"They do, but since I'm pretty sure they were fed by trolls closer to your inner circle—aka probably one of Simon's screwees—I bet they'll keep eating longer."

Jazz groaned. "C'mon, throw me a bone."

"Okay, here you go. You can't keep dancing around Gray forever. If I were you, I'd use this vacation from Lila's clutches to my advantage. Call it an orgasm recovery plan."

Jazz rolled on her belly, taking the pillow with her. "In case Deak forgot to mention it, I'm exiled with him and the great manwhore at a spa. Nowhere near the secret cabin where Gray and Nick are going."

"So find out where they're headed, and in the grand tradition of all cabin exiles, sneak in. Hopefully wearing something skimpy enough that all of Gray's brain cells disintegrate upon sight."

"Harp, he kissed me and left with some chick last night. But he claimed he didn't sleep with her."

"Do you believe him?"

"I want to."

"Then go with your gut. And follow your heart."

"My heart leads me to Gray." Jazz sighed. "Always."

"Exactly. Now let your body follow suit."

Jazz sat up again and heaved the pillow aside. She'd collapsed on her dress, probably wrinkling it all to hell, but who could worry about that at a time like this? "You're serious. You really think I should do this."

"I do. Absolutely. You have to give it a try. You've wondered all these years. If you don't go for it, balls to the wall, you'll always wonder what if. Fifteen years from now when Oblivion's broken up and you're married with a pair of adorable babies, you'll log onto Facebook and start a madcap instant messaging affair with him, thereby homewrecking both of your families. This is much more expeditious. Trust me."

"I don't want any adorable babies if they aren't his." Jazz frowned and smoothed her hand over her minidress. "I definitely don't want to be married."

"Proving my point. Pack some hot clothes, head off to the spa and tonight, attack."

When Harper started humming the Jaws soundtrack, Jazz laughed. "There's one little problem. I won't have transportation for this little sneak attack plan of yours."

"You can use the catering truck. It'll be at your service."

"Won't you need it?"

"Between the hours of midnight and seven a.m.? Nope. I don't have a job until eight a.m. tomorrow. So get there late and leave early." Harper made a purring noise. "And make the most of all the hours in between."

"Aw, damn, you've sold me." Jazz grinned and jogged over to her closet. "Now help me figure out what to pack."

Twenty minutes later, she had a head full of sex advice, a packed suitcase, several cases of instruments and her notebook under her arm. Operation Sex-up-Gray achievement unlocked.

On her way out of her bedroom she stopped by her guinea pig Ratt's cage and stuck her finger through the bars. "Hey there, munchkin. Auntie Harp is going to make sure you and your sister George have plenty to eat and drink while we're away. So don't go riding that wheel of yours all night long and getting your cage dirty til I get back. No wild parties, you hear me?" She pressed a kiss to her finger and placed it on Ratt's furry head. "Be good for mama."

Hearing herself, she sighed. Yeah, she really did have baby fever if she was actually mothering a damn guinea pig. But along with being cute, he was well-behaved. George, Simon's kitten, was much more of a miscreant.

She headed down the hall and knocked on Gray's bedroom door. Hopefully his and Nick's car hadn't been early. She'd been so busy squirreling away necessary items for her trip— naughty lingerie, check and condoms, check—that Nick and Gray could've split without her knowing. Normally Gray would've stopped by to say goodbye, but maybe he was taking Lila's warning seriously.

More seriously than she was anyway.

On her second knock, he opened the door and gave her a careless grin that didn't diminish the strain around his eyes. His silver eyebrow ring gleamed, adding a little edge to his casual outfit of jeans, a T-shirt and a vest. While the jeans were snug, the T-shirt seemed a little baggy, but he'd always had energy to burn and a crazy fast metabolism. She gained weight just looking at food and he could eat double cheeseburgers at every meal and not gain an ounce.

"Hey." He leaned on the doorjamb. "You defying a direct order?"

The amusement in his voice helped ease some of her nerves. She'd been planning for this day for a long time. Now that it was actually here, she couldn't stop fussing with the hem of her shirt and bouncing around on her Keds. She wasn't a raving beauty but normally she was fine with her appearance. Sure, her eyes weren't quite even and her nose was a bit too tiny and she was ridiculously short. She'd gotten used to all of those things.

Yet all of a sudden she couldn't stop analyzing her boobs or how her butt looked in her jeans.

Not that it really mattered. He'd been in her sphere for close to a decade. If he didn't find the goods up to snuff, there wasn't much she could do about it. She'd just have to work what her mama gave her and hope for the best.

"You okay, J?"

This zoning out problem she was developing wasn't going to up her hotness quotient. "Sure. I'm fine. Uh, yeah, about the direct order." She gave him a bright smile and waved her notebook. "If I keep this in my hand at all times, that makes this within the boundaries of Oblivion biz, right?"

He scraped his hand over the back of his head. "Sure. So, ah, you're off to the spa soon, right?"

"Yes." She reached up to toy with the ends of her hair. "I'm thinking of dyeing it again."

His grin bordered on indulgent. "No kidding? That happens so rarely with you."

"No, I mean something shocking. Like...platinum blonde." She tipped her head to the side. "What do you think of that?"

He jerked a shoulder. "It's a color."

She frowned at his back as he disappeared into his bedroom. Really? *That* was his idea of a response?

"I might pierce my nipples and get a nose ring too," she called, stepping back at his surprise reappearance in the doorway.

"You've pierced enough of yourself, don't you think?" He moved into the hallway, forcing her backward.

Hmm. Which piercing was he thinking of? "You mean my ear piercings?" she asked coyly, flipping back her hair. He'd definitely gotten to know her clit piercing too. Briefly. So freaking briefly.

He hoisted his duffel higher and clutched his guitar in one hand, pulling the door shut with the other. "Yeah."

Wow. Seriously? She was trying to act flirty and even directing his attention toward sexual areas—nipples, clits, come on—and nada. "I'm pierced other places too."

"Uh-huh. So did you need something? I think we're supposed to head downstairs soon."

She grabbed his arm before he could start down the stairs. "I wanted to know if you had the address for the cabin yet," she said in a low voice, keeping an eye on the hallway. The last thing she needed was for someone to overhear her setting up an illicit tryst.

"No. We won't know until we get there, and that's if they even tell us where we are. Much mystery afoot." He flashed her a distracted smile and adjusted his grip on his guitar.

"When you find out the address, text me."

"Why?"

Jazz sent up a quick prayer that she wouldn't be soundly rejected. "So I can, um, pay you a visit." She tossed her hair. "You know. At night."

His eyes narrowed. "Are you okay? You're acting weird."

"Yes, I'm fine. Jeez. Just text me, okay?" She gave him a light shove down the stairs. Clearly she needed to adjust her plan of attack, because her casual flirtiness didn't seem to be having much of an effect.

"Okay. Fine." He backed down the steps, smiling up at her in that way that caused her belly to twist like a knotted up Slinky. "Have fun getting girly."

"I'm already girly, you jerk." She grinned and waved, waiting until he turned around to descend the stairs to cover her stampeding heart with her hand.

This had to get easier. If it didn't, she'd stroke out before she managed to get naked.

A moment later, Deak yelled up the stairs. "Pix? Car's here. You ready to go?"

"Coming," she called, returning to her room for her stuff.

Here went everything.

* § *

His life had been circling the drain for a while. Today, Lila had flushed.

"So this is it, huh?" Nick strode across the living room of the rustic cabin where they'd be holed up together for way too long. "These are our luxury accommodations while the three glam girls get their toenails waxed?"

In spite of his dissatisfaction, Gray choked a laugh into his fist. "Two of those three glam girls would kick your ass for saying that. And I don't think toenails can get waxed."

"Whatever. I can take Deak and Simon."

"I meant Deak and Jazz. I think Simon would probably correct you for mixing up your metaphors then show you his manly manicure."

Nick shook his head and ambled over to the giant fireplace that appeared to have been dug by hand out of the wall. He braced his hands on the mantel and dropped his head. "This really fucking blows."

"Yeah." Gray dropped into the nearest leather wingback chair and propped his guitar between his knees. "Have to agree."

Nick turned away from the fireplace and prowled around the cabin while Gray popped open the case and pulled out his Epiphone. Though the drive from the Hollywood Hills hadn't taken that long, he still felt too edgy to just calmly check out his new surroundings. He needed something to unkink the knots in his gut and distract him from the urge for a fix. He used to be able to go days between them. Now in less than twenty-four hours, he was jonesing again.

He'd hoped to get a hold of Cricket before the car arrived to pick them up, but Jazz had been talkative and Cricket hadn't answered his texts quickly enough. When she had, she'd made it clear she'd be providing no more freebies.

If he didn't pay up his past-due amounts—and/or fuck her brains out, which probably would buy him a week or two and another hit at best—he'd be cut off. And that couldn't happen. He wasn't about to put out feelers for another dealer when his name had already been thrown to the media wolves for the Jazz thing.

Bottom line, he needed to get her some fucking cash, fast.

"These bedrooms aren't bad," Nick said from down the hall. "I'm claiming the one next to the—holy shit, man, come check this out."

Sighing, Gray set aside his guitar and got to his feet. He truly didn't give a crap what Nick had found nor did he care which bedroom he ended up with. Sleeping was pretty much optional for him nowadays, and he didn't have a need for a bed otherwise. It wasn't like he'd be getting laid during this misfit toys vacation.

His weird conversation with Jazz popped back into his brain. She'd said something about visiting him tonight. For what? Maybe she figured they could work on some songs away from the rest of the group. They'd always had their own vibe and style of collaboration. It had been a while since they'd tried to write something new on their own, but the whole "Captured" discussion during the band meeting last night had probably reminded her of all the fun they used to have making music together.

"Hang on," Gray replied, dragging out his phone. "Gotta text someone."

He'd overheard the address when the driver had been calling in to some kind of dispatch and now Gray typed it out quickly to Jazz. He still didn't get why she wanted to flaunt Lila's decree on the very day she'd made it, but his best friend had been a little rulebreaker for as long as he'd known her. He'd always been attracted to the side of her that prompted her to sneak out of her bedroom window to go to a concert or to dye her hair blue with Kool-Aid when no one at school was doing it. She'd never walked the straight and narrow, and damn, she made the crooked seem so fucking sexy.

That even extended to her personal jewelry. He still couldn't believe she'd pierced her clit. Earlier it had almost seemed like she'd been goading him into mentioning that particular piercing. Something must be up. Maybe he'd figure out her game plan after she showed up.

If she even did. That'd be his luck to get his hopes up for no reason at all.

He texted her the addy and she sent back an answer almost immediately.

I'll be there by 12:30. One level?

His lips quirked. Was she planning a reverse Rapunzel? His hair had grown longer than he preferred but he wouldn't be able to use it as a trellis for her to climb up from the ground anytime soon.

Yes, one. At least he was pretty sure there was just one. That's how it had looked from outside.

Where's your bedroom?

I'll let you know in a bit. How's the spa?

So far I've had a kelp smoothie and I'm baking in a green clay face mask. Simon is hitting on Diane, the esthetician, and Deak keeps texting Harper while they do something to his feet. Later I guess we're gonna try to write.

He smiled, hearing her enthusiastic voice as he read her words. Seeing Jazz happy made up for so much of the toxic shit in his world. He'd give anything to keep her that way.

Glad to hear it. Me and Nick are just checking out the house. Is it nice?

Yeah, it's sweet. His thumbs hovered over the keys. He didn't want to seem desperate, but man, the idea of spending some time with Jazz alone—relatively anyway—sounded better and better. *So I'll see you later?*

You will. Text me when you know which room is yours.

KK. Enjoy getting even more beautiful, beautiful.

The smiley face she sent back made him grin until he glanced up into Nick's amused face.

"A little busy there?" Nick asked, jerking his chin at Gray's cell.

"Nah, all good. So what does the rest of this place look like?" He tucked his phone in his back pocket and ventured down the hall, stopping in the doorway to a gleaming black bathroom. The tiles, spacious tub and floor were all onyx. And damn, the tub looked like it had a million jets. It was definitely made for two.

He shut his eyes and tried to ignore the sudden pressure below the waist. Two wasn't a possibility. Hell, he'd probably be hiding out in the shower as much as possible just to avoid Nick's smirk.

"This place is a fucking wet dream. And dude, I already claimed the bigger bedroom, so you're out of luck."

Gray gripped the back of his neck and turned to face Nick. This wasn't just about disliking the guy. He needed to make this work for the band. That was more important than his urge to plant his size twelve boot right on that sneering face.

"That's cool. I don't sleep a whole hell of a lot, so go for it."

Nick tucked his hands under his arms. "Wow, I think that might be the most words you've spoken at one time in...well, ever."

Don't rise to the bait. "If we're going to be writing together, we're going to be talking, right? Unless you want to try out the whole telepathy deal."

Before Nick could respond, he slipped past him into the hall and headed into the rustic bedroom on his left. Obviously this was the one Nick hadn't claimed, since it looked untouched. A thick plaid spread covered the double bed and a plush loveseat and pair of chairs made up a small seating area. The old-fashioned carved armoire opened to a pair of thick white robes. Clearly this place was made for couples.

One more reason to put sex in his head. Fabulous.

He walked to the window and flipped the lock, then dragged up the sill so he could haul in a breath of humid air. Beyond the cabin lay what appeared to be miles of woods. His gaze drifted back to the deck and he did a double take at the huge Jacuzzi. Best of all, a door beside the closet allowed direct access to said Jacuzzi without having to go through the rest of the house.

Shaking his head, he stepped away from the window. Yeah, lovers would have a fucking awesome time here. Him? He needed a hit.

He tugged out his cell and tapped in another quick text to Cricket. She couldn't leave him high and dry with Nick. Maybe he hadn't been clear enough about the desperate straits he was in.

Or maybe he'd have to dig out the weed Jere had given him and settle for that. He wasn't a big fan of pot, but shit, his nerves were jumping under his skin. If he touched his arm, he was certain he'd feel them wriggling beneath the surface. A few tokes would take the edge off.

"So? What's the verdict?"

And that right there was a big reason why. Damn Nick. Damn Jazz. Damn everything right now.

"Verdict?" Gray finished his text and tossed his phone on the bed. "On what?"

"On the place. I think—holy shit, look at that Jacuzzi." Nick strode over to the door and pulled it open before tossing a grin over his shoulder. "Man, dragon lady is nuts if she thinks I'm going to spend the entire time strictly dickly in a tricked-out place like this. This house is practically begging for an orgy."

"Dragon lady?"

Nick's grin spread. "Yeah, fits Lila, don't you think?"

In lieu of replying, Gray dropped to the mattress. He cast a sly glance at his silent phone. What the hell was Cricket doing? She never went this long without answering. Yes, he owed her money. He had a little bit left in his savings account stashed away for the next few months of rent so if he had to, he'd use that. If Cricket ever bothered to return his text.

"You heard Lila," he said vaguely, still fixated on his cell. "She wants us to concentrate on coming up with material for the album. We need to bond or some shit."

Nick snorted. "Lila can kiss my ass. She's not here, and I'm not wasting this kind of setup."

"So you're already bailing on the plan. Why am I not surprised?"

"Look, Boy Scout, not all of us do real well at taking orders. I know for a fact that you're not nearly as lily white as you pretend, so go fuck yourself." Nick crossed the room and slammed the door hard enough to shake the foundation.

Shaking his head, Gray balled up his pillow. He shoved it under his head and stared at his phone, willing it to ring. He couldn't do this week without blow. If he had to empty his savings and offer up his dick as a goddamn consolation prize, he'd do it. He had no choices left.

A text came through and he leaped on his phone. Excitement surged and banked as he realized it was from Jazz. Not that he didn't want to hear from her too, but at the moment he had another priority. Even his gorgeous, perfect best friend couldn't compare with a sweet white pile of powder.

Simon just got the esthetician's number. He said it's a new personal record. I think Deak's too disgusted to laugh.

Gray waited, unable to reply. But she wasn't done.

Back in high school, I saw girls give you their numbers way faster than that. Though you always tried to hide them from me. You always joked that I was hotter than they were.

He swallowed and shut his eyes. Jesus, how had they gotten to this place? She'd been the cornerstone of his life for so long. The reason he wanted to be a better man. The answer to all the questions he'd never been brave enough to ask when he wasn't high. They mattered too much, and he was a goddamned coward.

Now she was asking him to remember a simpler time, one where his longing for her had been pure and untainted, while he had a hard-on for a mirror and a snow-white smile.

His thumbs moved over the keys. *You are hot. The hottest girl I've ever seen.*

Without giving her a chance to answer, he shut off his phone.

Chapter Fifteen

Then

Holy crap, what had she gotten herself into?

Standing in the foyer of Beth's parents' house, Jazz glanced around with wide eyes. She wasn't a stranger to parties, but this one was a freaking rager. The place had already been completely trashed and it wasn't even ten o'clock yet. The front door stood wide open and a steady stream of people poured in and out, most of them laughing and shouting and guzzling their drink of choice.

And those drinks were all alcoholic.

She didn't balk when one of the senior guys pressed a bottle into her hand. Why should she? She could tolerate her liquor. She'd been sneaking sips from her mother's stash since she was ten. Yet another reason her mom had said she was such a bad influence on her little sister.

What kind of example are you setting for Molly? Drinking and slutting around.

At the pang in her chest, she lifted the beer and took a sip. Bad influence. Right. That was her label, so she'd wear it proudly.

"This is incredible," Stacey said, bumping into her side. "There are so many sexy guys here, oh my gawd, I can't stand it."

Jazz giggled, and not from her friend's statement. Stacey's glazed eyes and slack mouth gave her a shell-shocked appearance. Of course that also might've been from the pills she'd been popping on her way over, claiming they were some kind of muscle relaxant for bad cramps.

"Who're you planning on nailing tonight?" Jazz asked, leaning her head on Stacey's shoulder as she took another gulp. This beer didn't taste like any she'd had before. It had a metallic flavor to it rather than a yeasty one. But if it worked to ease her nerves about putting the moves on Gray—any kind of moves at all—she was down with it.

"Who am I *not* planning on nailing is a better question." Stacey patted Jazz's head like a child's before she snagged a beer from the same senior who had hooked up Jazz with one a few moments ago. He'd reloaded both hands with a pair of bottles that were already uncapped.

Jazz took another bolstering sip, fearing repercussions, but instead of seeming pissed, he stopped and turned back to give them both a leisurely look. "You two come as a set?" he asked, licking his lips.

Shaking her head, Jazz stumbled back. "N-no, of course not."

She wasn't positive what he was asking, though she had a pretty good idea. A girl didn't land in a handful of foster homes in two years without picking up a thing or two about the dirty, depraved things that people did for fun. And heck, she wasn't slamming it. If more than one person was your scene, aces. But she only had one guy in mind. Even Toby didn't garner more of her interest than a passing thought.

Stacey shot her a sharp glance. "Depends what you have in mind, Mike." Her tone turned flirtatious. "You bring some party favors with you tonight?"

Jazz backed up again, straight into a hard chest. "Hey there. You heading somewhere?"

She looked up at Toby's smiling face and her stomach tumbled. It wasn't desire that caused that shaken-marble sensation in her belly, but nausea. "No. I don't think so." Was she? How was she supposed to remember?

He chuckled. "Let me know when you figure it out."

"'Kay."

The noise was getting to her. The music wasn't something she was familiar with, all screaming guitars backed by a vocalist who shrieked more than sang. Normally she enjoyed any kind of rock or metal. Not tonight. Her temples were pounding like hammers into wood. She swallowed to wet her dry throat before remembering she still held a bottle in her boneless fingers. She took another swig, letting the off-tasting liquid flow down her throat. Why was her face so hot all of a sudden?

"Jasmine, isn't it?" He leaned down and ruffled the hair she'd teased into blue spikes at her crown. "You want to go somewhere a bit quieter? Maybe we could talk a little, get to know each other."

"Okay." She nodded again and regretted it when her head spun. Jesus, she was becoming a lightweight. Couldn't even handle one beer. She let out a tipsy giggle, pleased at how Toby steadied her with his iron fingers. God, his strength was hot.

But when he started to head toward the stairs, she planted her boots on the carpeted floor. "Uh uh. Don't know you. Can't go upstairs with you 'til you buy me dinner."

His amused smile made her offer a goofy smile back. At least it felt goofy to try to make her lips work. "Is that so?"

She firmed her wobbly chin. "Yes. My mom taught me that."

"Your mom sounds like a smart woman." He flashed her a lethal smile, one she'd heard the girls talking about as a panty-dampener. She couldn't tell if she was still wearing panties, never mind if they were wet. "How about the basement? Other people are down there, but it'll be easier to get better acquainted."

It was getting harder to argue. Maybe she shouldn't. She wanted so badly to make friends, and here was a chance.

She glanced over her shoulder to tell Stacey she'd be downstairs. Except Stacey wasn't anywhere in sight. And neither was Mike.

Swallowing hard, she faced Toby again and gave him a smile. She could do this. Perhaps she'd even have fun. "Sure. Lead the way."

Chapter Sixteen

Now

On the back deck of the cabin where Gray and Nick were staying, Jazz tugged down her slip dress and peered at her phone. It was late. She debated texting Harper, then decided she needed an urgent pep talk that involved actual speech.

She was about to seduce Gray. All alone. Him and her. And Nick, except he'd be in a different room. That was a whole other kettle of hot mess. Her guilt on that score alone made her want to turn and hide. But she wasn't hiding. She was going for it.

She was almost sure.

Ducking behind the hot tub, she called her partner-in-crime. It was chilly tonight so she sway-rocked on her high-heeled boots to generate body heat while she waited for Harper to answer. And maybe because she was nervous. Just a tad.

"Help me," she whispered as soon as her friend answered.

"Let me guess. His zipper broke?"

"Ha ha. So not funny. I'm on the verge of chickening out. He's not answering my texts and I'm dressed like a—" She glanced down at the insanely expensive scanty red dress she'd bought at the spa's gift shop. The boots were on loan from Harper from a few weeks ago, but this was her maiden voyage in them. "I think I might look like a hooker. A scared one. Harp, I'm *blonde*. What the hell was I thinking?"

"You know, I've heard blonde is a perfectly respectable hair color. Sometimes blondes even have more fun."

"I'm not having fun right now. My scalp still hurts from all the bleach and I'm getting drafts in places that should never feel cold air. Why am I doing this again?"

"The hair thing, I couldn't tell you, since you were plenty hot as a brunette and a rainbow and every color in between. If I had to guess, you thought becoming blonde would help you score. But I seriously doubt you needed to bother, since your scoring is in the bag." Harper paused. "Where are you anyway?"

"At this very instant?"

"No, last Tuesday. Yes, right now."

"Kind of crouching behind the hot tub. Gray's window overlooks the deck. It's sunken. The hot tub, I mean, not his window—"

"Jasmine. Go inside and talk to the man. You're going to get pneumonia if you stand around outside half-naked."

"Aww." Jazz couldn't help but smile. "You sound like a mom. How cute."

"Do I?" Harper asked, clearly pleased.

"You so do. I have to get knitting. I found this pattern for the most adorable booties—"

"Jazz. Stop stalling."

"But he hasn't texted me back since this afternoon. He was supposed to tell me which room was his and instead I had to guess. What if he doesn't want me here?"

"What was the last thing he said to you?"

Jazz gripped the edge of the Jacuzzi to adjust her position. "Uh, something about me being the hottest girl he's ever seen."

"And you're still outside? Did that bleach fry your brain or what?"

"I'm scared. This is so huge. And—and Nick's here."

"Oh Lord. Don't tell me you want a repeat of that threesome, because I swear to God, I will come there and—"

"No, no, of course not." Jazz had to laugh. "Believe me, once was plenty. It wasn't even a normal threesome. I told you, there wasn't penetration by both, just Nick."

"The words *penetration* and *Nick* should never be in the same sentence. Just FYI."

"Nick's not that bad. Okay, fine, yes he is, but he has redeeming qualities."

"Do not mention his penis. Na-na-na, can't hear you," Harper said in a singsong voice as Jazz choked out a giggle.

"I'm not. I'm just saying, I feel bad for doing this while he's here. It doesn't seem right. I don't want to hurt him if I can help it."

"You can be discreet, right? You'll be leaving early in the morning. Just try not to swing from the chandeliers—or the deer antlers—and you should be good."

Jazz peeked over the hot tub at Gray's window. He'd lifted it part way and the light was on in his room but from this angle she couldn't see if he was actually in there. Dammit, why wasn't he answering his texts? "I can be discreet, I just don't want it to be awkward."

"So wait for a less complicated time then. Bring back my catering truck and go back to the ginormous suite of rooms at the spa you're sharing with my delectable husband and the manwhore. Just keep on pretending that your heart isn't breaking every moment you're not with Gray. Go on, I dare you."

Jazz slumped behind the hot tub and tapped her head lightly against the side. If she kept doing it, maybe the pain would distract her from the knot of nerves in her throat. "Direct hit."

"Sorry, but it had to be said, sweetie. Dispensing tough love means I love you."

"Yeah. Yeah." Jazz blinked away the sudden film in her eyes. "Me too. And I know you're right. I've come this far, I might as well—"

"Actually come?" Harper offered helpfully.

Just like that, Jazz's grin returned. God, she'd missed having a girlfriend, and Harper was one of the best she'd ever had. "From your mouth to God's ears. Okay. I'm heading in. I'll have the truck back by seven a.m. as agreed. Or, you know, in fifteen minutes when he tells me I look like a skank and kicks my ass out."

Harper snorted. "Right. You're so getting nailed tonight."

"Thanks for that vote of confidence." Jazz smiled and flexed her damp fingers around her phone. "Later, chick."

"You better call me tomorrow. I want deets. Lewd ones."

"Pregnancy hormones kicking in already?"

"You know it. They're fierce. And where's my husband? Getting beautified, which is basically an oxymoron. He's already perfect." She let out a heavy sigh. "Luck, sweetie."

"'Bye." Jazz clicked off and shoved her phone in her boot.

She was about to stand when the scrape of Gray's window being raised hit her ears. She ducked even further into the shadows, but she finally gave up and peeked over the Jacuzzi.

Gray had his arm out the window, and he held a glowing cigarette. Or...maybe not. He blew out a breath then she caught an unmistakable whiff of what he was smoking. That was no cigarette. Since when had Gray started smoking pot?

She thought back over the last few months. The awkward silences between them, the unexplained absences, the unfocused expression in his eyes. She'd tried to play all of that stuff off as his being uncomfortable with the band, though she'd suspected deep down that there was more to it than that. She'd been afraid of how much that stupid threesome had influenced his behavior. Something had seemed to crack in him after that. But no, maybe she'd pegged him all wrong. Plenty of musicians got high on a lot worse things than pot.

Not Gray. Never Gray.

It had never occurred to her that he could be on something because he'd always been militantly anti-drugs. Back in high school he'd flipped out when she'd gone through her experimental phase. It hadn't lasted long. She'd tried a few different substances at parties. She'd also gotten fall-down-drunk more than once. She'd soon realized that she didn't want to lose control of her faculties—ever. His rants every time she touched the illegal stuff had certainly pushed along the process.

Now this. It was better than the alternative, though. *All* of the alternatives.

She nearly let out a peal of hysterical laughter. Damn, she actually felt *relieved* that he might have a pot problem. A few tokes she could handle. She'd been in bands since she was a teenager. It was almost a standard part of life on the road.

That didn't mean she approved of Gray developing a habit. She'd definitely try to get him to cut back or quit. She was just happy it wasn't something worse.

Like the heroin that Snake, Oblivion's first drummer, had gotten hooked on. She shuddered. Once that shit had its claws in you, it was almost impossible to tear yourself free without leaving some vital parts of your flesh behind.

She sucked in a breath and winced at the aroma that came with it. They'd discuss the pot situation, after. She hoped it didn't affect performance. Assuming he would be doing something that counted as performing because dear Lord, if he didn't, she might start toking up herself.

The time had come to find out.

She lurched to her feet. Luckily she had a firm grip on the side of the Jacuzzi because she wobbled on her super-high boots and nearly did a header onto the deck. Awesome. Naturally Gray picked that moment to glance her way—and to drop his joint. Whether he did it intentionally in the hopes of hiding it or due to her appearance, she couldn't say.

Swagger firmly in place, she marched over and picked it up, waving it back and forth. "So this is what you've been up to."

Her gaze dropped to his bare chest and the swirls of black ink that banded his upper right arm. Her focus slid farther down, stopping at the unbuttoned top button of his jeans. Swirls and shadows lurked behind his zipper. A tattoo? Just a really dense happy trail? Hard to say, but at that point, she forgot how to speak.

And breathe.

"Give me that," he snapped, leaning out the window far enough that she could watch his chest and abs ripple in perfect harmony. So many damn muscles. They would've struck her dumb again if he hadn't been about to snatch the joint.

She'd just have to ogle later.

She stumbled backward, retreating until her spine hit the hot tub. He was already hauling up the sill and climbing out, making her heart rate zoom up to dangerous levels. Soon she'd need CPR.

Mouth-to-mouth, yes, please.

"Seriously, you're not even supposed to be here. What the hell are you—Jesus Christ, what are you wearing?" He took one step toward her and stopped, reaching up to run his hand over his face. He spread his fingers over his eyes and swore. "Yeah, got it right the first time. Not hallucinating. Fucking thigh-high leather boots and blond hair."

"Nope, no hallucination. This is all real."

"No kidding. I don't know what you're here for, but I think you chose the wrong night."

"Because of this?" She lifted the joint to her mouth as he cursed again. Why the hell not? She'd never made a believable good girl anyhoo. "Friends should share."

Before he could make another grab, she took a deep drag. And started to choke.

"Christ, don't." He bolted forward and locked an arm around her waist, pulling her against him. She coughed again weakly, not even protesting when he plucked the joint out of her hand. She expected him to toss it aside, not to bring it to his perfect lips and take a deep breath. After inhaling, he blew out the smoke until it curled up lazily in the air between them. "Mine. Not yours."

"Is that how it is?" She swallowed to ease the burn in her throat and swayed again, though not from her boots this time. The weed had already hit her head, and wow, she had no complaints. Already her nerves were fading.

Now she was just *hungry*. And not for food.

"Yeah." He drew in and out, lightly blowing the smoke between them, squinting his eyes as the plumes swirled through the air, pungent and sharp. Intoxicating in their own destructive way. "This is a party for one, babe."

"You definitely sound high." She caught her fingers in his belt loops and ducked her head under his chin. His body heat radiated against her, searing and intense. Being this close to him was like stepping up to the edge of a cliff and staring down into an inferno.

She wanted to fall. To fly...and burn.

"Mmm-hmm. I can smell you. You're like burnt sugar, bubbling over the pan." His mouth moved against her hair. "What do you have on under that dress?"

Her heart squeezed. He wasn't in his right mind. She wanted him fully aware. And she wasn't all that aware herself. One toke had been enough to scattershot her thoughts like balls across a pool table. She should wait.

Wait.

Wait.

"I can't," she whispered.

"*Can't* what?"

"This." She waved a hand between them. "You've given off so many mixed signals, and I probably have too. We've been dancing around this for too many years. I may be making a huge mistake but I don't care anymore. We're both here right now, and I'm not wasting one more chance."

She drew her dress up over her head and let it fall.

* § *

Curves. So many curves. She was like a living G-clef made out of flesh and flawless diamond-crushed skin. The ruby red tips of her breasts peeked out from beneath the waves of her white-blonde hair. Thanks to the spill of light from the window, he could see that the same flush bloomed between her legs, beyond enticing. It would be so easy to move forward and take. To just drown himself in her until he couldn't remember anymore why this was wrong.

"Jazz," he breathed, shutting his eyes to block out the torch-light of her beauty in front of him. He couldn't breathe through his want. Couldn't think through the haze of the marijuana and his need. And his love.

He fucking *loved* her, and he'd fight not to do this with every fiber of his being. She deserved more than a strung-out bastard who'd turned to pot because he couldn't get ahold of more coke. For fuck's sake, even his dealer wouldn't return his calls.

Now she was here, and he couldn't get high enough not to feel each of the knives carving him up inside.

"Gray," she said, equally soft. He didn't open his eyes but her voice crept closer. "Look at me."

"No." The word burst from him on an exhale. "No."

Her hand touched his bare chest and he jolted as if she'd set off a stick of dynamite. Her chuckle rubbed over his nerve endings, sandpaper and silk, and he struggled to hold back a shudder. Only the steel beam he'd shoved in his spine held him upright.

"Back when I used to get high, it'd lower my inhibitions," she continued. "It made me excited. I know it's supposed to relax you, but it had a different effect on me."

He focused on each of her words on its own, so he couldn't take them all together and feel their impact. He couldn't let her do this. The man she was trying to seduce might've been worthy of her a year ago. He hadn't believed it fully then either but he knew without doubt that he wasn't now.

"As if you ever had inhibitions," he muttered, unable to summon the strength to raise his voice. All his blood had rerouted to his cock. All his air was fueling his starving cells. He could only not inhale for so long. But if he did, he'd smell her again, watermelon and sugar, and he'd be finished.

"Oh, you'd be surprised. I've wanted you for years. And I haven't done one damn thing to let you know." She started circling him, her body brushing against his. Hip to thigh, thigh to ass. Her fingers trailed from his chest to his arm to his back, sensual feathers of sensation that made his balls clench so tight he feared any movement would send him over the edge. "But I will tonight."

He gritted his teeth. "You can't. You don't know me anymore. You don't understand what you're getting into."

That made her stop. Her fingers pressed into his lower back as she processed his words.

Please, make them be enough.

She completed her loop around him and hooked her fingers in the front of his jeans. He groaned at the slide of skin on skin. Her other hand closed around his fingers, still gripping the joint, and she pried it free. He heard her inhale before the wisps of her breath kissed his mouth. "So show me."

To Jazz, he was just a recreational user. Never mind that he'd told her years ago that doing that shit would lead nowhere good. In her eyes, he didn't owe thousands of dollars to people who would break his legs—or his hands—if he didn't cough up the cash. He didn't have such a fucking thirst for blow that he'd practically broken down during his voicemails to Cricket tonight, begging for enough to get through his time at the cabin. Then he'd do whatever she asked.

He could do anything, survive anything, but he couldn't turn away from Jazz. She would sustain him where every other drug had failed.

Opening his eyes hurt. For an instant, the spill of light from his room haloed her head, glowed like dancing fire in her china blue eyes. He fisted his hand in her hair and watched it spill through his grip like liquid gold. With one tug, her head was back, those slightly glazed irises fixated on his. Waiting.

"I'm going to break you," he murmured, both warning and plea.

"Maybe we'll break each other." Her tongue flicked over her lips, an invitation more potent than even the siren's call of cut lines on a mirror, glistening and pure.

And he couldn't say no anymore.

Chapter Seventeen

Then

The room was spinning. Lights and shapes blurred, becoming one psychedelic mass. Guitars screamed and drums crashed, pounding between her legs. Echoing in her head. Her feet couldn't keep up. She moved faster, revolving through the thick, humid air. She wasn't just dancing, she *was* the music. The bassline simmered in her blood, as intrinsic as a heartbeat. If she exhaled, the rhythm would change. Inhaled and it would skip.

Don't look down. Don't look up. Don't stop.

She laughed when someone grabbed at her arms. *No.* She couldn't take time to think. This particular section required her to keep moving to hold on to the beat. She couldn't falter or the song would end too soon. Maybe she'd never get to play it again.

"Jazz. What the hell? What's wrong with you?"

That voice. Rough and urgent. It didn't belong here. She hadn't reached the chorus. This wasn't his part. That would come later, when she was prepared to share the melody with him.

Not yet.

"Baby, come here." Gentle fingers caressing her cheek, brushing aside her hair. The familiar scent of sage and cedarwood from his aftershave drifted over her, as warm as a blanket. He tucked her against him and she let out a sob, so close to shattering in his arms that hiding in the thick cotton of his flannel shirt seemed like the only oasis of safety she had left.

"Gray," she said, over and over.

"I'm here. I've got you."

She shook her head, knowing it had to be a lie. No one had her. Trusting anyone led to her being alone. She wouldn't be so stupid again.

"Are you here by yourself?" His knuckles slid under her chin, tipping it up. This close, she could taste the hops on his breath. He'd been drinking too, but he wasn't like Toby. His hands weren't grasping and groping at her clothes. She'd finally shoved him away and started to dance, and he'd laughed, wanting to see her show.

Everyone expected her to perform, as the pretty little doll who wasn't supposed to cause a fuss or as the blue-haired freak who played through her pain. Either way, she had a script.

She'd always sucked at not blowing her lines.

"Jazz. Look at me."

She struggled to focus on him. Why did Gray have four eyes? Four gorgeous gray eyes, but still, that was creepy as fuck.

"Jesus, baby, what are you on?" He drew her toward the nearest couch and pushed someone aside so he had room to sit. Then she was on his lap, and his thumb was on her lower lip, carefully stroking. "Tell me what you remember."

She tipped her head toward his, accidentally banging their foreheads together. A giggle erupted at the flash of pain before she angled her nose lower, lining her lips up with his. He exhaled and for an instant, the fog in her brain cleared away. He'd blown through the cobwebs just by enfolding her in his strong arms and offering her his air when she couldn't figure out how to inhale on her own anymore.

"I remember you," she murmured before everything went black.

Chapter Eighteen

Now

Gray lifted his hands to her face, spanning her cheeks with his fingers. She could've been made of glass, he took so much care in tilting her closer. He brushed his lips over her mouth, tasting smoke and toothpaste. A lick of his tongue against the seam and her lips fell open, her breath escaping on a moan. His hands trembled as he drove them into her hair, driving her backward into the hot tub. She let out a startled squeak.

"Sorry," he mumbled, rubbing her back where she'd made contact with the frame.

Then they were kissing again, and he couldn't focus on all the textures of her. Warm lips, slick tongue, rising and falling breasts. He cupped one in each hand, feathering his thumbs over the puckered tips, and lifted his thigh to force hers open. He hoped she was as ready for this as he was, because damn them both, he doubted he could wait.

He'd been waiting for eight years.

"It's okay. I'm okay. Oh, that feels good."

"It better because I can't spare a hand right now." He caught her laughter in his mouth and swallowed it down, desperate to get drunk on all the sounds she could make. It might take a lifetime to tease all of them out of her.

"I can." Lightly, she dragged her nails down his stomach before undoing his zipper. He groaned as she curled around him, groaned again as she tightened her grip. "This time you're not coming on my back," she said fiercely, pulling his lower lip between her teeth while her hand shuttled up and down his length.

Some part of him was shocked his pretty, perfect, innocent Jazz could be saying such things. Another part reveled in the dirty light in her eyes. He palmed her cheek, angling her head back so he could lick a pathway along her jaw to her ear. Hoops and dangles crowded the lobe, jangling together as he sucked the pliant flesh into his mouth. "Where do you want me to come?"

"Anywhere." She fumbled her small hand farther into his jeans and squeezed the base of his cock, making him hiss. "Everywhere."

"Jesus." Reluctantly, he let go of her breasts and bent to grab her dress. "Let's go inside before Nick comes back and sees you."

"He's seen it all before." He sent her a dark look over his shoulder and she flushed, clearly realizing what she'd just said. "Uh, I mean—so would this be a bad time to tell you I dropped your joint and it rolled away?"

He laughed and pulled her close again. "You're lucky I love you."

"I am. So lucky," she said, glancing up at him as if he'd just presented her with a bucketful of stars.

"Don't try to sweet talk me now. I'm supposed to be annoyed, remember?"

Her eyes twinkled up at him. "You can't be. Just like I can't be mad at you. It's our curse."

"Uh-huh." He dragged the sill higher and patted her very fine ass. The door was right there, but he couldn't deny he wanted a view of her from behind. "In you go."

"I thought that was your line. I mean, in you go in *me*. Oh shit. I'm high." She giggled and climbed in the window.

Gray smiled and shook his head. He couldn't even be annoyed at himself right now for letting her have some of the joint because she seemed so loose and relaxed. How could he ever wish that away?

He'd no sooner climbed inside and tossed her dress on a chair than she threw her booted foot up on the bed and yanked down the tiny side zipper. A dozen foil packets tumbled out.

"Wow." He cleared his throat. "Looks like you have plans for me."

"Oh, I do." She grabbed one between her teeth and used both hands to shovel the rest onto the floor. She unzipped her other boot and unearthed her cell phone, setting it on the nightstand, then toed off both boots and climbed up on the platform bed.

Something about her efficiency made him laugh in spite of the serious hard-on he was sporting. "Good thing I've been saving up."

A shadow passed over her face, a brief cloud in the midst of all the sunshine. "Have you? Really?"

"Really. I haven't been with anyone in months." He gave her a sheepish grin. "It's even been a while since I've been with myself."

Instantly the sun sliced through the momentary darkness in her expression. She flashed him a dazzling smile. "Me either." Invitingly, she spread her legs, revealing her swollen pink pussy. No hair to speak of, anywhere. "So. Where were we?"

"Christ almighty." He didn't smoke pot often enough to know what it normally did for sex, but with every passing second, his cock thickened more. He felt harder than the exposed beams overhead. Even walking to his bedroom door to lock it presented a frigging challenge, but he did it because he wouldn't risk Nick interrupting them—again. "Warn a guy before you do that, would you?"

"No. Because I don't want you to have control around me. I want you on the edge, like I am."

"No worries there."

He turned back and drank down the sight of her, all tumbling hair, hungry eyes and puffy lips. Without lowering his gaze, he shoved down his jeans and boxers. He stalked forward and leaned across the bed, banding his hand around her thigh to drag her closer. The simple movement made his head swim as if he'd downed a few six-packs. He had a light buzz going from the few pulls on the joint he'd managed before her appearance, but that wasn't the cause of his dizziness. He could smell her now, sweeter than springtime, more alluring than the most seductive drug.

Smiling at him, she picked up the remote he'd tossed on the pillow earlier and aimed it at the small speakers on the dresser. "Ripcord" from their EP flowed out. He'd been trying to write earlier—on his own, since Nick had taken off hours ago and hadn't returned—so he'd turned on Oblivion's music in the hopes of luring out the muse. That hadn't worked, so he'd turned to weed.

Now he would turn to Jazz.

He nipped her lower belly, causing her to drop the remote and lean up on her elbows. He learned her flesh from touch rather than sight, because he couldn't bear to look away from her eyes. That lust-soaked blue dragged him on a path straight into the heart of her, her lashes fluttering while his tongue parted her swollen folds. The pink crystals on her hood piercing nearly made him beg. Seeing that delicate flesh pinched and ready for his kisses made him want to send up a few thousand prayers of gratitude.

Unable to wait a second more, he shoved her legs open wide. He held her gaze as he licked her from her clit to her entrance and back again, but he couldn't maintain it when he pushed a finger inside and she trembled around him, her body yielding to his invasion. She moaned and flexed around him, inviting him inside her just as she'd done on the deck by licking her lips.

God. He wasn't going to survive this. He wouldn't survive without seeing her come, either.

He flicked her piercing, eliciting her high, thin cry, then focused on her clit. A rainbow of colors exploded in his mind. He swore he could hear her heartbeat, that wild, unsteady thud, and his own drummed in response, an endless beat that sped up at even the smallest movement. Razoring his teeth over the piercing and the plump bundle of nerves, he slid another finger inside her, pulling upward, coaxing that same melodic response from her throat, a delirious mixture of sigh and moan, more breath than actual sound.

In the background, his guitar solo dominated the song before her drums came crashing through, breaking apart the rhythm and making it something all new. Something all theirs.

Then a new sound, a new instrument to add complexity to the composition. Her sighing his name, over and over. She drew it out until it vibrated like the strings in his guitar. "*Gray.*"

He closed his eyes and savored, losing himself in the overwhelming pulse of their song, of her swollen, wet flesh around his pumping fingers, of her heart throbbing against his mouth. Tasting her pleasure as he created it felt more like making music than he'd ever known before.

Her body rose up, her full breasts lifting, her dusky nipples pointing skyward. Red from his fingers and her desire. He licked up the evidence of it between her legs, desperate to take it all, to fulfill every want she had before she found the voice to ask. Offering her bliss in small, steady doses until she quivered, her breasts shimmying, her muscles growing taut.

She gripped him relentlessly, pushing back against him with every thrust of his fingers. Her hips pumped, her heels dragging up the comforter, her head thrashing over the pristine bedding. Those rustling noises joined the rest, becoming a cacophony of need that surged blood into his cock and tore a groan from his throat. He wanted to hear only her, to know exactly that instant that she lost herself, but he couldn't stop the helpless convulsing of his hips.

"Fuck. Fuck. Jazz." He tried to apologize but he couldn't find the words within the unfolding spiral of warmth. She was everywhere. On his tongue, behind his eyes, in his hands. In his ears every time her drums cut through their songs to make them hers.

And then she was coming too, her hands driving forward to embed in his hair as she pulled him against her, her legs winding around him to bring him more fully into her clenching heat. His own release spun out, wringing him dry. He gripped her thigh and pressed his cheek to her belly, wondering if the floor was really trembling or if that was just him.

"Oh my God, the earth actually moved. That's an actual thing. Holy fuck." Her dazed laughter made him raise his head to give her a smile. At least he hoped it was a smile. His muscles felt like they'd gone numb.

"Guess so." He hauled in a breath and eased back enough to look down at the mess he'd caused. Technically, she'd caused it.

Though he hadn't used for all that long, he'd heard plenty of jokes about the side effects. Jere had regaled him with them the other night. Not being able to get hard, not being able to get off. But if tonight was any indication, Jazz could combat any substance.

He hadn't come on his lap without being touched since...ever. He'd *never* come that fast before, even back in high school.

"Yeah, this is fucking embarrassing." He shook his head in disgust. "I'm sorry."

"For what?" Noticing the direction of his glance, she scrambled up and peered over the side of the bed. She let out a laugh. "Oh, oops."

"Yeah. Oops. All your fault." He yanked on her hair, dragging her closer for a hard kiss. Instead of shying away from her taste, she chased his tongue, drawing it into her mouth with a long, slow suck that made his spent cock give a halfhearted salute. "Jesus. You're going to kill me."

"Let me make it all better first." Smacking her lips together, she slid to the floor in such a sensual move that he had to grab his dick again. "Uh-uh," she chided. "That's mine."

She licked her way up his thigh, catching every stray drop before treating the other one to the same treatment. By the time she finished, his balls were in knots again and the head of his cock had swelled painfully. She swiped her tongue over the tip, making an appreciative hum that might've rolled his eyes back had he not been fixated on her as if his life depended on it.

He wouldn't miss a minute of this.

She rolled her tongue down the side, traveling down to take teasing swipes over his sac. Her lashes dipped as she drew one of his balls into her mouth, sucking lightly while he fisted his hands in his hair and tried not to force her to take his length inside. She would get there. He might die first, but he'd let her find her own rhythm.

Her nails scraped up the outside of his leg and she applied the barest suction to his balls, one then the other, before she curled her super-strong fingers around the base of his dick and lapped at the head like she was in a champion ice cream eating contest.

Holy hell.

Her hair fell down around her face, hiding her features except for her reddened lips and smoky eyes. She could've been anyone. A sultry anonymous blonde. From this angle, she didn't look like his bright best friend. This woman had seduction down to an art. Then she smiled up at him, and the jagged puzzle pieces inside him shifted into place.

This was Jazz. *His* Jazz.

Unable to wait another second, he grabbed her elbows and pulled her up, clamping his mouth on hers. "I need you."

"Yes, yes. Please." Her tongue whipped over his, heightening his urgency. "Condom's too far."

"Fuck them. I want you like this."

He waited for her to balk. This was stupid. So stupid. She'd been on the Pill forever—when you lived with someone, you discovered those details about them whether or not you wanted to—but that didn't mean they should take risks. Right now he couldn't remember exactly why. His head felt deliciously light, and all the reasons for not doing what the hell he wanted seemed insignificant.

"Yeah. Me too." She panted into his mouth. "Have to have you now."

She straddled his lap, digging her knees into the carpet on either side of his thighs. Without another word, she impaled herself on him, sinking down to the root in a long, slow glide.

"God, yes," he groaned, losing his breath at the feel of her vising around him. Slick and hot, her pussy gloved his cock, enfolding him in a blast of heat that scalded him from his feet to the top of his head. Her piercing scraped him, adding a zing of pleasure that traveled straight through to the base of his spine. Something this amazing couldn't last long.

Neither would he.

Fluid and sleek, she rose above him, hands fisting in his hair as her mouth ghosted over his. "God, Gray. So fucking good," she gasped.

"Can't wait. Need more." He wound his arms around her, slamming her breasts into his chest, and still it wasn't close enough. He hauled her up in his arms and jockeyed her in his hold, stopping beside the bed to take her mouth. Her panting breaths echoed his, an unforgettable symphony.

Finally, they were together. All the way together.

She rode him wantonly, taking him deep as he rocketed upward. Goddamn, that piercing. She weighed next to nothing and with only a few adjustments, he managed to lock his arms under her thighs so he could surge into her again and again, rubbing over the crystals with each thrust. She took every bit of him, her sweet pink flesh swallowing his cock.

Riveted to the view between her legs, he tipped her backward, desperate to see more. She cried out and dropped her head back, exposing the long line of her throat for him to bite and kiss. Perspiration clung to her flushed skin, adding a faint sheen of dampness that he ached to taste. He couldn't kiss enough places. He wanted to be everywhere at once. Licking her, fucking her, touching each inch of her flawless skin.

More than anything, he wanted to own her the same way she'd owned him since he was sixteen.

Her pussy clamped around him, so wet and tight he couldn't see through the haze of his hunger, and he bent her backward, dangling her in the air while he hammered into her hard and fast. She held on for all she was worth, her moans escaping her along with her breath. As she started to spasm, he turned and dropped her onto the bed, climbing over her to drag her leg over his shoulder. He rubbed her clit and stroked into her, sinking in and holding while he slanted his mouth over hers. He whispered her name, the mystery and beauty of it, unable to hear anything anymore but the relentless beat of her heartbeat matching his.

That was the only music he needed. The only one that still made sense.

He linked his fingers with hers, gripping her hand next to her head on the bed. Swiveling his hips, he found a new spot inside her, sliding over it until she gasped and bowed up, her eyes going wide as she came undone. Her hot wetness gushed over him and he groaned and buried his face in her hair, his thumb still a blur on her clit, his hips still pounding. The song in his head wouldn't stop. All Jazz.

"Gray," she gasped, digging her nails into his back. "Oh God. It's too much. I'm so dizzy."

"Close your eyes. Feel." He nudged her chin up and kissed his way down her throat, pressing his lips to the wild throb of her pulse caged in by her delicate collarbone. "Feel me."

"I do. I can't stop." She clenched his hand and matched him stroke for stroke, her pelvis slapping against his with the force of his thrusts. Her slick heat spurred him on, driving him to fuck her so violently that his balls collided with her ass on every pass. And he still needed more.

"I can't get deep enough. Jesus. Get on top of me."

He switched their positions, pulling her over him, and latched his teeth on her swollen nipple, tugging on it without finesse. Crying out, she braced her fists on either side of his head and grinded on his cock, torturing them both with her piercing as she circled her hips in a frantic figure-eight. Goddamn, she was soaked. She bit her lip and moved faster, pushing more of her breast in his mouth. He grabbed her ass, yanking her down on him so powerfully that she whimpered. Such a delicious sound. He did it again, adding a twist of his hips, offering the counterpoint to her circling, and her whimpers increased.

"Don't you hold back on me," he growled.

"No. Can't. I'm coming again." She moaned the words as she fisted around him, squeezing so tight that he couldn't stave off his own impending orgasm another second.

"Yes. God, yes." He plunged one last time, grasping the full curves of her ass. He clung to her, his hands damp with sweat, while his release pulsed deep into her pussy. She shuddered over him, around him, finally collapsing on his chest.

But he still couldn't stop fucking her, his well-used cock seeking her hot slit without his conscious help. He'd probably die fucking her. And he'd die happy.

A few minutes later, he sank his hands into her hair and lifted her head, chuckling at the weak flutter of her lashes. "You okay?" He swallowed over the gravel in his throat. "Did I hurt you?"

"Yes." Finally opening her eyes, she flashed him a grin that was pure mischief. "It was absolutely glorious."

He laughed again and wrapped his arms around her waist. Now her watermelon scent brought him peace rather than pain. Her hair smelled of wildflowers, just as it always had, and that too only sweetened the moment. "I'm glad you think so."

"Oh yes. Give me five and I'll show you what else I think," she teased.

When she dropped back down to his chest, he caressed her cheek, her jaw, her shoulder. He couldn't stop touching her. Maybe if he kept touching her he could stave off the morning that had to come. It always did. "This meant everything to me," he said, voice ragged.

"Me too." She lifted her head. Tears brimmed on her lashes, nearly spilling over. "All I wanted was this. Just this."

Framing her face in his hands, he tipped his forehead to hers. "Yeah." He smudged his thumb under her eye, catching one of her tears. "You deserve so much more than me. But God, how am I supposed to give you up now?"

"You're not," she said fiercely. "Understand me? We've both given up too much for too long." She snatched one of his hands and held it between her breasts. "You and me, we're a team. Nothing can hurt us again."

There were so many reasons that wasn't true. But he went with the easy one, the one she wouldn't hate him for. "Lila—"

"Fuck Lila. This isn't about the band. This is about us. We were us before Oblivion existed. And we'll be us long after they don't."

He glanced away, wanting that to be true so badly that he couldn't speak. Until she said the rest.

"This isn't just a one-time thing. We're together now. Get that, Duffy? No going back. Tonight we made a promise to each other."

As much as he hated having to argue, he couldn't let this go. She needed to know what she was getting into. What he'd *brought* her into, willingly, because he wasn't strong enough to keep her out. "Baby, you don't understand—"

"Shh." She closed his lips with her fingers and kissed the cleft in his chin. "I understand you're mine. And I'm yours. Isn't that right?" she demanded, almost daring him to fight the point.

But he couldn't. Wouldn't. How could he fight something he'd craved for so long?

He exhaled, his self-loathing growing with every passing moment. "Yes."

"And we're overdue on proving that to each other." She shifted over him, rocking along his swiftly rousing cock. "I hope you took your vitamins today."

Worlds lived behind her glittering blue eyes, ones he wanted nothing more than to explore. With her. Nothing made sense when she wasn't at his side. The music had stopped, and right now, he didn't need it. She was his melody. His breath and his heartbeat.

His very *life*, and the reason he still wanted to live it.

"Ditto." He snagged his hand in her hair and flipped her over onto her back. Her giggle flowed over him, warm and precious and worth every sacrifice. "Better get ready, because I'm about to make up for a hell of a lot of lost time."

* § *

Jazz woke to a softly strumming guitar. Still half-asleep, she smiled and burrowed deeper into pillows that smelled like the man she loved. She'd know the sage-and-cedarwood scent of his aftershave anywhere. The slightest hint of sweet smoke layered over it, a reminder of what had occurred the night before.

As if she'd ever forget the best night of her life.

Gray started to sing, his voice still husky from sleep. But his fingers were magic, like always. She grinned at the double meaning of that—oh so true—and opened her eyes, unable to wait even a second longer to look into the eyes she adored so much.

He sat cross-legged beside her, his beat-up guitar held in a loose grip. He played with such grace that she fixated on his hand for a good minute before she realized he was singing Van Morrison's "Brown-Eyed Girl," except he'd changed the lyrics to fit the eye color of the girl in his bed.

She was in his bed.

She hugged that blissful reality to her chest, closing her eyes to allow it to fully sink in. He continued to sing, his deep voice caressing the words as deftly as the instrument he coaxed to life in his hands. Somehow he knew every word, though she'd never heard him play that song. When it ended, he slid effortlessly into his rendition of the Stones' "Brown Sugar." She tried to stifle her laughter but she failed.

"Okay. The first one I got. Lovely lyric change, by the way. I love it." She popped up on one elbow. "But 'Brown Sugar?'"

"You're awake." He sounded so pleased by that fact that she almost forgot her question until his smile turned wicked. "Sure you want to know why I picked that one?"

Now she wanted to know more than ever. "Yes. Tell me."

He set aside his guitar and leaned forward, brushing his mouth over her ear. "You smell like burnt sugar. Taste like it too. Sweet and sticky all over my tongue. I'm going to write a song." He licked the side of her neck and she shuddered. "But in the meantime, 'Brown Sugar' works."

"You're a dirty boy." Another laugh bubbled up in the middle of all the goosebumps. "I like it."

Expression playful, he sank his teeth into her bottom lip. "Oh honey, you have no idea."

"But I'm ready to find out."

"We'll see about that." The corner of his lip curled into that naughty smile she'd wanted to kiss since she'd first laid eyes on him. Now she could.

She could do anything she wanted with him. *To* him.

Accurately reading her thoughts, he tugged her on top of him, embedding his hand in her hair while the other coasted down her back to her ass. He cupped one cheek, hoisting her leg higher so that her slit flirted with the head of his prominent morning wood.

"Good morning to me," she teased, dipping her tongue into the laugh lines beside his mouth.

"Mmm-hmm. And I'm about to have breakfast."

He hoisted her up his body, making her squeal. He clamped his mouth between her legs, his tongue arrowing along where she'd already grown hot and damp. Just kissing him and crawling around on his body were enough to get her motor humming. But his teeth scraping lightly over her hood piercing represented a surefire booking pass to orgasm central.

She fisted his hands in his hair and wobbled as he pressed the tip of his tongue inside, scooping up her wetness and swallowing with such audible appreciation that she couldn't fight a blush. God, this man. How could she love him this much and not just shatter from it?

Everything seemed possible with hazy morning sunshine just beginning to trickle into the room, bathing the space in a romantic pink glow. Strong hands held her still, forcing her to take every bit of the pleasure he offered. He slid one hand around to part her folds, holding them open to lash her piercing and her clit with such focused attention that she scrambled backward and caught hold of his thighs to maintain her balance.

Bent backward, on the verge of a moan or a laugh—maybe both—she looked down to find that stormy gaze caressing her naked body. Suddenly she saw herself the way he must. Breasts lifted, nipples beaded and pink. Stomach quivering with every erotic kiss.

"You're so beautiful," he whispered.

She feathered her fingers through his hair, slipping her hand down until it skimmed his mouth. Until her fingers trailed over his on her flesh. He kissed the tip of her thumb, sucking on it so slowly that a shudder rolled through her. "Oh God. I'm going to—"

Her cell went off, playing the *Top Chef* theme song that was Harper's ringtone.

"Jesus. What the hell is that?"

"Oh shit, oh fuck, I forgot. It's morning." She tried to scuttle backward along Gray's torso, but he wasn't having it. He locked his arms around her thighs and did some kind of roll with his tongue that set off tingles all the way down to her G-spot. "Harper," she wailed as the phone went off and immediately started again.

"We're busy. She can wait."

"But I have her catering truck—"

"And I have your pussy, and I'm not done with it yet. So *shh* before you make me get rough." The teasing glint in his eyes accompanied his finger flick on her clit piercing.

Then he slipped his tongue inside her again, and she couldn't hold back her scream as he rotated her piercing in time with his excruciatingly slow mouth-fucking. He hummed in his throat and pressed on while Harper called a third time, clearly frantic.

Jazz was frantic too, for a whole other reason.

She snatched a handful of his thick, silky long hair and pulled, bearing down on his mouth without shame. He used his free hand to knead her ass, encouraging her to ride his face with abandon. There was no way she could stop now. She slipped her other hand over her breasts, tweaking her nipples as the liquid sensation in her belly turned to drowning heat.

"God, keep going." She squeezed her knees beside his head, rocking for all she was worth. "I'm so close." Moving over him faster, she closed her eyes and threw her head back, twisting her nipple. Almost at the crescendo. She cried out as her core contracted and scalding waves of pleasure suffused her body, going on way past the point of insanity.

And he still didn't stop.

"Oh no, I can't."

"You can. You are." His words rumbled against her drenched slit, amplifying the endless aftershocks. "On my fingers this time."

They slid inside her with ease, two and then three, working in concert with the same skill he employed on the guitar. He worked her hard, sliding in and out in a rhythm designed to cause her to lose her mind. Again. His lips closed over her piercing, tugging gently.

Gasping, she climaxed once more, her thighs vising to his ears as she flooded his mouth. He drank her down eagerly, licking up every bit of what she gave him.

When she was still shaking, still barely coherent, he scooped her up and flipped her on her back beneath him. "Fucking Gray sounds like an excellent idea," he breathed, slanting his mouth over hers.

Tasting herself on his lips had to be the gateway to heaven. "Yes. I want you."

He grabbed her thigh, pushing her leg straight up in the air. The tip of his erection nudged her where she still quivered and she moaned, already arching toward him.

A knock sounded at the door and he stilled, a mischievous light appearing in his eyes. He held his finger to his lips, indicating she should remain quiet, and shifted his hips, easing the broad head of his cock into her extremely sensitive entrance. She let out a whimper and he caught it with his mouth, swiveling his hips again to push in deeper.

"Dude, you ever coming out of there? It's almost fucking eight. We have music to make or else Dragon Lady will be up our ass."

Nick had to be the only rocker who didn't believe in sleeping away the day. Unless he was just being super-dickish.

"Gimme five," Gray called back, raising his torso and plunging farther inside her clutching pussy. "I'll be right out."

"Sure thing. Wouldn't want to interrupt you." Nick hit or kicked the door before letting out an audible curse. She might've been able to discern what that curse was if Gray hadn't picked that moment to suck her eager nipple between his teeth. Her attention blinked out to everything except the fullness of the cock inside her, shoving her wide open to accept his invasion.

He rubbed over her G-spot with each pass, traveling so deep that he grunted against her breast every time he bottomed out. The flashes of pain, the exquisite burn, only increased the pressure fisting in her belly, building so swiftly that she didn't have a chance of holding on.

"Oh fuck. You're coming again already," he rasped. From the bliss contorting his features, he wasn't far behind.

"Yes. Oh yes." Rolling her hips up to meet his strokes, she watched the storm break over his face. His jaw locked, his gorgeous eyes shuttered. And her name spilled out on the shout he muffled against her hair.

Nothing could ever be better than hearing him call out to her while he came. *Nothing.*

He continued fucking her, his movements languid now. Somehow they tripped the tangled wires inside her even faster than his rapid strokes had. God, she couldn't come again. She didn't even have enough breath left to cry out. Her hips flailed, trapped beneath his as the tension gave way. So deliciously trapped.

"That's it, baby." He nuzzled her neck, lifting his torso to plunge into her one more time. "Give me everything."

She reached up to cradle his head as the final punch of pleasure swept through her system and left her quaking beneath him. She bit her lip to stifle her whimpers, realizing once he eased back to give her a dazed grin that she tasted blood.

"Holy shit." She lifted her hand to her mouth. "I think I bit through my lip."

He bent to kiss the cut, so gently that her racing heart turned over before going still for a breathless moment while their gazes clung. She stroked the side of his face, shocked that for once, she didn't have to look for something to say after sex.

Between them, words weren't necessary. They had long looks and longer kisses. They'd have longer everything from now on.

This was just the beginning, and oh God, maybe even waiting had been worth it if she could get to feel like this.

"I have to go," she whispered as the phone started again. Guilt kicked hard in her chest. Poor Harper. She was going to kill her and rightly so.

"I know. When are you coming back to me?"

She threaded her fingers through his hair, marveling at the darkness against her pale skin. "As soon as I can."

"Not soon enough." He pulled out of her, causing them both to moan, and bent to grab her clothes. "No underwear? I sort of vaguely remember that but...no underwear?"

"No." She grinned. "I couldn't take any chances."

"Guess not. Though I would find you sexy in a parka and snow pants." He held up her dress and lifted an eyebrow. "I'm supposed to let you leave in this? Where'd you park anyway?"

"Two blocks down, behind some bushes."

"Damn, total spy mode. You walked two blocks in those boots?"

"I would've crawled on glass to get to you. Do you have any idea how long I've waited?"

He shifted toward her with her dress bunched in his hands. "Unless it's the better part of a decade, you're going to lose this contest."

"It is. Why did we waste so much time?"

From the way he set his mouth, she didn't get the feeling they'd be going down that road anytime soon. Maybe it was just as well. The future was what mattered now, not the past.

Swallowing deeply, she brushed her fingers over his jaw and tried again. "It's always been you for me. Always, since long before—before he—"

The melting warmth in his expression turned glacial. "Don't say his name. I don't want any part of that fucker to touch us here."

She turned her face away, hating that she'd brought even an instant of sadness into what had been such a wonderful night and morning-after. The sadness existed entirely on her part. She would never forgive herself for having any part in driving a wedge between them. From him, she felt only cold rage. "He's your brother."

"I don't have a brother anymore." He pitched what he held across the room, nailing the top of the still-open window. Her dress fluttered to the ground.

"Gray." She cupped his shoulder. "I'm okay. I swear. He didn't hurt me."

"Yes, he did. I heard you screaming. I hear it in my nightmares."

Tears filled her eyes, but not for her. His anguish ripped her open. "It was so long ago."

"Goddammit, *no*." He shoved to his feet. "It's like it happened yesterday for me. I don't care how many years pass, I'll kill that bastard if he ever looks at you again." He walked to the window and picked up her dress, clutching it to his chest before turning back and giving her a half-smile that didn't begin to mitigate the fury vibrating off his body. "Sure you have to go?"

His rapid mood shift knocked her off-kilter but she tried to return his smile. She wouldn't let anything ruin this, especially Brent. They'd fought too hard to get here. "Unfortunately, yes." She rolled off the bed and winced at the first step. "Ow. Ouch. Someone broke me."

That brought his grin back in full force. "Someone will make you better later," he promised, returning to her side to tug her dress over her head.

"I just bet." She yanked on her boots and zipped them up, then she grabbed her phone. "What am I forgetting?"

"This." He hooked a finger in the bodice of her dress and hauled her close.

His tongue slipped in to tangle with hers, and damn if she didn't still taste herself in his kiss. The thrill tingled from her nipples to between her legs, and she moaned, already halfway gone again. He grinned and kissed her harder, making her grin back even as their mouths moved together in perfect harmony.

Loving Gray was the easiest—and hardest—thing she'd ever done. But today it was easier than breathing. More right than anything she'd ever known.

Finally he eased away and nudged her toward the window. Must be the door to the deck didn't work or something. "Tell Harper I'm sorry too."

"Okay." Still dizzy, she started to climb over the windowsill then smiled dopily over her shoulder. "Same time tonight?"

"I'll be waiting for you." He leaned his forearm on the casing and drew his fingertip from her mouth to her jaw. "Think I'm going to write your song today. All that sugar on my tongue, I can taste it now..." He sang softly, making her flush and screech as she darted out the window.

His laughter followed her off the deck.

Chapter Nineteen

Then

Gray watched her sleep, tracing the tangled blue-and-black swirls of hair that flowed over her shoulder. She slept like the dead, never making a single sound. Even her lashes didn't flutter. But her heartbeat stayed strong and true under his other hand.

If that had changed for even a second during the long night he'd spent sitting with her on the lumpy couch in the Feldmans' basement, he would've hauled her off to the E.R. He wouldn't risk her health even if his parents found out and grounded her for a century. But that steady beat never wavered, so he'd called his worried parents shortly before midnight and told them Jazz was with him. She was fine. He wouldn't let anything happen to her, ever.

Except he already had. He should've known she'd be curious about the Feldmans' party, especially now that she was friends with Stacey. That girl liked to party. Hard. He didn't know if Stacey had been the one to slip something in Jazz's drink or if it had been some other creep—like that jerk Toby who'd been watching her dance until Gray showed up—but he recognized the signs of a girl who'd been roofied. Jazz never drank to excess. Though there was a first time for everything, his gut told him this wasn't it.

Someone had fucked with her, which meant they'd fucked with him.

She curled into his chest. Slowly, she opened her eyes. "Gray?"

Her weak, thready voice rekindled his anger. Whoever had done this to her would wish they'd never laid eyes on those fucking drugs once he showed them the error of their ways.

"Yeah," he gritted out, brushing his fingers over her cheek. "How're you feeling?"

"Stupid." Wincing, she sat up and seemed to realize that she was on his lap. "Whoa. What's going on? Where are we?"

Just as he'd thought. She didn't remember the end of last night. Sure, some blackout drunks experienced the same. That wasn't Jazz. He'd never believe it.

"You're safe," he soothed, tucking her hair behind her ear.

Her forehead puckered. "Why wouldn't I be?"

"We're in the Feldmans' basement. There was a party. Do you remember any of that?"

"Yeah. I came here with Stacey." She glanced around. "Where is everyone?"

"It's the next morning. Everyone's gone. Well, except for Beth, her boyfriend and a few friends sleeping it off upstairs."

She rubbed her temple. "My head hurts like I got loaded." She frowned. "I only had two beers. Why do I feel like this?"

"You're sure? You remember that part?"

"Yes, I remember. Some parts are fuzzy. The drinking part I remember, because the first beer I drank tasted funny. I took a second one, figuring that maybe I just needed to get used to the taste. The second one was even worse."

He smoothed his hand over her knee, avoiding her gaze while he hauled his ragged emotions back into line. He wasn't going to go off in front of her. She already didn't feel well and she'd had a shitty night.

A coppery flavor filled his mouth and he swallowed it away. He hoped it had only been shitty.

"Who gave the beers to you? Do you remember?"

She pursed her lips and looked off in the distance as if she was struggling to line up the details. "I don't know his name, but it was the same guy both times."

"I just bet it was," he said, idly stroking her jean-clad knee to keep from punching a hole through something. Anything. "Sure it wasn't Toby? The guy who was watching you dance?"

"I was dancing?"

"Yeah."

Her cheeks flooded with color. "Like on a table?"

"No, just here, in front of the couch. Unless..." He refused to think about any other possibilities right now. "Was Toby the one who gave you the beers, baby?"

She blinked up at him. "You just called me baby."

"Don't worry about that." That was for *him* to worry about later—that he'd let himself slip that much—after he made sure she was okay. "If you don't know his name, describe him to me."

"I don't know him. He's a senior. He was tall with dark hair and big shoulders." She shrugged. "That's all I recall. I'm sorry."

"Don't be sorry. Tell me what happened."

"Nothing, really. He gave me a beer and Stacey took one. Then later on, he came downstairs to talk to Toby and he offered to get me another."

"Did he touch you?" he asked sharply.

"No, I don't think so. Toby tried to—" She broke off, her flush increasing. "You think he did something to my beers. That's why they tasted weird."

"I think it's a good guess." He fought to keep his tone level. "He probably put roofies in them."

"Like...the date rape drug?"

"Yes." He rubbed his thumb along the seam of her jeans, not looking at her. "You don't remember anyone doing anything, do you?"

"Toby grabbed my boob but I think you mean more than that." She shook her head rapidly. "No. I'm pretty sure nothing more than that happened."

He swallowed, hating that he needed to press the subject but knowing he had to. For her. "There's a bathroom right down the hall. Can you go down there and...check? Just make sure you don't see any unusual bruises or anything out of place."

"You think someone raped me and I don't remember?" She shook her head again. "No. I'm sure that didn't happen."

"Jazz." He gripped her chin and forced her to look at him. "Go check as best as you can, all right? For me. If something did happen, we have to know now so we can..." Jesus, he couldn't do this. Couldn't say this. "...take the appropriate steps."

Her eyes filled. "What *we*? If someone hurt me, I'm all alone. I've always been alo—"

"No." It took everything he possessed to keep his voice firm. She was shaking now, and he wasn't far from it himself. "You aren't alone anymore. I'm with you, for everything. I'll wait for you right outside the door, and no matter what, we'll face it together. Okay?"

She closed her eyes and nodded, then she slipped off his lap and walked down the hall with her head held high.

True to his word, he followed and waited until she came out of the bathroom a few minutes later. The relief on her face caused the knots in his stomach to untwist all at once. "Everything all right?" he asked, needing to hear her say it.

"Yes. Everything's fine. No bruises, no...irritation or sign of anything anywhere. I'm fine." She let out a long breath as his arms came around her, hard. "God, why do guys do that? Why would someone be that desperate for sex?" She gazed up at him, chin quivering. "You wouldn't ever do that, would you?"

"Of course not. Never."

"You promise?"

He set his chin on her hair and tried not to let the indignation through that she even needed to ask. She was understandably shook up. "I promise."

"Okay." She pressed her face into his throat and exhaled shakily. "Okay."

"No, not okay. I get that you want to go to parties and all that, but I can't risk this happening again. My parents would never forgive me," he added hastily as she began to argue.

"You're not responsible for me."

"I damn well am. If you want to go to parties, fine. Awesome. But we'll go together."

She rubbed her eyes, smearing her mascara. The raccoon look only made her blue eyes more pronounced. "Why would you want to go with me? I'm a lame freshman. You're a senior."

"You're not lame." He pushed lightly at her shoulder. "Sometimes I even kinda like hanging out with you. Once a month or so."

The corner of her mouth curved. "What about when you have a girlfriend? Won't she get pissed you're hauling around a spare tire?"

"Didn't I already tell you I don't have girlfriends? Besides, friends look out for each other. Do we have a deal?"

She studied him for a long minute then nodded reluctantly before gifting him with a gorgeous smile. His Jazz's smile. "Deal."

Chapter Twenty

Now

Jazz called Harper as soon as she hit the freeway. "I'm sorry. Hugely, fantastically sorry—"

"Jasmine Edwards, where the fuck have you been? Meet me at the Vicenza. I got a ride over to your spa shindig when my truck went missing."

"I know I messed up, please don't hate me." Jazz flipped on her signal and switched lanes before bumping up her speed. It was handy that Harper had traveled to where they were staying. It was much closer than going all the way back to the Hollywood Hills. "Gray's sorry too. We'll totally make it up to you, I promise. And I swear, tomorrow I'll get the truck back to you on time. No, I'll get it back to you early. So early you won't even have to think about—"

"Hold it."

"Holding."

"You and Gray. You wanting to borrow the truck again—not happening, by the way. That must mean that you got thoroughly plowed?"

Jazz couldn't help the smile that stretched across her face. "Mmm-hmm."

"*Mmm-hmm?*" Harper screeched. "I help you set all this up, I even loan you my spare hooker boots and that's all you have to say? What in the actual hell?"

"You loaned me your spare hooker boots weeks ago, but yes, they were much appreciated."

Jazz steered with her knees while she put on her lipstick in the rearview mirror. She'd left her purse in the glove compartment last night and man, when she'd checked herself out this morning, she'd looked completely fucked. Fucked squared. But there was no denying the old-fashioned sex glow in her cheeks and the love shine in her eyes, so she didn't give a crap. Gray had seen her without makeup a zillion times, and he was the only one who mattered.

"Hello? I am waiting for details. What happened?"

"We made sweet blissful love...for a really long time." Jazz giggled and tossed her lipstick in her purse. "All right, it was more like fucking."

"Aw, damn, tell me more. For real?"

"Oh yeah, I'm talking serious fucking. The kind that gives you a crimp in your back and makes you walk bow-legged for three days."

Harper let out a long sigh. "I miss Deak. I'm on the way to the suite. So far he's not picking up his cell."

"They're probably in the fitness room. Deak threatened to punish Simon for getting drunk last night by dragging him to the treadmill first thing this morning."

"I'll check there next if they aren't in their rooms, but if I don't find him by the time you arrive, I have to head out. I'm catering a ladies' lunch and they'll revolt if I arrive a minute later than planned."

"I'll find Deak for you, don't worry. If it's after you leave, I'll make sure he sends you a dirty picture or two to tide you over."

"Even better, send him back to me and you can have the truck again tonight. I only need him for maybe half an hour."

"Half an hour? Girl, you slipping? Gray ate me out for longer than that. Multiple times."

"Shut up."

"Okay," Jazz said cheerfully, taking the exit that led to the spa.

"You better not. Your transportation to your secret lover hangs in the balance. By the way, you sound ridiculously smug."

"I am. I've never experienced anything even one-tenth as good as last night. And this morning."

"Ah ha! That's why you ignored my calls, you shameless hussy."

"I really am sorry. But I was unavoidably occupied when you called."

"Don't tell me. I don't want to know."

"He had his head between my legs," Jazz began. "His fingers are amazing—guitarist thing, you know—"

"Uh yeah," Harper replied drily. "Deak's a bassist, remember?"

"But his tongue is even more *wow*," she continued dreamily. "He has incredible reach. And skill. Did I ever tell you they called him Muffy Duffy in school? He had a rep for loving to go down on girls." She didn't mention that she'd seen the evidence herself that one time in his bedroom. She'd simultaneously been repelled and fascinated.

"That is both disturbing and oddly hot."

"Uh-huh. Let me tell you, his technique is legendary. I swear, my toes haven't uncurled yet."

"Damn you. You better hope Deak can take an emergency dinner break to bring me a hot salami sandwich minus the bun."

Jazz cackled and turned at the light. "I'll deliver that message. So, um, about tonight? Pretty please? I promise I won't be late again tomorrow."

Harper let out a long-suffering sigh. "Never let it be said that I'm not a hopeless romantic. Or whatever the equivalent word is for assisting my friend in getting lots of head."

"Thanks. I appreciate it. I mean, *we* appreciate it. You aren't too behind for your ladies' lunch, are you?"

"No. I don't have to be there to set-up until eleven-thirty. I have an idea how this secret sex thang works, you know. I built in a window for...well, climbing out the window."

Jazz had to laugh. "Good thinking. I'll see you in a few. Thanks so much for everything. Especially for giving me a push."

"And the boots," Harper reminded her. "I must've psychically known that you would need them."

"Oh yeah, definitely the boots."

"You're welcome. I'm happy for you guys. Though gotta say, I'm a little shocked about Gray being so good at...well, everything. He's super hot, but boy, he hides a lot under that semi-sullen exterior." Harper whistled. "Always the quiet ones."

"He didn't used to be quiet. You wouldn't believe it now, but back in high school he was outgoing and had tons of friends."

"I'm sure he had tons of girlfriends too. With that Muffy Duffy thing, he must've had to beat them off with your drumsticks."

"Pretty much," Jazz agreed. "God knows I couldn't get anywhere near him."

"You're near him now, so make the most of it."

"I am. And I will. Oh, and I don't suppose you have any of those chocolate coconut popovers hanging around, do you?" Jazz grinned. "We might want a midnight snack later after we get done...collaborating."

"Thin ice, Edwards. Thin. Ice."

"Sorry. I'm almost to—"

A loud crashing noise sounded before Harper let out a long breath. "I just found Simon. He's facedown in his bed with his earbuds in his ears. The room looks trashed." She sighed. "Deacon, however, is nowhere in sight. The door to his room is locked."

"Is mine intact? Check my door. I didn't lock it."

"Yes, yours looks fine. Guess this was party central. No wonder Deak probably holed up in the gym."

"Yep, can't say I'm surprised. Simon hooked up with our esthetician last night. And maybe one of the manicurists. The party sounded like it was raging pretty well when I left." Jazz signaled and turned into the parking lot of the spa. "I'll meet you upstairs in five."

Five minutes later, Jazz stood next to Harper at Simon's bedside and shook her head. He wore only a pair of black silk sleep pants and had what appeared to be a trail of lipstick kisses down his back. An empty—at least she hoped it was empty—champagne bottle had rolled against his side and two more were tipped over on the nightstand. The sheets were all over the floor and one of the pillows sat on top of the TV.

And the perfume. Good lord.

"That isn't you, is it?" Jazz leaned closer to Harper and took a healthy sniff. Harper smelled like a combination of yeast, butter and lemons, her usual scent when she'd spent time in the kitchen. "Oh, thank God. I didn't want to diss that perfume if you were the one who smelled so rank."

"I appreciate that. I think."

"It smells like something they'd bathe a poodle in before putting it in Paris Hilton's purse. Ick." Jazz kicked at the sheets. "This is what happens when I take off for a night. He needs a keeper."

"The door to his room was unlocked. Someone could've robbed him blind." Harper looked around the expensive French-influenced suite. The heavy gold drapes were closed tight against the morning sunshine. "Granted, it's not likely in a place this swank, but it's possible."

Jazz pounded on Simon's back and he jumped like a live wire. Still didn't open his eyes, though. "Wake up, asshat." She yanked out his earbud and shouted "good morning," in his ear, which finally managed to make him open one sleepy eye.

"It's the middle of the night. Why you botherin' me?"

"It's past nine in the morning. Get your ass up."

"Closer to ten now," Harper put in.

"A man's entitled to sleep. Especially since we wrote a new song last night while you were off playing Candyland, pixilicious, and it fucking rocks my socks off." He produced a battered notebook from under his stomach and thrust it in their general direction.

Jazz cocked a brow at Harper and turned the notebook right side up. "'Nailed'? That's your contribution to the album?"

"Read it," he said before disappearing under his pillow.

Jazz scanned the lyrics. The last stanza was particularly good.

All these voices hammering at my head
Wanting too many slices of me
Bit by bit I give them away
Until nothing but nails in the frame remain

"Wow," she said softly, passing the notebook to Harper. "That's pretty awesome. The chorus needs work."

"Well, duh," came the muffled reply. "You weren't here to give it your womanly touch and shit."

Jazz couldn't help laughing as she climbed on his legs and picked up another pillow to whale on the back of his head. "Get up, you jerk. We gotta go find Deak."

"Did someone say 'find Deak'? Because I—" Deacon broke off, stopping mid-rub on his damp chest. "Lawless." His gruff tone belied the wide smile that broke across his face as his wife headed straight into his arms.

"About time you showed up." Harper ran a fingertip over his wet pecs and cast a glance back at Jazz. "Cover your eyes. I'm about to lick this and claim it as mine."

"You did that already. About a thousand times or so." Deak lifted her off her feet and kissed her with enough gusto to have Jazz glancing away.

Simon, on the other hand, had emerged from under his pillow and watched avidly. "Hot," he proclaimed once they were through.

Jazz smacked him on the back of the head again, this time with the back of her hand. "Pervert."

"So says the one who snuck off for a booty call and didn't come home all night. All night," Simon repeated in a singsong voice, kicking his legs until Jazz tumbled onto her butt on the mattress. She quickly tugged down her dress, remembering she wasn't exactly dressed for horseplay. Or any kind of public play, period.

Deacon frowned. "Booty call? I thought you were visiting Gray's sick grandma."

Jazz flushed. God, she hated lying to anyone, especially her bandmates. She was about to apologize for her fib and come clean when Harper booted the door shut and linked her arm around her husband's waist. "She was visiting Gray's penis, and it's a secret from Lila the Romance Killer so *shh*."

Deacon unhooked Harper's arm and stepped closer to the bed. His jaw tightened, but that wasn't what caused the kick in Jazz's belly. For an instant, hurt flashed in his eyes. Deacon was a good man, the kind who believed in dealing off the top of the deck at all times. Of all of them, he was the closest to her other than Gray, and they'd bonded more after the contract brouhaha that had nearly ripped the band apart. She knew he felt protective toward her, and after Lila's decree, her starting something up with Gray now seemed ill-advised at best.

But that didn't mean she intended to do anything any different. She couldn't. As much as she loved Oblivion, she loved Gray more.

Hopefully her loves weren't mutually exclusive. Because she wanted—needed—both.

"That true, pix?" Deak asked softly, slipping his hands in his pockets as he waited for her answer. Even Simon had gone still and propped his head on his hand to listen.

"Yes." She made herself meet first Deak's gaze then Simon's. "I made a decision that could potentially harm the band if Lila finds out and flips her shit, as she seems likely to do. I knew that, and I did it anyway. If you want to know if I feel guilty, the answer is no."

"Jazz," Deak began.

"Let me finish. Please." She didn't speak until he nodded. "I've been in love with Gray since I was fourteen. It just took me this long to do something about it." She wrapped her arms around her midsection. "I won't give him up for anyone. I hope you can understand, and I'm sorry for lying to you about where I went. But I'm not sorry for loving him."

Harper sniffled from the doorway and waved her hands when everyone glanced her way. "What? I'm pregnant. I can cry at Lifetime movies happening right in front of me."

Jazz snorted. "Honey, what went on last night belonged on another channel other than Lifetime. Promise."

"Oooh? Do tell." Simon grinned and sat up, extending his fist to hers. "I say rock on with your bad self. It's none of Lila's damn business, and I, for one, am a card-carrying member of the fuck-who-the-hell-you-want club."

Jazz gave him a watery smile and bumped her fist to his. "Thanks."

"Ah, to hell with it. Come here. I need a good Jazz hug." He hauled her into his lap and made her squeal as he squeezed his arms around her ribs. "Much better," he said, laughing as she squirmed away.

She pulled her dress down her thighs and shot a sidelong look at a suspiciously silent Deacon. He'd moved back beside Harper and she was talking quietly to him, stroking his arm in a manner that reaffirmed how solid a unit they were.

Jazz stared down at the necklace she'd started working through her fingers without noticing. She wanted that kind of unity for herself. And dammit, she would have it. She wasn't going to give up on her dream of a life with Gray, not after she'd tasted what it could be like to wake up beside him. When push came to shove, nothing else mattered as much.

Not even the band she adored.

"Deacon has a response." Harper turned to face the room and not-so-lightly pushed on his back to nudge him forward. "Don't you?"

"Yeah." He gripped the ends of the towel around his neck. "You have my support, pix. Always. You and Gray both do."

She didn't dare breathe. Her sternum felt too tight, as if it couldn't possibly hold the bubble of relief and joy expanding inside her. "Really? You mean it?"

He nodded. "I mean it."

"Thank you. Oh God, thanks." Jazz scrambled off the bed and launched herself at him, hanging on as he raised her off the ground and made her giggle.

"I see London, I see France, I see someone isn't wearing any underpants," Simon sang from the bed.

With a yelp, Jazz extricated herself and ran out the door to her own room. Laughing the whole way.

Once inside her suite, she slumped against the closed door and let the happy tears come. She couldn't help herself.

Now everyone in the band had given them their blessing but Nick. That would be a little trickier for more reason than one, but she hoped that he would eventually be on her side if not hers and Gray's. Maybe they could actually make this work.

She pulled her cell out of her boot and fired off a quick text to Gray.

Deak & Simon know about us. They're cool.

His reply didn't take long. *For real?*

Yes. I wouldn't care if they weren't. I'm all in with you. She bit her lip and started typing again. *Okay, I would care, but not enough to stop.*

Me either. No one could make me stop.

She typed a smiley and grinned when he sent back a kissy face.

Aww. She replied once she'd stopped making gooey eyes at her phone. *I miss you.*

That statement couldn't have been truer. They'd been apart, what, an hour? Maybe a little longer? Surely not long enough to miss him. But already an ache was growing in the pit of her belly. She needed to see his smile. Hear his husky voice in her ear while he ranged his long, muscled body over hers and made her whole. She hoped she did the same for him.

I miss you more, sugar.

Her grin spread as her thumbs blurred over the buttons. *No, me.*

Doubt that. I'm writing your song. It's super-hot. It's making me hard.

Tell me more.

About your song or about being hard?

Laughing, she strolled to the bathroom. *Both. Definitely both.*

* § *

I have to go get beautified now. Time for pedis. I'll be thinking about you.

A few hours later, Gray smiled at Jazz's final text. God, he couldn't wait to see her again. It felt like too fucking long already.

He looked up as the front door banged open and shut. Nick stalked inside and kicked off his boots.

"Good morning to you too," Gray said, returning to the page of scribbling in front of him. He'd gotten into a groove since Jazz had left, no doubt because of last night. Now that Nick had arrived, he fully expected that to end.

The guy was like a thundercloud, pissing acid rain wherever he went.

"Good morning? It's past noon. As you would know if you'd dragged your ass out hours ago." Nick dropped into a wingback chair beside the fireplace and threw his feet up on the carved wood coffee table. He pulled out a crumpled pack of cigarettes and shook one out, lifting a brow at Gray's stare. "Got something to say? Words are free."

"Nah." Gray set aside his guitar and went back to his notebook. "Not worth the breath."

"Let me guess. You want to bitch about me smoking in here."

"As if you'd listen to me. Besides, maybe I'm worried about your health."

"Right. I'm sure you're concerned that I'm eating my Wheaties and upping my cardio to maintain my heart." Nick flicked his lighter and sucked in a breath of smoke, puffing it at the ceiling. "Since you're so worried about healthy living, let's talk about the smell coming out of your room this morning."

Gray froze. Had he smelled Jazz's perfume or something? Not that he particularly cared about hurting the guy's feelings, but Nick wouldn't hesitate to deliver the info to Lila just to be spiteful. Though he claimed to care about Jazz, Gray had his doubts.

Nick cared about one person and one person only—himself.

"I don't know what you're talking about." Gray crossed out a line of lyrics. He was already close to done with his song for Jazz, but that didn't mean Nick would want the band to touch it with a ten-foot pole.

The song was private, but it had come out pretty damn good. Since he hadn't written anything worth shit in months, he wasn't about to tuck it away in a notebook to rot. He'd see what Nick had to say then explain to Jazz later. She probably wouldn't be too mad. It's not like he named her in it or anything. She'd seemed pleased at the idea that he was writing a song for her. And from the increasingly dirty texts they'd been sending each other all day, she wouldn't exactly be surprised at the direction of his thoughts.

Damn, he couldn't wait to get his mouth on her again. To sing her the song he'd come up with and watch that flush creep up her cheeks. So frigging beautiful, that was his Jazz.

"Oh really. Did someone break in to smoke pot last night?"

Gray broke the tip of his pencil. "Don't start with me."

"Should I also start with you about the sexy little screamer you snuck into your room?"

Jesus. The Oblivion playlist he'd had playing had only lasted a couple of hours and he'd been too distracted to start it again. So much for thinking they'd mostly been quiet enough not to attract Nick's suspicion. He could only hope Nick hadn't yet figured out that the woman was Jazz.

"I told you to lay off," Gray said in an undertone.

Nick lazily blew out smoke. "Look, I know we're supposed to play nicey-nice and use this time to bond for the sake of the band. I think a smarter move would be to cut the crap."

"I didn't realize we'd ever done anything but sling crap at each other."

"Yeah, well, consider this my first step toward forging world peace." Nick braced his arms on his thighs and leaned forward, tension lacing his expression. "If you think I'm not well aware of the kind of shit you're into, you're dead wrong. You give off the vibe of a song we've all heard too many times before."

Gray's skin iced over. He could guess quite well where Nick was going with this. Deliberately, he pushed his notebook aside and grabbed his guitar again. He'd suddenly lost his mojo to write sexy times. "Spell it out, man. I don't have time to guess what you mean."

"Here's a hint." He kicked back again and waved his cigarette, probably tipping ashes onto the hardwood floor. "Cokehead musician, dead at eleven. Not happening in my *Behind The Music* episode, pal."

Gray gripped the neck of his guitar. "You don't know what you're talking about."

"Oh, I know way too well what I'm talking about. My family's made up of potheads and powder pushers, so don't try to blow smoke up my ass. And that's not even mentioning the baggie you dropped in front of me in the studio last spring."

When Gray only bowed his head, Nick chuckled softly. "Yeah. Thought so. You remember that day. You know, right after we had that threesome with the girl who wasn't your girl who isn't your girl who won't *ever* be your girl if you don't drag your head out of your ass."

"That threesome was a mistake."

"You were the party crasher, not me."

Gray braced a fist on his tensed thigh. "You don't have history with her. No one will ever care about her the way I do."

"Convincing me or yourself?"

Gray kicked out at the coffee table, sending it sliding across the gleaming hardwood floor. It crashed hard into Nick's legs but he barely flinched. "I saw the pictures the other night. I know you still want her. Why don't you just admit it?"

Nick blew smoke rings at the ceiling. "Don't think I ever denied it. That doesn't mean anything else is going to happen with us, or even that it should. When the timing's fucked, it's all fucked. And with her and me, it's been shit since day one for one reason and one reason only." He leveled his eyes on Gray. "I'm looking at him."

Gray linked his fingers behind his neck. The truth of what had happened between him and Jazz the night before lingered on the tip of his tongue. All he had to do was say the words and it would extinguish the last bit of hope he saw flickering in

Nick's eyes. But he couldn't do it. Not just because Nick might run to Lila, but because he understood all too well what it was like to love Jasmine Edwards and not think there was a chance in hell of her ever loving him back.

He didn't know if Nick loved her. He seriously doubted Nick had the capacity to love anyone. But he had feelings for her, and the idea of stomping on them wasn't nearly as much fun as Gray had always assumed it would be. Maybe his good mood was making him feel magnanimous.

Or maybe loving someone who loved you back had the power to change everything.

"She's the most important person in my life," Gray said quietly. "I know she told you some of our past. The situation with my family, I mean. She's my family now. Without her, I have nothing." *Am nothing*, he added silently.

Nick cracked his knuckles and steadfastly avoided Gray's gaze. "I told her on New Year's Eve to go after you."

"What?" Shock wound through him. "Why would you do that?"

"Because she's miserable without you. She can't make a move forward. Even beyond everything else, she's my friend, and I don't like my friends being unhappy."

Gray swallowed hard and ran a fingertip over the spine of his notebook. Was that what had sent her to his doorstep last night? *Nick?* Was his biggest rival—not only for Jazz, but within the band itself—part of the reason he might have a chance with the woman he adored? "Thank you," he said finally. "I don't know what to say."

"I didn't do it for you. I did it for her."

"I understand that."

"But don't think that I'm giving you my wholesale approval. I've got my eye on you. Not just because of her, but because of my fucking band."

"*Our* band," Gray muttered. "Last I checked, all of our names were on the contract despite the BS you tried to pull with Simon about getting the bigger cut."

"I've spent my life scrapping for everything I have. I don't expect you to get that, but you don't turn off a lifetime of having to protect your own interests overnight."

Gray didn't respond.

Nick swore under his breath. "Fine, yeah, it's our band, until you fuck up and the others find out. I've kept your secret this long because of Jazz. She doesn't deserve to find out that you're a cokehead from me. Besides, she'd never believe it." He tapped his foot on the floor in time to the ashes he drummed into a leftover mug on the side table next to his chair. "But Simon would believe me, and so would Deacon. Once he finds out, you'll be on a bus to rehab so fast that your guitar will spin."

Gray knew very well why they'd kicked their former drummer, Snake, out of the band. That opening in the lineup was what had led to him and Jazz being invited in. Well, invited, sort of. Deacon had wanted them, Simon hadn't cared and Nick had been vehemently opposed.

Sounded just about right.

"Jazz is a smart girl," Nick said, dangling his cigarette between his knees. "If you don't quit that shit you're into soon, she's going to find out. And if you kill what's between the two of you, I'm not going to step back twice. Fair warning."

"I hear you."

Nick hauled in a breath of smoke then puffed it out before crushing the cigarette against the side of the mug. "I hope you do, for her sake if not your own. She thinks you hung the fucking moon, man. Don't prove her wrong."

Gray nodded and thought of the text he'd received from Cricket an hour ago between texts from Jazz. He'd fought not to even look at it, for it not to matter. But that crawling-ants sensation under his skin that crept back when he went too long without a hit made him weak.

He'd cut back. He'd get the money together and start slowing down. It'd take some time, but he'd wean himself off it. Hell, if he had to smoke more pot in the meantime, even that was better. But he couldn't have Jazz *and* the coke.

He shouldn't.

"I've got it under control," he said softly, struggling to block out the text he'd sent to Cricket.

I've got some of your money. I just need more blow to tide me over. Then once I'm back home, I'll get you the rest of your cash. Promise.

Nick stared at him for a moment before crooking his fingers. "Let me see what you're working on."

"It's not ready for—"

Nick kicked the coffee table back into place, then grabbed the notebook and slumped back into his chair. He read the page of lyrics silently, lifting his brow at the end. "Well. That's not what I expected."

"I'm still working on it." Gray couldn't stem the defensiveness in his tone. "I haven't written much in a while."

"What's it called?"

"I don't have a name for it yet."

Nick dug a pencil stub out of his jeans pocket and crossed out something. His brows knitted together as he wrote and scratched out more. He drummed his fingers on the notebook spine and scribbled again.

"What the hell are you doing to my lyrics?"

"Ever heard of collaborating? That's what I'm doing."

"That song wasn't meant for collaboration. Especially not with you." Jointly writing a sex song for Jazz veered into weird-as-fuck territory.

For the first time since he'd arrived, Nick smiled. It was more of a smirk, but for Nick, it might as well have been a beaming grin. "If you didn't want to offer it up, you shouldn't have been fiddling with it when we're supposed to be coming up with material for the album. Besides, this has single potential."

Gray swallowed his protests. "You think so?"

"Hell yeah. Simon will be all over this. I'll prove it to you." He pulled out his cell and started typing, probably inputting some of the lyrics from Gray's song.

It didn't take long for Nick's phone to light up with text after text. Nick read them silently, his smirk deepening. "Yep. Simon's on board," he said, tucking his phone away.

Gray gripped his knees and leaned forward. "Really? What did he say?"

"He wondered why it took us so long to write an ode to eating pussy." Nick tossed the notebook back at Gray. "By the way, 'Sugar Kiss.'"

Gray was too busy scanning the changes Nick had made to the song to hear him at first. They weren't bad. Actually, he'd refined some of what Gray had come up with on his own, tightening it up and making it pop. He'd also reorganized a couple of lines, but it was still Gray's song. Just better.

Then he blinked as Nick's last words sunk in. "'Sugar Kiss?' Christ, that's perfect."

Nick grinned. "Helps when you have some familiarity with the subject matter."

Gray was about to grin back when he realized Nick definitely did—particularly with Jazz. His throat went tight but he shook it off, focusing on the words in front of him.

That didn't matter anymore. Nick and Jazz were ancient history. She was his now.

"Thanks, man. This is great."

Nick shrugged. "It's your song. It was all there. Awesome stuff."

"Yeah, but I couldn't pull it all together. I'm rusty."

He'd let too many things go the last few months. Songwriting had always been one of his favorite things yet he hadn't done it seriously since last summer. He'd lost the last few months in a blur of self-loathing and white powder.

No longer. He had plenty of reasons to get his head in the present and stop dwelling on the past. Jazz. The band.

Jazz.

Nick grabbed the guitar he'd leaned against the side of his chair. "That didn't read rusty to me. Now let's see what you've got on the rhythm side."

Gray dragged his guitar into his lap and started to strum his way through the chord progression he'd come up with between texts from his source of inspiration. "Here's what I've got so far."

Nick listened for a couple of minutes, joining in with him and adding an extra layer to the melody. He started to sing the lyrics, growled, and dug out his pencil again and the newspaper off the side table. "I can't work without paper. I can't just spin off notes in my head. That's what Simon does."

"I used to be able to do that," Gray said, rubbing his thumb over a scuff mark on his Epiphone.

Before the coke. Before the last few years. Just...before.

"Useful skill to have," Nick said at length. "Okay. Let's run through it again. From the top."

Chapter Twenty-One

Then

Jazz covered her mouth to contain her laughter. "I can't believe we're doing this."

"*Shh*. Gotta be quiet. We have an hour before they're due up yet." Gray stopped in front of the rarely used fireplace—they weren't often necessary in Southern California—and shoved his arm inside. He fumbled around. "Damn. Nothing. Last year this was a sure bet."

It had been a couple of weeks since the party at the Feldmans' house, and she and Gray hadn't mentioned it since. She hadn't brought up partying again. It would be too weird to go with him to a get-together when they weren't a couple. So she contented herself with playing her music—and lusting after a sweet, sexy boy she would never, ever have.

"You search for your presents every year? Why not just wait?"

Gray dusted off his blackened hands and shook his head. "Must I explain everything to you? There's a certain way we do things in the Duffy household. Since Brent and I were kids, we always snuck around and found our presents early. Now you're my partner in crime."

She shrugged in spite of the belly tingles his words caused. *You're my partner in crime.* "Seems like a lot of work when you're going to get them soon enough."

"Didn't you ever look for yours?"

Jazz scratched her bare toes over the back of her calf. It was hard not to squirm when Gray looked at her like that, his intense gray gaze probing into her head to ferret out all of her secrets. "I didn't really get that many," she hedged. "Especially after Molly came around."

"Yeah. I saw her picture in your room. She's cute."

Jazz nodded, smiling at the memory of the tiny blonde girl with huge brown eyes like their mother. "Everyone thinks that. Mama wanted to get her into modeling."

"Huh. I can see why. But she's not half as pretty as you," he said, turning away to poke at the leather ottoman.

His careless compliments always made her blush and now was no different. While his back was turned, she flapped her hands at her cheeks to try to dispel the heat coming off her face. "You need to get your eyes checked."

"I see just fine. Now come over here and help me feel around under this chair."

She scrambled to help. "*Under* the chair?"

"Sure. These recliners have a spot near the back where there's just space. Dad hid my new video game console in here last year." He tossed her a grin and went back to his task.

She knelt on the opposite side of the chair and began fumbling around underneath like he was, feeling more than a little dumb. "I'm not finding—" Her fingers bumped his and he gripped them, curling them into his warm, dry palm. She swallowed, expecting him to let go right away.

He didn't.

"Hey there," she said, voice shaky. She couldn't believe how good even this kind of abbreviated hand-holding with Gray felt. "Don't think my hand counts as one of your presents."

"Hmm. Don't know about that." He finally let her go and emerged from the other side of the chair. "Gimme your hand back. I think you need a palm reading."

"A what?" She laughed and tucked her fist into her side, strangely afraid to give it back. Her heart was beating so fast she knew he must be able to hear it.

"A palm reading. I'm about to predict your future. Now give me your hand."

She held it out and tried not to shudder when he cupped it with one of his. He used the index finger of his other hand to draw a line down the middle of her palm and nodded thoughtfully. "Yes. Just as I suspected."

"You can actually see something?" She bent her head toward his, peering at her palm. "I just see—"

"Jazz."

The urgency in his voice made her glance upward. Her pulse jackhammered in her head as he leaned forward, his mouth a whisper away. His eyes even closer. All that hot, misty gray. She'd happily drown there.

"There you are," his mother said from the doorway, causing them to break apart as guiltily as if they'd been caught half-naked. "Your father had to go into the office early today to wrap up some—" All at once she seemed to pick up on the strange vibe in the air, along with the fact that they were both half hidden by the hulking recliner. "What're you two up to?" Mistrust had crept into her voice and lined the fine-boned face so much like her son's. Gray's features were more rugged, but there was no doubt they were related.

There was also no doubting the disapproval that fell around her like a coat she'd worn too many times before. Not with Jazz. Never with Jazz.

Until now.

"Nothing." Gray squeezed Jazz's hand and set it back in her lap, as casually as could be. "Just showing Jazz how you and Dad try to outwit Brent and me every year with your creative hiding places. Luckily we can't be schooled."

Jazz remained where she was as Gray walked around the chair to talk to his mom. She shut her eyes and drew in a deep breath. Now she knew Mrs. Duffy didn't want her anywhere near her son, at least not like *that*. Jazz couldn't blame her. Mrs.

Duffy had been an amazing foster mother so far, a million times better than any other she'd ever had, but expecting her to be okay with her precious son taking up with someone like Jazz—if he'd even been about to kiss her, which might've been just her overactive imagination—was asking for way too much.

She was lucky Mrs. Duffy had taken her in at all. And it was time for her to stop asking for more when she already had so much.

After sucking in another breath, she emerged from beyond the chair and smiled her brightest smile. If it killed her, no one would ever know when her heart was breaking. She'd promised herself that years ago on the first night her mama hadn't come home, leaving her all alone while Mama spent the night at her boyfriend's with Molly. No one would see her cry anything but happy tears.

"Do I smell blueberry pancakes?" she asked, walking forward to give Mrs. Duffy a quick hug as she always did in the morning.

"You do. Never can hide anything from you." Mrs. Duffy flicked her nose and smiled, her momentary displeasure from earlier all but gone. Her eyes were still wary, as if she didn't know what to think of her anymore.

She'd overstepped her bounds. Again.

You're nothing but a fucking slut, Jazz. I can't even trust you around Jacob. That's why I don't bring you with Molly to his place. You try to tease him with those tits of yours.

Though Jazz's smile wavered, she managed not to shrink back behind Gray. She'd just have to try harder, that was all. She'd do more chores and do better in school. If she didn't give up, perhaps one day Mrs. Duffy would love her where her own mother hadn't.

Most importantly, she would stay far away from Gray.

Chapter Twenty-Two

Now

Jazz knocked on Gray's closed window, her heart throbbing with anticipation. The bubbling of the hot tub behind her didn't help calm her pulse rate. Had he or Nick been using the Jacuzzi earlier? Was that why the colorful spotlights and the jets were still on? Or was it for *them*?

Warm hands slipped over to cover her eyes. "You're late."

She shuddered at the thrill of having his hard body pressed to her back. "We were in the zone."

"Oh yeah? Tell me about it later."

"Why?" she teased. "Got something else in mind?"

"Maybe." He brushed his erection against her ass and slid his hands down to her breasts. "Maybe I'm in a hurry to get back in *your* zone."

"By all means." She turned and wrapped her arms around his neck, attacking his mouth with fifteen hours of pent-up need. She sucked his tongue between her lips and pushed her breasts into his chest, making sure he didn't doubt for a second how much she'd missed him.

"Mmm." He squeezed her ass and ground his cock into her belly. "I want to be in all of your zones at once. How am I supposed to pick?"

"You can have any of them in any order you'd like." She trailed her fingers down his muscled torso and toyed with his zipper. Damn shame that tonight he was wearing a shirt and jeans, but that just gave her more clothing to enjoy taking off him. "All-access pass."

"I like the sound of that." He hauled her up in his arms and she wrapped her legs around his waist as he carried her across the deck to the hot tub. "Kick off your shoes."

The gleam in his eyes made her dart a nervous glance over her shoulder. "Uh, Gray..."

He was already reaching behind himself to help her get them off. Luckily she'd only worn slingbacks tonight and not those crazy boots of Harper's. "Don't *Gray* me. You're on my turf. We play by my rules."

Amusement had her lifting her chin as he pulled off one of her shoes then the other. "Oh yeah? Is that so?"

"It's completely so." He dipped his head to bite her nipple through her top and she let out a moan. "If you're good, I'll sing you the song I wrote for you while I fuck you."

She couldn't stop the shiver. "You're in some mood tonight."

"Oh, you have no idea. It's almost like I'm an all new man." Stopping at the side of the hot tub, he cocked an eyebrow. "Want kind of underwear you got on under there, sugar?"

Already whipping out the *sugar* nickname. Damn. "Take a guess."

Apparently that was the wrong time to play coy, because he dumped her into the Jacuzzi, laughing uproariously while she squealed and sputtered. "I'd rather see for myself." He feinted left to avoid her wildly splashing hands, lifting his head only to proclaim, "Pink bra, huh? I approve."

"Gray Duffy, you are so dead," she shrieked, whipping her sopping shirt over her head and throwing it. He took the hit square in the chest, still laughing.

She couldn't help laughing too as she removed her soaked skirt and panties as fast as possible and dumped them on the deck. Then she moved to his side of the hot tub and grabbed the waistband of his jeans to drag him close for a hot, wet kiss. "I fucking hate you," she breathed between kisses.

"Liar. You know you love me." He didn't give her time to reply before he undid the clasp of her bra and filled his hands with her slick breasts. "And I love you. And these." He ducked his head and slipped his mouth over her nipple, drawing it against the roof of his mouth. "God. I've missed you today. I couldn't wait to get my hands on you again."

She wove her fingers into his hair and tipped back her head to smile up at the ceiling of stars. It felt like they were shining straight onto her. *Through* her. "We have a lot of time to make up for."

"We do. But we have forever to catch up."

He stepped back long enough to shuck his shirt and jeans then joined her in the hot tub. It took him all of five seconds to pull her on his lap and another five to slip inside her. She gasped at the sudden shock of his intrusion before the brief sting dulled into pleasurable fullness. She gripped his shoulders and rose up experimentally, sinking down again with a moan that he echoed in her ear.

"You feel perfect." He bit her lobe. "Like you're mine."

She'd never wanted anything more. "Yes," she whispered, fearing her voice would crack if she tried to speak any louder. She toyed with his eyebrow ring, riveted by the sight of his gorgeous face transformed by the same passion that was blossoming inside her. "You're mine too."

"I always have been." He grabbed her hand and kissed the tips of her fingers, the center of her palm, the inside of her wrist. "You own me. So..."

She rose up again and slid down, searching for the perfect angle to rub her piercing against him to generate more friction. She gasped as she found it, then swiveled her hips as she made the trip back up his erection. "So..." she repeated, licking the side of his neck. His skin tasted salty and he smelled like a different soap. This one held hints of cinnamon, like Red Hots.

She brushed her nose along his jaw, inhaling greedily, desperate for all of his scents and flavors.

"I was going to ask...what...you planned to...do with me, but I think I know. Ahh, fuck. That feels incredible."

"I can't believe I'm here, doing this with you. That it's you, and we're— God." She pressed her knees into his hips and rose up higher, letting her head fall back again as he sipped the water trailing off her nipples. His tongue swirled up over her breast, drawing erotic patterns, while he pumped inside her in long, deep strokes. He didn't rush, just applied that same focused attention he used for practicing guitar on playing her body.

"I can't get enough of you." He pulled her down and rubbed his thumb over her piercing, strumming her flesh as if he had lifetimes to make her come. He latched his mouth on her shoulder, nibbling his way across and up her neck. "Ah, baby, squeeze me, just like that. I want you all over me."

She rocked upward, losing herself in the heated bubbles frothing around her and the penetrating glides of his cock. His hands bracketed her spine, giving her the support to move, to drive them both wild as she dropped backward, trailing her hair through the water. She clamped down tight, her eyes closing from sheer bliss. She nearly bucked out of his hold when he adjusted his grip on her to tweak her swollen clit. Two flicks and she was squirming and panting, on the verge of an explosive orgasm.

"God. I can't come this fast." She tried to shimmy away from his questing fingers. "You'll break me before sunrise."

He chuckled at her evasive tactics and jostled her on his lap, lifting her and driving into her until she couldn't hold back her moan. "That's what I want. That sound, just like that." He ran his tongue down her throat, sliding over her stampeding pulse. "I wanna hear you scream."

"But Nick—"

She realized her mistake at the flash in his eyes. He knotted his hand in her hair and powered into her again, spreading his legs so that she dangled off him into the water. It rushed around her ears, as relentless as the pulsing in her core.

"He doesn't exist for us," he murmured against her breasts, speaking just loudly enough for her to hear him. "This is only about you and me." When she only whimpered, he brushed the edge of his thumb down to where they were joined, teasing her with a hint of contact. "And if he hears, then maybe he'll know that you're mine. I don't share."

She couldn't breathe, couldn't speak under his renewed onslaught. All she could do was wrap her slippery fingers around his tensed forearm and hold on for dear life. She braced her feet on the wraparound bench he sat on, levering up to give him more room to thrust. The nerve endings he scraped on every stroke created a whirling need inside her that matched the pumping jets that surrounded them. She finally stopped trying to fight her orgasm, giving in on a long, shuddering moan.

"So fucking sexy." He scooped her up and turned her around, sitting her on his lap and thrusting upward into the tight clasp of her thighs. She was still quaking from her climax and having his length rubbing against her so intimately while not sliding inside made her aftershocks spin on and on. "Reach down and use me the way you need to so you can get yourself off again."

God, he made her tremble so hard just by talking. The dirty things he said, the urgent way he said them—she couldn't have said no to anything he asked. Wouldn't have wanted to. She dipped beneath the surface of the water and encircled his cock, jerking upward and earning his hiss. His expelled breath stirred the wet hair along her nape and she dropped her head forward, encouraging him to brush kisses over the back of her neck.

Gripping him harder, she swept her thumb over the swollen tip of him and blew a stream of air that created a small current of bubbles over his length. He drove his hand in her hair again and pulled, bringing tears to her eyes. She blew again and his thighs bunched beneath her, the tension between them growing as she jerked him off with one hand and gave him an air-and-water blowjob with the other. With the slightest rock of her body, the heat emanating from the vee of her thighs enfolded him, tearing a sound that bordered on agony from his lips.

"God, your cock makes me hot." She arched like a cat, pulling him against her lower lips, swaying side to side so that her swollen flesh grazed his. "I want to suck it, ride it, feel it between my breasts."

She angled her body and dragged her taut nipple over the head of his dick. He groaned and used his hold on her hair to force her lower so she could slide her breast along his erection. He was so hard and thick that he throbbed in her hand. The leashed power she held made her whimper and rotate her hips, wishing she could have him inside her at the same time. Instead, she dragged the head over her clit, tantalizing them both.

He growled and grabbed her hips, impaling her on him in one smooth move. "Jesus, fuck me. I have to be inside you. Goddammit, I want to stay inside your tight pussy, always."

His teeth latched on to her shoulder and she vised around him, helpless to stave off the shudders that came just from having his thickness inside her once again. It had only been a few minutes since the last time and that was already too long. She rode him without hesitation, bouncing on his lap so violently that he sank too deep too fast. The flash of pain vanished swiftly, chased by an intense ribbon of pleasure. She bent forward, inviting him to seize her hips and hammer into her the way she sensed he needed to.

That was all it took to have him lifting off the bench to push her deeper into the water, forcing her up against the side of the hot tub. She gripped it in trembling fingers as he rammed into her from behind, his cock on the warpath on her still sensitive flesh. Crying out only seemed to spur him on more so she let every noise go, wanting him to hear what he was doing to her.

Fucking her into oblivion, stroke by stroke.

Her knees slammed into the wall and she lowered her forehead to the wet side of the Jacuzzi, savoring the unmistakable slap of skin on skin. Even the bubbling water couldn't mask it. Or maybe it was that she knew what their mating must sound like. The way his balls were hitting her ass on every thrust, she could only imagine the picture they made. Rough, crazed, wild. He rubbed her back, his long fingers stimulating points under her skin. His sensuous massage only fueled the tension overtaking her limbs. She couldn't climax again so soon.

She couldn't *not*.

"You know you want to come on my cock. So close." He leaned over her back, ruffling her hair with his warm breath as he started to pant out the lyrics to a song she'd never heard before. It shouldn't have made her hotter. She wasn't some groupie, and his normal tricks shouldn't have affected her to such an extent.

But between the siege of his cock and his raspy voice, the band of pressure inside her snapped. She wailed out her pleasure, her moans turning to screams as he battered into her without cease. His fingers fisted her hair and he growled in her ear, singing in a low, tormented voice that would remind her of relentless fucking for the rest of her life.

Up against the wall
Or on the floor
I'll take it anytime at all

She pushed back against him, letting out a whimper at the realization he still hadn't come. How could that even be possible? It felt like she had a stick of dynamite inside her, hard and unforgiving. Pulsing with every thrust. He pummeled her with his cock and branded her with his teeth on the side of her neck, tripping her into bliss one more time. And he still didn't find his own release.

When she managed to lift her head, she glanced over her shoulder, moaning again at the blur of his body pounding into hers. All those sleek muscles, flexing wetly. She tightened around him involuntarily and he groaned, throwing back his head. The cords in his neck stood out in sharp relief, highlighted by the colorful lights in the hot tub. His face contorted as he pumped into her frenetically, as if he was seeking something he couldn't find. She squeezed him again and reached down between her legs, stroking him hard every time he re-entered her. Bearing down, she rocked her hips, trying to give him the friction he desperately seemed to need.

Another orgasm built up inside her, the ripples in her core soon widening to encompass her whole body. She didn't even have time to warn him. Then she was lost again, the pleasure so violent that she nearly blacked out. She pressed her cheek to the side of the hot tub and hauled air into her starved lungs, barely able to focus on the swimming canvas of stars above her head.

Dear God. He truly intended to kill her.

He continued fucking her, shoving her past enjoyment to the cusp of pain. At this rate, she wouldn't be able to walk. Her legs were already quaking, and she couldn't stop gasping. His dick swelled impossibly huge inside her, earning her whimpers as he reached around to rub her clit and her piercing with those wicked fingers. She quivered, beyond the capability to cry out. All she could do was shudder through another endless climax.

By the time he picked her up and carried her inside, dripping water everywhere before he wrapped her in a thick, fluffy towel, she could barely lift her head. He placed her on the bed, covered her up with the sheet and slid in beside her, stroking her hair until she lifted her heavy lids and gave him a weak smile.

"Hi there." Her voice even sounded slurred.

He'd literally fucked her into almost unconsciousness. She hadn't believed that was an actual thing, but her limp arms and legs were more than willing to vouch for its existence.

"Hi." He brushed a kiss over the top of her arm. "Doing okay?"

"Yeah. I had an out-of-body experience for a few minutes there, but I'm reasonably sure I'm still in one piece."

"Good. Because I'm not done with you." He moved closer, nestling his length against her ass, and she realized with a start that he was still hard.

How could that be possible?

"What are—you didn't—you've gotta be freaking kidding me." She rolled on her back and stared up at the tensed planes of his face, tracing her fingers along his jaw. The faint tremor under his skin made her swallow hard and search again for her voice. "You didn't come?"

"Not yet." He turned his head to kiss her fingertips, not reacting to the sound of distress she couldn't stifle. "But the night's young."

Questions formed on her lips, trembling there while she walked her fingers down his neck to his shoulder and lower to his chest. Under her palm, his heart stampeded like a runaway locomotive, so fast that she wondered how she didn't see it pounding in his throat. Her gaze shot to his. "Did you smoke before I got here?"

It didn't make sense. He shouldn't be revving this hard from weed, but there had to be some explanation. Even while he was lying beside her, his body vibrated with pent-up energy. She could practically feel the need pouring off him.

And that wasn't even referring to his cock, which had felt like a baseball bat against her backside. Her poor abused pussy gave up a weak throb in protest.

"Nah." He skimmed his hand over her breasts. His casualness felt forced. Almost practiced. "Maybe I should though. Take the edge off."

Before she could open her mouth, he shifted away to dig through the nightstand. He rolled a joint in record time and returned to the bed. Shutting his eyes, he leaned against the headboard and took a long drag. Then another and another while she watched him with her own heart racing way faster than it should have.

Something was off, and she couldn't place what. More than his unholy staying power, more than his sudden ease in smoking up in front of her. She tried to line up her thoughts, to find a way to broach a topic she didn't want to touch with an eight-inch-still-freaking-hard cock. Even as he took hits off the joint, his erection curved against his stomach, so hard that she actually winced in sympathy.

Then his sleepy gray eyes landed on her and he passed her the joint without saying a word.

She started to object. Once was one thing. Maybe even more than once would be okay if it only happened occasionally. *Extremely* occasionally. But two nights in a row? She swallowed the bitter flavor in her mouth and shook her head. "This isn't a good idea—"

"But I feel so good." He pulled her against his side and gave her a heartbreaking smile, the kind she could use to keep her warm on cool nights. His soft lips brushed hers. "I want you to feel the way I do." He kissed her chastely. All sweetness and heat. "Let's share it."

Already she could feel some of the tension leaking out of his embrace. Her Gray was coming back to her. If that joint had somehow helped the transition, though she didn't know why, she couldn't fault it.

She couldn't say no.

Closing her eyes, she took a couple of quick hits. Like magic, the unexplainable fear that had gripped her insides began to dissipate. He chuckled beside her and turned his face into her hair, sighing as she reached down to cup his cock.

Guess she wasn't so tired after all.

She passed him back the joint and climbed on top of him, gripping the headboard behind his head. He leaned up to slip his mouth over her nipple, drawing it inside as she slid her wet flesh over his length. He groaned and palmed her hip, nudging against her with an insistence that echoed in his hungry gaze.

All she wanted was him. *This.*

Licking her lips, she inched downward, taking him in so slowly that he hissed out a breath. She flinched at the flash of pain and he set down the joint long enough to gently rub her clit, easing the sting.

"I can make this better," he said, his attention focused on what he was doing rather than on her face. "Just say the word."

She smiled and arched her back, moving into his strokes. Magic hands. They could heal her anytime she asked. "If you mean more of what you're doing right now, then yes."

"No. Something else." He shot her an unreadable look and reached for the joint, pinching off a quick hit. "A bit stronger than this. I wouldn't ever do anything that didn't make you feel good. I promise."

His sudden intensity made her frown. Worse, it chased away the happy little bubbles bobbing along through her bloodstream. She narrowed her eyes on his face and giggled at his sulky mouth. "Aww, pouty Muffy Duffy. What's the matter?" She kissed his stubbled throat and worked her way up to take a nip out of his lower lip. "I bet you want to fuck me."

"Yes." No hesitation. Nothing but those arrow-direct eyes stabbing straight into her soul. "Can you take me now?"

"Think the question is can you take me?" She rolled her hips and stretched her arms in the air, letting out a shrieking laugh as he clamped an arm around her waist and drove up inside her in one heart-stopping thrust. She stared down at him, dazed into silence, her hands falling limply to his shoulders. If she moved, she feared she would shatter.

"I can. I am. And this time I'm not going to stop until I come inside this beautiful pussy." He circled the rough pads of his fingers over her piercing and her head lolled on her shoulders, a moan of pure bliss tumbling from her mouth.

"Prove it," she whispered.

Chapter Twenty-Three

Then

"Are your eyes closed?"

"Your hands are covering my face." Jazz laughed and leaned back against Gray as they finally stopped walking. It was Christmas morning and he'd insisted on leading her downstairs in spite of the fact that she'd already gotten all of her gifts in the form of her bedroom set. She certainly didn't expect anything else. What she'd gotten already exceeded all—

"Okay, now stop. Open your eyes."

Smiling, she opened her eyes and gasped. In front of the Duffys' gigantic Christmas tree in the family room stood an enormous gift-wrapped box. Beside it stood another large, oblong box and a gift bag. "What the—what is all of this?"

"These are your Christmas gifts." He yanked a camera out of his pocket and knelt down in front of the fireplace, flashing her a grin that dazzled her even more than the array of presents. "Come on, open them."

"You shouldn't have done this. Oh my God." She dropped to her knees and ran her hands reverently over the largest box, her heart beating a staccato rhythm. "How did you afford all this?" As realization dawned that she wasn't similarly prepared, she flushed and let her hands fall into her lap. "I only have something small for you."

"Small gifts are the best. Haven't you heard that the best gifts come in tiny packages?" His grin turned crooked. "Like you."

Giggling, she hopped up. "Let me go get yours. Wait here."

She hurried up to her bedroom, grateful that Brent wasn't up yet. Since he'd given up his room to her, he was crashing in Gray's room while he was home on break. She moved as quietly as she could, hoping not to disturb him in the room on the opposite side of the adjoining bathroom. She grabbed Gray's gift from under her bed and jogged downstairs.

"Here," she panted, kneeling in front of him and holding out the package.

"Jeez, where's the fire? Did you think I would take off?"

"No. I didn't want to run into—" She broke off and shook her head. She didn't want Gray to know how she felt about Brent. The last thing she'd ever do was force him to take sides against his brother. Besides, she didn't have any concrete reason not to like Brent just a vibe.

Lots of vibes.

"Just open it," she said.

"Sure thing, boss." He tore off the bright green paper she'd fussed with for a good twenty minutes, trying to get the corners just right, and tugged out the box inside.

"If you don't like it—"

"Bite your tongue." His quick fingers flipped up the lid and he made a rumbling sound of pleasure in his throat that erased all of the weeks of saving her allowance and collecting bottles at the park. Whatever she'd had to do to be able to afford his present had been worth it. "A replica 1949 Fender Broadcaster? Fuckin' sweet." He dug out the ornament she'd had custom made and checked out all the details she'd insisted on being added, right down to the gold-embossed fret board. Then he lifted his head and grinned. "See? Tiny packages are the best."

She laughed and leaned forward to poke in the box he still held. "There's a little stand in there too beneath the foam so you can display it," she began, falling silent as he gripped her fingers in his viselike hold.

"This is the best gift I've ever gotten." Before she could slip back, his warm lips brushed her forehead. "Thank you."

"You're welcome." She sat back and stared at him, trying to ignore the sizzle in her skin where his lips had made contact. Her lips throbbed, wanting the same pressure and heat there.

God, he made her want too much.

"Your turn," he said softly.

Her turn for what? To kiss him? She ducked her head and he chuckled, gesturing to her gifts.

"Open them," he prompted.

Nodding, she shifted toward the tree and tugged the gift bag into her lap. She laughed at what she found inside. "An industrial bag of Skittles?" she asked, secretly thrilled he'd paid that much attention to her snack of choice.

"Taste the rainbow," he said solemnly, making her laugh even harder.

She moved on to the next biggest box, opening it swiftly before it vanished. She couldn't believe he'd given her so much. Her mouth dropped open as she peeled open the tissue paper inside and dragged out his battered white Stratocaster, his favorite of his two guitars. "Gray. You can't give me this."

"Sure I can. It's mine to give away." He leaned back on his hands and gave her his insolent smile. He had a whole range of smiles and she'd categorized them all. Insolent was one of her favorites. "Especially since I know I have a brand-new Epiphone waiting for me under that tree."

"But this is your baby—"

"It's a guitar. I can make any of them sing."

She couldn't argue with that. His magic hands had given her many moments of pause—and even more hot moments alone in her bed when she couldn't stop imagining them on her skin. "Thank you," she whispered, unable to say more.

"You're welcome. Now open the last one."

"This is too much already."

Lifting his brows, he gestured. "You don't want my gift? You'd hurt my feelings on Christmas?"

"Cheater." Smiling faintly, she carefully set aside his prized Stratocaster—*her* prized Stratocaster now—and dug into the largest box. When she pulled off the paper and glimpsed the contents, she fell back on her heels again with a loud thump. "Oh my God."

Grinning, Gray snapped a picture of her face. "Now that's the expression I wanted. None of this tame happy stuff. I wanted ecstatic, blown away, completely stupefied."

"You succeeded." She stroked her hand over the box that contained a Mapex M Birch 6-piece drum set, the very set he'd caught her ogling in Bradley's Music Shop just last month. It was way out of her price range and took up a ton of room. "Oh man, where am I going to put it?"

"In the basement with my gear. We're tricking out a whole Krystal Sword practice area."

"But I don't know how to play the drums. I've never even tried to."

"So you'll learn. You pick up every instrument in a nanosecond. Why do you think I bought you these? Otherwise you'd be kicking my ass on the guitar in no time."

She launched herself at him, wrapping her arms around his neck as he laughed and gripped her waist. "Thank you. Oh God, I don't know how to thank you enough."

He brushed her hair out of her eyes, his fingers lingering on her temple. "That smile just did."

Chapter Twenty-Four

Now

Getting the munchies at five a.m. when you really wanted nothing more than another hour's sleep and a quickie freaking sucked.

Jazz threw her legs over the side of the bed and winced. Yeah, so maybe a quickie wasn't the best idea. She'd had so much longie the night before that her vagina threatened to file a formal protest.

A smile snuck over her face as she glanced at Gray over her shoulder. He slept on his back with the sheets pooled around his waist and his arm thrown over his face. No wonder he'd finally crashed. Her thigh muscles were still trembling from how hard they'd gone at each other. She hadn't known it was physically possible to have sex for that long. It certainly wasn't something she was familiar with. Her previous max had been twice in one night, and even that was as rare as the dodo bird. Most guys just rolled over and that was it.

But not Gray. He just went...and went...and went. He'd fucked her a good three times before he'd even come, for God's sake. Which made his losing it on his lap while eating her out the night before even more adorable. Clearly the guy had the stamina of ten men, so if he'd gotten *that* turned on by going down on her—

She grinned. Yeah, she'd just float on that knowledge for a year or two.

Biting her lip, she rose and hobbled over to the armoire. She pulled out one of the robes and wrapped herself in the decadent terrycloth, brushing her nose along the collar. She'd forever associate that faint cinnamon scent with Gray and lovemaking from now on.

Hell, who was she kidding? She'd associate everything with Gray and lovemaking. Hot tubs, terrycloth robes, silky sheets rubbing over her naked torso while she slept. He'd slept nude for years but she never had before the last two nights, with him.

At this rate, she never wanted to put on clothes again.

She moved toward the door a little too fast and her head sloshed, making her giggle and slap her hand against her forehead to hold it still. Guess her high hadn't totally worn off yet. She couldn't say she minded. It was nice to walk down the hall toward the front of the cabin and not quite feel her toes on the floor. This floaty sensation she had going worked for her big time.

Nothing to worry about. No stress. Just afterglow and a nice, low-key buzz.

Trying to be quiet, she fumbled around in the dark, walking into walls, bumping into furniture. Giggling with every misstep. She finally found herself in the kitchen and flipped on the light. A gasp escaped her as she took in the sheer size of the space. And the appliances. Holy crap. She didn't cook or bake very often, but she'd probably be moved to more frequently if she lived in a place like this.

She padded over to the gigantic stainless steel refrigerator and pulled open the door. Inside there was everything she could possibly want. Wrapped sandwiches, a cheese plate, fruits and veggies. She pulled out the cheese plate and turned, intending to search for crackers.

Instead she came face-to-face with a very naked Nick.

Her hand slipped on the plate and she would've dropped it if he hadn't darted forward to close his hands around hers. She stared up at his face—which was much better than staring at his schlong—and blinked. "Uh, thanks. Um. You're probably wondering what I'm doing here?"

"Not so much. Close your robe, Jasmine. I might see something I've already had."

She thrust the plate into his hands and turned around, hurriedly tying her robe tightly enough to cut off her air supply. Guilt surged into her, thick and hot. She couldn't even say if she felt more guilty for Nick catching her in the cabin next to naked or because he'd seen her next to naked again, a fact Gray would not appreciate. While she puzzled it out, Nick stepped closer and loudly sniffed her hair.

"You smell like pot," he said flatly.

"So?" She turned around. "What's the big deal?"

He tucked his fists under his arms, evidently perfectly at ease with his nudity. What was up with the boys in this house? "Since when do you do that shit?"

She averted her gaze. "Can you please cover up?"

"I thought we were all friends here." She heard the smirk in his voice even without seeing it. "Fine." With a heavy sigh, he moved to the counter and returned with a couple of dishtowels slung immodestly around his waist. "Better?"

"Not hardly."

"Oh Christ, you've seen it, licked it and ridden it. The only thing you didn't do was play backdoor bingo with it and that probably wouldn't have been off the table if we'd had more time. At least judging from the screams coming out of Gray's room."

He was just goading her. Just digging around, looking for the weak spot. She knew better than to engage him, especially when she held a huge amount of the responsibility for this hopelessly awkward situation. But she was just blitzed enough not to care.

"We didn't do that. Yet."

Nick snorted and snatched a piece of cheddar off the plate before shoving it back at her. "No, you used the time to get high instead. Trust me, you'll hurt a lot less over the long-term if you stick to bottom-friendly activities."

She shouldn't laugh. Too bad she was still high enough to find him amusing rather than inappropriate. She choked on her chuckle and chose a piece of cheddar for herself, popping it in her mouth once her giggles had subsided.

Nick narrowed his eyes. "You look happy. Or is that just the high?"

"I am happy. And high," she admitted. "But not very. I didn't smoke that much and it's been a couple of hours."

"Enough to get the munchies at five a.m.," he said drily, holding a hand over his dishtowels as he strolled to the table. Unfortunately he hadn't done such a great job at covering his ass, which she got a healthy glimpse of before she turned her back.

"I'm sitting now. It's safe to look."

Without responding, she joined him at the table. She probably shouldn't sit with him while he was basically naked, but for God's sake, they were in a band together. They were sort of friends. And she owed him...something.

"That proves it," he said after a moment, his focus on the cheese. He selected another piece and flipped it between his dexterous fingers.

Damn guitarists. Everything was a pick to them. Though she wasn't much better, considering she was tapping her fingers on her thigh.

"Proves what?" she asked, stilling her hand in favor of grabbing another piece of cheese.

"We're sitting here, both of us almost naked, and there aren't any sparks between us."

"Oh, I wouldn't say that," she muttered.

He laughed. "Annoyance doesn't count. You're over me. And while I might be not so pleased about that for myself, I'm glad for you."

She tilted her head to gauge his sincerity. "You're serious."

"Yeah."

"Since when are you so altruistic?"

"I'm sitting here with a fucking boner, staring at cheese so I don't stare at your tits. Does that sound altruistic to you?"

There she went, laughing again. "Your boner must've gotten smaller, because I totally didn't notice."

"Ouch. The lady has a sharp tongue." His mouth quirked. "And knows how to use it."

"I'm so not a lady." She sighed and nibbled cheese off her thumb. "I'm sorry. This situation sucks sweaty balls."

"Can't say I'm thrilled with it." He crossed his arms on the table and leaned forward, his gaze snagging hers. "I'm less thrilled with you smoking up when I know it's not your scene. He doesn't have you doing anything else, does he?"

She rubbed her eyes, suddenly exhausted. All the excitement of the past two nights must be finally catching up with her. "Anything else like what?"

"Anything harder than pot."

Something in his voice made her drop her hand in her lap and give him a hard stare. "A, he doesn't *have* me doing anything, period. I make my own choices. I don't normally smoke but it's not like I haven't in the past." *Years ago, when I didn't know any better.*

Jeez, where was that judgmental voice coming from? There was nothing wrong with a bit of harmless experimentation now and then. She hadn't smoked in years but that didn't mean she had a problem with it. She definitely didn't see any issues when she was still coasting, though that floaty state was starting to wear off. Dammit.

"Sure you did."

"I did. And C, what are you insinuating? What else besides pot would he be 'having me do'? You realize how completely random that is, right?"

"You missed B, and it's not random at all. Users use. I've seen enough of that with my own relatives. Not saying all pot smokers take it to the next level, but plenty do."

"Maybe some do, but not Gray." She shoved another slice of cheddar between her lips.

"Sorry, I must've missed his halo the last time we spoke." Shaking his head, he laid his hand on the table as if he intended to get up. "Look, never mind. You're all abuzz with sex hormones and you're probably still higher than a kite. We'll talk when you're—"

"I love him," she interrupted, snatching Nick's arm before he could rise. "It's not sex or weed that has me buzzing. Well, not entirely. It's *him*. I've wanted this since I was a kid, Nick."

He didn't respond for a few moments. "I understand that," he said finally. "And I hope it turns out to be exactly what you've been wishing for. But if it doesn't, I'll be here."

"Here for what? To fuck me all better?" She let his arm drop and covered her face with her hands. Tears threatened, burning the back of her eyes, and beyond them lurked shame. For what, she wasn't even sure.

Was this the crash? Or did some part of her hear the warning in Nick's words, and know he was right to offer it?

"This isn't about fucking," he said quietly, and that only made the shame burn hotter, scorching her cheeks. "We've been past that for a while now. I told you to go after him, remember? Twice," he added. "I didn't want to. I still did it, and it sure as hell wasn't for me."

She lowered her hands into her lap and nodded, swallowing hard. It was all just overwhelming, is all. Even getting exactly what you wanted after so long cost a big emotional toll. No wonder she was reeling.

"I'd like to think that maybe we're even friends."

"Yes," she whispered, struggling to meet his gaze. "We are. At least I think so. But if you've got a problem with Gray, then you have a problem with me. I'm sorry. That's just the way it is."

Nick lifted his hands, palms out. "Hey, I managed to collaborate with the guy today. He's got some chops."

Her surprise dried the leftover dampness in her eyes. Damn, that was some really good pot if it had her reading this situation all wrong. Perhaps he was actually being a dick and she was still buzzing enough not to notice. "Swear you're not messing with me?"

"I swear. We came up with some good stuff. We were at it for hours." At her flush, he laughed. "Sorry, bad choice of words considering. But we're dealing with each other."

"Good."

He shrugged. "Not saying we'll ever be pals, but maybe we can keep it about the music and leave the rest behind."

"We all want the same thing. For Oblivion to rock."

"True enough. Hey, I'm inviting a friend over tonight. Serious hot tub time." He flashed her a crooked grin. "You should stop by earlier and we can all party together. Sound good?"

* § *

"You should stop by earlier and we can all party together. Sound good?"

From just outside the doorway, Gray heard only those two sentences, but they were more than enough. He stepped inside the kitchen and tried to keep his face impassive in spite of the cozy scene he found. Jazz wearing just a robe, her hair tumbled around her sleepy eyes and her mouth still swollen from his kisses.

And Nick was fucking naked from the waist up—*and* the waist down, something that became apparent when the other man stood to meet Gray's silent challenge.

"What the fuck are you wearing?" Gray asked, blinking away the haze from his mind. He'd crashed hard and slept better than he had in weeks—maybe ever—but now the light made his eyes hurt. "You're sitting around wearing fucking dishtowels while you're talking to my girl?" *And making plans with her tonight right under my nose.*

"Gray," Jazz began, pushing aside the little snack the two of them had been sharing. "Don't do this. Nick's cool."

Gray slouched against the doorway, fighting every instinct that demanded he cross the room and tug Jazz into his arms like a kid with his favorite toy. But he wouldn't do that, because if he and Jazz were going to have a real chance, he had to trust that what was between them could withstand anything.

Even Nick freaking Crandall.

"Is he now?" Amazing that he managed to sound so calm when everything inside him was raging out of control. Just seeing Jazz with her cheeks and neck softly pink from his own stubble burn made all kinds of crazy intense protective instincts surge to the forefront.

"Yes. We were just talking. He knows about us now," she added, somewhat unnecessarily considering her very presence in their cabin at this time of day. "It's all good."

Somehow he doubted that. Gray swiveled his head to give Nick a steady look. "That so?"

"Sure. It's not like I hadn't figured it out the first night we were here, what with all the screaming." Smiling blandly, Nick leaned against the wraparound counter and cocked his hip, probably to show off his barely covered attributes.

"Screaming's a bit of an overstatement," Jazz mumbled, making a sandwich out of her cheese before popping it into her mouth.

If he had his way, she'd scream twice as loud next time to wipe the smile off that smug bastard's face.

Gray pushed his fists into the pockets of his robe. "So what's this about a party tonight?"

"I invited a friend over. No orgy yet, though I also invited Jazz." Nick licked his lips. "And you, of course."

"Sorry to get in your way, man."

"It's kind of a habit of yours, isn't it?"

"Nick," Jazz said, not looking at either of them.

Gray plastered on his own thin smile. "I think we'll be busy tonight. Thanks but no thanks."

"Christ, this is way too much drama before breakfast. I'm outta here," Nick said, pushing his way past Gray into the hall.

Gray waited until Nick's bedroom door slammed shut before he inhaled, long and slow. The residual burn in his nose made him shut his eyes.

Every step forward with Nick always resulted in two back. Not kicking the guy's ass for openly coveting Jazz was bad enough. But knowing that he was silently—and not so silently—judging him, and waiting for him to fail so that he could swoop in and be the savior dumped even more gasoline on the fire.

Worse, he couldn't help wondering if the reason Nick's condemnation sliced so deep was because it echoed everything replaying on a constant loop in his head.

When he was sure he had a hold on his ragged emotions, he pulled out a chair and sat down beside Jazz. Rather than speak, he gestured for her to get on his lap. He half expected her to decline, but she sighed and folded herself against his chest, curling her small fist in the vee of his robe. Right over his heart.

"I'm sorry," he murmured, stroking her tangled hair.

"For what?"

For so much more than I can ever say. "That this is so unpleasant for you."

Her quiet laughter took him by surprise. "It's a clusterfuck for all of us, not just me." She straightened her fingers, brushing the smattering of hair on his chest. "This is all my fault."

"No."

"Yes. I knew better than to bring him into the middle of us." She kissed the dent in his chin. "I know you don't believe it, but it's most unfair to him. We're happy. He's not. Not because of me, I don't think, just in general."

He stared out the window above the sink at the towering firs tipped in morning silver. "I can't think about his happiness when you're in my arms. Honor no longer exists." He grabbed a fistful of her hair. "All I care about is making you mine."

Her lips tipped up on one side. "You did that years ago. All the years in between were us just getting it right."

It wasn't that simple. Couldn't be that simple no matter how much he wished he could rewrite history. Yesterday had provided yet another example why not.

Cricket had met up with him a couple of hours before Jazz arrived, and she'd doled out more blow than expected. It had helped that he'd given her a down payment on what he owed—also known as two-thirds of his savings—but she'd also been surprisingly understanding about the Nick situation. And when she'd hit on him again and he'd mumbled out an explanation about Jazz, she'd backed off.

She probably thought he was an idiot. As long as she kept supplying him, he really didn't give a shit.

Regardless, he needed to start trying to cut back. After last night, he'd proven he couldn't be trusted when he'd done a line. Not only had he encouraged Jazz to smoke with him, he'd been high enough to think that trying Jere's coke-on-pussy trick was a good idea. Thank God she hadn't taken him up on the idea of trying something more adventurous.

Next time, maybe she wouldn't turn him down. He knew all too well that he could manipulate her. She trusted him. Which meant he had to be responsible enough not to put her in another situation where she could be harmed when he was too amped to know better.

He loved her, and dammit, he needed to keep her safe. Even from himself.

Especially from himself.

Closing his eyes, he rubbed his hand between her shoulder blades. The way she cuddled against him made him feel like a hero. Too bad he wasn't anything close. "I like the way you think."

"I am pretty smart."

"No arguments there." He paused. "Do you think he'll tell Lila?"

She sat up straighter and yet again he had cause to regret his hasty words. "I didn't even think of her. I was more worried about—"

"Him," Gray said softly. "Because that's who you are. You hate hurting anyone." When she didn't say more, he let out another breath. "I know you cared about him. Care," he corrected. "It's okay. I don't expect you to deny your feelings."

"I'm not, at least when it comes to him. I care about him, yes, but I never loved him. We weren't about that." She sighed and toyed with the ends of his hair. "But you and me... God. We screwed up so badly. If we'd just been honest with each other at the beginning and pushed aside all the unimportant stuff, we could've been a real family by now."

Her eyes implored him, encouraging him to open up. It was so fucking tempting. If he just told her what he was dealing with—

No. Fuck no. She'd shut down on him. She wouldn't understand. Worse, she might try to make it into more of an issue than it really was. Maybe even bring up rehab or something crazy. He couldn't miss time with the band.

He had it under control. Sure, it didn't always seem that way, but he hadn't truly tried to stop yet. He still could. It was all his choice.

"Is that what you want?" he asked.

"I'm supposed to say no, right? To pretend all I care about is the band and my music and living wild while I can."

"You're supposed to be honest." *Like you are?* He squelched the voice in his head, letting his galloping heartbeat drown it out.

"Being in the band makes me so happy. I feel like I finally have a place that's mine. Where I belong. But I'd give it up in a hot second for you." She cupped his cheek. "For *us*."

His fingers tightened in her hair and he closed his eyes. His suppressed confession tasted bitter on the back of his tongue, like a pill he couldn't force down no matter how many times he tried. "We can have it all. I promise."

"Tell Lila that."

"I think it'll be pretty obvious to her what's going once we go on stage in a few days." Brushing a kiss over her ear, he murmured, "I'm going to sing your song to you."

"The pussy one? No way." Her shock made him laugh so hard that his stomach ached.

"What better way to tell the whole world that we're together?" He nudged her upright on his lap and shifted the chair closer to the table so she could brace her back against it. He unknotted her robe and spread it open, giving her a slow smile as he traced his fingertip from her guitar pick necklace to the silky skin between her breasts. "Other than the screams you're going to give me when you come."

Chapter Twenty-Five

Then

"Okay, from the top. And don't come in so quick after the bridge. Build up to it." Gray rubbed his arm over his sweaty forehead. "Follow my lead."

From behind her kit, Jazz huffed her damp hair out of her eyes. They'd practiced the same song ten times already, and Gray was never satisfied. She'd been all excited to not only get a chance to write a song with him but to show off her burgeoning skills on the skins—hopefully for him first then his bandmates in Krystal Sword—but her interest had plummeted fast.

She got being a perfectionist. She was too. She'd been practicing the drums a couple of hours a day for months. But for fuck's sake, his band wasn't big time. They'd only played like five real shows at clubs. So what if she proved her chops to Gray and he got her an audition? It wasn't as if this would ever actually be her career or anything.

The reality was that she'd probably end up at the waffle house she'd applied to last month, though she knew the chances of getting a part-time position there before she turned fifteen were slim. But she needed to start saving up cash. It wouldn't be long before Gray would be going away to college at Berkeley to major in their music program, which meant he wouldn't be around to keep slipping her money in spite of her protests.

Dammit, she couldn't think about Gray leaving. Couldn't even let the idea float through her mind. If she did, she'd screw up the practice even worse.

So she'd think about getting a job at the waffle house. She'd start there part-time and most likely end up full-time at some point. Eventually she'd start cursing life and "the man" like her mom. School sure wouldn't pan out for her. Gray was the brainiac, not her. She hated the monotony of her classes. If she had to do one more algebra problem—

"Jesus, Jazz, you in there?" Gray snapped his fingers and she jolted hard enough that she almost fell off her stool. "We need to get this song right."

"Yeah, yeah. Hit it."

"You sure you're ready? You keep zoning."

Her dissatisfaction bubbled over. "Hell yeah I keep zoning. I don't get the point why this matters so much. Music is supposed to be fun. You're turning it into drudgery."

"No, I'm turning it into what your talent deserves. What the hell do you intend to do with your life? You skip class constantly. Your grades are in the toilet. This is your way out."

His words slapped her in the face and in reaction, she slammed her sticks on the cymbals. "Better," he said, lips curving. "That's the kind of emotion I want to see."

"You wouldn't know what to do with all of my emotion, Grayson Duffy." She flexed her bare foot on the pedal and gripped the sticks tighter, rolling her shoulders. "Okay, let's go."

"Want to switch songs? We could try 'Placebo'—"

"No. We're doing 'Counterstrike'. Go."

Rather than seeming pissed, his smile only grew. "You're adorable when you're pissed." At her growl, he laughed and strummed his way into the song. "On three."

She was already counting, losing herself in the building rhythm. She shut her eyes and gave herself over to the song, letting his fast finger work carry her into the heart of it. Like Hansel from the fairy tale sprinkling a trail of breadcrumbs in the forest, he opened up the melody, taking her right up to the bridge before easing off to let her take over. He maintained the backbeat of the song while she slammed the skins, channeling her frustration into creating that floor-shaking sound.

Hell yeah, the floor was shaking. The walls quaking. Everything around her trembling and dissolving under the focused pressure of her hands.

Her voice lifted with his, their harmony soaring to the rafters. Vibrating at the pinnacle like a heartbeat before that inevitable drop that left her shaking as the last notes from his guitar faded away.

She opened her eyes and he was in front of her, his grin a kilowatt of light capable of illuminating the darkest space. It crowded out the confusion and frustration inside her, leaving behind only joy.

"You did it. You fucking *killed* it, baby." He came around the kit and hoisted her up off her stool, giving her no choice but to wrap her legs around his waist and her arms around his neck. Like a pair of drunken monkeys, they spun around the room until they were so dizzy that they fell back on the sofa, laughing.

Tossing back her sweat-soaked hair, she sank into the cushions and let her exhaustion win. And smiled as his fingers crept across the space between them and forged a link. Such a small, seemingly insignificant gesture.

Nothing had ever meant more.

Chapter Twenty-Six

Now

Jazz hopped from foot to foot backstage, grimacing more than a little at the stickiness of the floor. Her own fault for needing to play the drums barefoot. Not that she'd let a bit of grime change her show routine. Musicians were notoriously suspicious, and she wore the badge proudly. Especially since she was pretty sure she might ralph at any time.

She rarely got nervous before shows anymore, but tonight she was. That probably had to do with Gray's declaration that he was going to sing his song to her onstage, sight unseen. Or unheard. She'd only gotten a few verses out of the jerk, and those were plenty dirty. She couldn't even imagine what the rest would be like.

But Nick could. And Simon. And Deak. Gray had slipped their bassist and lead singer the change in their usual setlist and he'd banned her from anything but a music-only rehearsal of that song, saying he wanted to get her "natural reaction" to the words during the live performance. Apparently Nick had helped him refine the song even before Deak and Simon had gotten a look at it. Everyone in Oblivion had contributed.

Except her.

And, you know, there wasn't anything weird at all about her ex-boyfriend and her current boyfriend collaborating on an ode to having sex with her, or some variation on that theme. She couldn't be sure since she hadn't heard the stupid thing yet. The melody was freaking hot though. Lots of buildup on the guitar and a low, throbbing drumbeat that had made her squirm on her stool even without the matching lyrics.

Damn, she wanted to find out what he'd written.

She'd tried to tamp down on her frustration all afternoon. They'd agreed to throw a couple of new songs into the setlist to give the crowd at Tribute, a medium-sized club halfway between Santa Monica and San Francisco, an extra special treat. Lila had been appraised of the setlist change, with the exception of Gray and Nick's last minute addition, "Sugar Kiss."

That was their showpiece. Their crème brûlée.

Her Mylanta moment.

Screw it, she couldn't wait anymore to find out some of the song. If it was for her, she shouldn't be the last to know. If she had to, she'd put on her best pouty face and maybe flash a little boob Gray's way. She had her own bag of naughty tricks, and she wasn't above using them.

She marched toward the men's dressing room, well aware that only Simon and Gray still remained inside. Nick had vanished with one of the more regular groupies, Tori, and from the look on the brunette's face, she'd been prepared to take Nick's mind completely off the impending show. Deak had disappeared with his phone, probably to check on Harper.

Leaving her two victims behind.

After knocking on the dressing room door, she pushed it open, her statement dying on her lips as she heard the conversation taking place within.

"Okay, now you gotta layer the second layer on top of the first. Curl your wrist on the downsweep. That'll get more of it to cling to the end of your lashes."

"It's clumping. Is it supposed to clump like that?"

"Oh Christ, let me do it. Look up."

Covering her mouth, she stuck her head around the door to get a visual to go with the dialogue. It was even better seeing it than hearing it.

Gray sat on the stool in front of the lighted mirror and Simon perched on the dressing table, one of his hands tilting up Gray's face and the other deftly applying mascara to Gray's eyelashes.

At least she assumed it was deft until she screeched and Simon's hand slipped across Gray's cheek, leaving a giant blue-black smear.

"Jesus, woman, a little forewarning, hey?" Disgusted, Simon grabbed a makeup wipe and attacked Gray's face. Gray shoved him away but Simon wouldn't be deterred, ambushing him with a knee damn near to the groin to hold him still while he cleaned up the mascara. "Stop squirming! If I crush a nut, it'll be your own damn fault."

"Hey baby, what are you doin' in here? Wanna see me get maimed?" The grin Gray flashed her made her last bit of frustration about the song drain away.

Actually it was a tossup between the panty-dropping grin and the smokin' eye makeup.

"Holy fuck, you look hot in guyliner." She patted her chin. "Just making sure I'm not drooling."

"Come here and sit on my lap."

"Oh hell no. This space is not sanctioned for ménages and shit." Simon dropped the mascara wand and backed up, palms raised. "You're on your own, Ghosty boy."

"I think we can take it from here." She smacked Simon as he passed and giggled at his growl. "Ah, I do so love my guys."

It was Gray's turn to growl playfully. He hauled her onto his lap. "Guys, plural? I think not." His mouth was on hers before he'd finished the statement.

"I'm outta here," Simon said.

Jazz waved halfheartedly at him over Gray's head and rubbed her lips over Gray's, absorbing his low groan. She'd never get tired of kissing him. Or feeling his wicked fingers trailing up her thighs. He wandered past her exposed garters to her flippy short skirt and underneath to where she already burned for him.

"Mine," she whispered, sinking her hands into his thick dark hair. It was so long now and she didn't even care that it was a bit crispy with the product he'd put in it. All she cared was that she had her hands on him, and he had his hands on her.

All over her.

"Yours," he agreed, reaching past her to grab the mascara off the dressing table. "I look a bit cockeyed at the moment, but if you still want to claim me..."

"Fuck yes. Since when do you do the whole guyliner thing? In high school, you refused."

"Gotta change things up now and then. Don't want to get stale."

"No chance there." She eased back and studied his face, her heart speeding up even more with one glimpse into his smudgy gray eyes. "You are a little lopsided though." She grinned and took the mascara. "Let me fix you."

He palmed her ass under her skirt and settled her right on his stiffening cock. "Oh sweetheart, we don't have nearly enough time for that. Unfortunately."

"Funny guy." Catching her lip between her teeth, she uncapped the tube and took an experimental stroke with the mascara. It was only when she had to apply the makeup that she realized his body held a faint tremor, almost indistinguishable to the naked eye. But when she needed him to hold still, that slight shaking made a world of difference.

"Hey, are you nervous?" She laughed, though she didn't find it amusing at all.

He'd been performing for over a decade, and she'd never seen him with anything but nerves of steel. Crowds didn't rattle him. Being in the center of a bunch of screaming fans rattled him even less. Despite what the members of Oblivion probably would've guessed based on his disappearing acts and sometimes sullen behavior over the past year, Gray was a showman through-and-through.

"No. Of course not." His laughter sounded fake to her ears. "Why would I be?"

"I don't know. So why are you shaking?"

He went still. "I'm not."

You are. But she didn't say it, because he seemed to be mostly better now. He must be anxious for some reason. Perhaps it had to do with performing her song. Could be he thought she wouldn't like it.

No wonder he didn't want to share it with her ahead of time if he was wigging out that much.

"That's better." She gave him an easy smile. "Tilt your head back." Once he complied, she swept the mascara over his lashes a couple more times, smudging it a little beneath the lash line. "Why do boys always have such thick lashes? It's completely unfair."

"We need something to lure in you ladies."

She inched back on his lap and gave him a dispassionate glance, scanning for flaws. There weren't any. His bone structure could've made angels weep. His eyes were sexy and beguiling. His mouth...oh, his mouth.

And then there was his cock, hardening more beneath her with every passing moment.

"Don't think you have to worry about luring anyone, Duffy." She glanced down at tonight's costume. He tended to wear some outlandish things compared to the rest of them. Tonight he had on just a pair of navy suspenders and black lace-up leather pants with heavy black boots. She capped the mascara and snapped one of his suspenders. "You're not actually going out there like this, are you? Where's your shirt?"

"It's gets hot out there. Why bother? This saves me laundry." He hooked his hand around the back of her neck. "Now shut up and kiss me."

She couldn't help laughing as she covered his mouth with hers. He kicked his foot off the floor and sent their stool spinning, making her shriek and hold on tighter. When they finally stopped, he grinned up at her, the dancing lights in his eyes reminding her of the impish Gray from so many years ago. The one she rarely saw traces of lately.

She traced her fingertip down his nose. "I love seeing you like this. I missed you."

"I've been with you all along, baby."

"No, you haven't. Not like this." She tipped her forehead to his. "Promise me it'll always be just like this between us. Fresh and new and so hot I can't breathe when our skin touches."

"I promise." He rubbed the inside of his wrist along her bare midriff, and she shot him a sexy look under her lashes. Sometimes it amazed her sparks didn't erupt at the point of contact between them. "After tonight, everyone will know how I feel about you. How I spend every hour of the day wanting to be inside you and every hour of the night making that wish come true."

She swallowed hard. "Oh. Okay then."

His grin turned teasing. "I love making you blush. Knowing that I'm the one who always could, even when there was nothing between us but friendship."

"Was that ever true?"

"You did an awful good job of acting like my good buddy for too many years." The prune face he made caused her to giggle.

"If you ever want more insight into my perverted teenage mind, check out my composition notebook."

His brows lifted. "I've been through that composition notebook a million times."

"Not that one. My *secret* one." She smiled and hopped off his lap. "Come on, sexy. We're needed onstage."

He smacked her ass before snatching his hat off the dressing table and propping it jauntily on his head. Then he rushed ahead of her to open the door. Even when he was being salacious, he never lost his gentlemanly ways. "Tease. I'll get you for that later."

"I should hope so." Adding a flirty sway to her walk, she led the way backstage.

When the house lights came down half an hour later, he shot her that cocky grin that made her pulse turn frenetic. He faced her as he started the first frantic notes of "Ripcord", sucking her into his music with merely the power of his stare and his incredible skill. She played from rote, her hands barely aware of the sticks. Scarcely able to focus on anyone or anything but him.

All she could see was the boy she loved, playing for her and her alone.

From "Ripcord" they went into "Taste of Candy" and "Breaking It Down." They followed that with "Balls To The Wall," which transitioned well into one of their band camp collaborations "Lit." The new song was a party anthem, plain and simple, and Simon introduced it by tugging off his shirt and tossing into the crowd. When that wasn't enough, he tugged off his boots too and pranced across the stage like a drunken cheerleader, doing high kicks and gyrations to Nick and Gray's dueling solos.

Considering they'd only had a short time to rehearse the song as a group, they didn't have too many stumbles. Well, no one stumbled but her anyway. When Gray looked back at her after he came out of the finger-blistering solo with Nick, his grin mile-wide, she actually lost hold of one of her sticks. Only a quick save with her toes and a flip of it back into her hands saved that section of the song.

Worst of all? Gray knew his effect on her. He fucking laughed and added a little extra fingerwork to his part, nearly cutting Nick out in his haste to demonstrate to her that he could keep the beat. Ass.

An adorable ass, but still an ass.

Then her breath caught at the first chords of "Sugar Kiss." The drums throbbed, a low and erotic rhythm meant to make the crowd sway on their feet. And it worked too. Before Simon's low growl let loose with the first lyrics, the ones she knew because Gray had sung them in her ear that night in the hot tub, the fans were screaming. They could feel the change in the air.

Gray didn't look at her as one verse blurred into the next. He focused on his fingers, playing with a demonic sense of possession that made his muscles bunch tightly and gleam damply with sweat. His back flexed and his hand flew up and down the frets, pulling out slyly sexual chords. Because the song was new, she had to concentrate and missed some of the lyrics, though she heard snatches over the endless pulsation of her sticks against the skins.

She managed not to blush until Gray turned toward her to sing the last two verses. Simon's voice dropped away and he grabbed his guitar Cherry to pick up the rhythm section that Gray abandoned. Nick tossed a grin at Simon and they went back to back as they always had in the early band footage filmed before she and Gray had joined. Deak kept the bass line steady, adding a heavy heartbeat that ran through the song.

And Gray sang to *her*. Openly. He tugged off one of his suspenders, letting it hang, and the women in the crowd whistled and shrieked. Bracing one leg on the riser that held her drum kit, he added his own guitar to Simon and Nick's, his finger play a somehow carnal backdrop to the way his voice rasped over the lyrics he'd written. Through sheer will she managed not to lose the thread of her part of the song, but watching his sensual lips mouth words for her ears alone while chicks screamed only a few feet away nearly broke her a dozen times.

Instead of ending the song as they'd rehearsed it, he kept going, repeating the last verse, stringing out his guitar part until the other guys had no choice but to join him. Somehow she found herself singing louder, repeating the same sexy lyrics back to him, only aware that her mic had been turned up when her own voice echoed back over the track. She started to back off, but Gray's voice grew stronger, teasing hers out as if she were a turtle poking out of her shell.

His eyes stayed on hers, his stare strong and unrelenting. With one glance, she knew he was mentally peeling off her clothes and running his mouth down her body, playing her curves with his fingers with the same infinite patience he worked the strings.

She'd never been verbally made love to before. And she'd never reflected every bit of her desire right back.

As the song wound down, the hooting and hollering from the crowd shook her out of her stupor. But when Gray scaled the riser and locked his hand in her hair, hauling her mouth up to his for a hot, rough kiss, she succumbed to his spell.

Dimly, she heard the cheers and Simon's lewd laughter while he teased the audience about what they'd borne witness to. But the rest of her consciousness was completely centered on Gray and his slick tongue slipping over hers.

"I want to fuck you right here," he panted into her mouth, and God, she believed him. She wanted it too. More than she'd ever wanted anything before.

By the time he jumped back down and took up his regular space at Nick's side, she was shaking so hard that her sticks vibrated against the drums before she got hold of herself. Her nipples had beaded to painful points and between her legs, she was so soaked she didn't know what she'd leave behind on the seat. He'd fucking *melted* her.

By the time Nick ended the song with the solo of all solos, hunched over the guitar he gripped like it was a wild animal on the verge of escape, the crowd was on fire. A quick couple of hand gestures from Simon to Deak and the rest of the band and they changed up the setlist, going into a high energy cover they pulled out every now and then to keep the audience revved. As the first licks of Guns 'n Roses' "Sweet Child O' Mine" reverberated through the club, Simon grabbed Gray's hat and pitched it into the crowd, tempting him to lose his place. But Gray only grinned and kept right on playing.

Once the set was over, she'd search online for another velvet hat to buy him. Superstitions mattered. Tonight, when everything was going better than they'd ever dreamed—the band finally gelling, the audience vibe perfect, the music sounding better than ever—she wasn't about to alter any of their normal routines.

Including her post-show jump off the drum kit to grab a water and tease Gray. Tonight wasn't going to be any different—or so she thought until he waited through their three-song encore to turn to her, the look in his eye painfully intense. And obvious.

He intended to fulfill his fucking fantasy, right there.

The curtain dropped and the stage started to empty out, somehow faster than normal. Roadies scurried away with their equipment, calling instructions to each other, and Simon and Deak and Nick left as one, slapping each other on the back. This show would clearly go down as one of their biggest triumphs since last year's contract asshattery, in spite of the fact that they'd played for much larger crowds than this one. But hell, she seriously doubted they'd ever been more in sync and more amped than they'd been tonight.

Jazz rubbed her sweaty hands on her thighs and swallowed hard as Gray handed off his guitar to the stage crew. Then he was free to focus all of his attention on her again, his gaze burning her to the core. Each step he took toward her made her tremble harder until he stood in front of her. She couldn't even gather enough breath to say his name.

He didn't seem similarly afflicted. "What do you have on under that skirt?"

He jumped up on the riser and picked her up, spinning her around and settling her on his lap. She straddled his thighs, more than a little shocked that the normally proper Gray had pulled a page out of her rule-breaking playbook. He'd never been a goody-goody, but he'd also never been the kind of guy to go at it in a club.

Or on stage, with people still milling around, shouting and laughing, on the opposite side of the walls that surrounded them. Even the audience was still just a few feet away on the other side of the curtain. Most of them were probably dispersing fast to the bar area. Still, plenty of people remained behind, not ready for the party to end.

Neither was she.

She traced her fingertip from his sweaty throat down his chest to the top of his new Oblivion tattoo. Funny how something she'd teased him about didn't seem so humorous now. It peeked over the top of his low-waist pants, showing off way too much of that sexy-as-sin body for her liking. She caressed his happy trail and lower, cupping his cock in her hand while she nuzzled the sweaty side of his neck.

"Why don't you find out?" she asked against his skin.

He made a sound in his throat that verged on animalistic and slid one hand beneath her skirt while the other palmed her ass. When he found her bare beneath, he wasted no time in sinking two fingers inside her. "You do this a lot, sugar? Just sit up here and play and get your thighs all wet because you're not wearing any panties?"

"No."

She threw her head back, her hips lifting to give him more access. He rubbed her deep inside, massaging that secret place that always made her thighs shake. Now was no exception. His thumb toyed with her piercing, sending the longer crystals she'd worn tonight tinkling over her swollen folds. Already she was on fire for him.

"No? Then why'd you skip underwear tonight?"

Trying to respond was becoming increasingly difficult. All of her air was trapped in her chest behind her heaving breasts, the heavy tips brushing his chest without relief. She longed for him to lower his head and suck on one through her top, but he just kept the easy pace between her legs while he squeezed her ass.

"Because I wanted to tease you like this. I wanted to imagine you..."

His teeth closed over her earlobe. "What, baby?"

"I'm going to come," she gasped, shocked. How could she be there that soon?

Guess all the show foreplay had done its job.

"Uh-uh. Not until I'm in you. This is just the appetizer before the main course." Demonstrating it, he slipped his wet fingers out and painted them over his lips, making her moan as he licked up the traces of her excitement. His dark lashes lowered and he growled again. "New rule. I can't fuck you unless I can eat you out first. It's the worst kind of torture."

She glanced over her shoulder at the drums. He laughed and locked an arm around her waist, hauling her close for a scorching kiss. "You want it that bad, huh? You're willing to risk damaging the kit just so I can get my mouth on your pussy?"

"Yes." She didn't hesitate. "I'd even lay down on the floor. I'd need a decontamination chamber later, but yes." She framed his face between her palms and nibbled his lower lip, relishing her flavor on his mouth. Dark and sweet and so frigging naughty. "That's what I imagined," she added, unable to stop now that she'd started. She ground against his cock, needing that friction against her plump clit. "You just throwing me down somewhere after the show and shoving inside me, all rough and sweaty and wild..."

"My dirty fucking girl." He used a fistful of her hair to tug her head back and arrowed his tongue over her collarbone, tasting her skin with the same eagerness he would've gone down on her. "You ready for me, sugar?"

"Yes. So fucking ready."

He undid the laces of his pants with one hand and used to other to grip her throat, holding her in place with such erotic dominance that she couldn't restrain her moan. The quelling look he gave her only caused her to squirm harder. "I'm so hoping you soak through these pants," he said. "Then I can throw them out. Fucking leather."

"But it makes your ass look hot."

At his grunt, she laughed under his hand and rocked her hips against his in a bid for him to hurry. She loved how it was between them. No matter how urgent or erotic, they never forgot to laugh. Never lost that connection that linked them together so much tighter than simple sex.

"Screw it. You take me out." Eyes glittering, he let her go and she immediately bent to her task, fingers blurring over the laces until she reached the rigid prize inside his pants. She shuddered at the sheer weight of him in her hand and licked her lips hungrily. "Oh, baby, that's an invitation right there. Want me to put you on your knees?"

She didn't hesitate. "Yes. I want it in my mouth." Leaning forward, she bit the muscled cords of his neck and relished his ragged exhalation. "But I need you in my pussy more. It's aching without you."

"Christ. Do it now."

She shifted forward, taking him inside her in one slow roll. Her flesh stretched around his erection, the familiar quick sting from his size fading into a wave of pure longing. It cramped her belly and made her clumsy as she gripped his shoulders and bounced on his lap, too excited to take the time to ride him the way she should. He groaned and steadied her hips, lifting her up and easing her back down so slowly that she had to bite the inside of her cheek to keep from crying out. Blood bloomed on her tongue and involuntarily, she squeezed around him.

"Jesus. I gotta fuck you hard, baby. This isn't going to take long."

"Yes. Please." She wrapped an arm around his shoulders for balance and used the other to grab a handful of his damp hair. "I need it as hard as you can."

"Hang on." He spread his legs, changing the angle slightly, and lifted off the bench, surging into her so deeply that she nearly lost her hold on him. "That's not hanging on," he panted.

She dug her nails into his arm and squeezed him again, tilting into him and crashing her mouth down onto his. She fed on his lips and tongue, sucking and biting on them as he gripped her ass and set a manic rhythm. His air fueled her and she gave it right back, moaning at every powerful thrust.

Her skirt fell over his lap, hopefully hiding most of what they were doing just in case someone poked their head back onstage. But she really didn't care, because her world had narrowed to his long, thick cock moving in and out of her, scraping her clit and her piercing and pulling the rawest, dirtiest sounds from her throat.

"You've got thirty seconds to come. Otherwise I'm going to pull out and leave this beautiful pussy empty again, because I know someone's going to walk out here and see me fucking you. And baby, that can't happen." He dragged his teeth over her lower lip. "No one gets to see your face while you're on the verge of orgasm but me."

If she hadn't been on the edge—hell, dangling over it—his raspy demands probably wouldn't have triggered her to fall. But with that little nudge, she stopped fighting her climax. It hit her like a tsunami, destroying her awareness of everything but the feeling of her walls contracting in hard pulses around his rigid shaft.

She whimpered, her forehead bumping against his as she lost her precarious balance yet again. Her orgasm didn't seem to have an end. The pleasure overwhelmed her, shorting out her senses until she couldn't see anything but the naked need in his eyes. That need surrounded her, feeding her own. "God. Gray. God."

He groaned and buried his face in the crook between her neck and shoulder. His body quaked with his obvious struggle to restrain his own release. "Sugar, why you gotta test me?"

"Don't hold back," she breathed when she could form words again. "I'm still empty. You better fill me up. Now."

He hauled her back down, so roughly that the thrill zipped up her spine and intensified her aftershocks. He pushed up into her, hitting that spot that caused her to tingle from head-to-toe. She tried to focus on him, to help him get there, but God, he felt so good inside her, and his hands flexing on her ass added an extra bit of sensation. Those calloused fingers caressing her skin left sparks in their wake. He was touching her everywhere, inside and out, his heat overpowering her. She surrendered to it and to him, giving into another rapid climax with a cry that he muffled with a desperate kiss.

And then he rewarded her even more by thrusting deep one last time and spilling himself inside her. "Jazz." Still shaking, he dropped his damp forehead to hers and mouthed her three favorite words, imprinting them on her trembling lips and branding them on her soul. "I love you."

Chapter Twenty-Seven

Then

"How did I get stuck pushing a shopping cart when I was supposed to be auditioning tonight?" Jazz asked.

Gray tossed a bag of corn chips in the cart and hipchecked her into a row of brownie mix. Giggling, she grabbed a package with peanut butter chips and added that to their purchases. "Because the guys need to eat. Fuel, ya know? Once we start practicing, we usually keep at it half the night. Especially if Stevie's dad's out drinking. Then no one bothers us."

"But I can't stay out half the night. Your mom will kill me."

He grabbed a couple of bags of pretzels and added them to the growing pile. "So you should go home like a good girl and pull the covers up to your chin."

It was her turn to hipcheck him. He laughed and slid his arm around her waist, lifting her off the ground so effortlessly that she couldn't help but squeal. "Put me down, you oaf."

"*Oaf*?" He set her down with a thud. "Not exactly the kind of sweet talk I expected from the girl who is on tap to be Krystal Sword's first ever female drummer, thanks to me." He shook his head in mock disappointment and held his hand over his heart, approximately two inches from the beard of one of the members of ZZ Top. He'd found the relic T-shirt at a thrift shop and wore it gleefully in spite of all the shit he took from their classmates. "I'm wounded, truly."

She grinned and tried not to think of the reason spots were opening up in the band. Gray was heading away to college in not too long, as was another one of the guys who had a scholarship to a school back east. They wanted to get new people to fill in while the longtime members were off being scholarly. It was a fantastic opportunity for her to get some real band experience.

But all she could do was focus on the knee-weakening reality of Gray being gone. She couldn't imagine playing when he wasn't at her side. They were a team. He brought the best out of her, and now she was going to have to find her best all by herself.

"You don't know I'm going to be the drummer. I haven't auditioned yet. I could blow it." She stopped and tore open the bag of corn chips, shoving a handful in her mouth. "I'm going to blow it."

"Don't be stupid. You're gonna nail it." He took the bag back and set it in the cart. "Look, go read a magazine or something. I'm gonna grab a six-pack and pay for this stuff."

"Get me a—"

"A Sprite. Yeah, yeah. I know you, Edwards. Now go read about giving the perfect BJ in Cosmo or something." His teasing grin as he shoved her away made her laugh.

Dang, get caught just one time reading a dirty article and a girl was branded for life.

"Fine. Push your own damn cart." Still grinning, she wandered to the front of the Grab 'n Go and rifled through the rack of magazines. Nothing caught her eye, at least not of the magazine variety.

She ventured to the line of toy vending machines and played with her bamboo initial necklace, a holdover from her old life. She'd been wanting something new to replace it. A sign of a fresh start. But cash wasn't exactly plentiful, especially now that it was getting close to the beginning of the new school year. She'd need to buy supplies soon, and she needed to ration the money the Duffys gave her. She didn't want them to think she was some kind of spendthrift.

And man, she wanted one of these stupid guitar pick necklaces. A dollar a chance with the giant claw. She sucked at this game, but that didn't stop her from trying.

It's just junk. You wear junk, baby girl, people will think you're junk.

Forcing her mom's voice out of her head, she dug around in her change purse and finally came up with her last four quarters. She was just about to slip them into the slot when a rickety grocery cart rolled up behind her and bumped her gently in the butt.

"Whatcha doin'?"

"It's nothing." She started to laugh it off and turn away, but Gray grabbed her arm.

"Liar. Looks like something to me. You want one of these?" He tapped on the machine and dug out his quarters, dumping them in the change slot before she had a chance to pretend she really didn't want that purple guitar pick necklace.

It was cheesy. Flimsy. It'd probably turn her skin green and break in a week.

But she wanted it with all her heart.

"Yes." Her voice came out in a whisper, as if she were confessing something shameful. The foster kid liked to drape herself in junk jewelry and pretend she wore diamonds.

"Then it shall be yours." He shot her a cocky grin and braced his hand on the lever attached to the claw. A few deft manipulations later, he zeroed in on his target and dragged it out from the sea of plastic egg-enclosed treasures with a crow of victory that any sports hero would've recognized.

The sweet taste of success.

Still grinning, he plucked it out of the tray and popped open the top. He turned to her and held it out for her inspection. "There you go, baby. All yours."

Every time he called her *baby* her heart rioted. Sometimes she didn't think her skin and bones could hold it inside, not when his twinkling gray eyes settled on hers. She took the container and dug out her prize. She wouldn't cry. If she kept on smiling, he would never be able to guess how a small hunk of crap could somehow crystallize the totality of her life and everything she wanted and would never have.

"Thank you."

"Turn around. Let me put it on you. Hold up your hair."

Pivoting, she did as he asked. He slipped it around her neck and she lifted her hair higher so he could fumble with the clasp. Then she turned back to him and gripped the tiny guitar pick between her fingers. "Thank you," she said again, voice breaking.

His smile fell away. "Jazz? What's wrong?"

"Nothing." She started to move away but he grabbed her arm and cupped her cheek in his other hand.

"Tell me."

She shook her head but the momentum only made the words spill out faster. "I used to save my allowance for this stuff. I'd pile it up in my jewelry box because I didn't have anything else and I wanted to be a princess." She smiled. "Every little girl's dream, right?"

"You are a princess."

Her smile wavered. "It didn't matter that I had holes in my shoes, because I had this fake bling." She stared at the grimy floor to avoid meeting his gaze. "My mom found it one day and threw it all out. Called it trash. She said I was trash for wearing it." She dug the other necklace out from under her shirt. "This is the only one I managed to save. The rest she covered in spaghetti sauce after she burned our dinner."

He closed his fingers around hers. "It's beautiful. J is the best letter."

She turned her face away. "Thanks for not laughing at it." *Or me.*

"Jazz." He nudged her chin back with the tip of his finger and lowered his head to hers. "Someday I'm going to buy you that bling. I promise."

A harsh laugh escaped her. She didn't know where it came from and couldn't figure out how to shove it back down. "Why would you do that?"

His Adam's apple bobbled in his stubbled throat. "When I do it, you'll know why."

Chapter Twenty-Eight

Now

Being summoned to conference room A at Ripper Records three days later didn't surprise Jazz in the slightest.

What did surprise her? That it had taken Lila that long to pounce.

When Lila hadn't snagged them the morning after the Tribute show, Jazz had been relieved. Maybe she hadn't been paying that much attention to her and Gray's show antics. Though Lila attended every show she could as well as making sure there was ample footage for dissection later, it was dark behind the drum kit and she might not have been eagle-eyed enough to spot Gray kissing her.

Maybe and *might* weren't offering her a whole lot of comfort at the moment.

Lila finally sailed in, a sunny smile on her face. "Morning, children." She held up a silver decanter and set a couple of mugs on the table. "Coffee?"

"That shit is poison," Nick muttered.

Simon kicked him under the table. "Since when? You drink it constantly. And I'm pretty sure it's less poisonous than those cancer sticks of yours."

"I meant this particular coffee is poison, and keep your damn feet to yourself, Kagan."

Lila ignored them both and took her seat at the head of the table. She shrugged off her shoulder bag and withdrew her iPad, setting it before her. "So. What's new?"

They all looked at each other, silently communicating about who would be the one to speak. Deak, as usual, stepped up.

He cleared his throat. "We've come up with a lot of good, usable material in our time away, both in our individual groups and collectively. I'm assuming you saw the footage of our show at Tribute. It went well."

"Yes, of course, I saw it. That's my job." Lila scrolled her finger across the tablet's screen and smiled. "Your job is a bit different. You were given certain tasks and offered certain admonitions yet with my little eye, I spy that these were not followed."

Jazz shot a glance at Gray in the seat beside her, and he slid his hand under the arm of his chair to link his fingers with hers. Such a small thing, but so important.

"Lila, we—" Gray began.

"Don't bother explaining. I can see." She folded her hands on top of her tablet. "What I see is amazing chemistry that I want to exploit like a motherfucker."

Jazz blinked. "Excuse me?"

"You heard me. And don't pretend to be shocked. I'm hardly the first person to be blown away by what I saw on stage." Lila lifted her iPad and started scrolling again. "Check out YoloFan's YouTube clip, entitled 'Motherfucking Oblivion Hotness,' for example."

"YoloFan? That sounds like a true genius." If Nick had rolled his eyes any harder, he would've dislocated something.

"Regardless, Gray and Jazz's chemistry is exactly what this band has been needing. The magic ingredient."

Gray clamped his fingers tighter around Jazz's and leaned forward. "Look, I'm not sure what you're getting at, but we're not going to be 'exploiting' anything. This isn't a game to us."

"You think my paycheck is a game, Mr. Duffy? Au contraire. I take it very seriously."

Jazz glanced at Gray and lifted her eyebrows when he would've spoken again. He fell silent, giving her the floor.

"We realize that the timing of this could be construed as...inconvenient for the band, and we certainly don't want to be a distraction, but—"

"You're the best kind of distraction, Jasmine. Let me read some of the comments on YoloFan's clip. By the way, over two-hundred-thousand hits in two days for a show at a venue like Tribute is impressive."

"YoloFan can kiss my ass."

"Nicholas, are you really that upset at not being in the spotlight? Kindly hush." Lila slid the iPad toward Deak. "Actually, why don't you read some of them aloud, so no one thinks I'm stacking the deck."

Deacon picked up the iPad and started to read silently. Then one brow lifted. "When Gray climbed up on those drums to kiss Jazz, I swear I had an orgasm. Like...right then and there. Instant combustion."

Gray grinned. "Jeez, man, I never knew you cared."

Deak shook his head, laughing, before sliding the tablet back to Lila. "I'm not reading those out loud. Those chicks are seriously horny."

"Are you sure they're all chicks?" Jazz propped an elbow on the table and wiggled her fingers, indicating for Lila to pass the iPad to her. "There has to be some guys in the crowd, right?"

"There are. Men are excited too."

"Fabulous," Gray muttered, tightening his grip on Jazz's hand.

"Now Jasmine has become an accessible fantasy to them. The male mind works in fascinating ways."

"You can say that again." Jazz flicked Gray a sidelong glance and smiled when his broody expression never changed. "We're happy you're not displeased that we're together."

"Yes, but we really wouldn't have done a fucking thing different if you were."

"G, shush." Jazz squeezed his hand. "He doesn't mean that, Lila."

"Sure he does. He's in love and wants the whole world to know it."

Gray never looked away from Jazz as he brought her hand to his mouth for a quick kiss. "That about sums it up."

"Aww," Simon said, grinning. "That's totally adorbz."

Jazz took a shuddery breath and would've responded in kind if Lila hadn't cut her off.

"I agree totally with your plan to demonstrate it to the world. Clearly you two have explosive chemistry, and that shouldn't be kept behind closed doors. Neither should 'Sugar Kiss' be under wraps until the album comes out." She consulted her tablet. "I spoke to Donovan yesterday and we're of one mind. 'Sugar Kiss' should be the first single, and we want it out soon as possible."

"Say what?" Nick flashed her an incredulous look. "The album's not due to drop until—"

"June. Yes. Which is a damn long time for Oblivion to fade out of the public eye."

"I thought that's what these scattered club dates were about before we went into the studio," Simon said, spinning one of Lila's coffee cups between his palms.

She snatched it away from him and set it beside Deak's elbow. "That's china, Kagan, and those are hand-painted roses. Moving on. Yes, you're right. And that is a good plan until you can get back on the road later this year. But nowadays, many artists are dropping advance singles. In fact, I want you to give me another one I can release in a few months. Preferably a ballad."

"'Finally' would be perfect." Gray spoke up, his attention focused on Lila. "I've been working on that one on and off for the last week."

"Uh, hello, why didn't you mention it to me?" Nick asked.

"Or me," Jazz put in.

Gray's cheeks tinged pink. "Because it wasn't ready yet. Now it almost is."

"Almost," Lila said. "Once it is—and once your band has given their go-ahead—I'd like to hear it. In the meantime, I want to get going with 'Sugar Kiss'. Donovan and I had a strategy session and we have some preliminary ideas for the video. Specifically, we'd like it to feature Jasmine, covered in sugar. Or a sugar-like substance, since I think that might be difficult to work with under hot lights."

Silence descended around the table. Lila, however, didn't seem to notice.

"We think conceptually that this might be just the song to shoot the band into superstardom. Think of what 'Cherry Pie' did to Warrant back in—"

"What? Now we're taking our cues from freaking hair bands?" Nick slapped his palms on the table. "Newsflash, lady, Oblivion isn't Poison rebooted. Simon's lips are way too small."

"Hey." Simon touched his fingers to his mouth. "Don't hate on the pout."

Deak leaned forward. "Lila, I'm not sure this is the direction we want to proceed. 'Sugar Kiss' is already an extremely sexual song. To add a salacious video—"

"I'm certain we don't want to proceed that way," Gray snapped. "Jazz isn't a sex doll."

Lila pursed her lips. "A doll, huh? I didn't think of that angle."

Abruptly, Gray let go of Jazz's hand and crossed his arms. "Not. Happening."

Jazz twined her fingers together in her lap and tried not to let Gray's sudden distance bother her. She understood he didn't want her to be sexualized, but what did he expect, writing a song like that? That they'd braid her hair and have her skip down a hill of flowers like in Mary Poppins?

"This is your song," she said quietly, unsurprised when he didn't look her way. "You came up with it, now you're mad that Lila wants to capitalize on it?"

She stared at his stony countenance and frowned. He'd totally shut down.

"It's not entirely his song," Nick said. "I improved upon it. Simon named it. And yes, it's highly sexual, and yes, the crowd loved it. But couldn't we go with a different concept than the typical naked chick vid? Didn't that jump the shark in oh, about 1992?"

"What do you propose then? Jasmine in a pinafore, maybe, and the rest of you in suits? I know, I know." Lila snapped her fingers. "How about Robert Palmer-style videos? Hot babes in classy black dresses? Then it just implies sex without pushing the envelope?"

"Who the fuck is Robert Palmer?" Simon asked.

Nick ignored him. "So you want us to be like every other band out there."

"No, I want you to deliver on the promise you made by creating a song like 'Sugar Kiss'. Jasmine is a beautiful woman. There's no reason she should be hidden behind—"

"I don't want her to hide, but I also don't think she should be objectified."

"More objectified than what you did by writing that kind of song?" Jazz shoved her hands under her thighs so she wouldn't lean over and whack Gray in the head. As much as she loved him, he could be a pigheaded chauvinist at times. Sure, it was so wrong for her to decide to be sexual—if she did, she still hadn't agreed to do it yet—but it was fine if *he* made that decision for her. "Maybe you shouldn't have shared that with Nick if you really wanted to keep me under lock and key, huh?"

"I didn't share anything with Nick that you hadn't decided to share first."

She sucked in a breath. The pain came fast, as it always did. Pain that she'd hurt him, even unintentionally. And the deeper pain that the threesome they'd had would remain a splinter in their sides, a weapon to be dragged out in arguments probably for the rest of their lives. "It always comes back to that with you, doesn't it?"

"Kids," Nick said from the other end of the table. "I think we're getting off-topic."

"It comes back to it because everything seems to keep shoving it in my face. And no, I didn't share it with Nick. I was going to," he acknowledged, "but I hadn't gotten that far. I was still writing it when he grabbed my notebook and called Simon."

She pushed her hands through her hair, sending the beads at the ends of her braids clinking. When she'd done them that morning, she'd grinned at her reflection in the mirror, so stupidly happy that she couldn't stop from beaming at herself. Gray had come into the bathroom and hugged her from behind, pressing kisses on the back of her neck she could still feel if she concentrated.

Now they were arguing about nothing.

"I don't really want to be powdered in sugar," she admitted.

"I don't have a problem with it," Simon said, laughing when Nick kicked him again. "I meant me. I'd be fine with being turned into a piece of fried dough. As long as there's a hot girl to lick me clean."

Nick snorted. "Lick yourself."

"I'm not quite *that* flexible. Those Pilates classes can only do so much."

Lila sighed. "It's a song about giving oral sex to a female. Not sure if powdering you would have the same effect, Kagan." She tapped her nails on her cheek, her eyes brightening. "Actually, maybe that's a good idea. Jasmine can get up a ladder and dump the sugary substance on Simon. It'll be a trend-setting role reversal. I like it. Good thinking."

Before anyone could blink, she popped to her feet. "I'm going to run this by Donovan and get a vid shoot set up. Kagan, don't cut your hair. Women like it long."

Nick touched the ends of his own short cut. "I don't seem to have any trouble."

"Discriminating women," she corrected, skirting the table and heading for the door. "Keep up the good work, Oblivion. Time's running down and I want enough material to take into the studio next week, so don't start slacking now." The door clicked shut behind her.

Gray unfolded his long frame from the chair and had taken two strides toward the door when Jazz called him back. "Gray, wait."

"Guess this is our cue to leave." Nick grabbed a handful of the back of Simon's shirt and shoved him toward the door.

Deak shot her a sympathetic glance and followed them, shutting the door with a decisive snap.

She drew up her legs and hugged her knees to her chest. One of the benefits to being small was that she could imitate a pretzel when she wanted to hide from the world.

Except she never wanted to hide from him.

"I'm not going to apologize, because I don't know what I did," she said quietly. "If you expect me not to be sexualized, then you shouldn't have ever invited me into this band. That's part of the rock and roll image. As you well fucking know. Girls scream after you all the time, and I've never put a bag over your head."

His silence felt as brutal as a slap. No, actually, it hurt worse. She'd been slapped before. Mrs. Beetle, her second foster mother, hadn't had a problem with meting out her form of justice with an open palm.

This sting lasted longer.

After a moment, he heaved out a breath and dropped into the seat he'd vacated. He locked his hands behind his head, staring off somewhere she couldn't see.

"Nothing to say, huh?" She swallowed hard and picked up the cinched purse she'd set down beside her chair. "Okay. Guess that's that."

He let her get to the door before he spoke. "It feels like I've shared you my entire life. Is it so wrong of me to want you to myself for a little while?"

"No." She closed her eyes and gripped her purse tighter. "But it's wrong to expect more from me than I expect from you. If this situation had been reversed and Lila had asked you to do something crazy for a video, I would've bitten my tongue."

His laughter scraped down her spine, as cold as an icicle. "Yeah, well, guess what? You're better than I am, in so many ways."

"Not in my eyes."

"Your eyes aren't getting an accurate picture, sweetheart." Instead of sounding sarcastic, he sounded tired. So very exhausted.

So was she.

"No, perhaps I'm only seeing what I want to. Just like every time I think we can put what happened with Nick behind us, it comes back again to kick us in the ass."

"We're in the same band. It's not like I can forget when he's staring me in the face."

"Or when you're collaborating with him on songs about doing me? Ouch. Awkward. For me anyway. The two of you seemed cool with it."

"Jazz—"

"Forget it." Too annoyed to hold back her frustration, she yanked open the door. "I'm going back to the spa to see if they'll fit me with a shroud so no one notices I have tits."

* § *

For two days, Jazz didn't respond to his calls. Oh, she didn't ignore him. She'd never be that cruel. She spoke to him civilly, even laughing as she regaled him with Simon's latest adventures involving a glycolic peel and a pedicurist. She'd gotten a full-body detoxifying seaweed wrap and purchased another dress. This one was champagne-colored, like her hair.

God, he missed her hair and all the rest of her.

She explained not visiting by saying that she and the guys were in a good rhythm with their songwriting and she didn't want to alter their streak. The underlying message, however, was obvious. She hadn't forgiven him for his highhanded tactics and she wasn't going to bend until he proved he would bend too.

It was probably smarter that they faced this issue now. They were so new, and it was bound to be a problem going forward. One way or another, he'd figure out how to kill his jealousy. They were both part of the band. And if Lila had suggested the sugar thing to him, he would've laughed but he wouldn't have thought twice about it. Because he was a guy, and that made it okay.

It was oh so fucking different when it was *his* Jazz. Finally she was his.

Right now it didn't feel that way. He hated not being able to touch her and hold her close late at night when, after a long night writing and playing with Nick, the shakes came back. They pushed him out of bed to the baggie he hid in his shaving kit. The first night without her, he resisted.

The second, he gave in.

The next morning they had rehearsals for their show that night at Rave, another medium-sized club outside of LA. Somehow even the tension between him and Jazz didn't affect the band's vibe. It helped that the material the spa crew had brought to the table was really good, especially "Nailed."

Jamming together buffed away some of the rough spots. By the end of the session, he and Jazz were even laughing.

He headed back to the cabin to grab his stuff before heading out to Rave in a much better mood than when he'd left that morning. Until his cell rang while he was tugging on that night's outfit of extremely tight jeans, a leather vest and the new hat Jazz had found for him. He smiled, clutching the hat in one hand while he reached for his phone with the other.

She couldn't be *that* pissed if she was still buying him stuff, right?

A quick glance at the Caller ID made his smile fade. He didn't recognize the number. "Hello?"

"Gray Duffy. Nice to speak to Oblivion's rhythm guitarist in the flesh."

Gray's shoulders tensed. "Do I know you?"

"No. Not yet. But I know of you." The male's voice held a thread of menace made even more potent by its deceptive pleasantness. "You're a very talented young man. Capable of achieving many things, assuming you don't stray from the path you're on."

"Who the hell is this?"

"Don't curse at me, boy. Right now I'm the only thing standing between you and a shattered hand. Both hands. That would be truly unfortunate."

Cricket. Obviously this had to do with her. Christ, how much did he owe altogether? Not a small amount, but not one so large that the spinecrackers should've been circling.

Though, fuck, what did he really know about how this crap worked? He'd spent the bulk of his life in frigging Vista View. He'd never even smoked weed in high school. For God's sake, back then he'd practically been a Boy Scout, and deep down, he probably still was.

He was way, way out of his depth.

"I know you're looking for money," he said, running calculations on what was left in his savings account.

So much for trying to hang onto a portion of his money for rent. Not going to happen. He needed to clear his debts, fast. He'd pick up a couple of shifts at the transport company next week once they were done at the cabin. That would help. And maybe he could take one of his spare guitars down to the pawn shop. He hated to do it, but better to get rid of one of them than to look over his shoulder constantly.

As for what he'd do without the access to blow, well, he'd just have to ration what he had left, that was all. He wanted to cut back. Hell, he had to, if he intended to have Jazz in his life. So he'd just start limiting himself now—

The other man chuckled. "Money, yes. But I'm guessing you don't have a lot of access to that right now. Something you do have is a very pretty girlfriend."

Gray's throat closed and he sank to the mattress, crushing the hat Jazz had bought him against his thigh. "I don't have a girlfriend." His voice came out shakier than he'd planned so he cleared his throat and tried again. "Don't know where you're getting your information, man, but it's all wrong."

"Oh, really? So that sweet little drummer girl you were kissing onstage the other night at your concert, she's just a friend, right? Doesn't matter at all to you." He lowered his voice. "So you won't mind if I—"

"Don't. Just don't." He could barely breathe through the ice coating his lungs. "Look, I'm going to get you your money. Cricket told me I needed to get her a third of what I owe her."

"Try half, asshole. And the rest better not be far behind, or I won't be making phone calls to communicate."

"Okay, okay, half. Just give me time to get it together. I promise you'll get what you're owed, but you gotta give me the space to make it happen. Oblivion's management is intense. They watch us like hawks."

"They aren't the only ones watching you. Don't make me regret giving you more time." The other man clicked off, leaving Gray staring at the phone.

Christ. This couldn't be happening.

What the hell had he been thinking, instigating a public display like he had with Jazz the other night? He'd practically put a goddamn target on her back. He hadn't forgotten that Cricket had indicated there would be consequences if he didn't make more of a dent in his debt. Sure, he'd paid some of what he'd owed, but he'd also gotten more coke. He was probably more in the hole now than he'd been before he'd practically emptied his saving account.

Even so, he could deal with paying half of it back, fast. Half was doable. He had a bit of money left, and he had his spare guitars, the ones he rarely played anymore. Every one of them counted as one of his prized possessions, but that didn't matter right now. The important thing was to show them they could trust him, that he was making a good faith effort to get them their money. Then he could catch his breath a little while he took on a few extra shifts at the transport company.

It wasn't like Deak and the rest of the band would toss him out on his ear if he was temporarily short on rent next month. Hell, he could even ask Jazz for—

No. He hissed out a breath and smoothed out the hat she'd given him. Real fucking drug addicts hit up their girlfriends for cash. That wasn't him. Would never be him. He'd handle the first part of what he owed and figure out the rest later.

At this moment, he had a show to worry about. The car would be picking him and Nick up anytime now, and he couldn't let any of this shit affect his performance. Jazz would be watching.

They would be watching, and they would be way too pleased to see they'd rattled him. He'd be damned if he gave them the satisfaction.

He set aside the hat and headed into the bathroom for a quick shave. Deliberately, he pushed aside the baggie of blow, not wanting to even be tempted. But fuck, just the feel of the powder sifting between his fingers and the plastic was enough to make him press his fist to his forehead.

How was he supposed to get through tonight without the help? They'd threatened Jazz. The idea of them—*him*, whomever the caller was—looking at her, even thinking about her, made Gray want to throw things. Rip the mirror off the freaking wall and pound his knuckles into the glass until they were as bloody and destroyed as the pieces of his mind.

Breathing hard, he braced his hands on the edge of the sink and faced his reflection. His bloodshot eyes looked like they belonged to a druggie.

Because you are one. Everyone knows but you.

And her. Fuck, he couldn't let her know.

It was bad enough they'd smoked together. That he could brush off as just partying. Just a good time. It had never been the way he'd had a good time, but as long as she didn't think more of it, he could rationalize. But this...it would kill her to know he had people threatening him because of his drug debts.

Threatening *her*.

Hands shaking, he took out his shaving cream. He went through the rest of the task by rote, finally returning to the bedroom to grab the hat and his wallet. At the last second, he grabbed the small folding knife he'd bought after Cricket had started her not-so-subtle threats and stuffed it in his pocket. It wasn't enough. How could he protect Jazz with that? He needed a gun.

He threw back his head and sucked in a long, slow breath. No, he didn't need a gun. Didn't need to panic, either. As long as he got them the money he'd promised, he had nothing to worry about. Just in case, he'd keep Jazz close to his side.

"Yo, man, you coming? Ride's here," Nick called through Gray's closed bedroom door.

"Yeah." Gray opened the door and clamped his fingers around the knob. The words were out before he could stop them. "Look, I need you to do me a favor. And I don't intend to say more about it than this, so don't bother asking."

Nick kicked back against the wall in his best *don't give a shit* pose, eyebrow lifted. "Okay."

"I know you care about Jazz, and her well-being is the most important thing. Just keep more of an eye on her than usual for the next few days, all right?" Gray swallowed, trying to force down the lump in his throat. How had he gotten to this point? "I'm going to make sure I'm with her as much as possible, but if I'm not, I need to know you'll have her back."

He expected Nick to argue. To demand to know how deep he'd gotten. If the positions had been reversed, *he* probably would have. But from the resigned lock to Nick's jaw and his hooded eyes, he already knew.

Nick nodded and walked down the hall. Abruptly, he stopped. "You owe it to her—if not yourself—to end this."

Gray hooked his thumbs in the pockets of his jeans. He didn't know if Nick was referring to the coke or to his relationship with Jazz, period. "I've got it under control."

Nick glanced back and smiled, the warmth never reaching his eyes. Then he kept going out the front door, letting it thud shut in his wake.

* § *

"How y'all doing tonight, LA?" Simon's shout to the crowd at Rave made them scream even louder. "Who's ready to fucking rock?"

From behind the kit, Jazz flexed her foot on the pedal. Something felt off and she couldn't figure out what. Between Gray's strange lurking around her and then his last second demand for a setlist change, he definitely wasn't acting right.

He'd insisted "Sugar Kiss" come off the list, and it wasn't hard to figure out why. She'd thought that over their past few days apart, he'd cooled off a bit from his sexist stance but evidently not. The weird thing was that he'd really seemed to be coming around yet tonight he'd backslid big time.

Even more oddly, he'd hovered around her offstage, while onstage he hadn't looked at her once. Normally they teased each other before a show, exchanging winks and quips to break the pre-performance tension. Tonight he hadn't even made eye contact. He wasn't engaging the crowd either while Simon went through his revving up routine. Normally Gray got into it too. His focus tonight remained entirely on his guitar.

"Get up on your feet, LA!"

At Simon's directive, she forced a smile and started the steady buildup to "Balls To The Wall." The song was fairly straightforward and didn't require a lot of thought on her part, just mainly keeping the beat, so she was able to watch Gray. He didn't respond to Nick's good-natured—usually—posturing and taunts and barely seemed aware of Simon's showboating across the stage.

Their lead singer was in rare form tonight, owning the space and sucking up so much of the energy in the club that it began to feel like they were Simon's back-up band. But that helped disguise Gray's lack of involvement beyond his manic playing. Rather than take part in the band's antics, he focused on the instrument he cradled like a lover, plucking out notes that shrieked and wailed and raged. All of his passion funneled through his hands and became something inescapably beautiful.

And throughout, she counted off the beat, serving as the backbone to the music that roared around her just loudly enough to quiet the questions in her mind.

They went through their modified setlist without faltering, but their crazy cohesive energy from the other night had vanished. On the surface, everything seemed fine. Nick even bantered a bit with Simon and Deak in between "Lit" and "Ripcord," which was about as rare as Gray not looking up from the strings.

Stylistically, he was perfect. Didn't miss a freaking note. His face, though, never changed. He wore a stoic mask, the playful Gray from Tribute driven so far underground that she wondered if she'd imagined the whole thing.

The end of the show took a lifetime to reach and also came way too fast. She wasn't ready for him to turn that mask on her. Seeing those eyes she loved so much frosted over like the coldest winter day hammered spikes of ice in her chest, making it hard for her to breathe. She didn't know how to reach him when he was like that—the way he'd been for much of the past year.

But God, since they'd been together, it had been different. Yes, they'd only had a string of days together so far. She'd hoped it was a beginning.

She refused to believe it wasn't.

As the stage cleared out, she peeled off her fingerless gloves and flexed her achy hands, waiting for the right moment to pounce on Gray. Turns out she didn't have to bother. Once Gray handed off his guitar to the crew, he appeared at her side, closer than a shadow.

"You were fantastic tonight." He stroked her cheek and gave her his beloved Gray smile, the one he saved for her alone. Not the public cordial one, or even the sex-personified rock star one. The one he'd been flashing at her since the first day in his parents' living room, when he'd discovered she played the guitar too.

The first link in a chain of so many. She wanted that chain to be unbreakable. To be too strong to weaken or corrode. Nothing—not her goals, or her ambition, or even her principles—mattered more than building a family with Gray.

She hoped she could have it all. She would try her hardest to make it happen. But if she had to choose, she would always choose him.

Because he had always chosen her.

"Thanks. So were you. You were kind of into your own thing, huh?" she teased, not expecting the flash of heat that came into his eyes.

"I'm into you, always." His thumb smoothed over her lower lip. "Come back with me tonight. Don't make me sleep alone again."

She knew she should ask questions. Maybe even tell him that this bit of distance between them was good. Everything was moving so fast. But after the years they'd spent circling each other, fast seemed to be the only speed that made sense.

And she didn't want to sleep alone anymore either. Now that she knew what it was like to fall asleep wrapped up in arms and wake curled against his side, she didn't want to go without.

Then there were all the hours they spent together before sleep...

She nodded and reached out to cup his jaw. "Are you okay?"

"Yes. I am now. Just stay in the cabin with me, baby. Please."

The tremor in his voice had her nodding again. He really had missed her. She smiled for his benefit and stroked her index finger over his eyebrow ring. "How can I say no to a sexy, sweaty rock god in denim and leather?"

"I'm not a rock god with you. I'm just a guy who's in love with a girl."

She launched herself into his arms and pressed her face into his damp hair. His laughter rumbled through her, sweet and reassuring, and his arms banded around her like steel, holding her up. He would never let her fall.

"Let's go." She eased back and grinned. "My plans for the night just got a lot more interesting."

Chapter Twenty-Nine

Then

"You can't just bring a couple of pairs of shorts and T-shirts. What if the Minors want to take you out to dinner somewhere fancy?"

Gray snorted and tossed a pair of rolled-up socks in the open suitcase beside her on the bed. "The Minors aren't going to be home. Think you're missing the point, squirt. This is the final party before college. A long weekend to rip it up on the beach—"

"Yeah, because there are no beaches here." Jazz dug a pair of his board shorts out of the suitcase. "These are surfer shorts. You don't surf."

"Sure I do. Just not particularly well." Grinning, he snatched the shorts and tossed them back in the suitcase. "You should be happy I'm leaving. Now you'll get a whole long weekend to yourself to practice Krystal Sword's latest material in the basement without me prodding you to take it up a notch."

She wrapped her arms around her updrawn legs and dropped her chin to her knee. Moping wouldn't do her any good. Her life was going pretty well. She'd recently joined Gray's band for real—no more probationary period—and she'd made it through the school year with nothing lower than a C. She'd gotten her job at the waffle house, and it wasn't completely sucky.

Hell, she even had a couple of friends. And none of them laughed when she brought her not-quite-brother with her to parties. They were kind of a fixture now. Gray-and-Jazz. Jazz-and-Gray. Where one went, the other wasn't far behind.

Soon, he would be so far ahead of her that she couldn't ever hope to catch up.

"I wish I wasn't so fucking young," she whispered.

"Say what?" He started to laugh, but then he must've seen her face because he fell silent.

"Nothing. Never mind."

He sat beside her, too close as always. The boundaries between them seemed to grow thinner by the day, and a part of her rejoiced at that. The rest knew she couldn't let it happen. Somehow she had to erect barriers strong enough to keep him out.

Not when it came to her body. Sex was easy. She'd finally had it for the first time a couple of months ago when Gray was gone for a weekend visiting Berkeley. It had been fine. No big deal. She and the guy were still friendly. But matters of the heart were a different story. She'd already let Gray in way too far, especially since he was going to leave.

Forget *going to*. Every time she looked into his eyes, she saw that his bags were already mentally packed. He was ready to move on from life in suburban Vista View.

Ready to move on from life with *her*.

"You know, it's not going to be easy for me either," he said quietly. "You're my best friend. Do you honestly think I want to leave you?"

She couldn't restrain her laugh. "Dude, you're so eager to go. Don't even try to hide it."

"I'm eager to go somewhere new, try something different. But I'm not the least bit excited about leaving you." He grabbed her hand and rubbed his thumb over her knuckles. "I have an idea."

"Uh oh."

He grinned. "Let's you and me spend the weekend together. Somewhere far from here."

She blinked. Blinked again. She wasn't sure what he was suggesting, but the possibility made her tingles have little tingle babies. "You don't mean..."

"Let's go somewhere and get a room—a couple of rooms," he said quickly. "Bring our guitars and sit up playing all night, writing fucking awesome music."

And fucking. Please God.

But she didn't say that, because that couldn't happen for a million reasons. Not the least of which was that she wanted the Duffys to adopt her. Her screwing around with their son wouldn't exactly show them she was worthy of the title of *daughter.* Plus, it seemed seriously squicky. She and Gray weren't related, but if she legally became his sister, that would change things. And she really wanted to be a Duffy.

She also really wanted to have sex with Gray.

"You already have plans. Why would you want to break them to be with me?"

Lightly, he pinched the back of her hand. "You didn't seriously just ask that, did you? Hello, I've broken plans this entire year to be with you. We have fun together." He bumped her hip with his. "Don't we?"

"Guess so."

"Jeez, a little enthusiasm, please."

"Yes, we have fun. Always." She grinned and tried to tamp down on her growing excitement. "But where would we go?"

The width of his grin matched hers. "Anywhere. My graduation money's burning a hole in my pocket so it's dealer's choice."

"San Francisco," she said immediately, thinking of the stacks of postcards she'd sent away for from Chambers of Commerce all over the country.

Imagining where else she could go had helped make the lonely nights in random foster homes seem more bearable. She dreamed of traveling all over the world, but the Golden Gate bridge had always called loudest and longest to her. She'd imagined standing on it so many times, looking out across the water, her hair blowing behind her in the breeze. Bright sunshine warming her skin, filling her up inside so nothing bad could ever touch her again.

"How come?"

"Because it reminds me of freedom." She hadn't meant to say it aloud. She waited for him to tease her, but he only nodded.

"Yeah." He squeezed her hand. "Let's go to San Francisco."

Chapter Thirty

Now

This was either her brightest idea or her worst.

Several days later, flush from a day of beautification—a manicure, a spa wrap and a new haircut and color, despite the warnings from her stylist that she'd probably end up bald—Jazz pulled up in the driveway of the cabin. She'd really found her groove working with Deak and Simon, and she wanted to extend that streak. Perhaps she could even start knitting the band back together. The two factions of Oblivion would only be separate for a couple more days, and if she could start linking the two groups ahead of time, that would make their upcoming weekend sequester so much more tolerable.

She dug out her phone to text Gray.

Come out and help me.

His answer was nearly instantaneous. *You're here?*

She smiled, reading his anticipation in the question. *I am. Now get your butt out here.*

Coming. Both ways soon enough, I hope.

Depends how fast you move. She sent him a winky face then hopped down out of the truck.

She'd arrived a couple of hours early tonight, hoping they could maybe get some practice time in with the new material she'd purloined from Deak and Simon. They didn't mind her role as the band go-between, and they even seemed cool with her wanting to get Gray's feedback on the latest stuff they'd come up with.

And Nick's too, of course, assuming he was in the mood to play well with others. That was always anyone's guess. He'd had

Tori, the girl groupie with really big boobs, over the last few nights and that had mellowed him out a bit. So Jazz was hopeful he'd still be in good spirits tonight.

Jazz had just opened the back of the truck when the front door opened. As Gray's familiar cedarwood scent drifted over her, she let out a relieved breath. No weed tonight or any of the other nights since their argument over the sugar video. Just her Gray.

Thank God.

"Hey you. After the long day I've had, you're a sight for bleary eyes."

"Ouch. Bad one?"

"No, all good actually. We worked on three more songs, including one that Nick's been working on solo for a while. It's looking like we might even have a surplus to take into the studio. But the day's a million times better now." He tugged her into his arms and covered her mouth with his, swallowing the laughter that followed. His tongue slicked over hers, quick and hot, stirring her moan before he moved back and swept a hand over her hair. "Red now? Christ, woman, being with you is like getting a new chick every night."

"Do you like it? Check out the streak of pink." She ducked into the light beam from the truck and shook her head. "I cut a few inches off too."

"I love all of your looks."

"And here I thought you never noticed," she teased.

"You're always gorgeous." He rubbed a hunk of her hair between his fingers. "I do have a particular preference though."

For unknown reasons, her stomach sank. "Oh yeah? Which one?"

"The one where you have beautiful all dark hair without a hint of color in it but night. Because you trapped all the sunshine inside." He skimmed his fingers over her chin and tipped her face up to his again, sealing the words with a kiss.

"Aww." She framed his face between her hands and sighed into his mouth. "You say the sweetest things."

His smile turned wicked. "Just buttering you up for the dirty."

"Ha. Like you even need to." She shivered at the cool wind that tinkled through the miles of trees around them. Uncharacteristically cold weather had settled into the area and she'd spent most of the day shivering and imagining snuggling with Gray under the duvet.

"Let's get you inside." He slid his arm around her shoulders and pulled her against his side. Then he let out a startled laugh, evidently noticing her cargo. "Dude, you brought your drums? You moving in with me or what?"

She cocked an eyebrow. "I already did, smartass. We share an apartment, remember?"

"Mmm-hmm. I've had the pleasure of living with you for a good portion of my life. But from now on it'll be in the same bed." He leaned in the back of the truck and grabbed her disassembled drum kit, hauling up the pieces with an easy strength that almost distracted her from what he'd said.

Almost.

It shouldn't be that shocking to hear him talk about them being a real couple. She'd already said she wouldn't settle for anything less, and he'd indicated the same. But it was still so amazing to imagine that it could be so.

"We can actually share the same bed now," she said softly.

He turned back, his arms full of her kit, and grinned. "The minute we get back to our place, your stuff's moving into my room."

She picked up her drum stand and slammed the truck shut, then followed him across the lawn. "What if I want you to move into *my* room?"

"Mine's bigger."

"Is this some kind of gender stereotypical reference? Because my uterus can carry a baby. Unless your sword of destruction can do that, I win."

"Point taken." He choked out a laugh and shouldered open the front door. "I can't wait to see that, by the way."

Her breath caught. "See what?"

"You pregnant." He tossed her another of those mind-erasing grins and shoved his way into the foyer.

"Hey Nick," he called out. "Give us a hand."

She stopped in the doorway, her arms going lax. First they were going to share a bed. Now he wanted to see her pregnant.

God, she was simply going to burst from happiness if he didn't stop saying stuff like that. And best of all? He seemed like he was just talking off the top of his head.

Hell yeah, we're living together.

Hell yeah, we're going to have babies.

Hell yeah, I'm going to make you my princess bride and we'll ride off on golden steers—

"Yo, gimme that." Nick grabbed the stand out of her hands and headed into the living room. "You planning on being a permanent fixture here until we go back? Well, more than you already are?"

"Nah, I'm not camping out here." She booty-bumped the door shut. "I just figured since you guys are collaborating, and the three of us are too, that I could kind of be the bridge between the two groups until we get our weekend all together before we head into the studio. Deak and Simon are fine with it. The club shows have been going well—" She broke off, thinking of the awkward show with Gray at Rave. But since that night, he'd seemed fine. Mostly. "Anyway, they want your input on the stuff we've been coming up with."

"Yeah, Vapor and I have had a few breakthroughs too. Lo and fucking behold." The doorbell rang and Nick's smile turned lascivious as he strode past her to the door she'd just closed. "Hold that thought."

"Well hello there—" Nick began, his voice low and suggestive.

After that tone, she definitely hadn't expected to see a hulking bald tattooed man in the doorway. From Gray's chuckle behind her, neither had he.

"Switching teams, man?"

"Shut the hell up." Nick opened the door wider, allowing Jazz to get a better look at the visitor's face.

Her stomach wobbled. This was *not* good.

Gray's hand landed on her shoulder an instant before Nick spoke again. "Snake, what are you doing here?"

"Now is that any way to say hello to your old buddy?" Snake muscled his way into the foyer and gave Nick a hug that Nick returned with little enthusiasm.

"And look at this, my replacements are here too. It's like old fucking home week." Snake swaggered across the hall and stuck his hand out at Gray, ignoring Jazz completely. "What's up, man? Greg, isn't it?"

"Gray," he responded, clamping his palm that much tighter on Jazz's shoulder. "You remember Jazz."

Snake acted as if Gray hadn't spoken. Jazz shifted, moving more securely into the circle of Gray's arm. Not for protection, but because he'd tensed like a wild animal on the verge of leaping for the kill.

"Where is Tori?" Nick asked, bracing his arm on the open door. "How the hell did you find out where we're staying?"

"Tori's waiting in the car. She accidentally let it slip about the cabin's location and I offered to give her a ride here, seeing as we're old friends and all. Guess you guys had a little hot tub soiree type thing the other night?" Snake circled his finger. "She just thinks you're the hottest thing ever. Which kind of sucks for me, since we've been hitting it since that party backstage last year. Guess a current Oblivion guitarist is worth more than a has-been Oblivion drummer."

Nick shot Jazz a look. Jazz flung one at Gray, who stared at Snake as if he were the same sort of creature that he'd taken his name from.

"Okay, so you've got a thing for Tori. Works for me. She neglected to inform me that you two were acquainted." From Nick's thin smile, he'd be sharing his displeasure about that fact with her soon enough. "If you want to take her and go, by all means."

"Really, man? That's where we're at after all this time?" Snake shook his head and glanced at Gray. "You ever have a friend you've known since you were kids, one you'd give your goddamn life for, sell you out for the flavor of the month? Fucking blows."

"Yeah, I know what it's like to have a friend I'd give my life for." Gray tightened his embrace on Jazz. "You're looking at her."

Jazz's heart squeezed and she glanced up at Gray, unable to suppress her smile. But he wasn't looking at her. His attention was locked on Snake, who was glaring at Nick.

"That's not what happened and you know it. I had your back long after Simon and Deacon turned theirs. I fought to keep you in the band. You promised me you'd keep clean and you broke those promises time after time."

"Speaking of promises, I ran into someone else you guys know recently." Snake walked over to the door and closed it, leaning a beefy shoulder against the wood as if he expected someone to try to forcibly shove him out.

No one moved.

Jazz figured the guys were as shell-shocked as she was. This was just supposed to be a relaxing night hanging out. She'd hoped to continue the good streak they were on, and now they had this sneering giant of a dude causing shit.

Nick pushed a hand through his hair, his frustration leaking through. "Yeah? Who?"

"Not sure you know her, Nicky boy, but my man Gray over there sure does."

Jazz went cold. She didn't look at Gray but she didn't need to. The rigidity of the arm around her shoulders told her everything she needed to know.

What was coming next wouldn't be good.

"About five-six, long blonde hair, blue eyes. Fucking stacked—"

"Mind your manners, asshole." Gray stepped in front of Jazz as if Snake had thrown an actual punch her way rather than a metaphorical one. She didn't even think she was his intended target, just a casualty of his war with Nick, Deacon and Simon. Oblivion would always be *their* band, and he'd never stop seeing her and Gray as outsiders.

But at least before she'd had Gray on her side. Always. Right now, despite his solid frame blocking her view of Snake, she felt very much alone.

"Gray." She nudged him back but he didn't move. So she sidestepped him and slapped her best *I'm fine* smile on, the one that had served her well from facing her first foster mother at twelve to looking Mrs. Duffy in the eye at sixteen after her oldest son had tried to rape her.

She would never break in front of anyone.

"No, you shouldn't have to listen to his obnoxious BS. He came here just to start trouble. He doesn't know what the fuck he's—"

"Oh no? I saw you get in her car, fuckwit. Sweet black vintage Mustang, tricked out rims. She waved something at you, and you took it like the greedy bastard you are." His smile turned lethal. "See, thing is, bud, we travel in the same circles. Carson kids never manage to make it too far out of the hood, do they?"

"I'm not from fucking Carson." The disdain in Gray's voice turned the chill in her bones to ice. "Try about twenty miles north, asshole."

"Oh, right. You're the suburban rich kid who started slumming with the cute little foster kid who's so good at shaking her...sticks." Snake smiled and narrowed his eyes on Jazz. "You like to play with powder too, sweetness? Is that what they teach you up north?"

"Shut the fuck up." Gray went flying at Snake so fast that Jazz barely had time to get out of the way.

Stunned, she stumbled into the side table near the door, righting it and herself in time to hear Nick heave a sigh of epic proportions before he waded into the fray. Gray had the surprise advantage because he'd attacked Snake with a damn near flying tackle, but Snake outweighed him by a good forty pounds and was now showing that by shoving his meaty fists into Gray's ribs. Nick muscled his way between them, finally managing to separate them just as Jazz grabbed the frosted hurricane lamp on the table and swung it, nearly hitting Nick in the face.

"Hey, watch it," Nick yelled, ducking just in time.

"Sorry. So sorry."

She would've dashed around him and taken a cheap shot at Snake while Nick had a hand on his chest, but the blood blooming on Gray's white T-shirt snagged her attention before she could. She dropped the lamp on the table and rushed at Gray, dragging him back with her into the living room.

"Where are you hurt? Where did he hit you?" Even as the questions burst from her lips she saw the source of his bleeding. His nose gushed like a fire hydrant, the thick red liquid pouring out so fast that she choked out a cry.

"Get him out of here," she screamed at Nick.

"Fuckin' nosebleed, huh?" Snake called from behind them, his disgust palpable. "I barely touched the bastard's pretty face. Goddamn cokehead."

The words drove nails into her back, striking soft tissue that gave way from the pressure. She clutched Gray's shirt tighter and pushed him down on the couch, blocking them out. Snake was just throwing taunts. More nasty shit like the stuff he'd tossed out a few minutes ago. All he wanted to do was hurt them.

It wasn't real.

None of this was real.

She fell to her knees in front of Gray and dragged off her shirt, beyond caring about the catcalls coming from the front hall. Nick's voice rang out, loud and sharp, as he tried to force Snake to leave. Snake jeered about "pretty white tits" and she didn't so much as flinch. Nor did she cringe when he mentioned tabloids and headlines and singing his little heart out.

None of it made one iota of difference right now.

With trembling hands, she pressed the material to Gray's nose and instructed him to lean back, her voice gentle in direct counterpoint to the harshness that surrounded them.

Only Gray mattered.

* § *

He woke up in his bed. Not his bed at their apartment, but the bed at the cabin. Soft, dryer-fresh sheets tickled his chin and he smiled, remembering how his mom had always tucked him in when he was sick. The smile faded as the pain in his ribs kicked in, followed swiftly by the sting in his nose. *Sting* was a kind word for the brushfire incinerating his sinuses.

Sweet bloody hell.

"You're awake."

That voice did not belong to his mother. Or Jazz.

He opened one eye and groaned as the back of an iPad came into view. No. Jazz loved him. She wouldn't send the first horsewoman of the Apocalypse to his bedside unannounced.

"Doesn't look too bad." Cool fingers pressed on his jaw, tilting his face this way and that. "Not broken. Can one sprain one's nose?"

"Maybe one can, but I doubt *he* did," Nick said from behind her. "He barely took a hit. On the other hand, I took a knee to the goddamn balls—"

"God forbid your best days would be behind you in that arena. Fear not, I'm sure you'll live to mindlessly bang again." Lila sat on the edge of Gray's bed and shook back her wheat-colored hair. "Grayson, I didn't expect you to be my problem child."

It shouldn't have made him smile, especially since he was riding the knife's edge of pain and he had no clue where Jazz was. "You were saving that role for Nick, huh?"

"Saving it? The boy was born for that role."

"I'm not anyone's child, problem or otherwise." Nick strode out of the room and slammed the door, causing Lila's lips to twitch.

The instant he was gone, however, her polite mask fell away. "How deep are you?"

"Excuse me?"

"Don't fucking play games with me, Duffy. Jazz called and told me what Snake was insinuating. Poor girl's still naïve enough to believe he's just trying to start trouble for Oblivion, but we know better, don't we?"

At Gray's silence, she stood and loomed over the bed like a vicious angel of mercy. "I don't like nasty surprises, and you've already given me too many of them. She'll be back in a few minutes from the store. Either you tell me now or you tell me in front of your little sweetheart, but rest assured, your secrets will be mine."

He coughed and directed his attention at the window. Dawn was breaking in the distance, casting a milky grayish pall over the room. He must've slept the night away.

And this question wasn't going to get any easier if he put it off.

Swallowing hard, he darted a glance at the closed door. "It's not a big deal," he began.

"My husband has been addicted to OxyContin for seven years. He's what you call a functional drug user. That's what *he* calls it. I don't believe such a thing exists."

"You have a husband?" He'd never really thought much about her personal life, but she wasn't much older than they were. Not that they weren't old enough to be married. "How old are you?"

"Twenty-five."

"When did you get married?"

"Seven years ago." She tapped her flawless French manicure on her iPad. "Now if we can—"

"Wait, you married your husband even though he was a druggie?"

"It happens. Jazz would marry you, and you qualify."

He flushed and hated himself for it. "She doesn't see me that way."

"No, her rose-coloreds are pretty much welded to her face. There's also a part of her that gets off on saving the bad boy. She's not nearly as innocent as you've convinced yourself. Otherwise she wouldn't have snuck over here to seduce you the same day I told her to steer clear."

"Water?" Gray croaked.

Sighing, she plucked a cup off the nightstand. He drained the mug and handed it back then threw his arm over his face, earning a stitch in his bruised ribs for his trouble. That fucker Snake had hands like ham hocks.

"I owe some people some money," he said finally, once it became obvious that Lila would wait until the end of time for him to come clean.

He'd emptied his savings and given the cash to Cricket as a down payment on the half he'd promised to get them in short order. She'd seemed pleased, and he hadn't gotten any threatening phone calls since.

He'd also kept Jazz at his side every moment that he could.

"How much money?"

He named a ballpark estimate of his remaining debt and Lila hissed out a breath. "What the hell is wrong with you? Do you want to get hurt?"

"I've got it under control."

"You're not seriously going to sit—I'm sorry, lay—there and tell me you're handling this. If Snake knows the kind of company you keep, so do other people. That's not even mentioning your dealer. How long before she contacts a tabloid and sells the story to make up for all the cash you're not giving her? And that's if they don't extract their payment from your flesh first." She shoved his leg. "Or worse, your hands. They might not heal correctly. And what about Jazz? Are you ready for her to have to watch her back every time she walks out the door? Like right now. She's parked at some corner drugstore, blithely picking up some Tylenol, and someone could be waiting outside, about to pounce—"

"Stop it." Gray shot upright in bed and fisted his hands in his hair. "Don't fucking do this to me."

He'd already been having nightmares about that very possibility. The only thing that made them go away was turning to Jazz in the night and draining all of his fear into making love to her, over and over. Reassuring himself that his beautiful girl was whole and strong and his, and no one would ever hurt her again.

Least of all him.

"I didn't do it. *You* did it." Lila dropped down on the bed and flicked her finger across her iPad screen before turning the tablet toward him. Jazz beamed out of the photo, her eyes brighter than the sky on a summer day. Smile blinding. "Look at her and tell me you could live with yourself if she paid the price for your sins."

He grabbed the iPad and scrolled to the next picture. It was another of Jazz, this one at their concert at Red Rocks. She sat behind her kit, her head thrown back. The pink and blue spotlights picked up the gold dust on her skin. The irony wasn't lost on him. She'd always sparkled. A jewel in a morass of rocks.

His island of safety in the center of a world covered in landmines.

"I won't let this touch her," he whispered, knowing he already had. He'd not only let it touch her, he'd invited it into their bed.

"It already is. If it affects you, it affects her." She took back her iPad and tapped the screen. "I'm transferring the sum you mentioned into your account. I want you to pay every penny to the spinecrackers you owe. Understand me?"

His hand went lax on the sheets. "But—"

"I don't want a Hallmark moment about this. You're a commodity I want to protect, as is Jasmine. But make no mistake. If I find out you didn't pay every red cent of this advance on your future income to those you're indebted to, or if you don't keep your fucking nose clean, you will not only be cut off, you'll be out of the band. End of story. I have no use for drug addicts." She rose. "If Jasmine is smart, neither will she."

The door squeaked open and Jazz poked her head in. "I heard my name."

Gray's shoulders relaxed, the tension that had gripped him easing away at the sight of his girl's tremulous smile. "Of course you did. You're my favorite subject. Get in here."

She slipped inside the room and waved a small white bag. "I brought you a couple of kinds of pain pills. Hopefully something will work." She set the bag down on the nightstand and bit her lip, her gaze pingponging from Lila to Gray and back again. "Are you okay? How are you feeling?" She moved forward to fuss with the sheets. "Your color's better at least and—"

"Baby, stop." He gripped her wrist and brought her hand to his mouth. "You've done enough. You need some sleep."

"How do you know I haven't slept?"

"Because he knows you." Lila patted her shoulder and walked to the door. "Thanks for calling me. I know it must not have been easy."

Jazz sank on the edge of the bed. "No, it really wasn't." She sent Gray a look under her lashes. "But Snake obviously intends to cause problems. Better we deal with them now."

"True enough. A wise woman faces an enemy head-on." Lila pivoted to face them once more. "Your work sabbatical is ending a couple of days early. From your shows and the material you're producing, it appears that you've made considerable progress, which is what this was all about. Bring your songs and yourselves to Ripper Records at ten a.m. tomorrow."

"Tomorrow as in later today? Or tomorrow tomorrow?"

Lila offered Jazz a rare smile. "Tomorrow tomorrow. Enjoy your last day and night in paradise." She gave Gray a glance heavy with things unsaid. "Make sure you come back prepared to work your asses off. One date remains on your club tour and we have a video to shoot, then you're heading into the studio. We want to keep this momentum going."

"Got it. Thanks, Lila."

"You're welcome. Feel better," she said to Gray, pulling the door shut behind her.

Jazz screwed up her mouth and gazed down at her hands. "So on a scale of one to ten, how pissed are you at me right now?"

He laughed and gripped his ribs at the twinge of pain. "Ow. Fucker. Next time I'm going to use his bald head to polish the floor."

"Sure you are, honey."

He laughed again. "I'm not pissed at you at all. Well, maybe a two. She didn't threaten to dismantle me from the balls up, so whatever you said must've smoothed over the waters pretty good." *And you inadvertently got me the money I needed.*

Definitely couldn't be pissed about that.

"When I told her Snake had tried to kick her guitarist's ass, she seemed to lose some of her interest in what Snake was spouting off about. Though she did ask me a kind of weird question." Jazz frowned. "When I told her I had something to tell her, the first thing she said was, 'it's not you and Nick again, is it?'"

"Hmm. If I didn't think she had more taste than that, I'd wonder if our uptight label rep had a thing for Mr. Personality Plus. But she told me she's married so that can't be it."

She snorted. "Yeah, because people never cheat."

He slid over on the mattress and held out his arm. "C'mere. It's been too long since I've held you."

"Are you sure? I don't want to hurt you."

"Holding you could never do that. Besides, hello, big tough guy here."

Her giggle as she settled in beside him eased the fist gripping his gut. "Oh, I know that. I almost didn't run out to get you pain pills. You're too hardcore to ever need them." She reached up to feather her fingers over his nose, as lightly as a breeze. "You bled so much. I wanted to call 911 but Nick stopped me. So I called Lila instead."

"She is the fixer of all of Oblivion's problems." He cleared his throat. "I, ah, about what Snake said—"

"I know he just wanted to cause trouble."

"Jazz—"

"I bet that blonde he described is the one I saw you at the club with, right? So that's not even a thing, because I know about her. You said you didn't sleep with her and I believe you."

"Jazz, listen to me."

"It's not like the rest even merits a mention. We're best friends. You wouldn't hide that from me, no matter what." At his silence, she lifted her trembling chin. "Right?"

He tightened his hold on her and fought to focus on her face rather than the cramping in his belly. "I need you to listen to me, okay, baby? Just let me say it all before I lose my nerve."

"Oh God." She swung her legs over the side of the bed and gripped her stomach, rocking back and forth. "No. Don't. If you don't say it, it's not real."

Swallowing hard, he rubbed her back. "I'm going to stop. I swear to you, this is the end of it." Her choked sob made him close his eyes. "God, don't cry. Please."

"I'm not crying. It's fucking allergies."

He scooted forward on the bed—pain be damned—and slid his arm around her waist before pressing his cheek to her back. "I don't want it between us. I don't want anything there. If I didn't quit for any other reason, I would for that one. How I feel about you is stronger than any drug."

The sound of her quiet weeping ripped a blade through his chest. "Why? You always warned me away from everything. You wouldn't touch the stuff, ever."

He exhaled, tightening his grip on her. She was so soft. So easy to break. "Something happened. I let it push me to a dark place, and I slipped. I messed up. And then I kept doing it."

"What happened?"

The image formed in his mind, as stark as the colored spotlights that had nearly blinded him that night. Nick coming out of a storage closet near the stage, still doing up his zipper. Jazz—his Jazz—following a moment later, still touching up her lipstick. Her hair tousled and wild, with that sleepy sex smile still curving her mouth.

But he couldn't tell her. Couldn't lay the blame at her doorstep when he'd made the choice that day and every day since.

"I thought one of my had dreams died," he said, fisting his hand against her side. "I never expected to get another chance. Now that I am, you can be sure I won't give it up for anything."

She turned toward him on the bed, drawing her leg up. One glimpse of her blotchy, tear-stained face and his heart convulsed. "Was it because of that stupid threesome?" She dashed at her tears. "It was the biggest mistake ever. I don't know what I was thinking—"

"No. That wasn't it. It was before then."

"B-before? How much before?"

"A little while. And I know what you were thinking. I always knew, as much as I hated that I wasn't enough for you." He cupped her cheek and closed his hand around the tears he caught in his palm. "You wanted love. He gave it to you before I could."

"No. No, that's not true. You always loved me better than anyone else. After Brent, everything got so fucked up. There was always this wall between us, and I couldn't find my way through."

"What he did was one wall. What I did to push him to that point was another."

"What? How did you have anything to do with Brent's actions?"

Her confusion just added another layer to the self-disgust coating his throat. "You never saw me the way I truly am.

Christ, I wanted to be a hero in your eyes. You saw me as selfless when the reality is I tried to be your entire world so you wouldn't notice I didn't measure up."

"No." Her shoulders hunched and she bowed her head, her cheerful hair only emphasizing the bleakness in her eyes. "I know you better than I know myself. The man I know never did anything to hurt me. Not once."

If only that were true.

"Come here." When she didn't move, he hauled her against his chest, tightening his arms until she gasped against his throat. Her tears came harder, racking her shoulders. He pressed his cheek against her head, rocking her as carefully as a child. "I love you with everything I am," he whispered once her sobs began to slow. "You deserve the best, and I'm going to give it to you."

She tipped her damp face up to his and drew her quivering thumb over his lower lip. "I love you too. And you're the best I could ever ask for."

He dipped his forehead against hers. "I'm going to stop. I promise."

She nodded so quickly that he would've chuckled if he hadn't been a deep breath away from tears himself. "Yes. We'll do it together. Whatever you need. I'll help you." Her lips lifted hesitantly, the double rainbow bonus after a destructive thunderstorm. "I'm good at projects."

Now he did laugh, hard enough to elicit the tears he'd battled back. He closed his eyes before they fell, but one snuck through, cutting a shameful path down his cheek. "I'm sorry. God, I'm so fucking sorry, baby."

"You have nothing to be sorry for. You gave up everything for me. Everything. Your brother, your parents. You turned your back on them to protect me and I let you down. I left you alone—"

"No." He grabbed her face, shaking her more than he'd meant to. "Goddammit, no. You aren't to blame for any of this. I did it. *Me*, Jazz. I knew what I was doing, and I kept doing it. I did it before the second night we were together. God, oh God, I even wanted you to try it too. So don't you ever *ever* say that you did anything wrong. It was me. I'm the wrong one."

"No." She shook her head, tears streaming. Breath hiccupping until each stutter echoed in the pit of his chest like an aborted heartbeat. "I won't let you face this alone. Let me share the burden."

"You are. You're here with me, and I can face anything now."

"*We'll* face it," she said fiercely. "Like we face everything. Together."

"Yes. Lila gave me an advance, and I'll get square with the people I owe. This is almost over." He gathered her in close and buried his face in her hair, smearing his tears in the silky strands. Hiding them like a humiliating secret. "Just don't leave me. Please."

"I won't. We're a team. Always."

Drawing strength from her words and her solid warmth in his arms, he swallowed and edged back. "In my shaving kit in the bathroom, there's a baggie. Flush it down the toilet. I don't want to see it or know it ever existed."

She didn't hesitate. She slid away from him and rubbed her palms over her cheeks before climbing off the bed and marching into the bathroom. As small as she was, she brought to mind a fierce warrior, ready to do battle in her off-the-shoulder top and skinny jeans.

He closed his eyes at the flush of the toilet, imagining all that pretty powder draining away. And when she walked back to him and whispered, "it's done," he realized she wore one of his shirts, wrapping his scent around her even as she faced the reality of his failures.

She'd used her favorite vintage Sex Pistols T-shirt to mop up his blood. Whipping it off without a thought to try to take away his pain.

Inhaling a ragged breath, he nodded and pulled her close. He pressed his face against her breasts, the gentle thud of her heartbeat as calming as the sound of the surf coming in at high tide. Jazz's love burned inside him now, and nothing else mattered.

He laid his lips on that steady beat, smiling as it sped just from his nearness. She scooped her hand through his hair, gently soothing, and he turned his mouth to her breast. He drew her nipple between his teeth through the shirt, drowning in her summery watermelon scent and the hint of cinnamon from the cabin's soap on her skin. Those two smells shouldn't have worked together, but on her they were the perfect mixture of spicy and sweet.

Pushing his hands under her shirt, he rolled it upward until he glimpsed her black-and-white bra. The tiny bow in the middle might've made it chaste, if not for the quickness of her breathing pushing her breasts up and almost over the tops of the cups. One flick of his fingers and they spilled free, hopelessly vulnerable, her skin flushing prettily before he closed his mouth around her nipple and sucked in earnest.

Her soft moan washed over him, barely loud enough to reach his ears. He slipped his hand between her legs and cupped her, relishing the pulse that built there too, a butterfly beat against his palm. He licked his way from one breast to the other, giving them both special attention, lapping at the taut peaks while their color bloomed from pink to a needy red. He continued down her belly, shifting onto his stomach on the bed, ignoring his aches and pains in favor of peeling away her snug jeans to reveal the boy shorts beneath.

The damp spot that bloomed on the material beckoned his tongue. He pressed it to her mound and swirled it up and down, chasing the flavor that he'd already become addicted to. When he couldn't wait another second, he pulled the side over and slid his mouth over her damp folds, absorbing the sigh that went through her and the pinch of her fingers on his hair as if they were as essential as breath. More so, because he'd felt like he'd stopped breathing for months and being there with her, feeling her swell and grow wetter with each erotic kiss, gave him a head rush unlike any other.

The roaring in his ears expanded, blocking out the world except for Jazz and the tiny, impatient pumps of her hips against his face. Knowing that she was trying to restrain herself made him chuckle, as did her growl and insistent tug on his hair, pulling him into her heat. He pushed her jeans and underwear down, freeing them from her legs. Then he banded his arm around the back of her thighs and drew her close, opening her up with the fingers of his opposite hand and teasing her clit and her piercing with the tip of his tongue. He moved down, seeking her entrance, closing his eyes at the suction of her flesh.

Pain raced along his scalp as she seized hold of his hair and gyrated against his face. So open and unabashed in her pursuit of pleasure. He dragged his fingers through her wetness and offered them up to her to lick off. A glimpse of her pink tongue slipping over the twisted silver ring he wore renewed the heavy pounding between his legs. He felt huge. Too sensitive to touch.

She gripped his hand in both of hers as she sucked him dry, swallowing her flavor without hesitation. Her tongue rode his knuckles, twined around his fingers. Just her stare and her wet kisses held him entranced. When her teeth grazed his palm, his cock jerked against his zipper and he groaned, impossibly lost.

Fuck, he could come just from the feel of her mouth on his skin. *Any* part of his skin.

Going any speed other than fast with her was basically a fantasy. He had a lifetime to make up for. Even spending the rest of his days inside her wouldn't be enough to settle the debt.

Unable to wait another second, he fell backward and tugged her with him. Curtained by her hair, lost in his need, he lowered his zipper and freed his cock, letting out a groan of gratitude as she took control. One flex of her hips and he was inside her, her body splayed on his chest, her mouth moving with his. She cupped the back of his neck and lifted up before sinking down and taking him deeper. So deep that he couldn't do anything but stare into the slumberous blue eyes that held him hostage while she started to ride.

She braced her hands on his torso and rolled him inside her, again and again. Slowly, sweetly, she ruled him. Her piercing scraped over his cock, sending a bolt of lightning down his spine, and he jolted off the bed. His ribs protested and he didn't give a shit. Glimpsing the tight red crests of her breasts playing peekaboo between her arms as her hips undulated and her pussy enveloped him, slick and hot, exceeded any toll on his body.

Hooking one hand under her knee, he pulled her leg up and drew her head down, savoring the hiss of her breath against his cheek. Her heartbeat thundered in time with his, a race they would both win.

Together.

"I love you," he murmured. She trembled with him, around him, and slid her hand up his abdomen to his heart. He laced his fingers with hers and brought them to his mouth, kissing her knuckles as she shuddered and tumbled over that final rise.

"I love you," she echoed, her words following him into the glorious spiral of oblivion.

Falling, falling until only peace remained.

Chapter Thirty-One

Then

"Keep walking. Straight ahead. Bump. Step up. Your eyes are closed, right?"

"Oh my God, you can't do this to me again. It's not Christmas."

"Good because I couldn't fit this in a box. Okay, slight left. Straight. No peeking. Step down...and open your eyes."

His hands dropped away as her eyes opened and the world spread out in front of her. Jewel-blue water glistened beneath the arches she'd dreamed about for so long that she'd taken to sketching them in her composition notebook. This was the bridge that would take her from her current reality to a whole new one.

And now it was almost close enough for her to touch.

"Oh Gray!" Jazz rushed to the railing of the balcony of their hotel room, leaning forward so far that she lost her footing. She gave a little screech but he was already hauling her back, his arms clamped securely around her midsection. She laughed and turned to face him, her hair blowing all over her face as the wind whipped it into a frenzy. And then it wasn't the wind whipping her up any longer but his intense gray gaze riveted to her face.

To her mouth.

"Is it everything you were hoping for?" he murmured, and she had the feeling that he wasn't only asking about the view. He was asking about *them*. About how it felt to have his hard, muscled chest against her breasts and his ropey arm holding her close. His heat surrounded her, chasing away the chill coming in off the bay. His lips were a fraction of an inch away, and if she inched upward, she'd be able to smell the scent of cherry cola on his breath.

"Better." It was. So much better than she'd ever dreamed.

Lights twinkled to life in the early pink haze of dusk, and the sky glimmered with an endless canopy of microscopic stars. Gray tilted his head and eradicated the space between them, his intent clear.

The kiss she'd fantasized about for so long could be hers, and *here* of all places. She'd never dared to dream this big.

Yet all she could think was she would never have a mother again if she didn't say no.

"Such a gorgeous view." She whirled away to press her hands on the water-spattered balcony. She leaned forward again and this time he didn't drag her back, just let her hang in the balance between the two lives she wanted with equal fervor.

The one where she was his sister.

And the one where she was his lover. His love.

"Jazz?"

She heard the uncertainty in the question, and it twisted another blade in her heart. How many nicks could one organ stand, she wondered, before it finally ceased to beat?

"I can't believe you got a room so close to the bay. It must've cost a mint. We'll have to rent bikes and ride them across. The tour guide I bought says—"

"Jazz. Look at me."

She wouldn't. She couldn't. Because he would see that she wasn't at all certain about the choice she had made, and then he would take the choice away.

She couldn't say no to him twice. Not when he held the entire scope of her dreams in his hands, like a guitar only he knew how to play.

"Jazz."

His hands touched her shoulders and she bowed her head, helpless to stop her babbling. She couldn't let the silence fill in the rift she'd opened up between them, simply because she wanted too much. "We have to go to Fisherman's Wharf. And oh God, the Art Institute. Did you know that—"

He turned her to face him and she couldn't bear to meet his eyes. So she did the one thing she always did when the world got to be too much. She burrowed her face against his chest and clung to his strong arms and hoped like hell he couldn't feel the heat from her face through his T-shirt.

"It's okay." He rubbed his hand over her hair, his gentle touch finally making her realize that she was shaking hard enough to rock them both. "We're okay."

"I forgot my sunglasses," she whispered, and he pulled her that much closer.

"No, you didn't. I have them in my suitcase."

Then she started to cry.

Chapter Thirty-Two

Now

Jazz rolled her tube of gloss over her mouth and narrowed her eyes at her reflection. She'd just finished a quick shower and was on her way to meet Simon and Deak in the steam room for a pow-wow on "Echoes" and "Undertow", their latest two finished songs.

Well, until the other guys got their hands on them. But at least they had good material to present to the team at Ripper Records. That might improve Lila's mood regarding Gray's substance issue, though she'd been remarkably composed when she left the cabin. Maybe things were finally looking up.

A girl could hope.

She dug through her purse and pulled out her birth control, biting her lip as she saw how many pills remained. She'd skipped a few days, what with everything going on. Truth be told, she often skipped a few days, because it wasn't like she was regularly sexually active.

Until now.

It probably wasn't a big thing to skip. As long as she caught up now, she'd be fine.

She swallowed her pills, chasing them with a bottle of water from the mini bar. Then she glanced at her watch and judged she'd have just enough time before she had to meet the guys.

Sitting on the bed, she pulled out her phone and tapped in the number she'd looked up online earlier. She felt vaguely seasick, but that wasn't surprising. She hadn't talked to Mrs. Duffy in years. She wasn't exactly making contact now for a social call. At any rate, she refused to reveal too much. She owed her allegiance to Gray. No matter her reasons for taking this step, she wouldn't violate his confidence.

The phone rang twice before Conchita picked up. Jazz smiled at the sound of the Duffys' long-term housekeeper's lightly accented, musical voice and asked to speak with Eileen without giving away her identity. Conchita pressed for it, but Jazz stayed firm that it was a surprise.

A surprise, yes, but she also didn't want to give Gray's mother a chance to refuse the call.

"Hello," Mrs. Duffy said after a moment, her tone coolly pissed. She wasn't used to people refusing her demands—or the demands of her staff. "Can I help you?"

Despite the edge to her voice, she still sounded like the woman Jazz had loved so much. Everything that had happened had sent that love into hiding, but it only took a few syllables to bring it roaring to the forefront again.

Now if only she could speak.

"Hello? Is anyone there?"

Jazz gripped her phone tighter. "Hi. It's Jazz. Jazz...Edwards," she added into the silence, trying to ignore the twist in her gut from the realization that perhaps Mrs. Duffy had shoved her into the back of her mind.

To Jazz, Mrs. Duffy had been a second mother. A *better* mother. In Mrs. Duffy's eyes, Jazz had been the girl who shattered her family.

"Jazz? Is that really you?"

Don't analyze her tone. She doesn't sound hopeful, and if she does, it's not because she wants to talk to you. And that's fine. Her priority is and should always be her son.

"Yes. It's me." Jazz cleared her throat. "How are you?"

"Better now. How are you?"

"I'm good." How could they talk so pleasantly when their last meeting had been so full of vitriol and pain? The intervening years acted as a kind of buffer, sheltering them both. "Gray's good too."

Lie number one. She hoped there wouldn't be half a dozen more before the conversation ended.

Mrs. Duffy exhaled, clearly relieved. "I'm so glad. I've called him so many times but—"

"You have?" Jazz couldn't smother her surprise. "He never mentioned it to me."

"He doesn't take my calls. Doesn't respond to my letters. I leave him voicemails and I send him notes, but I get nothing in return." His mother chuckled humorlessly. "That's my son. Stubborn to a fault." She paused. "I don't doubt he's been influenced to keep up his lack of communication as well."

"You think I've asked him to stay away from you?"

The knowledge shouldn't have wounded her. What else would Mrs. Duffy think? She obviously saw Jazz as the ho who had teased one son into going too far and cried rape then prodded the other son into breaking up his family.

Except she *hadn't* cried rape. Gray had hassled her about going to the cops so many times during those weeks she'd lived at the Duffys after the attack, and she'd always said no. She'd insisted it was a family matter. Brent had just slipped up.

She hadn't truly believed that. If Gray hadn't come in when he had, Brent wouldn't have stopped. He'd been so close to ripping part of her away that she never could've gotten back.

The first few months after, she'd thought he had succeeded anyway, even without completing the rape.

If drinking too much brought that kind of behavior out of a person, they obviously weren't fully balanced to begin with. But God, she hated being the reason Gray and Brent had stopped speaking. Gray had ostracized himself from the people he loved because of her.

"I'm not saying you specifically asked him to not to talk to his family, Jasmine."

"I didn't. I never would have. In fact, I asked him just the opposite." Jazz pressed her fingers to her eyes. "I took myself out of the situation. Brent's reaction to me was the problem, so I left. I fully intended to leave Gray behind permanently too. For the first couple of years, I didn't speak to him at all, so I didn't even know he'd stopped communicating with you and your husband. He moved out and into his own place without me even being aware of it."

"He believed he was upholding your honor."

"He's a wonderful man. You raised him that way."

Mrs. Duffy didn't say anything.

"I also didn't want to let you and Mr. Duffy go. Sometimes there aren't any choices."

"Yes, there are. Once you started talking to him again, you could've chosen to urge him to come back to us. But you didn't. You continued to lead him on, just as you led on Brent—"

"We're together," she whispered. "Gray and me. We're in love."

The silence that descended was so absolute that Jazz felt its echo in her chest like the reverberation from the amps. She wasn't on stage right now but she might as well have been. It felt like a spotlight shone directly on her, highlighting her flaws. She would come up lacking. She always had.

"Well," Mrs. Duffy said. "I can't say I'm surprised."

"You're not?"

"I always saw what was between you. That's why I didn't understand why you ever looked at Brent. Perhaps the first name didn't matter as much as the last."

Jazz pressed her fist against her mouth to stifle the cry that nearly escaped. *I won't cry. No matter what.* "I never 'looked at' Brent. He scared the hell out of me from the first day I met him. No, actually he scared me the first time I saw his picture. He needs help, and I hope he got it." She blew out a breath.

"Not for him as much as for you and your husband. And for Gray. I know you all love him. But—"

"Brent committed suicide last month. So no, Jasmine, he didn't get the help he needed, if he needed any at all. I guess we'll never know now, will we?" Mrs. Duffy let out a sound that bordered on a sob. "Thanks to you, I've lost both of my sons."

The dialtone blared in her ear until Jazz pressed hard on the End button to make it stop.

She glanced blearily around her luxurious suite, the details bleeding together. The thousand thread count sheets underneath her didn't register. The silk draperies hiding a slice of bright morning sun didn't intrude on the darkness that had overtaken her mind. She'd been staying there for the better part of two weeks, and she'd barely noticed any of the high-end amenities because she'd been so full of Gray. The suite had just been a place to crash in between spa visits and working with Deak and Simon. Now their sabbatical was almost over and she and Gray were about to go back to their regular lives.

What could ever be regular again?

Oh God, she had to tell him about Brent. Which meant she'd have to tell him about calling his mother. She'd planned to encourage Mrs. Duffy to push for a visit without actually saying why Gray needed his family back in his life, and she hadn't even managed to.

Instead she'd discovered something that might shatter Gray's newfound sobriety.

She knew the man as well as she knew herself—and his recent admission hadn't changed her conviction on that score—and she had no doubt about his response to what had happened. He wouldn't react favorably to her contacting his mother. No matter her reasons, he'd view it as a betrayal. And that wasn't even including what she'd learned about Brent.

Sucking in a deep breath, she gripped her phone as a text message came through. She nearly smiled at Simon's note.

Yo, purple pandemic. We are steaming out our impurities and you iz not here. Get a move on, luscious. xoxo

Only Simon could say *xoxo* and retain his over-the-top masculinity. The kissy face cat sticker he sent next turned her smile from tentative to real, at least until she headed into the bathroom to face her stark reflection. The mascara she'd put on made her eyes look sunken and morose. The streaks of green eyeshadow she'd chosen to go with her kicky new red hair color seemed garish.

Clown on the outside, crying on the inside. Isn't that always the way?

She couldn't tell Gray yet. It wasn't that she wanted to jealously guard their new coupledom for a bit longer. Yes, she'd waited forever to be with him, but that wasn't the point. His family mattered more. But she wasn't about to say anything so soon after he'd vowed not to touch any substances again. She'd be damned if she caused him to relapse.

Somehow she'd find a way to tell him. Soon. Once he had a bit better handle on things.

God, she'd just wanted him to have his family's support. He needed that. He deserved it. If she'd believed that telling him about Brent would push him to get closer to his family again, she would've hopped on it in a second. Despite how Mrs. Duffy felt about Jazz, she was Gray's mother. Jazz would never ask him to choose. He'd already chosen for too long.

But that wouldn't happen. The last thing she wanted was for him to think she'd broken his confidence. He'd hear "I called your mom" and immediately assume she'd gone to tattle about his drug problem. He'd made it clear years ago that he was done with his family, and he expected her to respect that decision.

At the knock on the suite door, she sighed. Probably Simon or Deak had come to collect her. She hurried to open it. On the other side stood a deliveryman with an enormous bouquet of wildflowers. She couldn't even identify all of the scents and colors.

"Ms. Jasmine Edwards?"

"Yes, that's me." She blinked, more than a little knocked off-kilter, and held out her arms for the bouquet. "Whoa, wow. These are incredible."

He smiled. "Someone must love you very much."

"I guess so. Thank you." She dug out a five from her jeans pocket and gave it to him, then shut the door and pried out the card.

This is only the beginning of our forever. Meet me at the Grab 'n Go in Vista View at five o'clock. Love, G.

The Grab 'n Go? What the hell? There was a blast from the past. And Vista View, his hometown. Last she heard the Duffys had moved farther north, but that was still too close for comfort.

Guilt surged, knotting her throat. She wouldn't wait long to tell him about the phone call. For a few days, she would help him get his bearings and deal with walking away from his addict—no, his *usage*—of coke. After he'd had a chance to regain his equilibrium, she'd tell him everything.

She lowered her face to the flowers and took a heady sniff. They both wanted forever.

Hopefully his idea of it looked like hers.

* § *

"All right, try that again. After we sing 'ooh, ooh, ooh' you should come in on the—hello? You alive over there?"

"Yeah." Gray pulled his hand out of his pocket like the guilty schoolboy he knew he must look like. He adjusted his hold on his guitar and strummed the strings, trying to loosen up his fingers.

His whole body ached. One part of that had to do with his first almost full day without coke, weed or even a Tylenol. Another part had to do with the box-shaped rock in his jeans. He'd driven out to the jewelers right after Jazz had left that morning, with the certainty he couldn't wait. The need to make this move now before anything else went wrong was an imperative he couldn't ignore.

He'd put her at risk with his actions. Now he'd begun taking the steps to prove that he could keep her safe and happy and give her more love than she'd ever dreamed.

"I think I need a couple minutes to limber up," he muttered as he stumbled over the frets and produced a sound that resembled a dying cat.

"You've been limbered for half an hour. What's the deal?" Nick shoved his guitar between his knees. "Man, if you're fucking using—"

"I'm not, okay? After last night, it's finished. I can't have people walking around talking shit about my...issue."

"It's not an issue, it's a habit. And every time you pussy around without calling it what it is, you show how deep you are." Nick dug his crumpled pack of smokes out of his jeans pocket. "See these? I'm addicted. Know how I know? Because when I'm stressed or pissed or even goddamn horny, one of the first things I look for are my cigs. They're my crutch. I toss them out and then when I can't hang, I go buy more. Pretending I can stop at any moment is just me being a lying addict instead of just an addict."

Gray dug his thumbs into the corners of his eyes. "Not the same and you know it."

"No, mine's legal. Which means I don't have any reason not to do it all day long until I run out of air and can't sing anymore. You know, my fucking job."

"You can't smoke all day long around Simon. He'd kick your ass for screwing with his voice. He's been touchy about it lately."

"Like I care? Addicts don't. They want their fix when they want it and to hell with the beautiful brunettes who love them."

The corner of Gray's mouth lifted. "She's a redhead this week."

"My sister had a saying. Only the color of the shag rug counts. All the rest is window dressing."

Gray tried not to laugh. He honestly did. "Jesus. You have a sister?"

"Yeah. A twin."

"Huh." Gray scratched the back of his neck. "She like you?"

Nick smirked. "If you're asking if she'd bust your balls too, the answer is hell yes. Ricki never took shit from anyone. Of course, it's easier to do that when you're high."

Something in his voice struck a chord and Gray set aside his guitar and leaned forward, rubbing his suddenly ice cold hands together. "You haven't asked me."

"About what?"

"About why I told you to keep an eye on Jazz."

Nick jerked a shoulder and tossed his cigs on the side table. "Why ask what I already know? You're worried the people you owe might take a cut out of her. You're right to worry. Those bastards don't mess around."

"But you didn't lecture me."

"What good would that do? If you don't want to quit, me saying you should means nothing. And you don't need to ask me to have her back. I've been watching out for her ever since I saw that baggie of yours hit the studio floor."

When Gray started to speak, Nick held up a hand. "Don't bother. It's not about me being in love with her. She's my friend. I may not have a lot of them, but those I have I fucking value with my life." He glanced off into the distance. "I already had to let one go that I wasn't ready to. That's one too many."

"Snake?"

Nick just nodded.

Gray encircled the fingerboard of his Epiphone, holding on when it felt like the ground beneath his feet could crack open at any moment. "Thank you for caring about her."

"Yeah." Nick shut his eyes and dropped his head back against the chair. "See, that shit right there is why she's with you, not me. You're a decent guy. You just got fucking lost. We all do. Some don't find their way back, mainly because they don't have a good enough reason to." He opened his eyes. "You do."

"Yeah." Gray tightened his grip on his guitar. "I do."

"Okay, well, uh, this has been some awesome spiritual crap and all, but I'm pretty sure my nuts are shriveling up the longer we talk. We gonna play or what?"

"I'm going to ask her to marry me."

Nick didn't say anything for so long that Gray had no choice but to look up and meet his gaze. "Okay."

"I thought you should know. Considering..."

"Considering she slept with me as a substitute for you?" Nick grabbed his cigs again and pulled one out with his teeth. "Now there's a sentiment you don't often see on a greeting card."

Gray shook his head and traced his thumb over the years of scars on his guitar. They held so many stories, ones he'd never find enough words to tell. "This is some seriously fucked-up shit. Most of all because I honestly think we could be friends, and that seems wrong."

"Why? You think you're supposed to bash my head open because I found your hot girlfriend hot?"

His mouth twitched. Damn Nick had a way of breaking it all down. "Something like that."

"You'd only do that if you thought I was serious competition, and we both know I'm not. So I'll buy a fucking bag of rice for your wedding and hope like hell you know what you're doing."

"I'm quitting. For real."

"And I'm the douche who wants to believe you." Nick bit down on the cigarette between his teeth, breaking it in half before he dumped the ends on the table. "By the way, I'm not fucking hugging you even if you say that the Pope is going to marry you at the Basilica."

Gray laughed. "You think they'd be cool with marrying a foster brother and sister? My guess is probably not."

"I think I heard that story in a country song once." Nick grinned. "So we playing or what?"

Gray dragged his guitar in his lap. He had a couple hours yet before it was time for him to meet up with Jazz. Might as well spend it doing his favorite thing.

He smiled and plucked the opening notes to "Sugar Kiss". *Second* favorite thing.

"Yeah. Let's play."

* § *

"Buy a kitten, miss? Don't you want to buy a kitten?"

Jazz stopped outside the supermarket and let out a squeal at the pair of furry, wiggling kittens. The kid manning the box couldn't have been any more than twelve. "Oh, I can't." She knelt to pick up a gray tabby trying to scrabble over the side and cuddled it to her cheek with a happy sigh. "I live with a bunch of boys. We already have a George and a Ratt."

The kid's eyes widened. "You live with a bunch of boys?"

She laughed at how that sounded. "I'm a band. They're my bandmates."

"Oh. What band?"

"Oblivion."

"No way. No fucking way." Before she could say a word, he'd hauled out his phone and taken a couple of pictures. "Man, Eli's not gonna fucking believe this." Then he gave her a pleading look. "You gotta buy one of my kittens. My mom's gonna kill me if I take them back home and they're only fifty bucks."

"Fifty bucks? Holy crap." This kid was hardcore.

She glanced down at the big green eyes staring up at her, and her heart softened into a puddle of goo. "If I take both of them, do I get a discount?"

"Yeah. Only one hundred bucks."

She laughed and scooped up a white one with a black dot on the top of its head like an inkblot. One of them would be perfect for Harper. The other...hmm. Maybe she'd give her to Lila. Lila seemed like she needed some snuggling time.

"Sold." She stood up and fished her wallet out of her hip purse. "I hope I have—"

The door to the grocery store swung open. "Christ, Jazz, there you are. I was getting worried."

Smiling, she turned toward Gray and held out her kitten. "Look. Isn't she adorable?"

"It's a he," the kid said.

"And I'm buying that girl right there too."

"That one's a boy too, miss."

"Man, striking out all over the place." Jazz went back to digging out her wallet.

"Uh, honey, what do you mean you're buying both of them? Where are we going to keep two more kittens?"

She scooped up the white kitten. "One's for Harper and one's for Lila."

He took the second kitten from her. "Do Harper and Lila want kittens?"

Jazz bit her lip and sorted through her bills. This kitten expenditure would just about tap her out until she got to the ATM. "Why wouldn't they?"

"Because not everyone's like you."

"What's that supposed to mean?"

"It means I remember when you brought home a frog in a shoebox and a bunny in a shopping bag. You collect pets, which is adorable but—"

Money in hand, she narrowed her eyes at Gray. Gray who just happened to be rubbing noses with the kitten he claimed to have no interest in. "Look, buddy, this is part of the package deal you're getting. I know what it's like not to have a home, and as long as I can help another creature not feel unwanted, then I will." She bit her lip and glanced at the kid. Maybe she shouldn't spend the last of her cash. "Do you take checks?"

"Marry me."

"Forget the check. I'll go to the ATM."

"Jazz. Marry me."

Still turned toward the now gaping kid, she shut her eyes. She must be hearing things.

"Uh, miss, I think the guy asked you a question."

"It'll take a second," Gray said, his voice drily amused. "She's processing. Jazz's mouth runs faster than the rest of her."

"I think I should get a better discount," she said, eyes still closed.

"Still processing?" the kid asked.

"Or ignoring me. Either's a good bet."

"You weren't on your knees when you asked," she said shakily, opening her eyes. The kid looked well and truly confused. "Isn't that how you're supposed to do it?"

"You're right. This whole kitten thing threw off my speech. I had it all planned. You were supposed to come inside—"

"The vending machine." She swiveled to face Gray, a laugh exploding out of her at the sight of him clutching two kittens to his chest while he knelt on one knee in front of her. "Oh my God. There's a ring in the vending machine. The stupid claw game. But what if I didn't grab the right plastic bubble? You know I suck at that game."

"We have all night. And apparently so do I, since I'm kneeling on the ground and people are taking out their camera phones to record this moment for the Daily Gawker."

"That's my job. I should be live tweeting my own proposal." When she dragged out her cell, she expected Gray to balk. But he didn't say a word as she took a quick picture and tweeted it with the caption, "Look who I found."

She'd found the best thing ever—the boy she loved more than life offering her the world.

But maybe she needed to stop and think first. Not only had they barely had time together as an actual couple, he was dealing with a serious issue. Adding a new stressor to his life, even a good one like an engagement, might not be a smart idea. And what if he fell off the wagon—

No. She wouldn't even let herself consider that. He'd promised her that he would stop, and he wouldn't lie to her. Whatever struggles he faced, she'd be by his side. Making this commitment to each other would prove that.

Then there was Brent and his mom. Should she accept before she'd told him everything? He deserved to know. Was she being selfish for thinking they deserved any bit of happiness they managed to snatch before the rest of the world intruded?

God, she wanted to marry him. If she was making a mistake, it was hers to make. She'd longed for this—just this—for so damn long.

She turned off her phone and dropped to her knees. "Do you really mean it?"

"Yes." His throat worked. "I want to marry you."

She swallowed hard, trying to get the questions out that she needed to ask. "When?"

"Tonight. Tomorrow. Two months from now. I don't care."

Tears burst from her eyes as she let out another laugh, this one verging on hysterical. "We've only been dating two weeks."

"Yeah, with almost a decade's worth of foreplay."

That made her laugh harder. "Lila doesn't want anyone else to get married."

"Oh. Well, never mind then. My bad." He made a show of struggling to his feet, his charges wriggling and meowing. Halfway up, Jazz planted her hand on his chest and shoved him back down.

"Uh-uh. You started this now you're going to finish it."

"Technically I can't, because the ring's in the store."

God, his grin and those sparkling eyes were like a gateway into the past, before everything had gotten so messed up between them. For this instant, she could pretend not to see the spiderwebs of blood fanning out in the whites of his eyes, and the heavy bags that rimmed them. He was too skinny, his shirt bagging around his torso, his jeans hanging off his lean hips.

But right then, he was just her Gray, and he was perfect.

"You didn't spend a lot, did you?" She nearly asked where he got the money, but the diehard romantic in her couldn't ruin the moment. Maybe Lila had loaned him enough extra to cover his debts and the ring. He'd never been a wasteful spender so he might've had some money set aside other than what he'd gotten as an advance.

Unless he used it all for drugs and that's why Lila had to bail him out.

"Shh. You can't ask that question about an engagement ring. By the way, still on my knees here." He flashed her a playful smile that erased the last of her questions and doubts.

"You haven't asked me anything that requires a ring yet. Just sort of demanded it. Next time try adding a question mark at the end."

"Okay." He tucked one kitten on each hip and faced her without an ounce of mirth in his eyes. "I love you. Will you be my wife?"

"Aww," someone said from behind them, but she didn't bother to look. She was too busy internally saying "aww" herself. And sniffling.

"I love you too. Yes." She gave him a broad smile in spite of the damp heat gathering in her eyes. Happy tears didn't count as a sign of weakness, and by God, she'd earned these. "Easiest question I've ever answered."

For a moment he didn't move. Barely seemed to breathe. Then he launched himself at her, crushing the kittens between them while he pressed his mouth to hers. "Yes?" he breathed once he moved back to haul in air.

"Yes. On one condition."

"Anything. What?"

She grinned. "That you fish the ring out of the vending machine for me."

"Ah, baby, I think we can arrange that." Laughing, he turned to the stunned silent kid. "We'll take these to go."

Chapter Thirty-Three

Then

She was singing again, loudly and off-key in her adorable Jazz way. It wasn't that she couldn't hold a tune. Far from it. The girl was pitch perfect. But she loved making up new lyrics to her favorite songs—for some reason, she was currently slaughtering Elvis' "Don't Be Cruel,"—usually while booty-dancing around her room.

In his bedroom, Gray grinned and adjusted his bowtie. He hated the stupid thing, but he'd gone all out and rented a tux, intending to surprise Jazz. The school year had gone by ridiculously fast. Now it was spring again and it felt like they hadn't spent any time together in forever. She'd mentioned a couple of times in her emails that she didn't have a date for her birthday party, and the date coordinated well with his break from school. So why not?

They were friends. Friends hung out together. Friends also grinned at the sound of each other's voices. And in his case, saved their friend's emails in a special folder in their account.

Sometimes they even stopped bothering to date college girls for the last few months, because what was the point? He'd tried doing the full college experience during the fall semester, and every one of the girls had come up short in comparison.

But that wasn't what tonight was about. After the kiss that wasn't during their unforgettable San Francisco trip in August, he'd gotten the message loud and clear. She didn't see him that way. He'd come up with and rejected a few theories why, but in the end, their friendship was the most important thing. He would never do anything to jeopardize it.

Tonight he intended to make sure his best friend had a fabulous time.

"Well, this is a surprise. Didn't expect you to come home for spring break."

Gray cringed inwardly. His brother. Great. Of course Brent wouldn't have expected him to come home, because he didn't think about anyone but himself and figured Gray was as one-track-minded. "Yep. Here I am."

"And you're all done up and shit. Big plans tonight, bro?"

So much for Brent paying attention to what was going on in his own house. "It's Jazz's birthday." Gray turned to look at his brother, slouching insolently in the doorway. He had a bottle of scotch tipped up to his lips. He wasn't twenty-one yet, but their parents wouldn't say a word to their precious first-born.

Even when he was being a dick.

"Oh is it? How'd I miss that?" He grinned. "Bet she'll need some spankings."

Asshole. "How about you?" Gray slicked a hand over his spiky hair. "Not like you to stick around home on a Friday night."

"I'm thinking I'll spend some time with Jazzy at her little party." Slowly, Brent licked his lips. "I heard she needed a man and you know I always try to assist family."

Gray's spine locked. Brent had dropped out of college right after Thanksgiving and he'd moved into the spare bedroom Jazz had used when she'd first moved in, one that was much smaller than the room he'd given up for her. She must've told Brent about her lack of a date. They must be friends now.

"Did she tell you that?"

"Does it matter? I know." Brent swaggered into the room. "So what's up with the tux? You trying to class it up? Gotta commend you, man. It won't get you anywhere with her, but keep trying."

When he would've pushed past Brent, Brent wrapped his meaty hand around his upper arm. "What the hell, man? Cool it."

"No, *you* cool it. You don't fucking live here anymore and you don't know what shit's been going down."

The back of Gray's neck went cold. "What is that supposed to mean?"

"It means you're not the only one who can get close to Jazz. You always thought you had some special freaking bond. Well, get a fucking clue, dude. Girls like her are used to latching onto whomever's around." Brent saluted him with his bottle. "You weren't here anymore. And I am."

Gray's eyes narrowed until all he could see was Brent's taunting expression. "I don't know what you're trying to insinuate but I talk to her all the time. We call and email—"

Brent barked out a laugh. "Yeah, you keep calling and emailing. Meanwhile, some of the rest of us are taking it up to the next level."

His older brother turned to leave, still wearing that sardonic smile, and something in Gray snapped. Why, he didn't even know. He didn't truly think anything was going on between Jazz and Brent. She rarely mentioned him, even if after he'd moved back in. Although maybe that was suspicious in itself...

No. They weren't anything to each other. And even if they were, Gray knew he had no right to be pissed. They weren't a couple. He'd barely even tried to kiss her.

She shut you down too fast for you to have a chance to kiss her.

"Stay the hell away from her," Gray said in a low voice. "You want a piece of disposable pussy, find it somewhere else."

"Why?" Brent tossed back another drink. "I think that particular pussy suits me just—"

Gray shot across the space that separated them and locked his hands around Brent's throat, driving him into the wall with a crash that displaced one of Gray's framed honors certificates.

Glass shattered on the floor, splattering his bare feet, and he didn't even care. "Touch her, fucker, and you'll answer to me."

Brent shoved him back and he rammed into the corner of his dresser with enough force to knock the breath out of him. "She's not yours. You don't own her. Besides, maybe the lady likes me. Ever think of that?"

It was all bullshit. Brent had always been fiercely competitive with him in everything from sports to girls to their parents' affection, and by showing how much he cared about Jazz, he was basically putting a bullseye on her forehead. Brent would direct one hundred percent of his attention at her just to piss Gray off. But he couldn't keep the sharply-edged words from flying from his mouth like bullets.

"She'd never want you more than me. Fucking deal with it. You always have to win, and this time you just can't." Gray gripped his stinging back and heaved out a breath. "No matter what you do, you'll never be me."

Chapter Thirty-Four

Now

"Do you know you have a constellation of freckles right here?"

Jazz leaned up on her elbows and laughed at where Gray had his head. It wasn't surprising. He had his head between her legs about half of the time.

She was a very lucky girl. A very lucky, newly *engaged* girl.

She glanced at the diamond ring on her finger. Tiny diamonds formed an X shape with an O of black diamonds, signifying the typical XO phrase. But to Gray, they'd represented sticks and a drum. He'd apologized for buying it off the shelf and not getting it custom-made, which boggled her mind. She'd never seen anything more lovely.

Dragging her attention from her ring, she focused on the sensation of his fingers tracing over the sensitive skin of her inner thigh. "Where?"

"Right here." His hand crept higher, creating a path for his lips to follow. "They're everywhere. I could spend a lifetime searching for them with my tongue."

"Pretty sure you've already found most of them, especially in that particular area." She sifted his hair through her fingers and sighed, dropping back against the mussed sheets. "It's official. I've had more sex in the past two weeks than in the whole of my entire life."

He nipped her lower belly. "Is that a complaint?"

"No. That's a *yay me*." She tugged on his hair until he got the memo and crawled up her body to settle on top of her, his cock heavy between her legs. "Not that I've done a complete study or anything, but I've decided engaged sex is way better than regular sex. Although that was pretty fucking amazeballs too."

"You seem to be overlooking all the ways my native skills in this area are probably influencing your opinion." He tilted her jaw upward and kissed the corner of her mouth. "How you could after all of the evidence I've presented, I don't know, but..."

"Dude, your evidence is against my thigh. It's way too hard to overlook."

His laughter as he buried his face in her hair made her laugh too, just from sheer joy. If she'd ever been this happy, she didn't remember it.

Her entire life had been building up to this moment. She was engaged to the man she loved. She was in a successful band with people she cared about and they were coming up with some kickass new material. And she had a terrific best friend who would make her into an aunt-by-proxy next summer. How could she ask for anything more?

"I want to show you something."

"I've already seen it from a variety of angles. Pretty sure we're on a BFF basis by now."

"Forget BFF. I'm thinking your name's tattooed there in invisible ink." He grinned and pinched her nipple before rolling away to tug a notepad out of the nightstand drawer.

"Invisible's not nearly good enough. I think your cock would look good with a nice big J." She turned onto her side. "Whatcha doin'?"

"Remember that song 'Finally' that I mentioned at the band meeting?"

She sat up, tugging the sheet with her. "Yeah."

"I wanted you to see it before I show the rest of the band. It's not complete but—"

"Gimme." She held out her hand.

He gave her the pad and sat back, propping his arm on his updrawn leg. Naked as the day he was born and casual as could be about it.

So she dropped her sheet. Hell, she could be casually nude too. At least she could work on it.

She glanced down at the words he'd scrawled, more conscious of her more than generous boobs flying free than what she was reading. At first. Then the lyrics snagged her attention and she forgot all about what he might be thinking about her curves.

A dream came true, finally
The moment you said you loved me too
And up until I take my last breath
I'll cherish what is mine, finally

Goose bumps popped out over her arms. The song was so beautiful and poignant. She should've been dancing around the room but instead she trembled, as if the sudden wind shaking the windows blew cold air straight onto her bones.

"Change that line," she said, pointing.

He propped his chin on her shoulder. "Which one?"

"The one about your last breath. Change it."

"Jazz," he said, chuckling. "It's just a saying."

"I'm serious. The rest of it's perfect but take that line out. Look, we can even say—"

His cell went off and he went still at her side before moving away. "Sorry. I have to take this."

He grabbed his phone and went into the bathroom. The sound of the door closing echoed, making her push aside the pad and draw her knees up to her chest. She was breathing too fast—had been even before the phone call—but now she would've sworn a panic attack was coming on. It had been years. The last time was since shortly after Brent had attacked her. Before then she hadn't had one since her foster care days.

But man, when they came back, they always knocked her flat on her ass.

She focused on her breathing, counting off her breaths like she did with the beat when she was playing the drums. Mostly, it was instinctual now. She didn't have to verbalize the numbers, she just naturally knew when to hit her marks. Her breathing was different. Every time she faltered and paid too much attention to what was being said on the other side of that closed door, her chest tightened and her lungs cramped.

When he returned, she'd almost gotten it under control. Her palms were still clammy and she couldn't quite meet his gaze, but she wasn't shaking anymore.

Until he spoke.

"I have to go out for a while."

She glanced at the bedside clock. "It's not even seven a.m."

They'd barely slept all night, just dozing in between rounds of Gray playing the guitar and making love. It was their last night in the cabin and their first as an engaged couple, so who needed sleep?

But now that he was pulling on his jeans and digging through his still unpacked suitcase for a shirt, her exhaustion hit her like a wave. She wanted nothing more than to burrow under the covers with him and hide from the advancing day. Sunlight trickled into the room around the curtains they'd pulled, and that scared her almost as much as who had called and where he was going.

Within these four walls, they were safe. Outside, anything could happen.

"I know, baby. I won't be long."

Once his usage of the word *baby* had pleased her so much. Now it felt like a way to delay the inevitable.

"We have a meeting with Lila at ten," she said, hating the plea she heard in her voice. But it couldn't be helped.

And he wouldn't be stopped. She just knew it. That didn't mean she wouldn't try.

"I know. I'll be back by then." He tugged on his shirt and leaned across the bed to kiss her. "I'll be quick, I promise."

She threaded her fingers through his hair and cupped his cheek with her other hand. It took every shred of will she possessed not to cling and beg. "It's our first full day being engaged. Can't it wait until after the show tonight, whatever it is?"

"I'm sorry, it can't. But this is a good thing. This is setting the groundwork for our future." The smile he gave her almost convinced her.

But not quite.

"You won't tell me where you're going," she said, not bothering to make it a question. She already knew the answer.

He drew back, his smile fading. "Just trust me, okay? I'll be back soon." He picked up his wallet and gestured toward the tangled sheets. "Get some sleep, all right? You look tired."

She nearly laughed. *Tired* didn't come close to describing how worn out she felt all of a sudden. And she wasn't even certain why.

"I love you," he said, hesitating in the doorway before closing the door behind him.

It was only after he'd gone that she realized he'd been waiting for her to say it back.

After a while, she rose and went into the bathroom to dig through her makeup case. She took a couple of Benadryl to help her sleep and followed them with a glass of water, nearly crushing the paper cup in her hand as it started to shake again.

Something was off. She didn't know what, but it was more than Gray keeping a questionable appointment. She wanted nothing more than to chase after him and insist she go too. They were a team, and that meant he shouldn't do the big things alone.

Unless this was a small, usual thing. Like meeting with his drug dealer and getting a celebratory line or two to tide him over.

She tossed out her cup and went back into the bedroom. Though she had no desire to sleep, she curled up in the messy bedding and tugged his pillow to her face. His scent comforted her enough to close her eyes.

When she opened them again, muted sunlight slanted across the bedroom and someone was pounding on the door. Not someone. Nick.

"Hey lovebirds, we got a show to do. Rise and shine."

She rubbed her eyes and reached out for Gray. It had already become a habit for her to touch him when she awakened. But no one slept beside her and the sheets were cool.

Dread combed icy fingers through her belly as she scrambled to her knees. She glanced around the room, getting her bearings. The cabin. Gray leaving. God, she must've slept the whole day away. It took her a moment or two to realize his suitcase was in the same place he'd left it on the floor that morning, the contents still spilling out. His wallet and cell phone weren't on the nightstand.

God, he hadn't come back.

She grabbed the sheet and stumbled to her feet a second before Nick pushed open the door. "Where is he?" she demanded, despite knowing he didn't have an answer.

How could he? From his question, he'd obviously believed Gray had been in the bedroom with her.

"He's not here?" Nick didn't appear to notice she was naked, which gave her enough time to wrap the sheet around herself toga-style. "Where did he go?"

"I don't know." She rubbed her hand under her nose and rushed to the nightstand to grab her own phone.

It only took her a moment to discover her only missed calls were from Harper, who was wondering when she'd get her catering truck back—luckily she didn't have a job today—and why Jazz had been under the mistaken impression that she wanted a kitten. Actually two kittens, since Jazz had foisted them onto Harper last night before hurrying back to the cabin with Gray.

"He hasn't called me. Oh God, what time is it?" Jazz answered her own question by glancing at her phone. Past three in the afternoon. Fuck. She'd slept through the meeting with Lila. "I missed the meeting. *We* missed it."

"Lila rescheduled until tomorrow. She had something come up."

"But rehearsal—"

"Simon bagged on rehearsal today. Something about a scratchy throat. He probably can't feel his legs after partying too hard last night and needed to sleep it off for a few more hours."

Nick's voice sounded too cheerful, as if he grasped that she was on the verge of losing it so he didn't want to say anything to push her over the edge. Too fucking late.

"He said he'd be back hours ago and he's not here. He didn't call me. Did he call you?"

"Uh, no. Why would he?"

"I don't know, okay? I don't know." She sat on the edge of the bed and sent off a quick text to Gray, trying not to panic. She wasn't surprised when he didn't reply. She'd known he wouldn't.

Goddammit, she'd known this was going to happen. Even without fully grasping what *this* was, she'd felt it coming this morning even before he'd gotten the call that had taken him away from her.

"I didn't say *I love you* back," she said dully, staring at her silent phone. "He said it to me and I didn't say anything back because I was pissed he wouldn't tell me where he was going."

Eyes painfully dry, she lifted her head. "He went to score, didn't he?"

Nick pushed a hand through his hair. "I don't know."

"You didn't find out he was using the other night from Snake," she said slowly, taking in the way his body stiffened degree-by-degree. "You've known for a while."

"Does it matter?"

"Yes, it matters. Yes, it fucking matters!" She hurled her phone. It smacked against the wall and dropped to the floor. "You said we were friends, that you cared about me."

"Christ, you're naked and wearing his ring, but I'm still standing here with you. Doesn't that fucking prove that I do?" he gritted out, pacing to the window.

She glanced down at her engagement ring and something inside her shattered, just broke in two. The sound that came out of her wasn't human. She clutched her stomach and bent over, scarcely aware of him kneeling at her side to stroke her back.

"Jazz. Listen to me. Get dressed and we'll figure this out."

She shook her head, eyes so full she couldn't see through the wall of tears. "No, no, no."

She hurt so deeply that she couldn't identify where all the pain was coming from. It seemed to originate both inside and outside of her body, as if hammers were pounding nails into her skin. Into soft tissue. Breathing was almost impossible over the lump in her throat. And her stomach. God. She felt violently sick, on the verge of throwing up everything she hadn't eaten all day. Just retching until she purged all of the agony taking up space inside her.

"Dammit, you're not going to break down on me. Do you hear me? Fuck it all, he's fine. He better be, because I intend to fucking kill him myself for this stunt."

Nick dragged her into his lap. All she could do was press her face into his shoulder and cling to his neck for everything she was worth.

"Y-you don't understand. He promised me. He never lied, never. Something's wrong. I feel it. Oh God, I'm going to be sick." She tried to shift off his lap but got tangled in the sheet and fell on the rug, landing hard on her ass. Even that pain barely registered over all of the rest. "They could hurt him." She stared blearily up at Nick. His helplessness poured over her, and she still couldn't find it in herself to get it together. "He could be hurt, and I didn't even tell him I love him."

"They have no reason to hurt him. He gave them the money he owed—" Nick broke off, his gaze dropping to her hand and back up to her face. "Get dressed, Jazz," he said, his statement nearly inaudible.

For a moment she didn't know why she couldn't hear him clearly. Then she realized she was crying again, even more loudly than before.

"Listen to me. I have someone I can call. She...knows people who might know the ones that Gray knows." He gripped her chin, holding on as she tried to shove him away. "Give me time to do some checking around."

"It's been hours." She crossed her arms over her chest, holding the tangled sheet in place. "What if he took too much? He could've overdosed."

"No. I don't think that's it." Nick crouched beside her, his fingers still tensed on her face. "But until he shows up or I talk to Ricki, we can't let anyone else know what's going on. We have a show tonight."

She stared at him, her mouth dropping open. "You think I give a flying fuck about the *show*?"

"You better, because if he doesn't appear, you're going to be playing rhythm guitar for him."

She didn't speak. Her tears trickled to a halt. "You've lost your frigging mind."

He chuckled, the sound forced and unnatural. "Yeah. I think you're right."

"Do you understand what this means? He's been gone eight hours when he said he'd be right back. I can't think of—"

"Let me break this down for you. If we don't do the show, Lila and Deak will get wise to what's going on. And that will spell plenty of trouble for your guy."

She dropped her head into her hands. "I haven't played guitar in years."

"Stop bullshitting me. You were playing it the other night just fine."

"I was tinkering with it for a new song! Not playing for real. It's not my fucking instrument anymore. I can't get up in front of all those people and pretend I'm him. I can't fill his shoes." She rubbed her streaming eyes and pressed a hand to her still-queasy stomach. "I can't do it. Especially when I don't know if—"

"You listen to me, Jasmine, and you listen good. I'm not your Romeo, sweetheart, and I don't give a shit if you cry your pretty little eyes out before and after that concert. But you will get up there and you will play your ass off, like I know you can." Nick's eyes glittered as he loomed over her. "If I have to carry you onstage and put the guitar in your goddamned hand myself, I will."

Her chin wobbled as she swiped away her tears. "You wouldn't."

"Don't tempt me."

Shocked into silence, she stared at the floor.

"Get up."

Her lack of response made him grunt. "Want me to dress you as if you're a little girl? Because I will. I've seen everything you have under that sheet and I guarantee I won't mind seeing it again."

Affronted, she hauled her sheet in tighter around her. She was trembling and nauseous and bleary-eyed and didn't give a crap what Nick expected her to do. Not until she knew Gray was okay.

God, he *had* to be okay. There was simply no other choice.

When she didn't move, he held out his hand. "C'mon. You're better than this. What would he think if he saw you this way?"

"He'd want to protect me." That only made her chin quiver harder.

"Yeah. But he's the one who needs protecting now. You and I are what's keeping him in this band. And when he comes back, he'll want his spot back. Won't he?" he asked quietly.

"Yes." She glanced up at Nick and fought to catch her breath. Another sob was building in her chest, and God, she was so tired of crying. "He's going to come back, isn't he?"

"He has to." He crouched before her again. "He has everything in the world going for him."

She shut her eyes at the renewed fists of pain pummeling her stomach. Only sheer will kept her from bolting into the bathroom to throw up.

"He told me he was going to propose to you." When she only shuddered, he gripped her hands, holding them tight. "The guy fucking adores you. I saw it all over him yesterday."

Sniffling, she nodded.

"Help me get through the show tonight, all right? I'll get someone to cover the drums and you and I will make it so no one notices he's gone."

"I don't know if I can do it."

"Look at me."

She shook her head. "I can't. You're disappointed in me for falling apart, and I don't blame you. But you don't understand what he is to me. If he's not there—" She couldn't finish.

"Look at me."

Eyes streaming, she looked. And found more compassion than she'd ever expected staring back at her.

"We'll get through tonight together," he said gently, rubbing her knuckles. "I'll help you, and you'll help me. Just like you did during those shows last year—" He broke off at her gasp and swore. "Christ, not like *that*. You're an engaged woman now. I don't fucking poach."

The corner of her mouth lifted. Saying nothing, she turned her hand over and lightly gripped his fingers before nudging him back so she could get to her feet. "Make your calls," she said in a voice that shook. It couldn't be helped. At least she was talking without crying. "I'll get dressed and be right out."

"Okay." He walked to the doorway and picked up her phone. He swiped his thumb over it before handing it back to her. "Still works."

She glanced at her background picture, a photo from years ago of her and Gray in San Francisco. They'd made so many plans last night in between rounds of making love.

Ones she refused to give up on without a fucking fight. But first she had to know exactly what she was dealing with. Turning her back on reality wouldn't work anymore, not if she wanted to save the man she loved.

"Tell me how long you've known."

"Known what?"

She set her jaw and met Nick's gaze. "You know what. Tell me how long you've known he's using."

His hesitation didn't last long. "Since last spring. The day after that clusterfuck threesome, he dropped a baggie in the studio. I called him on his shit and he said he was holding it for a friend."

"And you believed him."

"No, I didn't fucking believe him. But what was I supposed to do about it? The night before, you called out his goddamn name while I was inside you. I didn't want to be part of it anymore."

Shame heated her already scalding cheeks. "So you washed your hands of it."

"Maybe I did. It wasn't my problem. I warned him what he was risking, but fuck, Jazz, I'd just told him he could have you, that I wouldn't interfere. Everyone thinks I'm a bastard anyway, so why not play my part?"

"Because you're not a bastard. A bastard wouldn't have just sat with me while I cried. You wouldn't care if we saved a spot for him. You'd be hoping like hell he got thrown out."

"Yeah, so maybe I like the guy now, all right? Maybe I get it finally, that what's between the two of you had nothing to do with me. And so I'm not going to fucking cry in my milk and wish for him to get what he deserves. Because maybe he really does deserve you, more than I ever did."

She walked over to him and cupped his face. "Thank you," she whispered.

"Yeah." He gripped her hands for a second before letting go and stepping back. "Get dressed so we can practice." Without waiting for her to reply, he pulled the door shut behind him.

She still hadn't moved when she heard his voice on the phone.

"Ricki, I need your help."

Chapter Thirty-Five

Then

"Happy birthday, Jazzy."

She turned at the slurred voice behind her, her heart leaping into her throat at the sight of Brent in her bedroom doorway, his tie half undone and his jacket gaping open. He'd dressed up for the sweet sixteen party the Duffys had organized for her, but he was already half in the bag.

Didn't anyone notice? Or maybe it didn't matter. He worked now, and Mrs. Duffy treated him like an adult. It wasn't any big thing if he wanted to have a few drinks to unwind after he returned from his shift.

"Hi. Thanks." She tried to smile but the gesture fell short.

Nothing new when it came to dealing with Brent.

She tucked her hair behind her ear and turned back to her dresser. Tonight she would get to wear the aquamarine dangle earrings Mrs. Duffy had given her for an early birthday gift.

"I heard you singing, baby. What song was that?"

Ick, she hated when he called her *baby*. It made her skin prickle as if she'd gotten too much sun. When Gray used the same term, she loved it. That probably wasn't fair, but she couldn't deny her natural reaction. God knows she'd tried a million times.

"Elvis. Hey, is everyone here yet?" At the tickle between her shoulder blades, she turned, not feeling comfortable with him behind her. He'd moved up close—too close—and she bumped into the dresser, sending a few of her perfume bottles tumbling to the floor. She gasped and bent to see if the bottles broke, only to have Brent seize hold of her arm and tug her to her feet. "Hey, what are you—"

"Stupid slut. You think I don't know what you're doing?" He twisted her arm and forced her backward until she fell onto her bed. "Fucking tease. He thinks you want him. We'll see about that."

Panic spurted inside her, drowning out any logic she had left. She couldn't think straight when he was looming over her, the bottle in one hand and his other on his buckle.

Oh God, he was undoing his belt.

"Brent, no." She scrambled backward on the mattress and he grabbed her ankle, yanking her forward while she flailed and kicked. "Stop it, Brent! You got the wrong idea. I don't know what you mean—"

"Cunt. Stop your shit. I'm going to prove to him that you're not the sweet little bitch he thinks you are. I know you're not innocent. I hear you in here, fucking that Daniels kid." He moved to unzip his zipper and she went still, shock taking over.

This couldn't be happening. She'd finally found her perfect home with the perfect family. The Duffys were going to adopt her, she knew they would. All she had to do was stay still and take it, just not make a sound so they would never know what she'd let him do.

He was right, just like her mother had said. She was a slut. Always tempting the men. First Jacob, now Brent. She deserved this, and if she accepted it without making too much of a fuss, it didn't have to ruin anything. She could still become a Duffy. Gray didn't ever have to know either.

She'd never have to see the disgust in his eyes if she just stayed quiet.

"That's it, baby. I knew you wanted it," Brent crooned, bracing a knee on the bed as he tugged down his jeans. At the sight of his boxer-covered erection, she choked and turned her face away, covering her chest with her arms. "Don't hide yourself from me. Let me see those pretty tits—"

"No. Don't touch me. God, please, just leave me alone." She couldn't do it. Couldn't, couldn't, couldn't. She'd die first. She slapped and kicked, fighting for everything she was worth.

"Stupid bitch, you'll pay for that." His big hand clamped around her throat, cutting off her air as he pinned her with his heavy, hot body, and she screamed the only thing that came to mind.

The only word she could still remember.

"Gray!"

The door flew open, banging into the wall, and then the weight was being lifted off her, vanishing so fast that she patted her sides to reassure herself she wasn't imagining things. She still had her eyes squeezed shut but when she opened them, she didn't understand what she was seeing. Brent was fighting with...Gray? How could he be there? He was supposed to be at school. He'd apologized for not being sure if he could make it back home for her party, and she'd told him it was okay because she understood. He was busy, and she wasn't his whole life like he was hers. It was just a stupid birthday.

Stupid slut.

She covered her head with her arms and curled on her side, away from the fight. She knew she should get up and help Gray but her legs had gone numb and the sensation was spreading. Higher, higher the cold crept, taking away the pain. She wouldn't feel it soon. She could just float away.

She started singing Elvis again, louder and louder until she was screaming the words that only a while ago had made her giggle and dance around the room. Now they burned her throat as she shouted them, tears pouring down her face, anything to drown out the sounds taking place behind her.

Stupid cunt, you did this. You.

"Jazz, baby, are you okay?" Gentle hands smoothed over her back and she shrieked and rolled away, pressing herself to the wall.

"No, no, no. Don't touch me." She sang louder, rocking faster, anything to block out the hands pulling at her. She couldn't feel them. They couldn't hurt her now. Her knees banged the wall as she tried to ball herself up to make herself too small to be seen, but it didn't work. He was still there. His hot breath still blew over her skin. She shuddered and pressed her arms together. Smaller, smaller. She was tiny. She could disappear.

"I'm here. It's me, baby. Jazz, it's Gray. I've got you." He scooped her up and she turned into him, following his voice through the darkness that had claimed her.

"Gray," she whispered brokenly, clinging to his neck. A seeping wound marred his forehead and cheek. She touched the blood and shrank back at the sight of it on her skin. "Please don't leave me. Don't let go."

"I won't. I won't, ever." He buried his face in her hair and rocked them both. "Oh God, I'll never let him hurt you again."

She lifted her head, blinking through the haze of tears as Mrs. Duffy bolted into the room. "What happened?" She pinned Jazz with her accusing gaze. "What did you do?"

And just like that, the last of her dreams crumbled through her fingers like sand. She'd never had a chance in hell of anyone wanting her to be theirs anyway.

She was on her own.

Chapter Thirty-Six

Now

Backstage at Trix, the venue for that night's show, Nick gripped Jazz's hands. "How do you feel?"

"Like I'm about to puke."

"You're not going to puke. We ran through the entire setlist back at the cabin and you only flubbed a few notes. Completely unnoticeable notes, I might add. With me beside you, everyone's going to be too busy admiring my fingerwork to even notice yours." The smile he flashed her didn't do a thing to mitigate Jazz's nerves.

She flexed her fingers and tried not to think about how she was holding Gray's beloved Epiphone. She tried not to think at all, period. That was the only way she was going to get through tonight.

As soon as the show was over, she could—and probably would—collapse. But right now, she had to do this for Gray. She would make him proud of her and offer up every song she played tonight to whatever god happened to be watching out for them. And in every spare moment, she would continue to pray as she had since that afternoon.

Please take care of him. Please let him know how much I love him. Please bring him back to me.

Every hour that passed without contact from him increased her dread. There was no universe where Gray would've gone this long without calling her. He would never miss a show.

So he must not be capable of contacting her. That didn't mean he had OD'd. Once she'd realized he had taken Harper's catering truck, she'd started weighing other scenarios. It could've been a car accident. Not a fatal one—God no—but one where he had to deal with cops and other drivers and damage. Maybe his cell phone wasn't working. Dead battery. He might've run a light and gotten a ticket and fought with the police. Even imagining him in jail was preferable to any of the other scenarios scrolling through her mind.

Deak strolled up beside them and lifted an eyebrow at Jazz wearing Gray's guitar. "So you're our second guitarist tonight, huh? And the Brooklyn Dawn chick is filling in on drums?"

"Yes," Nick said, answering for Jazz. "Jamie. She's really good. Plus, she's super hot. Jugs for days, man."

As usual Deak ignored their guitarist and his sexist commentary. "And what's this about Gray borrowing Harper's truck? She's meeting with a new client tomorrow—"

"He had a family emergency and wasn't able to get back in time," Jazz said, reciting the speech that she and Nick had settled on. "He's really sorry for the inconvenience and promises to pay her for any loss of business. It was unavoidable."

"Another family emergency, hmm? Can we talk alone for a minute?"

"There's no need for that," Nick began.

"Yeah, it's fine." She shot Nick a calming look and led Deak a few feet away. Before he could speak, she held up a hand. "I know it all sounds weird, but please, Deak, just bear with me tonight and let's get through the show, okay?"

Evidently he heard the plea in her voice because he nodded and pulled her into a hug. "I hope like hell that whatever's going on doesn't get you hurt," he said gruffly.

She hugged him back and forced a smile as she stepped away. "Me too."

"You sure you're okay to play tonight? That's a lot of material for you to learn when you're used to being behind the kit."

"I started on the guitar way back when. It wasn't that hard to pick it up again." It had surprised her how easy it had been to play, especially since she'd had Nick at her side instead of Gray. But maybe he was helping her from wherever he was. He'd always given her a little extra boost, so why should tonight be any different?

So what if she didn't know where he was? He was out there. Okay. He had to be. If he wasn't, she wouldn't have been able to function. She would *know*.

"All right, if you insist."

"I do, thanks." She patted him on the arm then headed toward the stage, where the ladies from Brooklyn Dawn were trying to get her attention.

As always, Jamie wore a kickass outfit—lots of leather and denim paired with thigh-high boots and huge silver hoops. On another night, Jazz would've been jealous of her killer style. Tonight all she could do was lean in to give her a quick hug and a quiet "thank you."

Jamie was more of a guitarist than a drummer but Nick had said she'd offered her help without hesitation. Lindsey, Brooklyn Dawn's keyboardist, had done the same. The pretty blond wore a less flashy ensemble of an off-the-shoulder top and fitted pants but her beauty turned the ordinary into extraordinary. Nick had suggested Lindz add some piano accompaniment to a couple of their songs to make it seem more like a joint band collaboration, and Jazz had agreed. Why the hell not? Maybe if they crammed more people on the stage, she would stop looking at the spot beside Nick where Gray should be.

The spot she would be filling soon.

"Thank you too, Lindz," Jazz said, giving the blonde a quick hug as well. She hadn't talked too much to either of the girls before, but from the sympathetic looks they were giving her, she had to wonder how much Nick had told them about her missing fiancé.

Not that it mattered. They were there to help get them through the show. The rest had to wait until she'd put this night in the rearview mirror.

"No problem at all. We're excited to jam with you guys." Jamie slipped behind the kit without removing her boots and Jazz did a double take.

Wow, she was going to play in those? That chick was hardcore. Many of the drummers Jazz had known over the years were like her and preferred to play barefoot. But Jamie appeared supremely confident so Jazz had to assume she knew what she was doing.

"Absolutely. This is going to be one hell of a show. We already know a lot of your classics, so to get to play with you is incredible." Lindz squeezed Jazz's hand and moved off to take her spot behind the keyboard.

Jazz dampened her dust dry lips and looked down at the guitar she wore. It was too big for her and she'd probably be sore from playing by the end of the night.

But nothing could touch the numbing pain in her chest. It was slowly moving outward to encompass the rest of her body. She wasn't even nervous about what she had to do anymore. Her only thought was Gray.

When Nick joined her onstage, she struggled to give him a smile. He'd coached her through this, and someday she'd thank him for all his help. Right now getting through each minute taxed her to the point that speech had become impossible. She had no idea how she was going to sing.

"Jasmine, look at me."

She looked. She couldn't do anything else.

"Gray's going to watch this tape later and be so fucking turned on by watching you kill it on his guitar that he'll probably nail you in ways I haven't even thought of," he said, surprising a laugh out of her when she'd thought the laughter inside of her had finally run out.

"I needed that. Thanks."

"Don't thank me, show me up. I've never dueled with a girl before. Sounds fucking hot."

As soon as the finished speaking, the house lights went down and Simon swaggered on stage to greet the crowd. "How are you beasts doing tonight? A little cold out there, so we're ready to make it hot up in here!"

After the cheers died down, Simon tugged his old school mic up to his mouth and whispered, "Guys, I've got a secret. We lost our motherfucking guitarist, so we got ourselves an amazing replacement. Y'all give it up for our sweet Jazzy stepping out from behind the kit."

The cheers and whistling from the audience made it easier for her to step forward and give a bow. She didn't quite manage a smile, but at least she didn't freeze. The anxiety had bled away into a dull resignation. This was her band, and she would make it work.

Nick let the first few licks of "Taste of Candy" rip, her cue to shake off the rust and join him. She allowed the muscle memory to take over and focused on just getting out the right notes in the right order, following Nick's lead. He glanced over at her every couple seconds, almost like a papa duck checking on his duckling. It made her smile and try that much harder.

She wouldn't let Gray—or Nick—down.

Jamie had no trouble keeping the beat on the drums, adding her own sense of flair to the rhythm. Speeding up in places, slowing down in others. She had a sense of the dramatic and made damn good use of her hi-hats, slamming on them with a vigor that Jazz had to appreciate. The girl was fucking amazing with her black hair flying everywhere and that demonic grin stretching across her face. There was someone who was enjoying herself, not just getting by and getting through.

Lindz offered her own contribution to the music, providing a texture they hadn't had since the days Margo had sat in with them on their first big smash, "The Becoming". Lindz didn't have the same aggressive attitude that Jamie did but she was no less showy than her bandmate, easily bantering with the crowd in the few moments that Simon took a break to guzzle water and suck on throat lozenges. Guess his "scratchy throat" complaint hadn't been a fib after all.

Jazz just played her part, even going back to back with Nick on "Ripcord" as Gray always did. Having those firm shoulders behind her offered her a place to sag when she wasn't sure she could go on another second. Sweat dripped into her eyes and soaked her hair. The lights seemed way too bright, hazing her vision. Her arms vibrated from the unfamiliar stress of playing, and her whole body felt sore from crying. She tried her hardest to lose herself in the music, to let the hard, driving beats of the songs she loved carry her away, but there was no song that could distract her from the montage of terrifying images rolling through her mind.

Gray, hurt and bleeding. Those beautiful eyes forever closed. When the pictures hit her, stealing her breath and a cry from her throat she couldn't swallow back, Nick was there, dragging her through the songs with him, willing her to play. His solid form at her side helped her forge on when she didn't think she could pluck another note. When her voice ran hoarse because she was using all of her energy to try to hold back her sobs.

"You're doing fucking amazing," he whispered in between songs, nudging her arm in his version of a fistbump.

She shook her head, so disappointed in herself that she would've been on the verge of tears even without the Gray situation. She heard every missed note and hated that her fingers weren't as fast as they'd once been. Years ago she could've handled this setlist without difficulty.

Tonight she was a liability.

"You are. Keep your eyes on mine and keep playing for Gray."

She did, because she had no choice.

At the end of the show, after they'd played their final encore and taken their bows, she rushed backstage to dig out her phone. She'd latched onto the hope that maybe he'd called her during the time she was onstage. Perhaps he'd even made it back to the cabin or their apartment. Band camp was technically over as of today, but she and Nick couldn't go back to the apartment when they didn't know if Gray might return to the cabin. Well, *she* couldn't.

Gray hadn't called.

She didn't expect Nick to go back to the cabin with her but he did. As soon as the driver dropped them off, he unlocked the door and stood by as she ran from room to room, her momentary hope dwindling once again as it became clear that Gray hadn't come back. The light she'd left on for him only illuminated that she and Nick were completely, totally alone.

She stayed an extra couple of moments in the bedroom she and Gray had been intimate in, staring at the rumpled sheets and his suitcase. She wanted nothing more than to drop to her knees and bury her face in his clothes, to make sure his scent never left her for even a moment.

When she couldn't stomach looking around any longer, she wandered back into the living room and dragged the bands off her braids. She flung them in every direction, not caring where they landed. Her makeup was probably smeared from sweat and tears and she didn't give a shit.

"Come here," Nick said from the couch. "You look like you're going to fall over. You're too fucking pale."

She sat next to him, mainly because her feet felt like blocks and she doubted she could make it the few feet to the armchair.

"Have you eaten today?"

"No."

"You need to. I can make you a sandwich."

"Not hungry." Truth was, she was starving. It felt like her body was attacking her stomach lining for sustenance.

"If you faint on me, you're only going to piss me off. Give me five and I'll make you some bologna and fucking cheese."

"Nick." She stopped him with a hand on his arm. "We're going to have to call the police."

When he swiveled his head to look at her, a sound broke from her throat. "It's heading toward twenty-four hours. I'll have to file a m-missing person's report—"

Saying nothing, he hauled her into his lap. She slid her arms around his neck and pressed her face into his shoulder, her own shoulders heaving with dry sobs. She'd reached the point where she couldn't even cry.

"It's going to be okay. You have to believe me. My sister said she'd see what she could find out—"

"From her druggie friends. She'd digging through all the popular gutters, right?"

She hated the judgmental words tumbling out of her mouth, but she couldn't seem to hold back the rage that was geysering up in tandem with the gut-curdling panic and misery. She didn't want to think the worst. The very idea of Gray getting high in some random place—or worse, overdosing— made her want to scream. But what else was she supposed to think?

He'd walked out on her and left her alone in their bed. Naked. Wearing his ring. He'd promised her forever and then he'd gone off to be with someone who offered him something she couldn't. Probably that blonde babe Cricket, who smiled so prettily while she was sharpening the knife to hold at Gray's throat.

Nick's hand moved up and down her back as if on auto-pilot. "She'll figure it out. She knows Cricket—"

A thump from the doorway had Jazz lifting her head just as the door burst open. A guy wearing the clothes Gray had left in that morning stumbled through, his head tilting just right for her to glimpse the bloody gash that curved from his temple to jaw.

Horror bolted her in place. She couldn't be seeing what she thought she was. His torn, bloodied clothes were barely hanging on his body and his face was more black and blue than its usual color. There was so much blood. So much.

But when he managed to raise his head and fix his eyes on the scene on the couch, the racking laugh that left him sounded all too familiar. "Isn't this cozy?" he mumbled through cracked lips.

"Oh my God, Gray." She stumbled up, her paralysis finally giving way to action. She'd made it halfway to him with Nick right behind her when Gray barked out a command.

"No. Don't fucking touch me. Fucking liar."

She stopped so abruptly that Nick crashed into her back and almost toppled her. He grabbed her hip to right himself and Gray laughed again, the sound so agonizing that Jazz covered her mouth with her hand.

"I fucking dragged...myself back to you, and you're here...with him." Gray sagged against the wall, his eyes closing. "Hope you're fucking...happy."

"*Happy*?" she screamed, unable to stop herself. Relief rushed through her veins, mixing with something far more darker and destructive. "What the hell happened to you? Where did you go this morning?"

It was only when he shifted that she noticed the unnatural bump on the top of his shoulder. At her gasp, Nick grabbed the phone off the side table and pushed it into her hand.

"Call 911," he said.

"No," Gray whispered. "No cops."

Nick moved forward to offer his support to Gray. "She's not calling the cops, man. You need a doctor. Your arm's fucked up—"

"I said no fucking cops." Gray jerked back from Nick hard enough to crash into the wall. Jazz swallowed a moan at the pain that telegraphed across his face before he slid down to the floor, his ass hitting the carpet almost as hard as he'd hit the wall. "I just need to sleep it off."

"Sleep it off? Are you crazy? You're barely conscious."

"Oh I'm conscious." Gray's bleeding lips stretched into a macabre pantomime of a smile. "I'm conscious of what brought me to...this goddamn point. Never fucking changes." He coughed, his shoulders heaving.

She hurtled forward and fell to her knees in front of him, helpless to stop the tears. "Let us help you," she said, reaching out to touch his jaw with tentative fingers.

"You help me? Fat fucking chance. You and Nick are what got me here." He wiped his sleeve over his mouth. "Wanna know when I started this? Try the night you walked out of that closet at the club with this bastard." He jerked his thumb at Nick and shut his eyes.

She glanced at Nick in dawning horror and cupped her hand over her mouth again. The nausea was back, worse than ever.

If he was telling the truth, if he'd started the coke the night Gray had seen her and Nick come out of that closet before their concert, that meant this was all her fault. She'd done this to him. To *them*.

Nick shook his head minutely and crouched at Gray's side. "Listen, man, you need help. If not from us, let us take you to the hospital."

"Why?" Gray gripped his side, his pain so obvious that Jazz stumbled back and whirled away to try to get control of her traitorous stomach. "Want...me out of the way? Easier for you then."

"Oh Jesus, when you get cleaned up, you'll regret saying all of this, so I'm going to chalk it up to your injuries and ignore it. You can't make me cry with your taunts, but you can make *her* cry, so maybe stuff it for a while until you know what the hell you're saying, huh?"

"Big frigging savior, aren't you? Saving her from me." Gray laughed again, his breath wheezing through his teeth. Jazz moved her hand from her mouth to her belly, pressing there to try to calm the incessant rolling within.

When she was reasonably sure she was under control, she turned back, only to find Gray staring at her through narrowed eyes. "I got a phone call today," he slurred. "Guess who? Mommy fucking dearest."

"Oh Jesus." Had he gone to see his parents and not to see his dealer? If so, what had happened to him? She gripped the arm of the couch and sat down, incapable of standing. "You don't understand—"

"I never answer her calls, but something told me to today. You knew about my...brother, and didn't tell me. What else you keeping from me, baby?"

"It's not like that. It's not. I wanted to tell you—"

"You always want, you just never...do. I don't fucking care anymore. Get off me," he roared at Nick, who didn't move.

"Your shoulder is dislocated, at minimum," Nick said, his voice so calm that Jazz didn't know if she envied his strength or wanted to kick his ass. "If you ever want to play again, you'll let me drive you to the hospital."

When Gray didn't respond, Nick searched through Gray's pockets and pulled out the keys to Harper's truck. "Take these," he said, tossing them to her. "Go start the truck and we'll be right out."

"But I can help—"

"Go," Gray and Nick said in unison, making her eyes burn.

She knew she didn't have any right to feel hurt. Gray was in agony, and yes, he was angry—for some good reasons and for some stupid ones—but his reaction was marred by pain. She couldn't take offense at what he said in this state, and besides, it didn't even matter how he felt about her just then. The only thing that mattered was getting him help.

Nodding, she rose and swayed, digging her nails into the chair arm to maintain her balance. She glanced up to see Gray staring at her, his lips parting as if he'd been on the verge of saying something. As if maybe he wanted to know if she was okay. Then he firmed them and looked away.

She rubbed her thumb over the key fob in her hand and hurried outside, forcing herself to focus on what she had to do next. One foot ahead of the other, down to the truck. Start the vehicle and wait for the guys to appear. She quickened her steps, skirting the hood. She wouldn't analyze, and she wouldn't think. She'd just—

Something was on the hood, easily visible because Harper's truck was white and the substance was dark and sludgy. Mud maybe? She dipped her fingers into the wetness before she thought better of it. The coppery scent of blood hit her nose.

Blood. *Gray's* blood.

"Oh God," she whispered, barely making it to the grass before she emptied her stomach.

* § *

In the darkness, he could smell her.

Watermelons and wildflowers, fresh cut grass and sunshine. Her hair tickled his cheek and her heartbeat matched its rhythm to his, occasionally speeding up and slowing down before syncing with his once more. Her comforting weight on his chest abated his pain, more effective than any medicine. When she was with him, he could breathe again.

Gray opened his eyes, his mouth already curving in preparation of seeing her. But she wasn't there. The room was empty and dimly lit, illuminated just enough for him to make out the curtain pulled shut beside his bed. His *hospital* bed.

They'd taken him to the freaking hospital and left him alone.

As you asked them to.

He tried to lift his arm and groaned at the fiery pain between his shoulder and neck and the drag of an IV pulling on his forearm. Fucking hell. He tried to sit up to pour a glass of water and only managed to make it halfway to the jug on the bedside table before the myriad aches in his body forced him to be still.

Nope, no water. No anything. He was just going to lay there and listen to the guy moaning in the next bed and try to find his sense of gratitude that at least his soreness was manageable. Mostly.

The next time he woke, the room was full of light. The curtain beside his bed had been pulled open and his neighbor in the next bed was gone. He hoped he'd left on his own two feet.

Pale sunlight streamed in through the small window, making him blink. Maybe he could try reaching for the water again—

The click of high heels on tile caused him to turn his head. And inwardly groan. "Need some help?" Lila asked pleasantly.

"No."

He slouched against his pillows and rued the day he'd ever met Deacon McCoy. If he hadn't gotten friendly with him at some dive club, he wouldn't have ever tried writing with him. If he hadn't tried writing with him, they wouldn't have penned "The Becoming", the song that ultimately became Oblivion's first hit. Then he never would've met Nick and Simon, and he wouldn't have joined this godforsaken band.

That he loved, goddammit.

"Sure about that?" She stopped beside the bed and poured a cup of water before offering it to him.

"Didn't we run this scene before? I get messed up, you play angel of mercy and give me water and bail my ass out."

"That won't be happening a second time."

He finished drinking and crushed the cup in his fist, grimacing at the pain that traveled up his arm. "Yeah, well, I'm not asking to be bailed out. Worst they can do is fucking kill me, and then I won't have to think about any of this anymore."

Like how he'd discovered his brother was dead, and that Jazz had called his mother, probably to tell her all the ways he'd failed. That Jazz had let him propose without telling him. Then walking in to find *his* Jazz in Nick's lap, her eyes so blue and desolate as she clung to the man that Gray could never quite stop being jealous of even when it made no fucking sense.

She wore his ring yet all he could see was Nick's arms around her. Her head on his shoulder. Her hair caught in his fist...

"You're really that much of a ball sac, hmm?"

He blinked up at Lila. "What?"

"You heard me. I won't call you a pussy, because pussies are damn fucking strong. Right now you're being the kind of nut I could twist into a knot between two fingers."

"Are you seriously talking about my balls?"

"Not your balls per se. I'm comparing you to a nut sac in general. Weak, small and wrinkly."

He shook his head. "Your bedside manner needs a lot of work."

"Actually, I think my bedside manner is great. You're lucky I'm even here. No one else is."

The reality of that dried his mouth. He'd suspected it was true, but to hear it was another thing. "Yeah, so? What do I fucking care?"

"So you've broken up with Jazz then."

Even the words made him grip the sheets in a sweaty fist. "I didn't say that."

"Then you're still together?"

"I didn't say that either."

She sighed and pulled a chair up to the bed. "What happened?"

"What do you think? I fucked up, lost control and got my ass kicked—"

"Stop feeling sorry for yourself. It's supposed to be my job to feel sorry for you."

He didn't expect to be able to smile. "Are you going to tell me how bad they are?" He glanced at the shoulder where the bulk of his pain was radiating from. Well, not the bulk, but a lot. "My injuries, I mean."

"You'll live," she said shortly.

"Thanks."

"You're in rough shape but most of it is surface. You have a couple of cracked ribs and various contusions. The separated shoulder will probably require a sling and possible physical therapy. You won't be playing up to Grayson Duffy beast level for a while, but you'll get there again. The rest just requires sleep, a healthy diet and less contact with fists."

"Planning on it." Relief rushed through him. With his current level of soreness, he definitely hadn't been sure what the prognosis for his shoulder would be.

Looked like he wasn't permanently out of commission. Whether or not he'd have a band to return to...well, that was anyone's guess.

"Back to Jasmine."

"Sure. Why not? I'm already in hell."

"You think she believes that you went to get high and tangled with the wrong people."

"Doesn't she?"

"It's probably a good supposition, yes, because you didn't tell her any differently."

"Oh, and I suppose you believe something else?"

"Yes, I do. Through my magnificent powers of deduction after I saw that pretty ring on her finger, I decided I wasn't going to go with the obvious answer and did some checking around. Imagine my surprise when I located a jeweler near your apartment who sold a ring just like the one Jazz is wearing a mere two days ago, for a princely sum that equals roughly half of what I'd transferred into your account."

"What's your point?"

"Oh, you are a prideful one. Normally I respect that. In this case, you're being a jackass."

He tried to cross his arms and paid the price in the form of a shoulder spasm that would've buckled his knees if he'd been able to stand. "Thanks for the support," he rasped. "You can leave anytime now."

She lifted one perfectly arched eyebrow. "I'm dismissed then?"

"Yeah. Just like you warned me I would be if I screwed up." He gestured with his good arm. Even that movement pulled at his bad shoulder. "Take a look at me. Well and truly fucked. So consider this me resigning from—"

"I realize you had other things taking your attention three nights ago, but I wonder if you've given thought to who might've taken your spot at Trix?" she asked, smoothly interrupting him.

He reached for the sheets again, pulling them tight around his hips. "Three nights ago?"

"Yes. You were on some pretty powerful painkillers and you slept like the dead. I'm guessing you needed it. You probably didn't get a lot of rest the last couple of weeks, what with all that blissful bonding you and Jasmine were doing before you flamed out in a blaze of so-not-glory."

"Who played for me?" he asked quietly, though he already knew.

As soon as Lila had posed the question, he remembered the feeling of Jazz's calloused fingertips brushing over his skin. She'd never used a pick with any regularity, preferring to run her fingers down to bloody stubs no matter how many times he admonished her.

Damn stubborn woman that he loved more than his own life.

"I see you already know." Lila brushed invisible lint off her pale yellow skirt. "From what I've heard from your bandmates, she barely kept it together long enough to get through the set. But she did it for you, and she did a damn fine job. She and Nick concocted this stupid story about your granny again to save your ass. Little did they know they shouldn't have bothered. Guess you must like the smell of bacon frying in the morning."

Shame wound through his stomach, curling upward to encompass that hollow area in his chest that somehow still contained his heartbeat. He'd been so certain it would stop when he'd been lying in the fetal position in that shitty parking lot where Cricket's bastards had left him. His own fault for thinking they'd stick to the verbal deal they'd set. The money he'd offered hadn't been enough, so they'd taken their payment another way.

When he was lying on the ground, beat all to hell, he'd had plenty of time to replay where he'd gone wrong. He hadn't been dead yet but he hadn't been fully alive either. He'd been caught in a sort of purgatory, the option to die or to live in his hands if he chose quickly.

And he'd chosen the same way he always did. His choices *always* took him back to Jazz. He would've dragged himself there on his hands and knees if he had to.

He nearly had.

"She was in his lap," he murmured. "I'd just been beaten all to shit, and God, I hated myself in that moment. But when I hauled myself in the door, he was holding her, and I just fucking lost it. She's—"

"She's your drug, worse than any line of powder because you'll kill each other and claim it's in the name of love."

He started to argue until the truth in her answer sunk deep into his bones, way beyond where he could reach to fish it back out again. "Yeah," he said finally, rubbing the ache brewing behind his eyes. So many damn aches. "Yeah, I think you're right."

"She shares your addiction, by the way. She's no more capable of cutting the cord than you are."

He made himself meet her surprisingly understanding green eyes. "Is that...is that how it is with you and your husband?"

"Oh God no." Her light laughter shocked him. "Maybe it was once," she said after a moment. "I was young back then and idealistic. But life changes you, and now I scarcely remember what it is to love that desperately. That even if you gave every breath, every beat of your heart, it still wouldn't be—couldn't be—enough."

He nodded. "That pretty much sums it up."

"You need help," she began, holding up a hand when he started to argue. "Hear me out. I don't just mean for the coke. I mean you need help to bring some balance back into your life. *Your* life, Gray, not hers. Because if you don't have a life worth living, you have nothing to give her. Do you understand that? If you'd died, where would she be right now?"

His eyes filled and damn if he didn't hate himself even more for it. "Better off," he whispered.

"You don't truly believe that. I don't believe it either, not for a second." She grabbed hold of his hand and resisted his attempts to pull free with a shockingly firm grip. "The way you feel about her is the kind of love most women dream of. That, my friend, is some epic Titanic type shit, right down to Jack giving up the damn piece of wood, no matter how moronic that appeared to the more logical viewers in the audience." Her mouth quirked. "Us rational types might make fun of behavior like that but wish with our whole hearts that one day, someone might fall that madly in love with us."

He frowned. "I never saw Titanic."

"Figures." She laughed. "Perfectly good waste of an analogy."

"Jazz told me she hated that movie."

Lila sighed. "Kids today. Romantic subtext is completely lost on the lot of you."

He snorted. "Yeah, because you're so much older than we are."

"Maybe not chronologically, no." She let go of his hand to open up her dainty purse that was the size of Jazz's wallet. A moment later, she withdrew a slim silver case and sifted through the business cards inside until she found a cream-colored one and handed it over.

"Visions?" he asked, reading the line beneath the rolling hills that made up the company's logo.

Addiction treatment and recovery.

"You've figured out what it is, so I won't bother explaining. I will say that I've known several of the guests there, and they've made remarkable progress."

He shifted on the bed, trying futilely to get comfortable. That was difficult to do when it felt like his bones were being held together with a substance about as solid as gelatin. "Guests like your husband?"

She glanced away. "No. He doesn't believe he has a problem, so he hasn't sought treatment."

"Yet you remain married to the guy."

"Don't be so quick to judge unless you're ready to hop on the bus to Visions yourself. It's easy to see the flaws in others, much harder to recognize them in ourselves."

He tipped back his head to stare at the ceiling. It was only then that he noticed the cluster of balloons in the corner, decorated with get well wishes and cartoon characters. "Who sent those?"

"Everyone." She smiled. "Your bandmates and assorted friends and family have been in and out of this room constantly while you've been napping."

The surge of hope nearly stole his breath. Hell, it did entirely. "You lied to me?"

She patted his hand. "Selective truth."

"If I ask if she's been here, does that prove I need to go to Visions?"

"No, it proves you love her, and for good reason, because she's barely slept since you've been in this white-walled prison. I finally sent her home an hour ago to get some rest. She's worn out and on the verge of getting sick."

"Good. I mean, I'm glad you sent her, that she went."

"Me too." Lila picked at her nails. "So how long are you going to evade the question?"

"I didn't realize there was one." He let out a breath. "I've gone a few days without any blow."

"You've been unconscious for most of them."

He dropped his head to the pillow. "I'm not your husband—"

"Hey, am I interrupting?"

Gray glanced up at Nick's brush of knuckles against the doorframe. It wasn't even close to an actual knock but Nick expending even a modicum of effort in the manners department was big. Gray started to respond until he realized Nick's gaze was locked on Lila.

"Your husband, hmm?" He smiled blandly as he walked into the room without waiting for an invitation. "I must've missed that you have one."

She angled her chin. "I must've missed that it was any of your business."

Nick's smile never faltered. "Everything's my business, sweetness." He shifted his attention to Gray. "You look semi-alive."

Gray cocked his head, wondering if the pain meds he was on had influenced what he thought he'd just witnessed. Even now Lila and Nick were so noticeably *not* looking at each other that they might as well have been in a staring contest. What the hell?

Too bad Jazz wasn't there. She'd be able to weigh in—yeah, like that wouldn't be the least bit awkward.

It was all so fucking awkward.

"I'm okay," Gray said, tucking the card Lila had given him under the sheet. He had no intention of going down that road with Nick, today or any other day.

"Your color's better. Gray's not a good color for you." Nick grinned at his own joke. "See what I did there?"

"Impressive." Lila rose to her feet. "Think about what we discussed, Grayson, and get back to me when you've made a decision."

"What if I already have?"

She tucked her bite-sized purse under her arm. "Then my original terms for your loan repayment stand. You didn't use the money as intended, so you're out."

"Wait a second," Nick began, shocking Gray into silence.

"Butt out," Lila snapped. "If you were such a humanitarian, you wouldn't have caused trouble for him and Jasmine at every turn. I know what the hell I'm doing." She strode out of the room and shut the door. She didn't slam it, but it was damn close.

"Goddamn women." Nick grabbed the chair Lila had vacated and linked his fingers between his knees. "So about what you saw the other night—"

"I know it wasn't like what I thought. I wasn't exactly in my right mind."

"Yeah, and that news about your brother...I'm sorry, man."

"Me too. Not that the fucker's dead, mind you, but that I had to find out like that. That she knew and didn't tell me, probably because she thought it would send me headfirst into a mirror."

"Was she wrong?"

"Christ, I don't know. If a line was in front of me right now..." Gray shook his head. "I *am* sorry he's dead, and I feel like I'm betraying Jazz." He glanced at Nick. "You know what happened?"

"Yeah." Nick locked his linked hands behind his neck. "You only get one brother. I get it. My sister and I aren't exactly the Olson twins, but she's still my fucking sister. I still shared a freaking womb with her."

Gray snorted out a laugh. "Olsen twins gone really wrong, maybe." He sobered and rewound something in his head that Lila had said earlier. "Have you been around much the past few days?"

"Aww, worried that I don't care?"

"I wouldn't blame you if you didn't."

Nick jerked a shoulder. "I'm tired of looking back. Time for us to look forward, don't you think?"

"Yeah." Gray scrubbed his hands over his face and smothered the groan that nearly escaped him. A bit early for moves like that just yet. He dropped his hands and decided he didn't have much to lose.

Lies. All fucking lies. He could lose everything.

"Did my parents come?" he asked quietly, not meeting Nick's eyes.

"Yeah. I saw Jazz talking to them."

"Okay." He forced out the breath that had gotten lodged in his throat. "Okay."

"You could talk to them yourself, you know. It doesn't mean you don't love her."

"What does it mean then?"

"It means you're human, and sometimes you need someone. That simple. And that complicated." He paused. "She's still wearing your ring, you know."

"Christ." His breath left him on a shudder he couldn't stop. "I shouldn't want her to be."

"You know, it seems like you're not real comfortable with feeling how you actually feel. You could try relaxing and seeing what happens." Nick lifted his hands, his smile slipping into his trademark smirk. "Just a suggestion."

"I'll take it under advisement. I, ah, heard you covered for me at the show."

"She covered for you, and she kicked ass. If you're nice to me, I might hook you up with some really hot footage of your really hot fiancée playing your guitar." Nick waggled his brows.

Gray tried not to grin. "You're a frigging perv."

"So?"

Gray extended his fist, waiting until Nick bumped his knuckles to his. "Thanks."

"Yeah. You know, since you owe me, we could always try that threesome again..."

If anyone had ever told Gray he'd be able to laugh someday about one of the darkest nights of his life, he would've told them they were crazy. But somehow he managed it, even if it hurt like hell—at least physically if not emotionally. "Yep. Perv."

Nick grinned. "You know it, brother."

Chapter Thirty-Seven

Then

A knock on the door had Gray lifting his head. Jazz stood in the doorway, her normally bright colors and funky jeans exchanged for black shapeless pants and a black turtleneck. Ever since that day three weeks ago when Brent had attacked her, she'd worn little else. Her crazy braids and ponytails had been exchanged for a style that hid her face.

She was in self-protection mode and he couldn't stand the part he'd played in pushing his brother to that point. He'd known he was prodding a bear with his taunts, but he'd just never guessed Brent was capable of going that far.

He'd regret his mistake for the rest of his life.

"Hey there." She gave him a weak smile. "You ready to head back?"

"No." He pulled the zipper closed on his duffel. "I don't want to go."

"You've already been here way past your spring break." She shook her head and came into his bedroom, pulling the door shut behind her. "What are you going to do? Drop out of school so you can keep an eye on me?"

"Yes." He didn't hesitate. "But not to keep an eye on you, just to be together. I have a good amount of money set aside from birthdays and Christmas, and that's enough to get us started. We can move to San Francisco. We'll both get jobs—"

"You already have a life." She sat on the edge of his bed, a careful distance away from him. Since that day with Brent, she hadn't so much as let Gray hug her. "I don't want you to put that aside for me. We can't just run off together."

"Why not?"

She laughed, the sound as brittle as dry leaves. He'd begun to worry that he'd never truly hear her laugh again. "Because I got a better offer."

"What offer?" he asked, pushing his bag to the floor so he could sit beside her.

"My great-aunt Casey asked me to come live with her. She's older and needs help getting around. But it'll get me out of the system."

"You never mentioned an aunt before." He couldn't keep the suspicion out of his voice, especially when she ducked her head. "Why does she want you to live with her now?"

"She knows I need a place. And like I said, she's older and has a few health problems. My being there will help."

"You don't have to leave here. My parents won't make you go—"

Again she laughed, her gaze faraway. "They want me out. Brent wants me out. And to be honest, I need to go. This isn't—it isn't where I want to be anymore."

"So be with me." He grabbed her hand and held it to his cheek. She stiffened, and he knew he should let her go. But God, he couldn't. It felt like she was slipping away from him, and he'd be damned if he gave up without a fight. "You remember how it was between us in San Francisco. We had so much fun. Riding bikes, playing guitar, coming up with really bad drink concoctions from the hotel mini bar."

The last he added to make her smile, but she didn't respond. She'd retreated inside herself to a place he couldn't reach.

"We're not a couple." She met his eyes then, her chin firm even as her lips trembled. "We're just friends."

"*Just* my ass. I've never had a friend like you. No one matters to me as much as you."

"And that's not right." She tugged her hand back and stood. "You have a million friends at school and a full, busy life. God, you got all As this year so far. You're being offered internships and opportunities right and left. Why would you consider giving any of that up for me? Not to mention leaving your family—"

"You're my family," he interrupted. "I love you."

She shook her head. "I know we played brother and sister for a short while, but that doesn't make it real."

He rose and tugged on her hand, pulling her against him. Before she could evade the move, he cupped her cheek and lowered his head. "You're not my sister," he murmured.

Her pupils widened, the darkness swallowing the blue until only a hint remained. Her breathing sped up, her breasts rising and falling against his chest. He tried like hell not to be affected, not to even notice the points of her nipples pressing into his flesh through his shirt, but the reaction below his waist was instantaneous. From the sound of distress she made, she felt it.

She jerked back and turned away, covering her face with her hands.

Fuck, fuck, fuck. "I'm sorry," he gritted out. "I didn't mean to push you."

"No. You didn't. You wouldn't. It's just...it's never going to happen, Gray." She turned around and relief surged through him that she wasn't crying. Until he realized her face held no emotion at all. "You're always going to be part of some of the best memories of my life. I'll never forget you."

"*Forget* me?" He clenched his fist. "So, what, you're just going to move on like we never knew each other?"

"Of course not," she said, letting out a quick laugh. "I won't be far away. I'm just going to my aunt's."

"Where does she live?"

"In Carson. I'll be fine."

Something felt wrong. "Give me her address and phone number."

"I already wrote it down for you." She dug out a piece of paper from her pocket and placed it in his hand. "Go on. Your mom's waiting to say goodbye, and I'm on my way out too."

"You're leaving now? Today?"

She gave him a brief smile. "I don't want to be here without you, but that doesn't mean either one of us should stay."

He had to try one more time. He gripped her arms and poured every ounce of love he had for her into his expression, hoping to God she could feel how much he wanted to be with her. That nothing else mattered half as much. "You want freedom, baby, I can give you that. I'll give you everything."

"I know. It's just...the time's not right, okay? Maybe in a few years—"

"A few *years*?" The question burst out of him. "I don't want to wait any longer. We have no reason to." He rubbed his thumb along the inside of her arm and she trembled, closing her eyes. "We can have San Francisco. Just you and me."

"Maybe someday. Take care, okay?" She leaned up on her tiptoes and kissed his cheek, her lips sliding to the left for a fraction of an instant, ghosting over the corner of his mouth. "I love you," she said, easing back.

He held on for as long as he could, then dropped his arms.

During the drive back to school, he called the number she'd given him on a hunch. The call wouldn't go through. The line had been disconnected.

Chapter Thirty-Eight

Now

Jazz tapped her short fuchsia nails on the top of the table at Silas's Tavern and debated whether or not her touchy stomach could deal with iced tea. Apparently she'd stopped getting panic attacks in the face of stress and had moved right on to bouts of nausea.

After the night Gray had been hurt, she'd mostly been okay, not counting her horrifying replays of the way he'd looked when he lurched into the cabin. Then there was what he'd said, though she couldn't think about that part too much and stay sane. Even considering that Gray had turned to coke because of *her* hurt so much. But she couldn't go back and change things, no matter how much she wished she could.

She glanced around the dimly lit restaurant and pushed aside her menu. All she could do was this.

Leaning back against the booth, she stifled a yawn. Exhaustion dogged her constantly, but that made sense since she was barely sleeping. A likely side effect of her injured fiancé being in the hospital, she suspected.

A fiancé she hadn't spoken to for almost a week.

He'd been sprung last night and Nick—*Nick*, of all people—had picked him up and brought him back to the apartment. Like a coward, she'd cuddled her new kittens in her bedroom while listening to them laughing through the wall. True, they hadn't been yukking it up, just sharing the occasional chuckle, but still. When had the earth tilted off its axis?

It wasn't that she didn't want them to be friends. She did, absolutely. She wanted all of the crap of the past year to disappear entirely, including the awkwardness between the three of them. She just hadn't expected the two of them to become buddies while she tried to figure out how to even speak to Gray.

He hadn't made much effort on that score either. He'd called her from the hospital to thank her for the balloons and for sitting vigil. And he'd apologized for his "harsh words", of course, because his gentlemanly ways never disappeared for long. But the easy banter and enduring closeness that had always existed between them had disappeared, and she didn't have the first clue how to get it back.

She hoped this was a good first step.

Bypassing the iced tea she doubted she could swallow, she opened her purse and checked the contents of the bank envelope inside. She was taking a risk doing this, in every sense of the word. Growing up essentially on her own had made her excessively frugal, not counting her dependence on hair dye— usually store bought with coupons—and her thrift shop wardrobe. Today she'd practically emptied her savings account, and she'd also incurred a future debt to the absolute last people she wanted to owe money to.

The Duffys.

Bumping into them at the hospital had been about as difficult as she'd expected. She hadn't been surprised to see them, considering she'd called them in the first place. Telling them that Gray had a drug problem and had gotten hurt had been tough, mostly because she hated the feeling that she was betraying Gray. But his parents needed to know, and he needed them back in his life.

What he thought about her for making that decision for him didn't much matter. She'd opened the door for them to walk through again. If Gray chose to back right out, there was nothing more she could do.

In the meantime, she was going to order an iced tea, count her big stack of bills and try to look badass while she waited for her lunch companion to join her.

Ten minutes later, her dining guest finally appeared.

The blonde strutted up to the table, every inch of her from head to toe well-coiffed and perfectly presented. She wore an expensively cut business suit, one that highlighted her many curves and also gave her an air of professionalism. If Jazz hadn't known better, she might've actually believed the woman across from her was a lawyer or doctor or someone else important.

"Jasmine," she said, slipping into the opposite side of the booth. "I apologize for my tardiness."

"Cricket," Jazz replied, just as agreeably. "Don't worry about it. We're not friends, so manners aren't expected or necessary."

The waitress picked that moment to reappear and Jazz ordered her beverage. Cricket ordered a salad and diet soda while smiling and laughing with the woman serving them as if she couldn't be having more fun.

The moment the waitress left, Cricket leaned back in the booth and crossed her arms. "Out with your little proposition. My time is valuable and right now you're wasting it."

"You're the one who ordered lunch like we were old pals."

The corner of Cricket's mouth lifted. "I enjoy their salads here. I'm surprised you didn't get something too."

"I'm on a diet." She wasn't, but there was no damn way she'd ever eat with this woman.

"Oh." Cricket gave her a quick onceover. "Well, good luck. I always believe in being proactive and not letting a situation get too far out of hand before I deal with it."

Jazz set her teeth. "How much does Gray owe you?"

"Gray. Hmm. Now, that name does sound familiar." She placed a hand over her heart as she pretended to think it through. "Oh yes, I do remember him. He has a lot of...energy, doesn't he? I imagine you know that intimately."

"More intimately than you do, since you never slept with him."

"Is that what he told you?" Cricket smiled and thanked the waitress as she set their drinks down. She waited to continue until the waitress had moved away. "I'm glad to hear that you're so trusting. It's sweet, really."

"Cut the bullshit. If you know anything about his cock, it's because you played stalker and cut pictures out of a magazine. Don't bother trying to goad me."

"Hardly. I had my hand on it. That, darling, is sterling truth."

Which Jazz well knew, because she'd seen Cricket groping him on New Year's Eve. She pulled the wrapper off her straw and stabbed it into her iced tea, splashing some on the table. "Is that why you had your goons rough him up? Because you didn't get to do more than touch?"

"Goons. What an adorable word." Cricket laughed and unwrapped her own straw before sliding it into her soda much more delicately than Jazz. "What makes you think I have any idea what you're talking about?"

"I want to pay you what he owes. All of it, right now."

Interest fired in Cricket's dark eyes. "I'm curious. How did you get my number?"

"Off his phone, while he was in the hospital. He's out now. Your thugs didn't manage to kill him."

"If I wanted someone dead, you can rest assured they would be."

"Right, because you're so fucking dangerous in your expensive suits you buy with the money you make from other people's misery." Jazz sipped her tea to keep from throwing the contents on Cricket's seductively tousled hair.

"On the contrary. I make people happy. Why, you should've seen how happy I made Gray. Happier than I bet you've ever made him." Cricket smiled. "Though I'm sure you've tried."

Jazz set down her glass and counted off the beats to "Ripcord" in her mind in a vain attempt to stave off her fury. She hadn't come there to get into a bitch contest with Cricket. Whatever the other woman had done or hadn't done with Gray was the past. All she cared about right now was the future.

"How much does he owe you? I want the entire figure."

"Some big man he is, sending his girlfriend to pay off his debt."

"He didn't send me. He hasn't even told me he still owes you anything. I just assumed." Especially when she thought about the ring he'd bought Jazz just before he got hurt. She'd added up a lot of things and perhaps she'd reached the wrong total, but she figured she couldn't be too far off. If Gray had paid in full, Cricket's thugs probably wouldn't have messed with a lucrative cash cow.

"If you don't tell me, I'll walk away and you'll never get your money."

"Right. I'll just forgive the debt your boyfriend incurred because you told me to. Little drummer girl, trying to act all tough."

"You think I'm acting?" Jazz asked in a low voice. "I'm a product of the state of California's foster care system. I had men feeling me up before my breasts had fully developed. I've been on my own since sixteen. You don't scare me, and I don't give a shit if I scare you. I just want to pay you what Gray owes and pretend I never saw your motherfucking face."

Cricket fell silent as the waitress returned with her salad. She unrolled her silverware and set her napkin in her lap, as dainty as could be. Then she just looked at Jazz. "I was in foster care too."

"I don't care." She didn't. She absolutely would not allow herself to feel any empathy for this woman, not even for a second.

Cricket shrugged and speared a cherry tomato. "I'm not asking you to. I'm just saying it sounds like we come from the same place."

"No, we do not. Want to know how I know? Because I never would've stooped to selling to people who aren't strong enough to say no. I never would've bought my fancy clothes from blood money."

"No, you sit back and let the men in your band protect you. Sweet little Jasmine that all the boys want." Cricket scraped her fork over her plate. "I make no apologies for what I do. I provide a service to adults. If those adults can't control their fucking impulses, why is that my problem?"

"Because you're a human being and have a heart?"

"Maybe you still do, and if so, I pity you even more. Mine withered up years ago, and I can guarantee you that of the two of us, I'm suffering a lot less." She set down her fork and pulled her phone out of her purse. She tapped a few keys and glanced up, her face blank. "You asked me how much he still owes."

"Yes." Jazz tucked her now trembling hands between her thighs. "Tell me."

Cricket named a figure that caused Jazz's pulse to skip a dozen beats. She huffed out a breath and inhaled another. No big deal. She had enough to cover it. She'd planned ahead, and she was prepared.

"You look like you're about to hyperventilate, drummer girl." Cricket slipped her cell back into her purse. "Your boyfriend has a healthy appetite. His tab added up fast."

She wasn't going to think about exactly how much coke that money had bought. If she did, she'd probably get nauseous again, which wouldn't help her case for indifference. "That includes everything, right? Fees and interest and—"

"I don't pay taxes, so yes, that includes everything right up to this minute." Cricket smirked. "But the clock is running."

"Okay." Jazz withdrew the bank envelope from her purse. "I have about half of it here—"

Cricket sighed. "Same tune, different singer."

"Shut up. I have the rest, but it's in the bank." And it would tap her out completely. "I'll write you a check."

Cricket laughed. "Darling, mine's not the kind of business that accepts checks. We're strictly a cash-and-carry type of operation."

"Do you want your money or not?" Jazz pushed her iced tea out of the way. "I guarantee you I'm good for it."

"If you only had any idea how many guarantees I hear of that on a daily basis..." Cricket went back to her salad. "Fine. Give me the cash you have in hand and write me a check for the rest."

"I want it in writing that this satisfies the debt."

Cricket choked and reached for her soda. She took a long sip then shook her head. "You did say you were raised in foster care, right? Not with The Waltons on the farm? First you want to write me a check, now you want a signed note from the teacher. What's next, a handshake to show good faith?"

"You don't have any faith left, good or otherwise. As for the note, humor me."

Yes, it was stupid. She fully acknowledged it. But some part of her refused to see this as anything but a simple business transaction. When she paid a bill, she got a notice that it was paid. Simplistic, maybe, but she needed to follow the steps.

"You know, I like you. I have no reason to. Your contempt toward me is rather overpowering. But maybe it's our shared experiences." One side of Cricket's mouth curved. "And interest in men."

"You don't have an interest in him. You wanted to swallow him whole."

"Can't argue with that. He is one gorgeous package. And he has one, as well." Cricket held out her hand, her sly smile fading. "Now pay up."

Jazz handed her the envelope and wrote her a check for the rest. By then her stomach was threatening revolt, so she accepted the scrawled payment note Cricket gave her in return and stood to leave.

"It was nice doing business with you," Cricket said, returning to her half eaten salad.

Jazz started to turn away before some unknown impulse caused her to turn back. "Do you ever think about getting a real job? Something legit?"

Cricket didn't look up. "Something legit like banging on the drums in a rock band?"

"At least they won't be hauling me off to jail for it."

"I could walk away tomorrow and be set for years. Can you say the same?"

"I don't want to walk away," Jazz said, forcing out the words through her way too tight throat.

"One difference among many between you and me." Cricket saluted her with her fork. "Cheers."

Jazz drove back to the apartment with Cricket's words running through her head. For so long, she'd wanted nothing more than freedom. The ability to be able to pick up and go without any nagging foster parents or the system trying to tag her whereabouts. Eventually she'd admitted the reason she wanted freedom so much was because she truly didn't have a place to belong, so landing anywhere for long felt like the worst kind of lie. People like her were meant to go where the wind blew and the music carried them.

She'd once imagined becoming a traveling minstrel, strumming a guitar for pennies that people tossed in her case. Back then she'd been sure she could live on that kind of appreciation, hollow or not. In time, she might learn to stop *needing* so much, though her wants seemed simple enough. Love. Affection. A family.

Gray.

Without conscious decision, she headed straight to his room once she arrived back at the apartment. The door stood open and music played on the sound system on low, serving as a backdrop for him to strum along with. Not Oblivion. He'd chosen one of his favorite classic songs, "Wasted Time" by the Eagles. Listening to him sing along in his husky, haunting voice made her fumble for the guitar pick necklace she never took off. Touching it forged one more link with him in spite of the hesitation that bolted her feet to the floor.

She wasn't ready to have this conversation with him. Would never be ready. But it couldn't wait.

Once the song ended, she stepped into the doorway and tightened her grip on the chain. He sat on the bed, holding his guitar in his lap. His fingers ghosted over the strings, playing a silent melody she could hear though it had no sound.

She bit her lip, aching for him. For herself.

"You can come in." He lifted his head and gave her a smile tinged with a sorrow she understood all too well. "This was supposed to be your room now too."

She abandoned her hold on her necklace to start fiddling with her ring. "I wasn't sure that offer was still stood."

His lack of response created a chain-effect reaction in her body. Her skin prickled hot and a wave of dizziness rolled through her. But her unsettled stomach didn't so much as pitch.

Too bad she couldn't feel any relief through her dread.

"Come in and shut the door, okay?" He shifted to set aside his guitar, allowing her to see the suitcase tucked between the nightstand and the bed. The *packed* suitcase.

"That's from the cabin, right?" Her breath quickened. "You just haven't unpacked—"

"Come in." He gestured with his fingers for her to keep moving forward and she stopped, unwilling to make this easy on him. If he was going to break her heart, he'd have to travel the last few feet between them to do it.

Even if she suspected all he'd have to do was look, really *look*, at her to make her lose her last grasp on her composure.

"No. I'm fine here." She held her ground just inside the doorway. "W-where are you going?"

"Jazz—"

No *baby* this time. No sexy smile or hungry expression to let her know that he was undressing her in his mind even while he was talking about something banal. His eyes were guarded, his mouth set in a line.

"Just say your piece. Don't sugarcoat it." She clamped her arms over her chest and prayed for the strength to get through this. To not fall to her knees and beg him not to turn her away when they'd finally gotten so close to having everything.

It was all about timing, she'd told him once. Without it, it was impossible to keep the beat going. And theirs was always fucking wrong.

"Please, come sit next to me. Don't make this harder than it is already."

"Why not? Why shouldn't it be the hardest thing we've ever gone through? If I'd wanted easy, I would've stayed with Nick." His face closed off even more, but she couldn't regret her thoughtless mention. Not when he was about to trash their past and their future.

"It should be easy," he said, his voice barely audible. "That's what I always wanted for you. You deserve a man who can take care of you and treat you right. Who will never lie to you or hurt you or put you in danger for even a second. That's not me."

"I don't want to be taken care of. I don't need it. Newsflash, Grayson Duffy, I've been on my own for a very long time. If I let you share my life, it's because I wanted you there, not because I couldn't get by without you." She wasn't sure of that—not at all—but she was damn fed up with people acting as if she should hide out in an ivory tower all day. "Wanna know who I had lunch with? You might know her. She's tall and blonde and claims to have handled your penis."

Recognition dawned in his eyes and he jerked to his feet. "Why would you have lunch with Cricket? Or go anywhere near her?"

"Maybe I wanted a hit." She walked forward and slammed her hands on his chest, pushing him backward into the frame of the bed. "Ever think of that? Maybe I thought I should try it too," she said, pushing him again.

Too late she remembered his injuries. Fury burned in her, almost squelching out the fear. Beneath both simmered more love than she had any clue what to do with.

He didn't move, but the wildness in his eyes revealed the extent of his anguish. "No."

"*Yes*. I want to know what made you go that far. I want to feel that high that's worth throwing everything else away."

"I didn't have anything else." His voice lifted to match hers and he moved forward, going toe-to-toe with her. "I'd lost you, when I'd never even had you. All I'd gotten was a taste I had to share. What the fuck did I have?"

"How about these?" She yanked on his wrist. "You create beautiful things with these hands and this heart." She jammed her fingers into his chest. "Inside you, there's more music than anyone I've ever known. And you don't even hear it. You don't see what I see every time I look at you."

"What?" he roared, getting in her face.

"I see the sweetest, smartest, sexiest boy I've ever known. He's a man now, but when I look into his eyes, I'm a girl again and he's a boy. I never truly got to be a child or to stop watching over my shoulder, but with him, I did. Because he stood back to back with me every day. Not in front of me. Not shielding me. I just wanted someone to hold my hand." She panted out the rest. "I wanted it to be you."

He closed his fingers around her wrist and tugged it up to his mouth, pressing his lips to the center of her palm. "I let you down."

"Don't you dare say that." Tears blinded her as she shoved him once more, incapable of staying still long enough for his words to sink in. She couldn't allow them to travel deep enough that she couldn't dig them out again. "You're the best man I've ever known. I want to marry you, and have babies with you, and grow old with you. I won't let you keep me from getting what I deserve." She rained punches over his torso, not fully conscious of where her blows were landing. She'd just add this to her list of regrets later. "I won't back down. Not this time."

He caught her fists and pulled them up his chest, dragging her hands around his neck. Then he hauled her up in his arms, groaning loudly and swaying with enough force that she thought they'd end up on the ground. Somehow he maintained his hold on her and she held on to him, wrapping her legs around his waist monkey-style until he toppled them both to the bed. At the last second she tried to brace his shoulder but he groaned again anyway, his face going white for an instant before she crushed her mouth to his and offered him her breath.

She didn't expect him to respond. The guy was in agony. But his hands drove into her hair, turning her head the way he needed it, and his tongue stroked over hers, plunging deep. Feeding on her as if he was starving to death and she represented his last opportunity to sate his hunger. She gave him back as good as she got, biting his lower lip, sucking his tongue, pulling on his hair. He freed a hand to push under her top and she reared back to undo his jeans, her hands stilling at the soft but audible click of the door being shut.

She slid a glance sideways and yep, one of their bandmates had closed the door. Probably the one currently laughing like a loon in the hallway.

"Simon," she muttered, shaking her head. She glanced at Gray and found him grinning up at her, his amusement almost enough to disguise the leftover pain etched on his features.

He was hurt yet she'd whaled on him, and pushed him, and now she was sitting on him. She started to move away but he grabbed her arm, settling her directly over his definitely-not-ailing dick. "Stay put, freedom fighter."

It should've pissed her off to have their argument tossed back in her face. But it was hard to get too annoyed when she couldn't stop rubbing against his rigid cock like a cat in heat. "You're injured."

"And I know how you can take care of me."

She couldn't help laughing at his lecherous tone. "Well then, far be it from me not to...serve."

She shimmied down his body to peel off his jeans and boxers, yanking them down his thighs. She wasted no time in sliding her mouth over the head of his cock, then pleasured his shaft with slow swipes of her tongue. Getting him nice and wet. She traveled lower and buried her face in his groin while she nipped and teased his flesh. She toyed with his balls, rolling them between her lips, giving them both equal treatment, before licking his length right up to the swollen tip.

This time she didn't torment him with a shallow suck but took him down in one long swallow, taking as much as she could in one pass. At the sound of his grunt, she pushed herself for more, digging her nails into the insides of his thighs while she opened her throat and amped up her suction.

"Jazz, baby, c'mere."

Shifting her body so that he could see, she flipped up her skirt and pushed aside her panties, moaning around him as her fingers brushed her soaked piercing. She knew his mobility was more limited than usual due to his injuries, so she took advantage, torturing them both with the visual of her swirling her fingers in and out of her pussy. He grabbed her leg and bit the inside of her calf and damn if the jolt didn't zip right into the heart of her, where she was pulsing around her thrusting fingers.

"Fuck, baby. I can't watch this."

"So close your eyes."

His indignant huff made her grin before her desire demanded center stage. She fucked herself openly, spreading her thighs, giving him the show of her life while she smoothed wet kisses along his shaft. She exalted in every broken gasp he couldn't hold back and the way his hips jerked and his cock thrust helplessly into her fist. He was so close to the edge, and she'd taken him there. Just like she'd taken herself.

Power surged through her trembling limbs, heady and sweet. "Where do you want to paint me with your cum?" she murmured, pressing her thumb against the seeping slit on his erection.

He bit off a groan, his shoulders nearly coming off the bed as he gripped the sheets and stared fixedly at her pumping hand. "You know where," he rasped. "Inside you. I want it dripping out of you."

"Always gotta bump it up a notch." At his muffled laughter, she lapped up the fluid pooling on the tip of him and pulled her damp hand free to caress the base of his dick. His laughter turned into a moan when she squeezed. Having super strong fingers came in handy sometimes. "So do I."

"If only I could flip you on your stomach right now…"

"You can't flip me anywhere. And I think I like that." She caught her tongue between her teeth and crawled up his body to rub her lips over his, letting him taste himself on her mouth before she traced her wet fingertips over his lower lip. His broody eyes never left hers as he licked up what she'd given him, as he curled his tongue around her fingertip.

"You like taking control, huh?"

"I guess I do." She eased back to pull off her top, tossing it on the floor. Then she popped the clasp on her bra and leaned forward, trailing her nipples over his mouth. He growled and seized hold of one, biting down with a sensuous pressure that ignited a fierce drumbeat between her legs. "I can't wait."

"Then don't." He grabbed her hip and situated her over his cock. When she hovered over his length, a fraction of an inch away, he dropped his hand to the mattress.

The permission he offered her in his gaze stole her breath. She knew it wasn't easy for him to give up control, but he would—for her.

She scratched her nails over the Oblivion tattoo low on his stomach. "You know, I haven't teased you nearly enough about this tat. But since it says *this way to Oblivion*, I'm about to see if there's truth in advertising." She lifted up slightly then plunged downward, sighing as she took him in right to the hilt. "Oh yeah." She swiveled her hips and repeated the move. "That's fucking oblivion, all right."

"Christ, you're trying to kill me." He wheezed and gripped the sheet in his fist, his hips rising to match the violent pace she set.

She leaned forward and braced her hands on the pillow on either side of his head, brazenly riding his cock. Her breasts bounced in his face and she didn't even worry about excess jiggling because for the first time, she truly felt like a goddess. Sexy and free and so very loved.

Being loved made all the difference.

"So goddamn beautiful." His fingers spanned her cheek and he brought her mouth close, panting into it as he rocked into her again and again, their rhythm instinctual and unhurried. She didn't have to reach for the beat or urge him to speed up, because whatever she did, he countered, reading her effortlessly.

They were in sync, their bodies slapping and sliding together with the most delicious friction. God, she never wanted it to end.

Eventually beads of sweat popped out on his forehead and he swore, reaching down to grip her ass and pull on her onto him harder, faster. Her painfully swollen clit and her piercing dragged over his flesh, making them both curse, and she bowed back, locking her arms behind her head as she ascended that first peak and coasted into the thrilling drop, hurtling so swiftly that she didn't know if she'd find nirvana or a hard landing below.

Not caring, because he was inside her. Filling her up. Making her forget that anything existed except the two of them.

Still pulsing, she gasped as he sat up and wrapped his arms around her, holding her close as his body bucked and shuddered and hammered into hers. "God, yes. Come on me. Keep coming."

"Oh yes." She couldn't stop. She rode him like a wild thing, driven to wring out every drop of bliss. There seemed to be no end to the amount of times she could reach that pinnacle while he held back. Unlike her, he obviously had enough patience to spur her on to new heights for the sheer joy of watching her fly.

The harder he shook, the more demanding he became. He wanted more. Always more.

His control finally snapped, and she held on tight as he thrust one last time. And crushed her mouth to his to capture the unforgettable sound of him letting go.

* § *

He let her sleep for as long as he could.

As the day waned, Gray stroked her cheek with the backs of his fingers and tried to memorize every one of her features. The tiny dark mole above her upper lip, the spray of freckles over her nose. Her mouth formed a flawless bow, and without lipstick, it was a rosy pink like her cheeks. Even in sleep she was glowing. His stubble burn marred her jaw and neck, but it only made her more beautiful.

His gaze lowered to the guitar pick nestled in the notch of her collarbone. So much of their history existed in such a small, seemingly insignificant item. Her laughter and tears, his love and longing. He traced it with his fingertip, trying to imprint this moment on his mind for the endless days ahead. She would always be the most shining, perfect thing in his life, and he couldn't be anything but grateful that they'd had this time together. Whatever lay beyond today, he'd shared this with her, and no one would ever be able to take it away from him.

From either of them.

His gaze dropped to the hand beside her cheek and the ring on her finger. That symbol of what he felt for her was worth any penance. When he'd been lying on the concrete, his body in agony, his mind in turmoil, he'd still carried the light from loving her inside him. It was like a lantern, beating back the dark.

No matter how apart they traveled, he would never let the light go out.

She stirred, her eyelashes fluttering. Slowly, she smiled. "You're watching me sleep again."

"Busted." He shifted more fully onto his good side and swallowed the grunt of pain at the pull in his shoulder. Small favors that the bulk of his injuries were to his left side and he was right-handed. The bastards who'd fucked him up must've just gotten unlucky. He seriously doubted they'd spared his playing side.

She sat up and fussed at his shirt, smoothing it over his arm. "Your doctor told me you're supposed to wear a sling to help manage the pain."

"You talked to my doctor?"

Her eyebrow winged up. "What do you think?"

He smiled and cupped her cheek, rubbing his thumb over her lip. "I think you're going to make one hell of a wife someday."

He hadn't meant to say it. Not to mention the statement itself sounded kind of sexist. Damn, he'd been hanging around with Nick way too much.

At least that'd be over for a while.

She frowned and he braced for the storm sure to come. "What do you mean someday?" She held up her hand. "See this? I'm not waiting until I've gone gray."

His mouth quirked. "You went Gray years ago."

"Ha ha. I'm serious. If you think I'm down for some long-ass engagement—"

"We have to talk." He sat up and bit the inside of his cheek to avoid squealing like a little girl. Goddamn shoulder. The ribs weren't much better.

"So talk."

He glanced back to where she sat against the headboard, arms crossed, mouth sulky. "Hear me out."

"I'm listening."

"With less than half an ear." He stroked his eyebrow ring. "I'm leaving for a while."

She didn't say anything for so long that he looked back to find her staring at him, all the color in her cheeks gone. Her eyes were so huge and startlingly blue that his breath tripped before evening out again. "This is your home. We're your family."

"My family...Jesus, were you ever going to tell me about Brent?"

"Yes. No. I don't know." She tugged up the sheet then pushed it down again. "Yeah, I was, but I chose a different timetable than you would've probably picked. But I had a good reason."

"You were afraid of sending me into a spiral."

Once again, she grew silent.

He nodded, unsurprised. "Figured as much. That's another reason I have to do this."

"Do what? Walk away from everyone who cares about you?"

"No. I'm doing this *for* the people who care about me and depend on me. And I'm doing it most of all for myself. That's hard for me to say, because I've spent so many years living for you. But I can't do that anymore."

"I never asked you to."

"I know you didn't." He caressed her leg through the sheet. "I thought I could be everything to you. Make up for everyone who'd ever hurt you." His hand stopped moving. "Until I joined them, and I realized I'd been doomed to fail all along."

"I hurt you just as much."

He started to deny it. That was what he did. But this time, he couldn't. "Yeah. You did."

"You...you really started the night you saw me with Nick. That was true."

Yet again his first reaction was to deflect. He blew out a breath. "Yes." At her soft inward breath, he gripped her thigh. "That doesn't mean you're to blame. I made that choice. You and I weren't together. You had every right to be with him." He shook his head. "Just like I had every right to act like a complete dick and do something that harmed me more than anyone else."

"All those times I tried to talk to you about us in recent years, you blocked me and changed the subject. Ever since Brent, you never said another word about us. How did you expect me to know?"

"I never said I was smart."

She drew her legs up, out from under his hand. Always, *always* she curled into herself when she needed to retreat. He shifted to look her way, trying to stifle the flash of pain he knew must register on his face. But she reached forward just the same and cupped his cheek. "You need your sling."

"Later."

"You don't need a wife. You need a keeper."

"Yeah, for the last while I have, and I'm not about to shackle you with that."

"Isn't that for me to decide?" she asked, tucking her hands between her knees.

"No. Not anymore. I need to do this for me, and I'm asking you to understand. Just like I need you to understand why I didn't make another move toward you all those years."

"Because I'd turned you down so many times—"

"No. Don't get me wrong. That wasn't a walk in the park." He smiled faintly. "But I'm used to working for what I want. You could've told me no a million times and I never would've given up."

"Then?"

Of all the things he'd had to tell her, this was the hardest of them all. He sucked in a breath and discovered it didn't alleviate the pressure in his chest, so he rolled out of bed and paced naked to the dresser. He braced his hands on it and searched for a way to tell her that wouldn't make her hate him.

There wasn't one.

"Gray."

"The night Brent attacked you, I provoked him." When she didn't reply, he gripped the edges of the dresser and pushed on. "I came home early to go to your party with you. I rented a tux, whole nine yards. He goaded me by trying to make me think the two of you were involved. I knew it was bullshit. I knew it, and he still grabbed me by the balls. And I reacted."

"What did you do?"

Her quiet question, so full of confusion and hesitation, nearly broke him. For that moment, she was sixteen years old again, almost innocent and yet the exact opposite. And he was the one who'd nearly shattered her with his thoughtless taunts.

"I told Brent you'd never want him like you wanted me." He turned back, then crawled across the bed and framed her beautiful face in his hands. Even the aches in his body no longer could compete with the open wounds in her eyes. "It was my fault. I caused him to go that far. If I hadn't said—"

"If you hadn't told the truth, you mean?"

He fell silent.

"I did want you more than anyone else, and I'd certainly never looked at him that way. But I don't think he even cared about me. I was a pawn to push around. A weapon in his competition with you. And we all lost out because he didn't know when to back down and when to fight."

He sat back on his haunches. "Jazz—"

"You came onto me when I wanted to be adopted more than I wanted anything else. Even you," she said softly. "When adoption wasn't an option on the table anymore, *that's* when you decided to back off. Every time I looked at another man, you'd growl, but you never did one damn thing to indicate you still wanted me. Until Nick."

"Until Nick," he agreed.

"Then you decided the three of us getting naked together was a smart idea."

"Technically you decided that. I don't recall getting undressed first."

"Can you blame me? I never thought I'd get you undressed, ever. Even if the fucking Pope had been in the room, I would've stripped down to my birthday suit anyway."

"Back to the Pope," he muttered. "Seems to be a recurring theme lately."

"You know what else keeps recurring? You making your mind up for me and deciding you know how I must feel." She shoved her hands through her disordered hair. "By the way, your track record in that department sucks."

He had to smile. "Tell me how you really feel, honey."

"Fine." She stared him dead in the eye and held up her left hand. "I want to marry you. Now. No more bullshit. No more waiting."

His heart leapt and for an instant, he nearly agreed. The words were right there in his throat, aching to be spoken. But at the last moment, he lowered his head.

"Okay then," she said, sounding more defeated than he'd ever heard her. She tossed off the sheet and threw her legs over the side of the bed. "That answers that."

"Wait." He squeezed her shoulder. "It's not about me not wanting to marry you."

"Then what?"

"It's that I'm not in a place to make that decision. Honestly, neither are you. We've been together such a short time, and I'm a fucking mess. I'm going to get to the other side, but I'm not there yet. Anyone would tell us we're insane to consider a move this huge without making sure we have a firm foundation underneath us first."

"Anyone isn't us, and they haven't lived holding their breath for years like we have. I believe in you."

"You haven't even asked me what happened." He rubbed the heel of his hand over his sore ribs. "If I relapsed or blew the money Lila gave me or some combination of the two."

"I have my theories. If you ever doubted whether I want bling more than you, don't. There's no bling in this world that could make up for one iota of the terror I felt that night."

His shoulders slumped. "I'm sorry."

"You'll never be as sorry as I am, because it took both of us to arrive where we are." Squarely, she met his gaze. "Whatever happened, I trust you and I don't doubt for a second that you're going to kick this addiction. I may be naïve. I may be the biggest dummy going. But no one will ever accuse me of not putting one hundred percent of my faith in you."

"God, baby...I don't know what to say."

"Don't write an ode to me yet." She stuck her tiny hand in his face. "If you relapse or get yourself hurt again for *any* goddamn reason, I swear to God, I will fucking kick your ass harder than those thugs ever did. I will make it my life's work to bring you pain."

He laughed and kissed her palm. "You make it sound so simple. I wish it was."

"Here we go again." She sighed heavily. "Have your existential crisis some other day, all right? I'm not feeling too hot."

"But—" He broke off. "Why? What's wrong?"

"Nothing. Just some stupid nausea. Probably a side effect of having lunch with a drug dealer and getting dumped before dinner."

"Why would you be nauseous? Do you have the flu?"

"If I do, it's lasting a long time. It started the day you went missing."

"That was almost a week ago."

"Yeah." She dug her bra out from under the pillow. How it had ended up there, he had no clue. "Whatever. I'm going to go lie down. I'm too tired to argue anymore today. If leaving is your way of throwing yourself on your sword for being human, then that's your choice."

"Jazz." He grabbed her arm and somehow managed not to howl.

She stopped fumbling with her bra clasp. "What?"

His pulse kicked up. "Could you be pregnant?"

"Of course not."

"Have you gotten your period recently?"

Pressing her lips together, she yanked up her bra straps and bent to pull on her panties. She remained in a crouched position longer than necessary, her head lowered. She was breathing loudly enough for him to hear. Almost wheezing.

He leaned over to look at her. "What are you doing?"

"Having a panic attack." She peered up at him. "Do you mind?"

There was absolutely no reason in the world to laugh. Less than none. Yet it tore out of his chest and echoed in the room until she gave in and joined him, wiping her eyes as she rose to sit next to him on the bed.

After a few moments, he covered her hands with his. "Should we...I don't know, go find out? Make sure."

"What do you mean *we*?" Indignance filled her tone. "You don't have to pee on a stick."

"Have you ever done that before?"

"Take a pregnancy test? No. But I heard all about Harper's. And sat there and tried not to cry out of sheer envy."

He laced his fingers with hers. "It's not the right time for us to have a baby."

"I'd say not, since you just dumped me."

He laughed again, which earned him a narrow-eyed glance that only made her look more adorable. "I didn't dump you. I would never. Are you fucking kidding me? But they recommend limiting relationships as a condition of rehab."

"Rehab?"

"Where did you think I was going?" He withdrew the card Lila had given him from the front pocket of his suitcase and handed it to her. "It's an eight-week program."

"Eight weeks," she said, staring down at the cream-colored card. "But we're going into the studio soon."

"Lila said the band could work around me. I'll just have to make up the time extra fast when I get back."

She lifted her head. "You're coming back."

"Of course."

Shaking her head, she laughed softly. "Why didn't you just tell me that?"

"I was getting around to it. Speaking of getting around to things, why did you go see Cricket?" He gripped her arm, suddenly seized by panic. "You didn't actually buy anything from her, did you? It's bad enough you smoked because of me. If you're pregnant—"

"I smoked a small amount very early on. Not that it matters because I'm not pregnant. I'm also not enough of an idiot to covet a cocaine addiction." She winced. "Sorry. Can I blame pregnancy hormones without actually being pregnant?"

He let go of her arm. "Why do I love you again?"

"Because of my winsome personality? And because I give one hell of a blowjob, with and without happy ending?"

"The second one, definitely. The first...eh, I'm not terribly impressed."

"Funny. As for why I went to see Cricket, I paid off the rest of your debt. You no longer owe her a damn nickel." She looked around the floor. "If I can find where I dropped my purse, I'll show you the proof."

"Wait a second. You paid my debt? How? With what money?"

"Mine." She flushed. "With a little backing assistance from your parents. Yes, I called them and told them you were hurt. They came to the hospital, and we talked. They know about your...issue now."

"Jesus Christ."

"I asked them for a loan and explained why I needed it. I'll fully be repaying them once I get more money from the tour. And the album and the next tour. Then there's our merchandising." She smiled bravely. "See? We're going to be fine."

"You won't be repaying them. I'll be repaying them *and* you. You aren't responsible for my cash flow problems."

"That's a quaint way to put it, but hell yes, I am. I'd expect the same from you if I needed your support." She pulled the ponytail holder off her wrist and did her messy hair up in a quick bun that somehow looked sexier than the most artfully arranged style.

"You have officially exploded my brain." Then there was the fact that she was nauseous. Dear God. "I can't discuss any of this right now."

"There's nothing to discuss." She tugged on her skirt, fluffing the little kick pleats as if they were having an ordinary conversation. "I was overdue on doing my share of bailing out in this relationship."

"So you just called her up and met with her?" He shook his head, awe overtaking his initial irritation that she'd used her money to play savior. That wasn't even mentioning the potential danger she'd put herself in. "And I thought I had a pair."

She patted her chest. "I just store mine up top."

"That you fucking do." He expelled a short breath. "We're going to talk more about this later. In the meantime, do you think Harper will let us borrow her truck once more?"

"I think so, yeah. She'll also probably demand to come along and make me take the test in the convenience store bathroom."

"Why? Does she have a preggo fetish or something?"

"No. She knows I do, and she's my best friend. Other than you, of course."

"Oh." It took him a few more deep breaths to find the strength to put aside his own needs in favor of hers. "Would you rather she go with you than me?"

"No." She held out her hand. "C'mon. While we're there, you can buy me some Pepto-Bismol. You know, since you have to start paying me back and all." She rolled her eyes.

He grinned. "Is this what our life together is going to look like?"

"If we're lucky."

An hour later, they stared at the two pregnancy tests lined up side by side on the bathroom sink. "Well," she said, turning away. "That settles that."

Without saying anything, he gathered her in his arms.

"I shouldn't have wanted it to be positive." She pressed her cheek against his chest. "Right? Tell me I'm wrong to want that. It's a mistake. The timing is horrible."

"It's not the best," he agreed.

"But I wanted it just the same. I never let myself believe it could be true, but I almost willed those two lines to show up. And they didn't."

He tipped up her chin and caught her single tear with his finger. He couldn't sort through everything he was feeling, not yet. Not today. "No. Not this time."

"When do you have to go?"

"Soon." He swallowed hard and turned his cheek against her hair. "Will you come with me when I tell the rest of the band that I'm going to Visions? They're waiting downstairs."

"Sure." She was already walking away, her unshakable mask slipping back into place.

"Jazz. Wait."

She glanced over her shoulder. "Yeah?"

There was one thing he didn't have to sort out. One truth he wasn't willing to deny her for any reason. "I was willing those lines to show up too."

Her smile only made her tears more poignant as she offered him her hand. "Let's go."

Chapter Thirty-Nine

Then

Jazz stepped off the bus and tucked her secondhand iPod in her pocket. The ink on the shred of paper gripped in her other hand would probably run soon. Her palms were so damp she couldn't stop wiping them on her jeans.

Just do it. One foot in front of the other. Keep walking.

She dug out the address and made her way to the end of the block, biting her lip the whole time. She should've called first. A landline phone number had been included in the listing, so she should've used it.

I could call from outside.

No, she didn't have many minutes left on her phone and she wasn't going to be that much of a coward. It had been two years since she'd seen him, but that wasn't all that long in the scheme of things. Only seven hundred something days. Barely a blink.

When she stood beside the patchy lawn of the home Gray now lived in, she flexed her fingers and imagined limbering up for a lengthy session behind the kit. It was about mental endurance as much as anything else. Playing on past the point of pain and frustration and exhaustion, even when the notes wouldn't fall right and nothing sounded the way it did in her head. She never buckled, never stopped.

No matter what greeted her on the other side of this door, she would be fine. Unbreakable. Fucking granite.

Then he opened the door, his dark, wavy hair falling past his bare shoulders—he'd lost his shirt somewhere along the way—and his jeans hugging lean hips, and she forgot all about being stone. One glimpse was like hot lava, melting her on sight.

The cool frost burned away in his eyes, leaving only heat. "Jazz." Her name sounded like a prayer.

"Yeah." She smiled and adjusted her knapsack over her shoulder. "You look good."

"Thanks. So do you." He rubbed his hand over his mouth. "Uh, do you want to come in? You look hot. I mean, thirsty. It's brutal out there. Want a drink? Not alcohol. Like lemonade."

When she started to laugh, he grinned. "Fuck this noise." He locked his arms around her waist, hauling her straight off her feet and over the threshold. She laughed harder and locked her arms around his neck, wondering how it could still feel this right. Nothing had changed. He was the lock for her key. The hand for her glove.

Fuck it, he was her everything. Still. Always.

He finally set her down, though she doubted her feet would ever truly touch the ground again. "How are you? What are you doing now?"

"Not much. I'm working at the waffle house. What about you?"

"Teaching music theory to some kindergarten kids as part of an internship." The corner of his mouth lifted. "I still have one year left at Berkeley."

"That's awesome. And you're no longer living with your parents."

His face closed down. "No. I haven't since it happened." He held up a hand. "Don't ask me how they are, because I don't know. We don't talk anymore."

"Gray," she said, barely unable to speak. He'd given up his family for *her*, and they hadn't even been in contact. She'd never met anyone more selfless.

"Don't. It's done." He scratched his chest and she tried not to watch his muscles ripple. So many freaking muscles. "What else are you up to?"

"I just finished school."

"That's great. Where'd you end up?"

"Trawler Community College. I finished up my high school credits and got a certificate in Early Childhood Development in one fell swoop." She gave him a sheepish smile. "Turns out they have programs for fuckup dropouts like me."

"Shut up. You weren't ever a fuckup."

"But I did drop out."

"It isn't dropping out if you end up somewhere better." He tucked her hair behind her ear as he always had. "I'm so proud of you."

She fought not to blush. "Thanks. I'm in a band."

"Huh. Imagine that." His grin grew. "Me too."

"Oh yeah?" She knew exactly which one. She'd only stalked him to clubs in the area about ten times over the past year. "Maybe we should compare notes."

"Maybe we should." He frowned, tilting his head as he rubbed his fingers over her crowded earlobe. She was up to half a dozen piercings. "What the hell did you do to your hair?"

"Took you long enough to notice."

"Oh, I noticed." He rubbed his hand over the shaved part of her head that transitioned into long pink and green waves on the side. "You look fucking amazing."

"But not hot," she teased.

He started to respond when a door shut down the hall. She'd assumed he lived with a couple of roommates, so that didn't surprise her. But when a curvaceous blonde came down the hall wearing just a nightshirt, carrying a basket of laundry that clearly contained a pile of boxers, Jazz stumbled back. Her heels hit the floor, hard.

"Hey, I couldn't find the dryer sheets you bought. Are they in the—" The blonde trailed off and smiled at Jazz. "Hi. I didn't realize we had guests. I'm Amber." She anchored the laundry basket against her hip. "Man, your hair is sweet."

Jazz laughed because what else could she do? Cry? Well, yeah, but that'd be later, when she was alone. "Thanks. I'm Jazz."

"Awesome to meet you. Are you one of Gray's music friends? You look like one of them." She pursed her lips. "Oh my, that sounded bad. I mean, you dress funky like they do, with the ripped jeans and the cool hair and all. Of course your ass is half the size of mine." She paused, apparently noticing Gray had yet to speak. He actually didn't seem to be breathing, so that wasn't too surprising. "Notice he's not arguing with me," she added.

"Jazz is my foster sister," he said, almost robotically.

Jazz flinched before she could control it. *You walked away. Remember that.* "Used to be," she said, making her voice as cheery as possible. "Now I'm just the girl with crazy hair he used to know."

She turned to reach for the door, surprised to find it was still open. They'd just started talking without even closing it. Forgetting everything around them, just like old days.

Not anymore.

"Jazz, wait."

"I wish I could hang out longer, but I have practice. You know, us wild music types have to play as much as possible." She smiled at Amber over her shoulder. "Nice to meet you."

"I'll be right back," Gray said to Amber, following Jazz onto the sidewalk.

When she just kept walking, he grabbed her arm and spun her back. "That's it? You're just leaving?"

"What do you expect me to do? You have a girlfriend. She's even pretty."

He frowned. "Did you expect me to have one that's not?"

"No, but it would've been more considerate."

"Woman, I don't fucking understand you. You took off for two years without a word. You gave me a fake address and a fake phone number, swapped cell numbers and dropped out of school. You did everything you could to break contact with me. What the hell did you expect me to do? Hold my dick for two years?"

"I'm not supposed to think about your dick. Because I'm your foster sister, remember?"

He swore under his breath. "What am I supposed to do? Tell me."

"It's already done." She shook her head and kept walking, anchoring her knapsack higher on her shoulder. "I'll see you around. Maybe on the cover of a magazine. Or maybe YouTube. Lots of artists get discovered on there nowadays."

"Jesus, Jazz, wait. I couldn't just hit the pause button on my life."

"I know. And neither can I."

"So that's it? This is really the end." He let out a harsh laugh. "I got you back only to lose you all over again."

She stopped at the end of the sidewalk and turned back, sucking him down one last time. Bathed in unrelenting sunshine, he seemed to glisten with life and vitality. The golden boy she would always love, no matter what.

"With us, you never know."

Chapter Forty

Now

Gray adjusted his guitar on his good shoulder and stepped onto the set where they'd be shooting the "Sugar Kiss" video. After eight weeks in rehab, his first task involved stepping in front of the camera.

Nothing like a trial by fire.

The crew bustled around the room, arranging cameras and set pieces. There was a big four-poster bed in the middle, piled high with a thick duvet and piles of fluffy pillows. He frowned. No one had mentioned a bed to him.

Then again, Lila wasn't exactly forthcoming with details. Her instructions had been along the lines of "here's where we're doing the shoot, get your ass there at ten a.m. and don't be late."

He considered it lucky she'd given him until ten a.m., since he'd been released at eight.

Technically he could've gotten out last night, the official end of his two month stint. But he'd taken the last night away from the band to plan how he wanted things to go. He'd coasted for too long, just doing whatever it took to get by. Eight weeks of talking more than he'd ever wanted to in his life had helped him to realize that he couldn't do that anymore. He'd always been someone who had concrete goals and a step-by-step way of reaching them. His ability with the guitar and 4.0 average in college hadn't been accidents. He'd worked his ass off.

Now he had a new subject to master. Well, a couple of them. He wanted to take his skill to the next level, both with the guitar and with songwriting. He'd discovered a whole new way of making cash on the side, and that meant he couldn't take the slacker's way out when it came to coming up with new material. His A-game wouldn't cut it. He needed an A+.

Then there was the even bigger goal. The one where he settled down with the girl of his dreams and they finally made it work.

It wouldn't be easy, but he was committed to doing things the right way this time. No more two-week courtships and a proposal outside a grocery store. This go-round, they were going slow. They would date for a long while and really hit all the levels. No quickie moving into the same room, no skipping to the good stuff first. It was *all* good stuff, and he'd be damned if either them were cheated out of the whole experience. She was it for him, and this would be the one and only time he headed toward the altar. So they could take the scenic route.

Assuming she was on-board, of course. They hadn't spoken much during the past eight weeks by mutual agreement. She'd been busy in the studio, and he'd been busy cleaning out his system and his mind and going more than a little stir-crazy. Once he'd found his songwriting outlet—and had started making serious use of the fitness facilities at the center— everything had started falling more into line.

Even mental exertion and physical exhaustion hadn't stopped him from wanting coke. He didn't think of it as often as he had before, especially during the time right before rehab. But he still thought about it way too much. That would be his life now. He had to be constantly vigilant. There would never be a time he could relax and "recreationally" use any kind of substance. He had an addictive personality, and using any of his drugs of choice was a slippery slope leading to the same pit.

Including the woman he'd had to learn to love differently. Not less. That wasn't possible. But he'd begun to figure out that she had her own life, her own decisions to make, her own world that he didn't have to be privy to twenty-four/seven. He couldn't shield her from everything. And that was okay, because she was a fucking wonder in every way. Her strength astounded him.

Now he had to be just as strong.

"You're here."

He turned at the sound of Lila's voice and smiled. "I am."

"Gained some weight. And some serious muscles." She surprised him by poking his belly. "You look good."

"Thanks. I feel good too."

"And you kept growing out your hair. Nice." She fluffed the ends, viewing him with an objective eye. "You'll look great in the video, especially since it requires a little physical work, shall we say."

"What's that supposed to mean? Last I knew, the concept involved Jazz pouring sugar on Simon."

"Oh, that was just a wild hair." She glanced down at her tablet and waved her bright red nails. "We went round-and-round about it. Donovan had a different visual in mind, but I convinced him to go with the sure thing."

"And what's that?"

She gave him a smile that could only be construed as wolfish. "You and Jasmine on a bed, making out."

"Say what?" He set down his Epiphone between his feet. "She agreed to that?"

"Actually, it was her idea."

Had he only been gone eight weeks? Sure didn't feel like it right now. "Hold up. Jazz hates to be out front for long."

"Really? You should check out the footage from Trix. She has quite the stage presence."

"I never said she didn't. Of course she does. She's a goddamn knockout and no one plays better than she does. Not even me."

Watching the footage from the night she'd covered for him had brought him to that startling conclusion. He'd been strictly on guitar for years yet she still had a competence with the instrument that seemed to outweigh his hours of practice. There was no beating a native understanding of rhythm and an ear for music, and she had both.

And beyond that? Nick had been right. She'd looked so fucking hot playing his guitar.

The tightening in his groin made him clear his throat. Yep, he didn't need to be thinking about that right now.

"I think Jasmine is just coming into her own. So perhaps what might have been usual for her yesterday isn't the same as today." The knowing smile she gave him caused alarm bells to clang in his head. "Give it a chance, okay?"

He grunted. So much for his taking it slow plan with Jazz. That had included treading gently with sex, but he hadn't anticipated rolling around on a bed with her first thing. Good intentions only went so far. How was he supposed to remember his vow to prove to her how much he cherished her when he wanted to fuck her blind?

"Go on and get freshened up in dressing room C. There are clothes in there for you to wear. I might have underestimated your pants size, though." Thoughtfully, she tapped her nails against her teeth. "Then again, that might be helpful."

"Only from where you're standing," he muttered.

She laughed and started walking away. "It's great to have you back, Grayson."

"Lila, hang on." He grabbed his guitar and jogged after her. "Something weird happened this morning. I tried to make sure the payment plan with Visions was all set up and they told me I was paid in full."

She aimed her attention at her iPad. "Hmm. How irregular."

"You paid for it, didn't you?"

"TKS Enterprises paid for it, if you must know." She patted his arm. "And TKS can more than afford it."

"Who's that?"

Her lips tightened. "My husband's company."

"Lila," he said softly, gripping the neck of his guitar. "How am I supposed to thank you for that?"

"You're not. In fact, I demand that you don't."

"But I owe you—" He owed so many people, Jazz and his parents the most. He was on his way to earning the money to pay them back. He'd manage to pay Lila back too.

"You want to repay me?" She turned her direct, pull-no-punches gaze on him. "Don't fuck up again."

"Don't worry." His voice held the conviction that stiffened his spine every time he'd felt his resolve slipping. "I won't."

"Not just because of Oblivion, but because of Jasmine. If anyone deserves to be happy, it's her."

"Yeah." After a moment, he smiled. "You're not going to liken this situation to Titanic again, are you? Because I watched that movie in rehab, and dude, the guy frigging dies."

"I told you. But it's a good cautionary tale. At any time, the woman you love could banish you to icy cold water so watch your step."

"I guess so. Do you—"

He lost the thread of what he was saying as Jazz sauntered onto the set from a door across the room. She wore a floor-length robe with furry piping, and instead of it making her resemble a miniature wrestler in the WWE, she looked like a pinup queen. Her banging body didn't quit. She had serious curves from head to toe. And her hair. It was back to glossy unrelieved black, a wavy curtain that tumbled over her shoulders and framed her heart-shaped face.

"Wow," he managed once he'd unglued his tongue from the floor.

Lila laughed and gave him a light shove. "Not yet. Go get ready for her first."

"I'm more than ready for her now."

"I just bet," she said drily. "Save it for the shoot, stud. We want this video to be hot enough to fucking crash YouTube."

"I'm not wearing a penis sock. Just so you know."

"Nah, we figured we'd have you perform au naturel." When he gaped, she shook her head and pointed down the hall. "Outta here or you get the sock."

"Most interesting threat I've ever heard." He picked up his guitar and snuck one more quick glance at Jazz as she talked to one of the cameramen, gesturing with both hands as she often did. The sight made him smile.

God, he'd missed her. He would've agreed to exile in an igloo in Antarctica if a glimpse of her was his reward.

"There's the Titanic smile. Been waiting on it." Lila sighed. "Damn you people and your epic loves."

He flushed. "Can I get a sock for my head too?"

"You wish. Scram."

Gray found the dressing room she'd indicated and walked into a zoo. Simon was spinning around on the swivel stool in front of the mirror, his legs kicked out as if he was on a ride at the fair. Nick slouched against one wall and laughed hysterically at something on his phone. Deak, the only sane one of the bunch, stood near the window, talking quietly on his cell.

He also happened to be the only one who was dressed.

"Jesus H. Christ, if nudity is required, I'm leaving."

Silence descended. Simon stopped spinning like a mad top, Nick stopped laughing. And everyone stared at Gray as if they'd seen a ghost.

He smiled. Well, they kind of had, if his occasional nickname counted.

"Holy fuck. He lives." Simon bolted off the stool and pulled him into a hug, clapping him on the back hard enough to dislodge a vital organ or two. He stepped back and gripped Gray's shoulders. "You look great."

"Thanks. And you look naked."

Simon laughed and grabbed a pair of leather pants off the dressing table. "When you've got it, flaunt it, bro."

Gray lifted an eyebrow at Nick. "That your theory too?"

"Nah, I just got distracted. Not like I haven't been at a wang party before." Nick tossed aside his phone, pulled on a pair of faded jeans sans underwear and extended his fist, knuckles out. "Good to have you back, man."

Gray smiled. "You actually sound like you mean that."

"I do." Nick shrugged. "When you're not around, I gotta practice with Leather Loins over there and he preens more than plays."

"Don't hate me because I'm beautiful." Simon leaned toward the mirror to line his eyes. "Want?" he asked over his shoulder.

"Hell no, I don't want. You think I'm a damn female?"

"Not you, jackoff. I meant Gray."

Gray grinned. "Goddamn, it's good to be back." He met Deak halfway across the room to slap hands. "How you doin', Pops? Lovin' all over that woman carrying that baby of yours?"

A shadow passed over Deak's face though he recovered quickly. "Yeah, yeah, you know it." He laughed and gripped Gray's shoulder—the good one, thank God. Deak could've killed him with a careless shoulder clap. "You look incredible. Doing all right?"

"Yeah." He cleared his throat and met the other man's gaze squarely. Of everyone, Deacon had been the most militant about kicking Snake and his drug habit out of the band. Gray certainly hadn't expected a hero's welcome from him. "I know you probably don't have a lot of faith in me right now, man, but I want you to know that I'm straight."

"Pretty sure we all knew that already." Simon leered over his shoulder. "Isn't that why you get to bang the hottie on camera? Prior knowledge and shit?"

"I'm not banging her on camera." Though the more everyone kept talking, he was seriously starting to wonder what kind of video shoot he'd wandered into. "I haven't turned to porn yet."

"Don't rule it out, buddy. Times are tough."

Nick shoved Simon hard enough to upend his stool. "Christ, shut the hell up."

Gray shook his head. "Sorry," he said in an undertone to Deacon.

He just laughed. "I'm the one who should be apologizing to you. I'm the one who invited you to join this fucking chaos."

"Misery always loves company."

"You got it. And about the other...listen, I'm betting on you, man. I always have been. Whatever it takes to get you back to a good place, I'm behind you."

"Thanks. That means a lot."

"You and I gotta stick together. We're outnumbered here—"

Gray glanced back as Nick began coughing and flailing against the wall. "What the fuck is wrong with him?"

"Some new syndrome that's twice as bad as Tourette's. In a minute, he'll start foaming at the mouth and pissing his pants."

Nick managed to stop coughing long enough to glare at Simon. "What'd I tell you about shutting up?"

Gray glanced back at Deak. "Those two are something."

"Best friends. It's basically a sickness for two."

"Guess so." He'd never had that issue with his best friend, but she also didn't have the maturity of a ten-year-old, so that probably made a difference. "Where are my clothes?"

Deak pointed to another dressing table on the other side of the room. "Right there. Underneath the shirt is a surprise from Harper." He grinned. "A little birdie told her your favorite."

"Booyah. That almost makes up for the hell I'm about to endure." He went over to the dressing table and pushed aside the clothes to pick up the plastic-wrapped plate with a sticky note on top. "Look, she gave me a heart." He pinned it to his shirt. "Think she likes me more than you, man."

"I don't doubt it at the moment. Morning sickness is kicking her ass. They never like us too much then, fair warning."

Gray peeled off the plastic and took a heady sniff of the chocolate-coconut popovers Harper had made for him. Sin on a fucking plate. "You are a lucky man, my friend."

"Tell me about it. But you're pretty lucky yourself." Deak grinned and headed for the door with Moe and Curly in tow. "Enjoy."

Gray already had one halfway to his mouth. "I probably won't be able to fit into my damn pants."

"Just leave them open. Easier acc—" Simon began, trailing off when Nick yanked him through the door and slammed it shut.

Shaking his head, Gray grinned and finished his popover. So fucking worth it.

* § *

The hour of reckoning was close at hand, and Jazz had swollen ankles. That seemed particularly unfair.

Panning her iPhone around the set, Jazz waited until she had a good-sized clip before hitting pause on the recording and uploading it to Oblivion's social media accounts with the caption "Guess what we're doing today?" Answers immediately flooded in, from the zany to the downright nuts. But they were fun to read regardless.

She'd been slacking on the social media front for a while. Sure, she still tweeted now and then and took the occasional selfie to throw up on Facebook, but by and large, she'd let that part of her life lapse ever since things with Gray had gotten so crazy.

The last few weeks, she'd started easing her toe back in with candid pictures of Simon posing in his latest designer duds and Nick practicing like a maniac. Last night she'd caught a close-up of Deak and Harper sharing a smooch worthy of the hottest porno, and boy, had the Oblivion peeps enjoyed that.

But right now, she couldn't concentrate on being cute and chatty with their fans. Not when it felt like her entire life rested on the line.

"How does he look?" she asked Lila finally.

"Is there any appropriate way for me to answer this question?"

"Come on, drop the appropriate for a minute. You're a female. You have eyes."

"So I won't be risking life and limb if I admit he looks fucking incredible?"

Jazz frowned and went back to fluffing pillows. "You could've left off the *fucking*."

"I wanted to make sure you had the word in mind before upcoming events." When Jazz narrowed her eyes, Lila sighed. "See? Lose-lose proposition."

"No, I'm just nervous and taking it out on you. Who thought this was a good idea?"

"You. And you. Oh, and still you."

"If I throw up, I'm going to aim for your expensive duvet."

"I wouldn't expect anything less." She sighed. "Besides, I'm getting rather used to a disordered environment, thanks to Killer."

Jazz grinned. Harper had named her cat Whisk. So adorable. "I can't believe you named an innocent kitten Killer."

"I can't believe you gave me a kitten."

"Touché." Jazz leaned against the bed and reflexively tightened her belt. She was keeping it together mostly—both her robe and her thoughts.

Worrying wouldn't do her any good. She'd set her plan into motion and now she had to see it through. It wouldn't be much longer now.

Today was a good day. No, an *excellent* day, because Gray was home. If the fates were kind, it would end up amazing.

"Can we get this show on the road soon?" She tried and failed to temper her peevish tone. "I'm hungry."

"I thought you just said you were going to throw up."

"Hello, both thoughts can occupy my head at the same time."

"Did someone say they were hungry?"

Jazz squealed at the sound of Harper's voice and toddled off in the direction of her best friend. She probably looked up like a sexed-up penguin at the moment, but hey, penguins were pretty cute. "What did you bring me?" she demanded. "I hope it's full of chocolate."

"Nope. You need something healthy."

"Aww, man, that's no fair. You gave Gray chocolate."

"You can have some for dessert, young lady, not for the meal itself."

Jazz grinned. "It turns me on when you talk mom."

"Stop lying. You're turned on all the time." Harper giggled and opened a plastic container full of wrapped sandwiches. "Tuna salad for the boys, chicken salad for the big guy. And for you and me, a nice turkey with cranberry mayo."

Jazz poked in the box. "Do I see pickles?"

"You sure do." Harper nodded proudly. "I know my girl."

"Now I'm really hot for you. I may strip down in a second."

"Hell yeah, now this is what I'm talking about. All my women, getting naked for me." Arms spread wide, Simon strutted into the room wearing just a pair of leather pants and a smile. "And sandwiches too? Banner fucking day."

When he stuck his hand into Harper's box, she shut the lid on his fingers. "It's not lunchtime. Keep your grimy paws to yourself."

"But they're wrapped."

Jazz had to laugh at his hurt expression. He was so damn adorable. "I'll sneak you a couple of my pickles, manslut," she soothed, taking his arm.

"I don't like pickles."

"How do you feel about cranberry mayo?"

"I don't care," Jazz said to Harper. "He has his own sandwich. He can't have mine."

"Pernickety females." He kissed the top of Jazz's head. "Good thing I like that particular variety."

"Watch it, Kagan." Lila strode up to them, iPad in hand. The softer side of her that seemed to emerge when she and Jazz were alone had disappeared entirely. "Speaking of females, I have news on that score."

Simon perked up. "Oh goody."

"In honor of the great progress that you've been making in the studio, I've invited someone to sit in with all of you next week. Between Gray's return and her presence, I think it'll really round out the sound of 'Echoes'. We'd really like to recreate some of the magic from 'The Becoming' and 'Echoes' has a similar feel."

At Jazz's side, Simon went rigid. "They're completely different songs."

"I know that, but why argue with success? 'The Becoming' broke out Oblivion, and we'd love to take you to the next level with this album."

"Who're you bringing in? That violin chick?" Jazz snapped her fingers. "Margaret, right?"

"Margo," Simon said quietly.

"Margo, that's right. She was so talented."

"I think we're gelling just fine on our own." Simon rubbed his hand over his bare chest. "Besides, I seriously doubt she wants to slum with us again. I got the feeling she wasn't too into the experience last time."

"Funny, she seemed happy for the opportunity when we contacted her people. If all goes as we hope, we may even bring out for selected dates on the tour." Lila shifted toward Jazz. "We're also looking into a few different things to change up the dynamic of a few of the songs. Like taiko drumming."

"Really? I'd love to try that."

"Your enthusiasm is appreciated," Lila said with a pointed glance at Simon.

"Yeah, well, see how much her enthusiasm helps when she can't stretch her arms over her stomach to play the kit."

"Jerk." Jazz elbowed him and glanced over her shoulder at a noise in the doorway. Her belly rioted for a moment until she realized it was just Nick and his slinky brunette friend, Tori.

So much for Nick being concerned about sharing Tori with Snake. Though why that surprised Jazz, she didn't know. He was just a sharing kind of guy.

Snake. Just thinking that name nearly made her shudder. He hadn't resurfaced since the cabin incident, but she knew it was a matter of time. Lila had warned her as much. Now that Gray was returning from rehab, once Snake saw he wasn't being kicked out of the band—as Snake had been—that would probably lure him out of his hidey-hole.

But they were prepared. The media blitz around the video should be enough to distract the public from anything Snake had to say. Their fans knew Gray was in treatment, and everyone seemed to be supportive. If this video turned out as hot as they hoped, everyone would see Gray was back at full strength and anything Snake said would get lost in the noise.

Of course, that all depended on Gray coming out of his dressing room someday soon.

"What the hell." Lila aimed a death ray at Nick and charged across the room. "This is a closed set," she snapped. "No groupies."

"Groupies? I don't see any groupies." He glanced around, eyebrows lifted. The perfect lying picture of innocence. "Tori here is my special friend. Totally different."

Tori nodded eagerly. Lila did not appear impressed.

When Simon wandered off muttering about needing a drink, Harper leaned in close to Jazz. "How're you holding up?"

"Not awesomely." Jazz lifted the bottom of her robe. "These garters are cutting off my thigh circulation."

"Look sexy as hell though."

"So will the permanent band tattoos on my legs."

"Speaking of band tattoos, I'm thinking of getting the Oblivion O right here." Harper pulled down the collar of her shirt to reveal the top of her breast. "Maybe add a whisk."

"Sounds good. I still need to get mine too." Still holding her robe up, Jazz peered between her legs. "I'm thinking inner thigh." Gray liked that area on her. "What do you think?"

Harper didn't answer.

"Harp?"

"Not Harp." Gray's husky voice rumbled over her skin. "By the way, that's some pose. Don't feel like you need to change it on my account."

She whirled around and grinned widely enough that her cheeks hurt. "Where did you come from?"

"Today, rehab. Originally, my mother's wo—" The rest of his statement disappeared under her lips as she attacked him right there in the middle of Lila's set. He laughed and grabbed her hips, pulling her even closer while he stroked his tongue over hers and reminded her all over again just what that mouth was capable of.

Her panties soon bore the proof.

"Mmm, missed you."

Grinning, he dipped his forehead to hers. "I'd say me too but I think you can feel that without me saying a word." He tugged lightly on the belt of her robe. "This is some outfit."

"You haven't even seen the best part yet."

She waited for his eyes to darken with jealousy that everyone else would soon be seeing too but he only pressed his lips to hers again. "Yeah, I have. Nothing is better than your face."

God. This man.

"How are you?" she whispered between kisses. "You look good. No, you look great. You gained weight. Your color's back." Not caring who was watching, she reached around behind him and grabbed his ass. "Oh yeah. Everything's exactly right."

He laughed against her mouth. "You're trying to screw up the big plans I have for us, aren't you?"

"Big plans for screwing?" She arched against him and buried her hands in his thick hair. He'd grown it even longer and hot damn, her nipples solidly approved. "I'm down. Or up. Pretty much any position you want me in."

"Uh uh. No screwing. That's my big plan. I want us to go slow." He edged back and drew his fingertip over her parted wet lips and down her throat to her guitar pick necklace. "This time, we're going to do it right. No rushing ahead. I want to do the old-fashioned thing and, you know, court you."

Uh oh.

She cleared her throat. "I'm not sure that's possible, all things considered."

"Sure it is. We'll reset the clock and do everything all over again. Start from the beginning."

"Two minutes until I'm closing this set," Lila shouted as the crew hustled around, doing final adjustments. She wasn't the video director but she'd taken over as usual. "Necessary personnel only."

Jazz bit her lip. Oh shit. Damn, damn, damn. This was not going well at all. So much for her big surprise. He was liable to dump her again after she dropped this present on his doorstep. Not the present itself—that was wonderful—but her timing left something to be desired. Best of all? She'd actually *planned* this stupid set-up.

Other women arranged an intimate dinner for two. Her? She invited a camera crew.

"I have something I need to tell you. Like...now."

"We have all the time in the world." He tucked her hair behind her ear. "Back to brunette. I love it."

"It's vegetable dye. I can't use the real stuff right now."

"What, is there a shortage or something?" He grinned. "Doesn't surprise me. You change your hair practically daily."

"Places everyone. Simon, don't touch that. Jazz and Gray, get on the bed."

He grabbed her hand and tugged her with him. "Be gentle with me, okay? I've had a long eight weeks."

"You're not the only one," she mumbled, prepared to climb the three steps to the platform bed. But he turned and plucked her up, setting her down carefully on the mattress and lying beside her as if were the most natural thing in the world.

She stared up at him, dizzy for a whole different reason than her usual one lately. "Gray," she whispered urgently.

"Hmm, baby?"

"Jazz, move your leg. That angle is not flattering. Gray, put your hand higher. Pretend you actually like her."

"Was this really your idea?" he muttered in Jazz's ear, doing as requested. His hand slid up her thigh and she bit her lip to keep from moaning, though she wasn't sure if it was from desire or distress. Probably both.

"I'm not sure I properly conceptualized it."

"You think?" He turned his face into her hair. "Sweet hell, you smell like a fucking wet dream."

"That's good." The bearded cameraman loomed over them, his breath reeking of the meatball sub she'd seen him eating a few minutes ago. Jazz's stomach roiled. "Roll half on top of her. Think the hottest makeout session of your life. When we come into the bridge, Simon's going to take center stage for a moment and that's when we want you to slide down her body. I think we all know what we want you to simulate."

Gray lifted his head. "You can't be serious."

"Don't worry, with camera angles, it will all still be classy," Lila said from a few feet away.

"Oh yeah. This shoot is fucking exploding with class," Nick said. "Too bad I forgot my pearls."

"Bet we could arrange a pearl necklace pretty easily," Simon said.

Gray choked with laughter and gripped his side. "Ow, fuck, that still hurts."

Jazz eased up on an elbow and touched Gray's jaw. "Want me to get on top?"

"I do."

"Shut up," Jazz and Gray said to Simon.

"No, stay where you are," Lila commanded. "If everyone cooperates, this will be done by lunch."

"You mean I'll be done for," Gray breathed in her ear, making her laugh. He traced small circles with his thumb on her upper thigh, rekindling her lust and easing her nerves at the same time.

The set crew continued to yell instructions to each other and to the members of the band. Nick, Simon and Deak were supposed to rock out on their instruments in the corner like a bunch of voyeurs while she and Gray rocked out on the bed. At the end, a sugar-like powder would be dumped on them from above. Whether that would turn out sexy or dopey as hell was anyone's guess.

At the moment, she had bigger problems.

When the recorded track to "Sugar Kiss" started and Gray nuzzled the side of her neck, panic really set in. She'd bungled this so badly, and keeping this secret from him any longer felt like a huge mistake. She'd wanted to do something sexy and unique that they would never forget. Hell, their most important moment would even be memorialized for all time on video. But her sexy was in short supply and after his pre-shoot declaration about wanting to go slow, she couldn't hold back one second more.

"Gray." She guided his face up to hers, well aware the cameras were still rolling. Not really caring. She rubbed her mouth over his and slid her hand along his jaw so it blocked the movement of her lips. She hoped. "I'm pregnant."

For a moment, nothing happened. Had she overdone the whole hand blocking thing? The recorded music was freaking loud, and the guys were playing for real in the corner because Nick had insisted he couldn't simulate.

She wet her parched lips and inched closer to Gray's ear, about to try some seductive lobe action while yet again imparting her news, when his head reared up and collided with hers. Hard. Stars swam in her vision and she reached up to grab her throbbing face.

It was wet. That probably wasn't good.

"Cut!" The cameraman shouted as a slew of curses erupted around them.

"Oh Christ, get ice. We've got a bleeder," someone called.

Gray, however, didn't appear to notice her fluid loss. "What? What did you say?" She cupped her nose and tried to speak but evidently he'd decided to pry the words out of her by force if necessary. He dragged her hand away from her nose and pressed his there instead, holding it away from her mouth. His eyes were wilder than she'd ever seen them. "Say it again."

"I'm pregnant." Something about saying the words to him made her eyes fill. "We're going to have a baby."

He stared at her, a huge range of emotions playing across his face. So many she couldn't track them all. His lips moved but no sound emerged.

"Say something," she pleaded.

He dropped his hand as a crew member pushed a plastic bag toward her nose. "Ice's here," he said hollowly.

Normally she would've thrown some snark back at him. But she couldn't, because a boulder the size of Rhode Island had taken up residence on her chest.

"Let's see your face," Lila said, crawling on the bed on her opposite side. "If there's bruising, we're fucked."

"It won't show up yet," the cameraman said. "If we finish the shoot now, we can make it work."

"I'm still bleeding," Jazz said in a small voice, but no one seemed to care.

"Let me see." Lila nudged aside the ice and probed her face gently with her fingers. "She looks fine. Time to boogie."

"Still bleeding," Jazz said again, waving her ice bag.

She was resoundingly ignored.

For his part, Gray had slumped on his side and was staring vacantly into space. That didn't bode well.

"Everyone, places. From the top. Gray?"

He moved like a robot, assuming his position half on top of her with about as much enthusiasm as a child on the way to the dentist. He slid his hand up her thigh, shifting it up so it rested on both of his legs. She soon realized his erection hadn't abated. Nor had his stricken expression.

At the cameraman's cue, he went back to kissing her neck, his fingers still doing that stroking thing on her thigh that had worked well to start her engine before. It had the same effect the second time around and she arched again, getting into it in spite of herself, when he suddenly lifted his head and stared into her eyes. "You're pregnant," he said without lowering his voice. At all. "We're really having a baby?"

"Yeah." She swallowed. "We are."

"For fuck's sake, cut," the cameraman yelled. "How am I supposed to shoot a video under these conditions?"

"Give them five. You get five," Lila said, appearing in Jazz's line of vision just long enough for her to nod. Lila moved back, clapping her hands. "Clear the set, people. Time for a short break."

"Oh thank God. I'm so tired from playing six notes." Nick's sarcastic reply carried across the room just before the slam of a door signaled the group's exit.

Jazz chanced a look at Gray, who'd finally regained some of his color after her bombshell. "You okay?" she asked hesitantly.

"Yeah. Are you? How did this happen?" His gaze traveled down to her partially undone robe—they hadn't gotten to the big reveal yet—and back up to her face. "The tests were negative."

"We took them too soon. Within a few weeks, I didn't need them to tell me anyway. It became obvious pretty fast."

"The band knows?"

"Yes. I'm sorry I told them first, but I kind of had to. I was throwing up constantly while we were in the studio and Nick started making jokes about me having an eating disorder."

"So that's why the guys were acting so weird in the dressing room. Deak said we had to stick together, him and me. I thought he just meant because Simon and Nick are nuts." Gray's throat bobbed. "Lila didn't freak out over what it means for the band?"

"A little. She chided me for not coordinating the birth with the upcoming tour. I don't think she understands the meaning of the word *unplanned.*" She rolled her eyes. "But as soon as she figured out her spin angle, she was fine. She decided she would put out a big press release when I start to show about our 'love child.'"

"'Love child'? Only Lila." He shook his head. "Are you still sick in the mornings?"

"It's more morning and afternoon sickness. Sometimes evening. Harp and I keep joking about needing matching sinks wherever we go. Oh, guess what? Deak and Harp finally bought a house. It's the cutest place—"

"Save that for later. One life changing event at a time, please." His lips twitched. "What other symptoms did you have?"

That was her Gray, always needing to know the details. He'd never be the kind of man who didn't get involved. "Well, I couldn't even put on a bra without wincing—" He jerked back from her like she was on fire and she had to laugh, though it made her nose hurt more. She touched it gingerly. "I'm okay today."

"Oh. Good." He frowned, studying her chest so intently that she couldn't help squirming. "They're bigger."

"Yeah. So's my belly, though you can't probably won't be able to tell yet. But I can."

"Let me see."

She undid her robe and revealed the skimpy lace teddy beneath. He laid his hand on her stomach and her pulse skipped from the heat of his palm and the intimacy of the gesture. She felt more naked with him touching her there than she ever had in her life.

"I can tell," he breathed, and the wonder in his voice brought back her tears. He gave her a sidelong glance and let out a shuddering exhale. "So...guess slow's out, huh?"

She shut her eyes, thinking back to one of the hardest days she'd ever gone through. It hadn't been an ending for them, though it had seemed like it at the time. But somehow they'd found their way back to each other as friends even while they'd dated others. Then they'd broken up with those other people and grown closer all over again.

And then they'd joined Oblivion.

"I couldn't hit the pause button on my life," she said, blinking her eyes open as a tremor went through his body.

He remembered.

"I'm so fucking glad," he said hoarsely, lacing their fingers together over her belly. "I'm not waiting for any damn thing anymore. We've waited plenty."

"I know you just got out of Visions, and you're dealing with big life changes."

"Yeah, but I've been clean more than sixty days. I'm taking it one day at a time. Believe me, staying away from coke and everything else is my number one priority."

"I know, and I'm so proud of you for deciding to go to rehab. It wasn't easy." She bit her lip. "There are other concerns too. Financially, we're still finding our footing, but more of the money will start rolling in soon."

"Actually, we're not doing too badly there."

"Huh?"

"While I was in rehab, I started pursuing another avenue to make some extra on the side. I want to pay you and my parents back as soon as possible, and now I can."

"I don't understand."

"I started selling some of my songs." He smiled. "Lila hooked me up with some producers and artists who liked what I have. I worked on more in between therapy sessions and courtyard walks. You'd be surprised how much you can come up with when you're alone so many hours of the day."

"That's amazing." She stroked his cheek, smiling as he turned his head to kiss her thumb. "I can't wait to see all the new material."

"I'm stockpiling it. Once I got back into the groove, it felt natural. It reminded me of when you and I used to write together. I'm hoping maybe we can get back to that. Get a few Edwards-Duffy collaborations out there."

She glanced at her belly. "One's already cooking."

He pressed their joined hands to her stomach. "The best one yet," he murmured.

"You're really okay with this? Even though the timing sucks?"

"The timing must be right, because it happened. This is exactly what we both wanted."

She couldn't deny it. Even with the alternating bouts of worry and panic over his reaction that she'd suffered through since learning she was pregnant, she'd savored every single moment of their baby's life. "Yes," she said, throat thick. "This is exactly what I want."

"I know the extended family thing didn't work out for us the way we would've hoped. The situation with my parents..." He trailed off and shook his head. "I've talked to them a couple of times recently, and we've even tried to discuss Brent. It's just not happening."

"This baby is going to need grandparents. Look, they're not perfect, all right? But they're the only parents you've got. And I think—hope—that maybe this child can start to build a bridge. Brent's gone, Gray," she said gently. "It's over."

"They sided with him. They never even considered that he tried to hurt you. You had to leave, and it wasn't fair."

"They didn't make me leave. It was my choice." Not that she'd had many of them, since after what had happened with Brent, the Duffys had never looked at her the same way again.

"You didn't feel safe staying in the house with him. What option did they give you?"

"You paid a much bigger price than I did. God, you turned your back on them to show your solidarity with me, even after I left." She rubbed his hand. "Sweet, stubborn man."

"I won't stand for anyone hurting you. Not while I have anything to say about it."

"Then I guess we'll have to figure out this whole grandparents thing somehow, because I know all too well how it is to grow up without a family. I don't want our baby to go through that. If they don't like me, that's fine. As long as they treat our son or daughter well." When he turned his face away, she tenderly turned it back. "I honestly think they will. Your mom made mistakes, yes. Big ones. Mainly because she loved her son too much to see who he really was. I want my baby to be loved too much too."

He let out a long breath. "Give it some time, okay?"

"I will." She smiled. "We have plenty of it."

"That we do, and I want to make the most of it." He stroked her engagement ring. "Still want to get married now?"

Yep, there went the waterworks. "Yes."

"Me too." He shimmied down the bed to speak to her abdomen. "Baby, this is your daddy. We've gotta shoot a dirty video and then I'll be back to talk to you some more. But in the meantime, remember that the guitar's a better instrument than the drums, though your mom can kick my ass on both. Oh, and I love you." He met her gaze. "I love you both so much."

She half laughed, half sobbed and gripped her nose. "Ouch."

He frowned. "Sorry about the head bump. I was a little surprised. Are you okay?"

"I am now." She smiled as he shifted back on top of her and fisted his hands in her hair. "I don't think I could be better."

"Challenge accepted. Later. But first..." Grinning, he called out, "We're ready."

"Video for Oblivion's 'Sugar Kiss' crashes YouTube" - *headline in the entertainment section of the Los Angeles Wire, April 9th, 2014.*

There's more to come! Jazz and Gray's story continues in UNTWISTED, on FEBRUARY 12, 2015. ORDER NOW!

UNTWISTED

Falling in love was easy...figuring out the rhythm of being a couple, not so much.

Now that they've pressed play, life is going way too fast for Gray Duffy and Jazz Edwards. A super hot video has boosted their band Oblivion's popularity even higher, and suddenly Gray and Jazz are the reigning prince and princess of rock. But as their private wedding ceremony in their most special place approaches, they realize they can't go forward without facing their roots.

With new family members coming into the mix and old unresolved dramas coming to a head, one thing is for sure—the harder they rock, the bigger the drop.

LET YOUR VOICE BE HEARD

HIT OR QUIT: After you finish TWISTED please consider leaving an honest review on your e-tailer website or on Goodreads.

COME PLAY WITH US: We have a blast on our Facebook group, Word Wenches. It's all about the teasers, giveaways, music, hot guys...oh and books. Join us!

BE SOCIAL: Taryn & Cari are all over social media.

GET INFORMED: Sign up for our Lost in Oblivion NEWSLETTER for contests, advanced notice on new releases & other fun at www.lostinoblivion.com.

Lost In Oblivion

the Series
SEDUCED (intro)
ROCKED (book #1)
ROCK, RATTLE & ROLL (book #1.5)
TWISTED (book #2)

Coming soon

UNTWISTED (book #2.5)
DESTROYED
If you'd like more information about the series &
extras please visit **www.lostinoblivion.com.**

ANYTHING BUT MINE

WHEN YOU'RE GONE TRILOGY
BOOK ONE
By Taryn Elliott

Rock star Logan King has come home to Winchester Falls for the annual Summer Festival. Only this time he's hauling a helluva lot more baggage than a few suitcases and vintage guitars. His closet contains more than the usual skeletons...and if he doesn't keep the door firmly locked, someone might get harmed. The specter of what haunts him forces him to turn away from anything more than one-night-stands.

Until Izzy and her topaz eyes finally give him a reason to try again.

Since moving to town Isabella Grace has found friends and a place to belong for the first time in her life. Running the Summer Festival is the perfect way to show how important her new community is. She just never planned on a whirlwind fling with a man too used to saying goodbye. Or to fall for a guy who has as many secrets as he does hit songs.

Logan is used to protecting himself, but protecting Izzy is all new territory. With everything that matters to him at risk, he refuses to let her get hurt—even if that means he has to walk away. For her own good.

SHADOWBOXER

Book 1 in the Tapped Out series

by Cari Quinn

She's in for the fight of her life...with the man who only wants to be her lover.

Fighter Mia Anderson has faced the dark side of life and survived. But just getting by is no longer enough. To fund her new life with her baby sister, she's determined to beat the reigning king of the male fighters in New York's underground MMA circuit, Tray "Fox" Knox.

Tray refuses to fight a woman, until he learns Mia's tougher than anyone he has ever known. He soon realizes he wants more from her than blows and blood, and he's willing to hit below the belt to get it. He'll fight her, but if he wins, she spends the night in his bed. All night long, his rules. No tapping out.

Mia agrees, certain that he'll lose. What she doesn't realize is that Tray loves to fight *dirty*...and that this match may end up being the most important one of their lives.